The Day All Hell Broke Loose

by
Clarence M. Jackson, II

AuthorHouse™
1663 Liberty Drive, Suite 200
Bloomington, IN 47403
www.authorhouse.com
Phone: 1-800-839-8640

AuthorHouse™ *UK Ltd.*
500 Avebury Boulevard
Central Milton Keynes, MK9 2BE
www.authorhouse.co.uk
Phone: 08001974150

This book is a work of fiction. People, places, events, and situations are the product of the author's imagination. Any resemblance to actual persons, living or dead, or historical events, is purely coincidental.

© 2007 Clarence M. Jackson, II. All rights reserved.

No part of this book may be reproduced, stored in a retrieval system, or transmitted by any means without the written permission of the author.

First published by AuthorHouse 2/15/2007

ISBN: 978-1-4259-8167-9 (sc)

Printed in the United States of America
Bloomington, Indiana

This book is printed on acid-free paper.

Acknowledgements

I would like to take this opportunity to thank every person that has ever positively impacted my life and aided in my personal and spiritual growth and development. Whether it was a kind deed or much needed encouragement, thank you for thinking enough of me to sow what you had into me.

I want to especially thank my wife Dee. For a little over ten years, your unwavering support of my every endeavor has given me the confidence to aspire and dare to achieve heights I never thought were imaginable. You've stood along side me, never once desiring the light that was shown upon me, but always deserving of the adulation you've garnered. For, it was you and your love for reading that inspired me to write and I wrote this book for you. I also want to thank my children Jaelen Allen, Joana Alexandria and Jan Adolphus Jackson for sharing daddy with the world and understanding that my love for you transcends any and every thing you've ever allowed me to accomplish. You all are three of the most beautiful people in the world and I can only hope that you are as grateful for me as I am for you.

To my mom, Lessie M. Jackson; thank you for allowing me to be a momma's boy. Thank you for looking out for me even when you knew I deserved the worst of my daddy's punishments. Thank you for teaching me the importance of perseverance and the value of a face of strength. You are strength and though we don't always show it, our family knows and appreciates what you mean to us. Daddy, thank you for raising me to be a man that understands the importance and the historical relevance of being a provider. If we were ever poor, I never knew it. And I never knew it because whatever our family needed, you always provided. I hope this book makes you both proud to call me your child.

Marsha thanks for being more than a big sister. Thanks for being that down for whatever friend of mine. And to my brother Nathaniel, you'll never understand the kind of gratification I have for your willingness to expose your failures to me for the purpose of your baby brother's success. Man, I thank you for always being proud of me and I'm proud of you too.

Tonya Washington, Archie and Nicole Bouie, you all have inspired me in so many ways and your friendship means more to me than either of you know. Our connections are so much stronger than those of mere friends. You're my family. Thank you for allowing and trusting me enough to speak into your lives. And Archie I especially want to thank you for speaking into mine.

And to the educators that helped sculpt a country boy from Gretna, Florida into the well rounded man he is today; thank you. Mike Figgers, you never gave up on me and you wouldn't let me give up on myself. Thank you. And Mr. Carl Daniels; that hard earned "D" in that government class really did pay off. Thank you for teaching me the value of not settling for anything less than my potential said I could have or become.

To Tommy Mitchell and the entire staff of the Black Male College Explorers Program at Florida A&M University, thank you for exposing me to a world I didn't even know existed and opening my eyes to the concepts and strategies that have ultimately led me down this rather enjoyable path. Thank you for teaching me the importance of reputation and integrity. Thank you for teaching me how business men wear their pants.

Last but not least, I want to thank the greatest church family in all the land; Greater Bethel Missionary Baptist Church of Chattahoochee, Florida. I am so grateful that you've allowed me to pastor you for seven years and have trusted my sometimes radical brand of leadership. All of you have been so kind to my family and I and so many of you have unselfishly given of yourselves so that our church could maximize its potential. Unlike the fictional church in this book, you've made my job as pastor very easy and enjoyable and your respect for God's call on my life is evident. I couldn't be in a better place nor can I ever imagine being the pastor of any other people. To Queen and Ralf Jackson and the E1R1 team of Atlanta, thank you for thinking enough of my ministry to allow me to travel alongside you as you've and ministered to and fro. I love you all as well.

And I can't forget Uncle Roy. Thank you for teaching me the art of fishing. I really don't believe I would be as sane as I am right now if you hadn't and you couldn't have spent so much time teaching me without Aunt Linda's permission. Thank you all and I pray that this book finds each of you in health, peace, and prosperity.

> *"Life is a grinding stone.*
> *Whether it grinds us down or polishes us up*
> *depends on us."*
>
> -Thomas Holdcroft

Introduction

Chauncey Evansworth Pennington was born in relative obscurity and raised in a quaint town in northern Ohio just off the shores of Lake Erie. But from an early age he dreamed of forgetting his hometown and vowed never to return if by chance God would ever hear his humble plea. For Chauncey, dreaming of moving far away and never returning wasn't just childish imagination, but it was what he considered to be the best possible avenue to escape the shame of a horrific past, the blame associated with what that past had stolen from him, and the consistent internal bouts he had with guilt and depression. The torment this boy faced from his early existence was enough to cause any grown man's ruin, but Chauncey Pennington was no ordinary boy. He was an overcomer and would eventually rise above the nightmarish pre-teen years he spent, living without his biological parents, under his loving aunt's roof. As he grew into a man he learned to stare the trials of life in the face and daily he dared them to serve him up greater challenges. For a while it seemed as though he embraced his past because, though discouraging at times and embarrassing at others, he knew that his past was what gave his life character. One would think that that kind of perseverance and a willingness to survive would ultimately pay off but, trouble would never forget his name and his past always knew where to find him. This is his story.

CHAPTER 1

Born May 8, 1970 to the Reverend Wallace and Mrs. Suzanne Pennington, Chauncey was the apple of his mother's eyes. And as an only child he enjoyed the kind of early aged pampering reserved for royalty. When Chauncey's Aunt Eunice, who had raised him from age 7, was asked to describe what her younger sister was like, she replied with a smile "She was a beautiful, slender, bright-eyed, pecan tanned girl who loved that baby with every ounce of her soul. She had tried to have children before Chauncey finally came along, but every time something went wrong and it seemed like every time her pregnancy failed she would become more and more depressed," Eunice said as she remembered her sister's desperate desires. "But Ohhh… when that Chauncey was born it was like Suzanne was reborn. She was proud to be a momma. But to tell you the truth, I think she was more proud to be Wallace E. Pennington's baby's momma," Eunice said with a chuckle.

You see, before Wallace ever knew who Suzanne was, he was already a very popular man, primarily because he was a gifted preacher who pastored one of the largest churches in northern Ohio. A tall, dark, handsome, curly head, well spoken man, Wallace E. Pennington was adored by the many who knew him. And if he wasn't adored enough for his gift to preach, he was certainly adored by the women in Ohio for being one of the finest black men they had ever seen. "He would have churches filled to capacity when he would run those summer revival meetings." Eunice replied, still chuckling, when asked to share her thoughts about her brother-in law. "He would have those women flocking behind him in droves, and all of them wasn't looking for the Lord either, if you know what I mean. Everybody was after that boy. I mean everybody. Single women would come down there to that church all dressed up and get as close as they could to that pulpit. But, then he met my sister and I guess it was love at first sight. Some folk had always wondered how could a man like Wallace Pennington, who was so handsome be single for so long and not have a First Lady at Mt. Carmel? Some would say either he wasn't interested in women, you know... or maybe he was just damaged goods. I always believed that he was just waiting on a good girl like my sister". Eunice said.

They were a perfect couple by all indications and when it was announced in church that they were engaged, the congregation was understandably excited because they knew that their deserving pastor, who was by this time already thirty-seven years old, needed and desired a help meet and who better to fill that role than Suzanne Dawkins, a gorgeous thirty-one year old elementary school teacher formerly of North Florida.

Once Wallace and Suzanne were married and officially Mt. Carmel's first couple and after six long years of trying they finally gave Mt. Carmel it's official heir to the elder Pennington's legacy; Chauncey Evansworth Pennington, a bright-eyed, curly-head, brown baby boy who was as handsome as his daddy and who grew up to be as charming as his momma. Life was good in the Pennington house or so it seemed. Wallace was still excelling in ministry and Mt. Carmel, which once boasted of being one of northern Ohio's largest churches with only 350 members or so, grew rapidly into a grand ministry of nearly 1,000 members. This family enjoyed the luxuries of life primarily because they enjoyed the support of a loving church family.

Suzanne, a 1954 graduate of Florida A&M University, flourished in her career as well. She was an elementary school teacher and from the time she began her teaching career she always received glowing evaluations and had even been named school district teacher of the year. They lived in an exclusive suburban community, drove only the best vehicles and gave Chauncey the best education money could pay for. But all of that changed one still June day in 1977.

The Day All Hell Broke Loose

Eunice described it as the "darkest day of my life. I was at home on a Friday, at about five in the evening. I was cleaning some greens and watching the evening news when the phone rang. It was Chauncey", Eunice said slowing her speech dramatically. "When I recognized that it was him on the phone I said, like I always used to, hey Auntie's Baby. But I could tell something was wrong. It sounded like he was crying and I just asked him; what's the matter baby? And he wouldn't say anything. Then I asked him where his momma was and he told me in a soft innocent little voice, that I can remember like yesterday, "My momma is on the chair bleeding and my daddy is in kitchen."

"When he said that, I told him to put his daddy on the phone. And that's when he told me he didn't think his daddy could talk. "He's bleeding too." That's what he told me and that's when I just started screaming and just started saying Lord Have Mercy! I remember dropping the phone, getting my car keys, and even though I drove as fast as I could to my sister's house it seemed like I would never get there.

But when I did, I got of my car... and ran up those steps... and when I opened the door... When I opened that door I saw Chauncey sitting on the chair in the living room with the telephone still in his hand, his little face and clothes were just covered with blood. It was his momma's blood. He was trying to pull his momma up off the chair and he just kept on saying "Get up momma!" but she wouldn't move. She was just laying there all bruised and beaten and bloody. She was just laying there not saying a word. I tried talking to her but it was bad; she was still breathing a bit but I knew in my heart it was real bad." Eunice recalled. "I was in a panic and I was screaming and I didn't know what else to do. That's when I ran into the kitchen to look for Wallace and when I got in there I saw him. He was already dead. He had been shot. That was real hard for me to take. All I could do was call for an ambulance and cry of course."

"I did go back to the living room to see if I could help Suzy though. I remember pulling Chauncey off of her because I didn't want him to have to see no more of that. Her face was all beat up and I don't know why, but almost all of her hair was just ripped from her head." Eunice said as she wept at the remembrance of the gruesome sight. "I was just thinking to myself; what kind of person could do something so bad to somebody like my sister."

"Other than just cry like I had lost my mind, I couldn't do anything. So I just held her in my arms and cried out to the Lord, praying that somebody showed up before she was gone. That was all I could do. I was just holding her and that's when it seemed like she was trying to gasp for air... she was trying to breathe... and then I thought she was coming around because she actually reached out and grabbed hold to my arm like she was trying to tell something. But then she just started to shake. I tried to hold her and I called her name. Suzy! Suzy! And then she just...you know."

"I won't ever tell Chauncey, but I know exactly what happened that day. The police told me. And if their police report is true, I know why it happened too. I've never talked to him about it and I probably never will, but I know. For the most part, everybody else that had heard different versions of what happened, just kind of kept quiet too, because people around here really loved Wallace and Suzy and they knew that little boy had been through enough all ready. Pretty much everything was just swept under the rug for Chauncey's sake. Of course, there were some who would whisper or stare as we walked by and some still talk about it today; I know it. But, none of that stopped me from raising that child to cherish his parent's memory and it didn't stop him for reaching for his little dreams either."

"Even though he never just came out and talked to me about what happened in that house I do know that he felt like what happened was his fault. He would have these real bad dreams and he'd just wake up in the middle of the night in cold sweats, screaming "I didn't mean it." You know stuff like that. But it wasn't his fault. He was just at the wrong place at the wrong time and saw things that no child should ever have to see."

"Chauncey wasn't but seven years old when I took him in and from that time I did the very best I could for him. I won't lie; it was rough at times; for him and for me. But I'm real proud today because he's grown up to be a fine young man".

Chauncey is no doubt one of Aunt Eunice's greatest accomplishments. She raised him well and by all accounts he's still proving that he is an over comer especially considering his horrible past. Most people from his hometown initially adored him because of his mother and father's legacy at Mt. Carmel, but as he's grown older people respect what he's been able to accomplish in spite of his circumstances. They used to feel sorry for him when they saw him, and shed tears of sorrow for him because they knew how hard it must have been to grow up without parents that he saw die on the very same day. But now when they see him they shed tears of joy because they know that little Chauncey has made the best of his bad situation and if his parents were alive they'd probably be proud to call him son.

"When Chauncey was about eleven years old or so he looked up at me with Wallace's hazel brown eyes and said, "I want to be a pastor just like my daddy, but I want to be better than my daddy Auntie." and I smiled at him and told him "your daddy was some kind of preacher, but baby you can be anything you want to be if you are willing to work hard for it. And my baby worked real hard."

It was almost as though Chauncey immersed himself in his interests to hide himself from what was a terrible reality. He was an excellent student and even from an early age he seemed to be mesmerized by his father's vocation and studied the bible intently, as if he knew he was destined to be a preacher. By age eleven he was turning his Easter speeches into little preaching opportunities and by age thirteen he was announcing to the faithful at Mt. Carmel that God had indeed called him to preach too. When Chauncey made the long awaited announcement the people cheered as if he was a reincarnation of his daddy and Pastor William T. Montgomery, who succeeded the elder Pennington, embraced the young boy and shouted to the congregation "Our prayers have been answered church. We knew it was in him all the time".

From that day forward Chauncey studied hard and though he preached sparingly, was extremely active in Mt. Carmel's youth ministry. Some in the congregation often called him Pastor Pennington in hopes that one day he would fill the enormous shoes left by his father. But Chauncey had other ideas. He never wanted to pastor his father's former church, matter of fact Chauncey never wanted to live anywhere near northern Ohio. He always told his Aunt that he wanted to move far away to California, Texas, or Florida, not only because he didn't won't to live in a place that bore so many bad memories, but because he absolutely hated the cold weather. "He hated the snow, and he hated cold weather. If and when the Lord called him to pastor it wouldn't be anywhere up north", Eunice said with a chuckle.

As his young ministry progressed so did his scholastic career. Chauncey graduated with honors, from the prestigious Thornburg Religious Academy for Boys at the tender age of sixteen and completed his Bachelor's degree in Theology by age nineteen. Just two years after that Chauncey earned his Master's of Divinity Degree from The State University of Ohio where he met his wife to be, Miss Jada Alexia Blaylock, a beautiful, rosy check twenty year old who just happened to be majoring in Elementary Education.

Chapter 2

It was a romance made for a Disney movie. They were both very young. They were both relatively successful in their collegiate studies. They were both seeking another to share quality time with. But more importantly they were bound together by something more strange; a chord of tragedy. Like Chauncey, Jada had suffered the loss of her mother. After a long bout with breast Cancer, Jada's mother died and left the girl with a gaping hole in her heart when she was just twelve years old. But, like Chauncey, the girl was surrounded by people who loved and supported her and no one loved her more than her father Benny, a Methodist minister and her step-mother, Cora, who treated Jada like her own biological daughter.

From the moment he met her, he knew that the possibilities for romance to brew were enormous because Jada's physicality and personality just fit his taste. She was five foot five with big brown eyes. She was vibrant and outgoing and always giggly, and it didn't hurt that she was an ex-cheerleader who could've easily been the poster child for daddy's girl international. But what made her more appealing to him was the fact that she seemed to know what he needed and when he needed it most. Jada and Chauncey had an emotional and spiritual connection. Unlike some of other girls he had talked to on campus, she respected the calling that was on his life and knew how to facilitate atmospheres conducive for his times of desired biblel study. Jada had grown up in the house of a minister and she seemed to already know the role of a woman in love with one of God's men. And by this time she was in love with the tall, dark, and handsome preacher from northern Ohio studying for his master's degree.

She knew nothing of Chauncey when they met at the library during a late night study session. But after the chance encounter they quickly developed a strong bond, which was made even stronger after every intense discussion about their pasts and aspirations for their future. They both missed having their mothers around and to some extent Jada desired to fill the motherless emptiness Chauncey often exhibited. Though seven months and six days younger, than the man she loved more with the passing of each day, Jada often viewed herself as Chauncey's on campus mother figure and offered him much needed advice and career direction. She saw in him, a boy needing to be nurtured, but she also saw her father in him. He was affectionate like her daddy, loving like her daddy, successful like her daddy, and treated her like a queen just like her daddy. She wanted her future to include being Mrs. Chauncey Pennington just as much as he desired to be her husband.

After only six months of dating, and with her father's approval, Chauncey invited Jada to go back to northern Ohio with him for a surprise Mother's day weekend visit with his Aunt Eunice. That weekend would prove to be one that they'd remember for the rest of their lives.

When they showed up at Aunt Eunice's house after the three and a half hour trek from the university, they brought joy to the woman's heart just as Chauncey had thought. And she was surprised because she didn't think she would see him until she came down to the school for his graduation ceremony. "Why didn't you tell me you were coming home?" She asked joyfully, before noticing that she had another big surprise. "You must be Jada."

Delighted by her pleasant surprise and absolutely floored by the pleasantness of Jada, Eunice invited them both in and treated them to her famous pecan pie and ice cream before inviting them to a night air conversation on the front porch.

It was on the front porch that she became more acquainted with Jada and it wasn't long after, that she began to tell Jada all the funny stories of Chauncey's childhood as they all sat, watching the crescent moon and rocked like retirees in old chairs. It was a good time, a reflective time and it wasn't long after those stories that Jada began to loosen up and talk more openly with Aunt Eunice about her own childhood experiences in Odessa, Texas.

After only about an hour of candid conversation with the two love birds, Aunt Eunice fell in love with Jada, just as Chauncey had only six months earlier and begin to plan for her two days with her "Baby and his girlfriend".

Upon Eunice's suggestion that they should visit the flea markets and mall "tomorrow", Chauncey smiled because he knew how, both his Aunt and Jada loved to shop and spend money which was an even greater indication of how well the women he loved would get along. But his countenance quickly changed when she suggested that they all attend church on Sunday at Mt. Carmel and celebrate Mother's Day at the church which held so many memories for him.

"What's wrong Chauncey?" Aunt Eunice said noticing a change in his demeanor, as Jada looked on in concern.

Chauncey hadn't been to Mt. Carmel in nearly four years and since he'd been away working on his masters degree, he'd forgotten how difficult it was every time he stepped foot in that church, especially on Mother's Day.

"It's okay Auntie, I'm just thinking about momma and daddy. Going to church would be a great idea." Chauncey said agreeably, but reluctantly, as he was being consoled by Jada, who already knew of Chauncey's battles with going back to that church.

"Chauncey there's something I need to ask you", Eunice replied as Jada stepped off the porch to grant them a moment of privacy.

"Ever since your mother and father died, you've never asked to see their grave sight or anything. Even when I've wanted to take you up there you never wanted to go. Why? Don't you think that will help you deal with your feelings a little better?" she said in a calming tone.

"It's always been tough, Auntie. I think about that day, everyday, and even though it's been a while, some things make what I feel a little harder to deal with; that's all. Like going back to the church, I love that church, you know that. But it wasn't until I left here that I realized my life could be more than just what happened to my momma and daddy... I can't explain it...I just wish everyday they were still here, that's all."

"Chauncey, as long as you live, life will always present you with difficult problems, but you can't solve them by yourselves. And I think you've been running away from what's real for way too long. You can handle it. You just need the Lord to help you baby." Aunt Eunice solemnly spoke into his spirit as Jada listened on as she stood timidly in the distance, nodding her head unnoticeably in affirmation.

"I know Auntie."

"If you know then you'll go to church with me," she said smilingly as she placed both her hands on his knees. "And since you're going to church with me, I might as well call Reverend Montgomery and ask him if it would be okay if you bring the Mother's Day message this Sunday, since you're in town. I know the people at Mt. Carmel would love to see their proud Pennington prince." she continued as Chauncey managed a chuckled.

As Aunt Eunice scurried into the house with gladness, to call the Reverend, Jada walked back up the steps to the porch and hugged Chauncey and told him, "I heard what your Aunt said and she's right. You need closure and I just want to let you know that I'm glad I came here with you. And Chauncey I want to be with you every time you feel the need to express whatever it is you're feeling. Besides, I want to hear what a proud, Pennington Prince sounds like." Jada said, grinning and tugging on her love's cheek.

Chapter 3

After a big day of shopping and allowing Aunt Eunice to fall further in love with Jada, Chauncey was preparing for the greatest preaching engagement of his young life. He had been favored to preach at other churches before and most, when questioned about his ability to preach would often reply "He's a good preacher, but he ain't' Wallace yet." He had even preached at larger churches before, but nothing like this. He was going back to his father's church, a place that the elder Pennington built into one of Ohio's greatest churches.

The sanctuary was still immaculate, and every corner bore the imprint of his father's tremendous legacy. The foyer of the octagon shaped facility featured a dedicatory wall which displayed a four by six foot mural of the Pastor, Suzanne, and a five year old Chauncey. The, sometimes, overbearing painting was a duplicate of a photo that reminded the faithful of the good ole' days.

Chauncey was going back to a place where he hadn't preached since he was sixteen years old, where everyone including Pastor Montgomery expected him to follow in his father's footsteps. Some actually believed that Chauncey should be the Pastor of Mt. Carmel even if it meant voting out that "no preaching, hard to look at W.T. Montgomery". One of the older saints, Sister Betty McElroy even told the stuttering Montgomery after a heated discussion over the churches mounting financial problems, "The only thing you have in common with the man I knew as my pastor for twenty years is the W in your first name".

Since Wallace and Suzanne Pennington's untimely death, the church was in consistent decline. The church that easily seated 1,000 was now attended by only about three hundred on good Sundays. But, none the less preaching in this venue would be a major milestone for Chauncey.

On that Saturday night, Chauncey went to sleep as he often did, lying in Jada's arms. And as he drifted into a deep sleep, Aunt Eunice said to her new found buddy, "Let the boy sleep, Jada. You and me can go out back for a few minutes and play cards and talk about what we're wearing tomorrow."

As Chauncey slept, he dreamed. And it was yet another dream about his parents, but in this dream his mother was the central figure. She normally appeared in his dreams but never like this before. She wasn't all bloody this time with those patches of hair missing from her skull. Nor was she screaming as she did the very day she fought to save her own life. This time she appeared in all white as if she was an angel of some sort and she was as beautiful as she ever was. She wasn't lying on the living room furniture at the old house and he wasn't trying to get her up. This time, it was as if she was actually at Aunt Eunice's house, walking around when she stopped by Chauncey's bedroom to utter much needed words of comfort.

"I've always been here with you watching over you and protecting you," she said as she sat at the foot of his bed side. "But tonight I decided to stop by to encourage you and to talk to you and let you know that I'm okay now. My death was not your fault. Don't blame yourself and don't be afraid to go back to your daddy's church. Go back and be proud and do one thing for me Chauncey…preach like you know you can. And if you really want to be a better man than your daddy, you must first tear down the very walls he built to protect himself from the realities of his own life. You preach the truth tomorrow and continue to live the life that you preach about. And if you do, it will be the best Mother's Day gift I ever had."

And just like that the dream was over. But Chauncey didn't wake up out of this dream in a cold sweat nor was he kicking and screaming. This time when he awoke he was emboldened, getting out of bed in the wee hours of the morning repeating to him self "I can do this. I can do this." It was early, 4:30AM early, but Chauncey was preparing for a day that would make his momma proud. As he ironed his shirt, just before shining his shoes, he hummed as he waited for the morning to bring with it, an opportunity to substantiate the call of God on his life.

Sunday Morning

"Chauncey, it's almost 9:30. Come on out of there and let's go! I can't stand to just sit down when I know we running late for Sunday school."

"Okay Auntie!" Chauncey shouted back. "I'm on my way!"

When Chauncey finally entered that room he was glowing from head to toe. His smile was as bright and as wide as his mother's. And Wallace's brown eyes gleamed with confidence as he strode in to meet the loves of his life. His dark hair was wavy as usual, but this time he parted his hair on the left side of his head, which eerily resembled his father's trademark look. A three piece black and gray pen striped suit draped his shoulders and his hips as if there was only one made in the whole world and that one was made for Chauncey Evansworth Pennington.

"Chauncey you are really handsome", Jada said in awe, never before seeing her man so dressed up.

"Child you better grab hold to that man and don't let him out of your sight until he gets to that pulpit. Those old women at Mt. Carmel will eat him alive." Eunice said as Chauncey and Jada both embarrassingly chuckled. "When they last saw Chauncey he was just a little bumpy faced critter who was Wallace's son. Now he's a grown man. Go head Auntie's Baby!"

After serving up accolades to each other, they loaded up in Eunice's almost new 1990 Buick Lasabre and were off to church. As they made the fifteen minute drive to Mt. Carmel, the car was unusually quiet and stayed that way until they entered the church's half acre parking lot. At long last, they had made it and Chauncey braced for meeting his church family again for the first time in nearly four years. He took a deep breath and said to the ladies, "Well, we're here and I'm ready."

When they entered the church facility they were greeted by many well wishers from the church including Sis. McLeroy, now eighty-one years old, who grabbed him by the neck and said, "Boy we sure is glad you came back to get this church from that fool. He done tore it up!" she ranted. "All it takes is two-third majority vote and you can finish what yo' daddy started"

"No, mother McLeroy. Not Yet. I haven't been called to pastor yet." Chauncey said with an appreciative, but cautious grin.

Mother McLeroy's comments, if heard by the congregation, probably would've been seconded immediately, but to Chauncey her comments were only a sign of her love, which was shown by others as he was hugged and kissed by all who greeted him as if he was a returning former King.

Sunday Morning Service

Once the church service began and after the Choir's pitiful A & B selections, Pastor Montgomery stood before the congregation and said "Ladies and gentlemen, it gives me great pleasure today to welcome to the pulpit one of Mt. Carmel's favorite son's. I'm sure God has given him a word for the church, so let us stand and receive our son, the Reverend Chauncey E. Pennington."

As Chauncey stood to take the podium, the waiting crowd of over 500, a rather unlikely number on a regular Sunday, stood with him and cheered mightily. Aunt Eunice, who was sitting on the front row with Jada, gleamed with pride as he acknowledged her and introduced Jada as his college sweetheart to the appreciative congregation.

Aunt Eunice recalled that Mother's Day Sunday in 1991, saying "it was one of the best days of my life." As she and Jada looked on in anticipation, Chauncey began to preach what turned out to be an inspiring sermon entitled "She's not the Girl She Used to be"; a powerful sermon about the woman who was healed after she lost everything she had as a result of an issue of blood. He was brilliant. He dazzled that congregation and with a Hammond organ backing him up, shouted with tears streaming down his face. "When she met Jesus, everything was alright. I've come to tell you today that Jesus is able to heal any issue that you have!" People looked on with amazement and many shared tears of Joy as he preached as though he was finally free from his past. Others praised God with him as he danced across the pulpit, a scene that put the finishing touches on a magnificent message.

After the service, Jada rushed to the side of her man with tears streaming down her own face and said, "Chauncey you were great today and I really felt blessed to hear you. But, I'm more blessed to say that I know you and I'm proud that you've overcome a major barrier in your life. I've never said this to you before but, I really do love you Chauncey".

At the hearing of those words, Chauncey smiled, then held her close and said "I love you more." Pressing her way through a congregation that was anxious to shake the young Pennington's hand, Aunt Eunice finally reached Chauncey, but didn't say a word. As she was holding him closely with her head firmly planted on his chest, Chauncey whispered in her ear "I'm Ready Now, I want to go see my momma and daddy."

She knew exactly what he meant and without hesitation, nodded and took him by his hand and led him as he led Jada from the throng of well wishers to the car, where she gave him directions to the cemetery.

Chapter 4

It was a beautiful day. The sun was shining as bright as it ever had in May in Northern Ohio and by the time they all reached the cemetery, a nice breeze hovered over the area and eased the temperature just enough for the weather to be called perfect. The cemetery was well manicured and if not for the tombstones, it could be mistaken for a garden. As they walked closer to the place his parents were buried, Chauncey slowed his pace, eventually stopping, and said with a nervous voice, "Auntie, please wait here with Jada for a moment. I need to go by myself. I just want to be alone for a moment."

After getting the okay from Aunt Eunice, Chauncey slowly approached his parents' burial sight. When he reached the plot of ground that held his beloved mother and father, Chauncey became overwhelmed with emotion and told his parents he was sorry for what happened to them. As his nose began to run, he sniffled and said to them, "I wish you were here, it's been hard living down here without you."

Afterwards, he removed his coat and placed it across his right shoulder and stared intently at the tombstone which towered over the others in the cemetery and bore the inscription, Pennington, Wallace Evansworth, II, December 25, 1927 - June 19, 1977. Suzanne Yvette, Oct. 19, 1933 – June 19, 1977. Wiping his eyes with his right hand, Chauncey caressed his mother's side of the tombstone with his left hand and whispered, "I couldn't save you but I tried and I want you to know that I'll never forget you and I'll always love you and I'm gone make it momma; for you I'm gone make it."

Being freed, momentarily, from his grief, Chauncey slowly lifted himself to an upright position, wiped his face, and called out to his aunt and girlfriend "Ya'll come on!"

When Jada and Aunt Eunice joined Chauncey at the tombstone, they both hugged him as he gave them both reassuring caresses and smiles. "This is the happiest day of my life. I feel like a weight has been lifted off of my shoulders." Chauncey continued. "Auntie, thank you for caring for me and raising me to be the man I am. I know I lost a mother, but in you I've found the true meaning of motherhood and it is a blessing to be able to look at you and see the strength that you've instilled in me. Happy Mother's Day Auntie," Chauncey said as he presented her with a gift wrapped box.

"I didn't know what I was in for," Aunt Eunice recalled, "But that boy made me feel so special. He gave me a silver necklace with a pendant that held one of the few pictures we'd ever taken together after his parents died, and it was inscribed, "To My Momma".

But that was just the beginning of the day's surprises. After Chauncey presented Aunt Eunice with her gift, he turned towards Jada with that foolish grin of his and said. "I've only known you for a short period of time but it seems as though I've known you all my life. We fit together like hand in glove and I am deeply in love with you. I love your smile, and you remind me so much of my momma. Not just because of your smile, but the way you hold me, the way you console me, the way you speak sweet inspiration into my soul when I'm faced with life's most difficult challenges. I want to take care of you Jada, I want to love you and give you everything this world has to offer. I want to be there for you at your most vulnerable moments, just like you've been there for me." Chauncey said as he went down on bended knee to gasps of the girl who didn't know what was about to hit her. "Jada will you marry me? Will you let me be your husband? Will you let me show you how bad I need you in my life forever? Will you?"

As Aunt Eunice looked on excitedly in astonishment, Jada gazed at Chauncey with those big brown, tear filled eyes and said slowly and softly "Yes... Yes... Yes... Chauncey, I love you too."

"An engagement at the cemetery, Honey I done seen it all." Eunice said laughingly, with a gaping smile on her jolly face as Jada and Chauncey ignored his aunt as they hugged and kissed. "It looks like we need to start planning for a wedding. But first you got to talk to this girl's daddy. Chauncey you hear me."

Chapter 5

After that terrific Mother's Day weekend, Chauncey and Jada joyously traveled back to school to prepare for their biggest weekend as a newly engaged couple. A few weeks later, with their families in attendance, they graduated among the class of 1991, with honors from The State University of Ohio, Chauncey with his Masters in Divinity and Jada with a Bachelors degree in Elementary Education. After the ceremony, the proud groom to be and future educator dined with their relatives, where they shared with Jada's father and step-mother the good news of their engagement for the first time. After Jada and Chauncey finally spilled the beans to her family, Aunt Eunice acted surprised all over again and said, "You two make a marvelous couple. Now how soon can I expect another little Chauncey?"

"Auntie that's not appropriate, I haven't even received the blessings of Mr. and Mrs. Blaylock." Chauncey replied biting his top lip.

At first, Mr. Blaylock grimaced and was apprehensive about the prospects of loosing his only child to marriage at age twenty to a man she'd only known for a little over a half a year, but he quickly warmed up to the idea once he took into consideration Chauncey's evident affection for his daughter and the boy's academic success and lofty career aspirations. "He's a good boy," said Mr. Blaylock. "He'll make you a fine husband Jada and if you're happy then I'm happy Baby Girl," he said as he hugged and kissed her.

After the graduation dinner, life was on a fast track for the newly engaged couple and within four months they were poised for an elaborate wedding ceremony in Jada's hometown of Odessa. With her father officiating the wedding at the Bethel A.M.E. church where he served as an associate minister, the wedding was as beautiful as the new bride, who walked down the isle with a gorgeous pearly white wedding gown that was embellished with a beaded bodice, a flowing organza skirt, and a long train that seemingly filled the sanctuary. With her face covered with a pearly white veil befitting a princess, she slowly made her way to an anticipatory Chauncey, who was dressed in a charcoal tuxedo with an embroidered silver vest. He was dashing and after the wedding march played a second too long and Jada had failed to reach him in a timely fashion, Chauncey, without warning just left his place at the altar and met Jada in the isle, to the surprise of their nearly two hundred guests.

As the joyous crowd watched in adoration, Chauncey grabbed her by the hand, lifted her veil prematurely and proceeded to kiss her passionately. While onlookers whispered and laughed at the boy who must be foolishly in love, Reverend Blaylock said, as he laughed and covered his eyes "Boy bring her on down to the altar. The ceremony hasn't even started yet." When they finally reached the altar, they both recited vows they had written and in a very sincere moment of life dedication they each said to the other "I Do". Jada's father then said jokingly, "Now you can kiss the bride." As they embraced like they would never see each other again, Chauncey leaned his six foot three inch frame over and kissed his expectant, much shorter bride passionately as sweat poured from his forehead.

Sister McLeroy, now suffering from the beginning stages of Alzheimer's, was in attendance. She had traveled all the way from northern Ohio with Chauncey's Aunt Eunice to witness "her pastor's son's wedding." She sat near the isle to accommodate her frequent trips to the restroom and when Chauncey and his new bride, during the recessional, approached the area where she was sitting she reached out and grabbed them both and whispered encouraging words of wisdom to each of them "Now baby, if you really want to get pregnant right away, soak yourself in some pure Epson salt and mayonnaise the night before relations and when he's ready for relations you give him some

The Day All Hell Broke Loose

sugar water so he can stay strong a long time." she said as Jada covered her mouth in embarrassment.

She then whispered a few words of encouragement to Chauncey. "That William Montgomery ain't but fifty two years old and I ain't got but a few mo years left myself. But Baby I want to see you get your daddy's church back before I die. It's just about torn up now. If you want that church, I'll bust a cap in his ole swole lip and won't nobody know but you, me and the Lord." she said as Chauncey laughed out loud and pulled away to complete the recessional with his new bride.

After receiving well wishes from their family and friends, the newly weds embarked on an all expense paid honeymoon to the beautiful Island of Jamaica, where they bathed in the Sun and frolicked on the tropical beaches for seven days and seven nights. They made passionate love every morning, every night, and every chance they got in between. They enjoyed each other and took advantage of the free life of love birds, because they knew that they would soon loose that freedom to the trappings of the responsibilities of life.

While in Jamaica, however, they did make a few decisions concerning their immediate future and one of those important decisions was to move back to Odessa so that Jada, who already had a job offer from her former elementary school, could begin her career as Chauncey struggled to find direction in his career path. But Chauncey made, arguably, the most important decision of his life as he enjoyed an evening massage with Jada in the pool area of the resort. As he lay on his stomach being greased down by the professional masseuse, Chauncey turned his head toward Jada, who was lying on her back partially covered with a towel and said, "Baby ever since I preached at Mt. Carmel and visited my parents' grave sight I haven't had those crazy nightmares that I've been telling you about, but I have had dreams where God has visited me. And for the first time in my life I know that I've received clearance from the Lord to pursue pastoring as my full time occupation." he said with sincere eyes, waiting on a response.

"I knew one day God would lead you to pastor but I didn't know when it would happen." Jada said with a smile as she reached for his hand. "I know it's gonna be difficult for us for a while, but I fully support your decision. I just want you to be the man God called you to be, and if you do that you'll be all the man I need or could ever desire."

Once back in Odessa, the newlyweds expected a long, bright, future, together, and finally begin to see some of the fruits of their collegiate success. Jada was quickly hired as a second grade teacher at the very elementary school she had attended as a child and Chauncey, though not earning the salary adequate for one who holds a Masters degree, was hired and worked tremendously hard as an adjunct professor at a small local bible college to help make ends meet. It wasn't an easy time for the Pennington's, but they loved each other and enjoyed roughing it as relative newcomers to the realm of employment. Jada knew that this uncomfortable lifestyle wouldn't last for ever because Chauncey hadn't even begun to maximize his gifts or resources. Their future was so bright together that they both could see it; though it seemed far in the distance.

Chauncey was passionate about his call from God to be a pastor and he knew now more than ever that his destiny was to pastor in his father's footsteps. After seemingly conquering the demons of his past, Chauncey hadn't had those haunting, depressing nightmares about his parent's death since he'd preached at his father's church and visited the grave sight. To him that coincidence served as confirmation that he was now ready to walk as his daddy did; but greater than his daddy did.

With excitement and expectancy, Chauncey and Jada mailed out resumes to several vacant churches in pleasant climate areas across the country. But after months of no response, Chauncey began to pray for any response and even took his warm climate stipulation off of his desires and mailed resumes north of his imaginary border. The wait was on. But, surely someone would call.

One day while working late at the bible college, Chauncey did receive a call, but it wasn't from any church. It was Jada, and she was as excited as a cricket in the sunshine. When he picked up the phone he was greeted by a giggly Jada who shouted "Chauncey! You won't believe this!"

With concern and optimism in his voice, he replied, "What is it Jada? Did somebody respond to my resume? What?"

"No Silly! It's even better than that!" She said, anxious to deliver the news. "You're going to be daddy!"

At that very moment Chauncey quickly hang up the phone and raced to their tiny, two bedroom apartment and greeted his little mother-to-be.

Nine months and plenty of pain later, Chauncey and Jada were the proud parents of a beautiful little girl, whom they named Elizabeth Yvette Pennington; Elizabeth, after the first name of Jada's deceased mother and Yvette, after the middle name of Chauncey's mother who had been killed.

Nothing really changed in the Pennington household over the next two years other than the baby's diaper size and by mid 1993 Chauncey was twenty three years old and really exhausted with his search for a pastorate. He was really frustrated more than anything because over the past two years he had been interviewed on several occasions only to be told he's too young. By this time Chauncey was content with being Jada's husband, he was enjoying the privilege of being Lizzy's dad, and finally settling in as a country professor in Odessa. His focus shifted from wanting to be a pastor and he focused more on being the very best family man he could be. But as Chauncey turned his attention away from his search for a church, a little church in a small north Florida town had turned their attention on him.

Chapter 6

"All ya'll crazy as hell" yelled the Reverend Woodrow Elliot, pastor of the small Greater Mt. Carmel church located in a little town just north of Tallahassee. "If you think I'm gone keep preaching up here every second and fourth Sunday while ya'll pay everybody but me, ya'll got another thang coming" he said as his wife Wilma sat confidently with her arms folded, thinking that the deacons would surely give her husband a raise from the $50 they gave him on the Sunday's he preached.

"Now Woodrow, you just hold your horses!" shouted Sis. Lula Penny, the church's over weight piano player, as the deacons looked on with mischievous grins on their faces. "I earn every dime I get! You keep my name out yo snaggled toothed mouth, you ignant fool!"

"Now wait a minute!" yelled Deacon Walter Picket.

"This is a conference meeting and we are in the house of the Lord and as long as I'm Chairman of this deacon board, I won't stand for it. Now Reverend Elliot, the deacons have decided not to pay you a dime until you learn another sermon!" he asserted, as the other six members of his deacon's board nodded in agreement.

"I tell you what. Today ya'll gone have to make a believer out of me cause I ain't goin' nowhere till ya'll give me a raise and I get the $300 what ya'll already owe me!", ranted Reverend Elliot, as the other thirteen members nervously embraced for a showdown.

Mother Snelling, one of the oldest members of Mt. Carmel, who normally sat quietly during the always heated conference meetings, rose slowing out of her pew and chastised both the pastor and the deacons for their rude behavior in God's house saying, "I've been in this church for over sixty years and it has got rough sometimes. But I ain't never seen it get as bad as this. You deacons ought to be ashamed of yourselves and Woodrow as a man of God, you ought to be ashamed too. This don't make no sense. I make a motion that that we pay the Pastor, he earned it, even if it was the same ole dry sermon bout' Lazarus every week."

"I can do you one better Mother Snelling." answered the fifty nine year old Pickett "I make a motion that we give Reverend Elliot $500 dollars and tell him good riddance. All in favor signify by the sign "I"."

"Now wait a minute" rebutted the disgruntled, but pitiful pastor. "Ya'll ain't got to do me like that. I just want to be treated fair."

"All in favor say I!" Deacon Pickett shouted overshadowing Elliot's pitiful pleas for mercy.

With over two thirds of the angry congregation standing and shouting "I", Pickett moved carefully from his customary seat in the deacon's corner and inched his way towards the pulpit and looked Reverend Elliot squarely in the eye and said with a smirk "That settles it. The church has spoken. Get yo hat, yo coat, and get the hell from around all us crazy folk".

"Ya'll can't vote me out! I ain't done nothin' but try to be ya'll's pastor"

"You getting out today Woodrow!" Deacon Pickett shouted back as two of the churches much stronger deacons approached the impeached pastor.

"Why ya'll doing this to me? Get ya'll hands off me!" shouted Woodrow as the two deacons drug him from the pulpit and proceeded to shove him out of the back doors of the church.

After crying and asking the Lord why, Wilma looked back at the silent congregation, who seemed to turn a deaf ear to her husband's pleas, and said "As long as ya'll let Pickett run this church ya'll will never prosper! God have mercy on the soul of the next man who tries to pastor this church."

With the same smirk that he gave her ousted husband, Deacon Pickett squinted his eyes and answered slowly but surely, "Wilma don't be bitter. Even teeth and tongue fall out sometimes. If you don't believe me ask Woodrow. A whole lot of his teeth done fell out", he said with a grin, as some of the members sniggled, other members, including Mother Snelling, frowned on his distasteful farewell to the Elliots.

"Now what are we going to do Deacon Pickett?" questioned Ruth Anne Dunn, who totally disagreed with the ousting of Pastor Elliot and was the only college graduate to attend the rural church. "We just can't keep treating preachers like this and expect our church to flourish!"

Her husband Billy echoed her sentiments and said convincingly "What ever we do we need to find a pastor fast, a man that can take this church to the next level and lead us out of this mess!"

"I know exactly what we're gone do." uttered the elder statesman. "There was a boy out of Texas that submitted a resume to my first cousins church in Tampa. They didn't want him because they said he was too young. But my cousin tells me he's a educated fella and felt like we'd be a good fit for a up and coming preacher. So I got his papers in a file back there in the business room and I thank we ought to look at him. Yea, I know he's a young preacher but, I say the younger a preacher is, the more we can mold him and shape him into the kind of preacher we want. Them older preachers like Woodrow, you can't tell 'em nothin. We need us somebody we can learn how to be a good preacher."

"We don't need anyone to pastor this church that needs to be taught how to lead us Deacon Pickett. We need someone seasoned in ministry, someone who can teach us. I recommend that we form a new search committee tonight and include older ministers as possible candidates", lamented Ruth Anne, who by this time was willing to go to war with Pickett and his cronies to save the church she grew up in.

Ruth Anne's embolden statement was a result of her knowledge that Pickett wasn't foolish enough to anger her because she and her husband were two of only a handful of members paying tithes while the others continued the tradition of paying the five dollar a month membership dues. Pickett once chastised his wife, Eloise, who angered the thirty five year old accountant during a choir rehearsal saying. "Eloise, you need to stop your foolishness. We got to be careful how we treat that girl. She is one of the ones who paying the bills up there at the church. Ruth Anne and Billy gives at least $700 every month and we can't afford make her upset. You leave Ruth Anne alone!"

After Ruth Anne spoke her piece with authority, Deacon Pickett quickly granted her request. "I tell you what; I make a motion that you and me can be the search committee. I'll bring all the information on the boy from Texas and you go and find and bring back information on as may old preachers as you want. The next conference will be scheduled a month from this day. All in favor signify by standing", he said confidently, knowing he had the required majority. All stood but the three members in the Dunn family, Mother Snelling, and Sister Penny, who was just too lazy to get up out of her seat.

"That settles it. The Church has spoken, and by a vote of 16-4, a search committee of myself and Sister Dunn has been formed. With that being said, the two of us will report back to the next church conference meeting, to be held the Friday before the first Sunday in next month. This conference is adjourned. God bless you and God bless this church and oh, I almost forgot… God bless America"

With the meeting officially adjourned and many of the members exiting the sanctuary, Ruth Anne approached the gleaming deacon who was standing near the altar, and said with the voice of a woman determined to make a difference, "Now you know that wasn't right Deacon Pickett, but I will respect the will of the church and I look forward to working with you to find the best possible candidates to fill our vacancy."

"Ruthie you grew up in this church and you know I don't know but one way to run this church and that's the Lord's way. Acts 6:3 says it is the deacon's responsibility to run the business of the church and over the past twenty-five years, as the chairman, I thank I've done a pretty good job or I wouldn't still be chairman", Deacon Pickett said with authority.

"I don't know what your standard for success is," responded a furious Ruth Anne, "but if causing confusion, and running pastors off, and not seeing this church grow in twenty five years is your standard, I guess you're correct. But I beg to differ." She continued, "This church is in ruin because of you and those deacons and I won't continue to stand by and allow that to happen as long as God gives me strength. I pray that God leads you as you bring appropriate candidates to the table for us to discuss as possible replacements."

"Did you say appropriate candidates, Ruth Anne?" the confident deacon questioned. "I thought I made myself clear to you and everybody else. I only have one man in mind as a possible replacement. If history repeats itself, as it has the last six times we've voted on a pastor in the past five years, that boy from Odessa gone be our next pastor. We need a young man Ruthie. Somebody that we can show how to be just what we need. Trust me. He's educated and he's not from 'round here and my deacons will treat him just like he's one of our own sons. He'll be good for us and we'll be good for him."

As the dumbfounded pastor's search committee member listened quietly in disbelief, her husband Billy stood afar with his back planted firmly against the wall of the sanctuary witnessing his wife's frustration. "Ruth Anne!" he called. "It's time to go; only God can deal with these hellions." he continued as his voice drifted off as if he was talking to himself.

But before she ended her one-sided conversation with the man who helped baptize her at age eleven, she looked at him and said, "Dec. Pickett have it your way. I don't want to participate in any proceeding that will be unfair to the faithful people of Greater Mt. Carmel or might lead to any embarrassment or any more stress to me or my family. I just pray that someday soon you'll understand that there's a way other than Pickett's way. According to my recollection your way has been wrong many times more than it has been right. Until that time, I have no problem with attending other churches until I find a place that I can worship freely without all the chaos of Mt. Carmel. You have a nice night Sir."

"Now I don't want you to leave, but if you want to leave, leave", he said with joy hidden just beneath his breath. Joy, because Pickett knew that Ruth Anne would be his only major opposition to bringing the inexperienced preacher from Odessa to be their next pastor. "But I'll make you a promise, if I make the wrong decision this time, I'll step down as chairman and beg your forgiveness. But if I do..." he said smiling while pausing to grab both her hands. "I want you, Billy and that little girl of ya'll's to come back, not to apologize, but to help us turn this church around."

Without as much as a sigh from the stunned, soon to be fugitive, she pulled her hands away from the proud deacon, and walked hastily away to meet her husband, who by this time was on his way to end the meeting himself.

After Ruth Anne and Billy exited the sanctuary, Deacon Pickett went into the "business room" of the church and began to look into an old file cabinet to find the information of the young boy from Odessa. As he rummaged through the file cabinet he finally came across what he was looking for. "Ahhh, there it is, Chauncey Evansworth Pennington.", he said as he devilishly smiled and murmured to himself. "Boy if you still available, you 'bout to be made a man."

As he turned out the lights of the small office, he walked out slowly into the sanctuary, grabbed his bible, his John Deer hunting cap, put a fresh chew of Red Man tobacco in his mouth, and made his way to his brand new 1993 Cadillac Sedan Deville singing verses of one of his favorite hymns. "Hallelujah, Hallelujah, I know the storm is passing over, Hallelujah!"

CHAPTER 7

Living modestly, but extremely happy in their small, but comfortable confines in Odessa, Chauncey and Jada was the perfect picture of America's small family. Although Chauncey hadn't reached his economic peak and Jada's salary as an elementary school teacher was sometimes just enough, they lived as though they had more than enough, primarily because they both knew the best years of their lives were yet to come. No, Chauncey wasn't where he wanted to be professionally, because teaching at the local bible college wasn't his passion nor did it provide the type of lifestyle he dreamed of giving his wife and daughter. But just because he wasn't where he wanted to be professionally, didn't mean that he had any plans of treading down the cloudy road to the persistent state of depression that had plagued and characterized so much of his early childhood.

He would often call his beloved Aunt Eunice to seek guidance when faced with the displeasure of not being the kind of provider he desired to be, and on one occasion she shared with him that, "A whole lot of love is greater than a whole lot of money any day." And from the start, Chauncey and Jada had plenty of that. Love filled the Pennington's little two bedroom, town house styled apartment where the couple spent many entertaining days and enchanting nights with the new love of each of their lives.

They felt blessed to be the parents of Elizabeth Yvette, and little did Lizzy know, she was blessed too. With a charming, highly intelligent, handsome father, coupled with a gorgeous, petite, educated, ex-cheerleader mother, Elizabeth Yvette could boast when she's older that she has the pedigree of the an Ebony Fashion Fair model and the next Nobel Peace Prize winner.

Time shared with Elizabeth always made Chauncey's bad days better and his good days extraordinary. Just one smile from daddy's little dumpling made mountains mole hills and stormy waters peaceful. She didn't know it, but she put life in perspective for her daddy. No matter how hard times got in the classroom or how many disappointments he encountered due to a lack of response from vacant churches, when he looked into her hazel brown eyes Chauncey knew that his ultimate responsibility was being a good husband and good father. With one stroke of Lizzy's tiny hands across his face, he knew that there was at least one person on the face of the earth that loved him unconditionally, who didn't know enough about anything to care about his faults or failures.

On most Saturday mornings after eating a nice breakfast, Chauncey and Jada would spend time in deep conversation about their weeks at work, make plans for an exciting weekend, or sometimes they would even travel the fifteen miles or so to Jada's father's house to share their morning and Elizabeth with the proud grandparents, as was the case on a bright sunshiny day in the Spring of 1994. Jada was washing dishes as Chauncey held Lizzy in his lap as he sat comfortably on the couple's old black pleather living room sofa, when she asked, "What are we doing today Chauncey?"

"I was thinking that we could go to Home Depot, buy a few flowers, and do something with that ugly flowerbed out front" he replied as he looked uninterestedly at Toon Disney as Lizzy bounced out of control on his knees.

"That sounds good, but we really don't have any extra money to buy flowers, we need to get more groceries. You and Lizzy eat like dinosaurs," she answered back with a grin.

As Chauncey turned towards Jada he gazed at her as if he had found the master plan, he offered "Well how about this." He said with a childish grin. "What if we call your dad, ask if we could bring Lizzy over for an extended stay, and we come back home for an all day affair. That won't cost us a dime and we can finally make love without the interruptions from you know who." he said slyly as his eyes shifted toward and unknowing Lizzy.

"That sounds fine Chauncey but you and I both know that Lizzy is a handful and we can't afford to be pregnant again; not now anyway"

"Aw, Jada" He replied looking pitiful. "I just want to love on you; I miss my quality time with you. I'm starting to get a little jealous of Lizzy anyway. She gets all the sugar, all the hugs, and she's even taken my spot in my own bed." He said as Jada walked sexily toward the pleading lover.

"OK, Chauncey. I'll call my daddy, we'll take Lizzy, and then momma is gonna come back and take care of her oldest baby" She said as she leaned over to kiss both of her children on their foreheads.

After dropping Lizzy off at the Blaylock's, Jada and Chauncey rushed back home for a moment of romance. As they both jumped out of their 1990 Ford Explorer they raced towards the entrance of the house and once in the front door they embraced and kissed as love dripped from their brows. With a sense of urgency Chauncey lifted his little wonder girl and planted her firmly on the stairwell for a love making session on the stairs. As he lifted her skirt and pulled her panties to the side, Chauncey began to thrust his sweaty fingers into that special place as if to lubricate it and prepared the runway for a long overdo landing. As he penetrated the spot that only he had penetrated before, he pulled her hair as she dug her nails deep into his rippled back. For the first time in months they were making love like savaged beasts. Then…the phone rang.

"No. Don't answer that." Jada whispered as she grabbed Chauncey's waist to intensify the speed of his slowing pace.

"I got to.", he moaned as he restrained a premature ejaculation.

"Nooooooo.", she begged.

"It may be your dad." he replied.

"Well answer it but please don't stop baby." she compromised.

With as much composure as he could muster, Chauncey answered the hallway phone. "Hello. Pennington residence." with a slight gasp.

"Yes. May I speak to the Reverend Chauncey E. Pennington please?"

"He's speaking", Chauncey answered as he slowly pulled himself out a pre-climactic, disappointed, silently protesting, and pouting Jada.

"Reverend this is Deacon Walter Pickett, chairman of the board at Greater Mt. Carmel Missionary Baptist in Florida."

"Hello Deacon Pickett", he responded as he looked curiously at his wife. "How may I help you this morning?"

"Well, I know you don't know who I am or where I get your number from, but you sent a resume down to my cousin's church in Tampa when they was looking for a pastor."

"Um Huh.", Chauncey replied as he gave thumbs up to Jada and requested a pen and paper.

"He told me that you was a highly qualified young man and that you had graduated from a big school in Ohio. At the time that you sent your resume in, you were a little too young for St. Mark. But he did know that we were having problems with our own pastor and suggested that if we ever got rid of him, for stealing church funds of course, we should contact you."

"I'm sorry to hear that Deacon Pickett", Chauncey replied as his heart begin to race at the very thought of his dream coming true.

"Naw don't be sorry, he had it coming to him", the chairman said with a slow southern drawl. "What I really called you for, Reverend, was to know if you was still interested in becoming a pastor. If so I would love for you to come down here to beautiful north Florida to do some catfish fishing and chit-chattin' and hopefully sway you to be our next pastor. Now we ain't as big as St. Mark; we just a few of God's humble chirren trying to make it in. And because our last pastor, Rev. Woodrow Elliott... do you know him?"

"No Sir I don't believe I do"

"I figured you didn't, but he was demon possessed. He the reason why we don't have no members now. But I figured, with you being a young man, you'd have plenty of time and energy to build us back up a great church". The confident deacon continued.

"Deacon Pickett, I'm absolutely honored that I was recommended and I thank you for so graciously extending the offer to me," Chauncey replied as he chuckled at the deacons bad grammar and country accent. "But to be honest with you I don't know much about the church and I'll need to talk this over with my wife and of course pray about it. Let me get your phone number and church's name again and I'll call you as soon as I make any decision."

"The church name is Greater Mt. Carmel and my number is area code 850-666-2476". Deacon Pickett answered with anticipation, hoping that the young preacher would be interested in the vacancy.

"Now I just want to tell you, young man, you take all the time you need. I already told the members at our last conference meeting that I felt like you was our man and we prayed long and hard that night. Every one of 'em supported what I felt in my gut. That's why I called. If you choose not to consider our church, I'll still appreciate it if you send another young preacher our way 'cause God knows our little church can't take another Woodrow Elliot. You just call when you hear from the Lord."

"I'll surely do it Deacon Pickett." Chauncey said as he joyously grinned at Jada and prepared to end the unexpected conversation.

After the deacon gave his carefully crafted closing statements, Chauncey thanked him again and said "Have a nice day." to the reply of "You take care and tell your family that I said be blessed." from the deacon.

When Chauncey hung up the phone, he was almost motionless, though he had the biggest smile on his face since he heard the news that he was going to be a daddy.

"Jada, you won't believe it." He said as he spoke in a tone that epitomized the emotional state he was in.

"It better be really good..." She replied with her hands on her hips and rolling those big eyes. "...especially since you've gone into the business of starting fires that you can't put out mister."

"Destiny called me today. My destiny called me." He repeated with a voice of confirmation. "That was a deacon from a church that I didn't even send a resume to. And what makes it so amazing is that the name of the church is GREATER Mt. Carmel. Baby don't you see, this was God's way of showing me my place of destiny. It's the same name as the church my daddy built, but to the second power and Jada it's in Florida. This must be my destiny." He said as he lifted his wife above his head.

"Chauncey you know that I'll support you in anything you undertake and I can see by the look in your eyes that you are really excited about this opportunity. But slow down for a moment baby," she said, looking into his eyes as he slowly lowered her to the living room floor.

"Every thing that glitters is not gold." She continued. "Let's be patient and obedient to God's voice and if it's for us He will give us confirmation."

"He already did Jada." Chauncey said as he walked with a swagger back to the place of their three minute sexual encounter. "I agree that we need to pray, but I can't go into prayer knowing that my wife thinks I'm unable to finish what I start. So why don't you come on over here, and give your baby a second chance to do it right."

"Praying can definitely wait." the lusty eyed damsel said, as she crawled on top of her anxiously waiting husband.

"Take the phone off the hook!"

Chapter 8

Nearly a week had past since Chauncey had spoken to Deacon Pickett and though Jada constantly urged him to ask God for confirmation, Chauncey knew this was the place for him. Though he had never stepped a foot on the grounds of Greater Mt. Carmel, Chauncey was convinced that what ever challenges lay before him, he would be able to conquer them and besides this church was in Florida. Yes, it was a small city and yes it would probably mean a significant decrease in salary, but as he often told his hesitant wife, "when destiny calls, she'll provide for the respondent."

On a rainy Friday evening following the promising Saturday conversation he shared with Greater Mt. Carmel's chairman deacon, Chauncey was traveling along with Jada and their active young daughter to meet Jada's father and stepmother for dinner at Friday's. While driving cautiously to prevent any bad weather accidents, Chauncey's cell phone began to vibrate violently in the console of the Explorer.

"Jada will you get that please" OK she responded as she tried vehemently to quiet a squirming Elizabeth, who had grown hungry and impatient in her car seat.

With one hand stuffing a pacifier in Lizzy's mouth and the other grasping her husband's cell phone, she answered with a slight bit of frustration in response to the baby's uneasiness. "Hello."

"Have you all lost your ever loving minds?" ranted a jokingly bitter Aunt Eunice as Jada whispered to Chauncey "It's Aunt Eunice and she sounds mad."

"I called all day Saturday and the line was busy. I called all through the week and that crazy answering service came on. Ya'll know you could've called me by now."

"Well Auntie it' really been crazy around here and we were going to call as soon as we got a breather."

"Just hush Jada. You're probably just covering for that knuckle head husband of yours." Eunice said as Jada smiled.

"Well how are you all doing?"

"We're doing just fine Aunt Eunice, but I think you need to talk to your Miss Lizzy, she's becoming a handful." Jada answered as Eunice laughed.

"Her daddy said he's going to have to spank her if she doesn't stop being a big baby."

"You tell Chauncey, if he lays a hand on my precious Lizzy, I'll call protective services. Better yet. I'll skin his curly head myself. He's the one who needs the spanking. Where is he any way?" Aunt Eunice said laughing, with anticipation of talking to the son she never had.

"Your little man is right here, driving his ladies through a thunder storm for a night out on the town. I'm sure he wants to talk to you because he has some very good news, even though we haven't decided if we should accept the offer yet".

"Well put him on Baby and I'll talk to you and Lizzy a little later."

"OK" she said as she handed the phone over to Chauncey, who knew his Aunt was probably a little upset because she hadn't heard from him in a couple of days.

"Auntie before you blast me out for not calling this week let me tell you what happened on Saturday." an excited Chauncey said as he pulled into the packed parking lot of the restaurant.

"I think I got the break I've been looking for. A man called me from north Florida and offered me the opportunity to interview to be their next pastor. I didn't even send a resume, but I was recommended by another church in Florida that overlooked me initially."

"How great is that?" Aunt Eunice replied glowing with pride.

"But that's not all." he said as Jada and Lizzy waited patiently for the conversation to end so that they might join the rest of the family. "The name of the church is Mt. Carmel, Greater Mt. Carmel."

"Is that right? That's the same name of the church your daddy built. How ironic would that be? Chauncey this might be the place for you; especially if it's in Florida."

"That's what I've been telling Jada, Auntie. This offer is too good to be true even though the church has to be much smaller than what I'm used to."

"Go ahead and tell me about it." An overjoyed Eunice asked an equally overjoyed Chauncey. "Where is it? And better yet, who are some of the people there? You know, your mom and I spent a little time down that way just before momma and daddy moved up here to Ohio. But that's been years ago."

"Well Auntie I don't know much about the church or the town. I've looked the area up on the internet and the only thing I've found is a city website that, unfortunately, is still under construction. I can't tell you for sure anything but the church name, but from my conversation with Dec. Pickett, I've visualized it as a beautiful little place where there's a whole lot of fishing going on. I think this is the place." Chauncey said as he motioned for Jada to go on into the restaurant if she wanted.

As Jada mouthed "We're fine." Aunt Eunice said with a bit of cautiousness, "Son that name Pickett is very familiar to me and if your momma was alive she'd remember too. When I was a teenager and Suzy was just a girl we worked on a tobacco farm called Pickett Plantation. A prejudiced old white man owned the property and me and your momma worked in the drying barn with daddy, hanging the tobacco."

As Chauncey put his right hand on his forehead as if to say, "not another tobacco farm story.", Aunt Eunice continued as if he didn't have a scheduled appointment.

"That old man was always nice to your granddaddy and never said a bad word to me or Suzy because he knew that our daddy didn't play the radio when it came to the mistreatment of us. But old man Pickett did have his way with some of the other black girls and even had a slew of children by one of his maids. I was crazy about Miss Ethel's oldest boy by Pickett. That boy had the prettiest brown caramel skin and because he was Pickett's son all the other boys looked up to him and he always told them what to do." She said as Chauncey grew tired of the impromptu history lesson.

Interrupting his aunt, who has a long history of rambling and to respond to his father-in-law's urgent wave to come on inside, Chauncey insisted "Auntie, I don't mean to cut you off. But Jada's father is standing at the entrance of the restaurant. He's been waiting for us and I can only imagine that his patience is running real thin by now. I promise I will call you as soon as we're done with dinner so we can finish up. OK."

"OK Baby I'm sorry. You should've told me they were waiting for yall."

"Don't be sorry. But I do want to hear about old man Pickett's son. I never knew you had any love interests other than me." Chauncey replied laughingly.

"Bye boy." Aunt Eunice replied childishly. "You tell Jada and my Lizzy, I said I'll talk to them later and tell the Blaylocks I wish them a wonderful evening. And when you talk to that Deacon Pickett again ask him for your old single Auntie; is he related to them Pickett boys from the plantation? If he is, ask him how that old Walter is doing. "

As a hysterically laughing Eunice abruptly hang up the phone, Chauncey's pleasant facial expression, which was decorated with a smile as he walked into the restaurant, slowly changed to a look of confusion as he approached the dinner table.

As he sat down in the booth adjacent to his in-laws, Chauncey stared at his phone in unbelief and whispered to himself, "That's it."

"Is everything alright Chauncey?" asked, a curious, Mrs. Blaylock.

"Oh, Yes." he replied as Jada shoveled Lizzy off to her father and snuggled next to her husband. "Everything is just fine. Matter of fact I'm more convinced than ever that we're about to move to Florida."

"Chauncey we haven't discussed any new developments. How can you be so sure especially since I haven't received my confirmation?" asked Jada.

"You've been looking for confirmation and now I'm about to give it to you." Chauncey replied as the Blaylocks sat, listening interestedly at the playful, but squabbling couple.

"I was just on the phone with Aunt Eunice and she told me that she and my mom actually worked for a while on a tobacco farm called Pickett Plantation."

"As in Deacon Pickett?" asked Jada moments before she widened her already big eyes and dropped her jaw.

"Yes Baby. She told me that Pickett's father actually owned the plantation and that she had a crush on him years ago, before they moved to Ohio. Now if that's not enough for your confirmation, I don't what is. My daddy's church name and the place where my momma grew up, that's the confirmation Jada!"

As the two sat quietly for minutes pondering their major decision, Mr. and Mrs. Blaylock stared at the two and Benny even gave a rather fatherly response. "You just got married and you seem to be settling in just fine. Don't you all think that you're moving a little too fast? Chauncey I know you want to be a pastor, but you're still young and there will be plenty of opportunities in the future. You all really need to think about this."

With an authoritative but somber voice, Chauncey eagerly replied as the waitress delivered their food. "Mr. Blaylock, you're right. I have been thinking about becoming a pastor since I was a little boy, but not for the reasons you may think. I have a master's degree and I can find a well paying job anywhere in the country. But for me it's bigger than that and it's not about the money. It's my destiny and Jada and I have prayed long and hard for God to give us direction. I feel like this is it. It's no coincidence that my mother grew up working on a tobacco farm owned by the chairman deacon's father. Nor is it a coincidence that the church's name is Greater Mt. Carmel. This is my destiny and if I'm right, destiny will provide for us."

"Daddy Chauncey is right." said Jada who spoke in agreement with her husband. "We haven't had the time to tell you guys everything, but for the past week we have been praying and asking God for guidance and I've been personally seeking God for confirmation and he gave me that confirmation tonight. We don't know how the interview process will go or if Chauncey will even be granted one. But, I do feel now, after what Aunt Eunice said that it's an opportunity worth looking deeper into. It may be a struggle and it may it may be a difficult transition, if he's chosen, but you and I both know that Chauncey loves Lizzy and I more than the world and he wouldn't knowingly lead us into a situation that wasn't right for all of us. My confirmation only gives him my consent to pursue the opportunity and only God knows what'll happen after that. Daddy, trust us on this one."

"I didn't share that with you to discourage you." said a sincere Benny as he wiped barbeque sauce off of the corner of his mouth. "I just want the best for both of you all; especially Lizzy."

As Mrs. Blaylock cleaned Lizzy's saucy hands and Chauncey and Jada prepared to leave a tip for the waitress, Mr. Blaylock, now picking his teeth, continued playfully with a toothpick hanging from his mouth; "If you all believe that this is God's way of leading you, you have my blessing to see what the end will be. I just hope that if and when you're given an interview, you fall flat on your face and those southern deacons send you and my babies running back to Odessa."

After dinner, the Blaylocks and the Penningtons said their goodbyes and with hugs and kisses they departed in opposite directions to retrieve their vehicles. Once Chauncey buckled Lizzy into her car seat and made sure Jada was securely settled in the passenger's seat, he entered the vehicle and told Jada how much he appreciated her for understanding his heart's desire.

"Jada you don't know how much it means to me to have your support. I would never have even considered leaving Odessa or even returning Pickett's phone call if I knew it would ever cause you any discomfort. I just know this is for us and I'm glad you're in my corner on this one."

"Enough of all of that stuff Chauncey. You know I'd support anything you chose to do anyway." Jada said smiling as she peered out of the sunroof to take a glimpse of the stars. "I'm really excited now. I want to go to Florida. I want to see what this little place is like. You may not believe me," she said as she turned toward Chauncey, "but ever since you told me about what Aunt Eunice said, I've had butterflies in my stomach."

As Chauncey gleamed at his wife's excitement he looked at her as if he had a bright idea and said. "Baby Lizzy is asleep, the clouds have gone away, and the night has turned out to be quite nice. I was just wondering if we could just sit here a few minutes under these Texas stars and fool around."

"No Sir!" an anxious Jada responded. "What you need to do is crank up this car and drive as fast as you can to 180 Lucid Avenue and find that man's number so we can let him know that Greater Mt. Carmel is about to have their chance to nab one the world's best kept secrets. Florida here we come!"

Chapter 9

After what turned out to be a night of confirmation, Chauncey and Jada deemed it too late to call Deacon Pickett and agreed that it would be better if they called him early Saturday morning, although they both were overly excited to have such a great opportunity.

That Saturday morning Jada rose early, as she normally did, but on this Saturday morning there was no need to wake Chauncey. He had been up virtually all night pacing the floor, constructing what would be his acceptance of Pickett's offer. After breakfast, Chauncey, who was still dressed in his Joe Boxer pajamas, prepared to make his long awaited phone call. But before Chauncey sat down at the breakfast table to make the call, Jada voluntarily escorted Elizabeth to her upstairs bedroom so that Chauncey might have a moment of privacy to talk with the deacon without any interruption or distraction from their little rambunctious rug rat.

"Here goes." Chauncey said as he let out a sigh of anxiousness.

As he held the couple's black cordless phone in his left hand, he begin dialing the eleven digit phone number with his right index finger and afterwards, waited patiently for someone to answer at the Pickett residence.

"Hello!" shouted Eloise, the wife of the chairman deacon, who must've been in a heated discussion before answering the phone.

"Yes Ma'am, may I speak to Deacon Walter Pickett please?" Chauncey asked with apprehension, due to the rude manner by which Eloise answered the phone.

"Who is this?" shouted an irritated Eloise.

"My name is Chauncey Pennington, minister from Odessa, Texas. Deacon Pickett called me last week and I'm just returning his call."

"Oh excuse me son. He's right here. Hold on for a moment." Eloise said apologetically.

"You better be glad this preacher called, you old heathen." Eloise muttered as she passed the phone to the deacon who was sitting in his favorite recliner with only a t-shirt and boxers on. "I should knock you in your selfish head with this telephone."

After quieting his belligerent wife, Pickett composed himself and answered with a scraggly morning voice "Hello Reverend. I've been waiting on your call. All I need to know is, have the Lord spoke to you yet?"

"Yes Sir he did."

"Well I'm anxious to hear what he told you son."

"Deacon Pickett, after much prayer and deliberation, my wife and I have decided that it would be an opportunity missed if we didn't take the time to come to Florida and pursue the pastorate of Greater Mt. Carmel and if everything goes well, we're prepared to leave Texas and help you all build a greater ministry there."

"Reverend, I'm so pleased to hear that. I can't wait for you and yo' family to come down for a weekend to meet the people, enjoy the great north Florida outdoors, and preach for us. How soon will you be available to travel?" Pickett asked as he gestured to his uninterested wife that he had his man.

"To be honest, my wife won't be available to travel for at least another two weeks. She's an elementary school teacher and classes won't end for her until the end of May. But I'm certain that the first weekend in June will be a perfect time for us both." Chauncey said as Jada and Lizzy re-entered the kitchen area and sat opposite of him at the breakfast table.

"Well, I tell you what. Let's make plans for ya'll to come the first weekend in June. That's a fine weekend to come because that's our communion Sunday and the people can see how you give the Lord's Supper and see how you preach too before we vote."

"Vote?" Chauncey asked with slight hesitation in his voice.

"Yes. See after you preach we gone have a meeting, of course you know I'm the chairman of the board, and if the congregation like you, and I'm sure they would since they know I'm the one recommending you, we'll name you the pastor effective that day."

"That sounds very interesting Deacon Pickett, but what about the selection process? Don't you all want to interview me along with any other candidates? I'm new at this but I thought the process was a little longer than that." Chauncey said as he looked at Jada in bewilderment.

"Reverend Pennington you'll be glad to know that there ain't no other candidates. After the last conference we had, I told the congregation about you and we prayed long and hard and fasted all that night and God showed us all that the job was yours if you wanted it. All we have to do now is set up a meeting between you, me, and the other six deacons, hear you preach, and take a vote for our records, and that'll settle it. That's the way we do it down here and so far ain't nobody objected."

"OK." responded a clarified Chauncey. "So who should I contact for traveling arrangements and hotel accommodations?"

"Now I told you before the church is in a little financial bind because of our last pastor and we really don't have nobody who can do that kind of stuff round here. But, I can tell you that if you can get here, we'll make your trip worth while and give you a little spending change to help out with yo' expense."

"Well Deacon Pickett, I'm sure we can make our own arrangements and I look forward to meeting you and the Greater Mt. Carmel family within the next few weeks and hopefully everything will all work out just fine." Chaunccy said as he lifted himself from the breakfast table, preparing to hang up the phone.

"I sure do hope so Reverend. We need a change and I feel deep down in my spirit that you the man to do it. You have a nice morning and tell your lovely family I can't wait to see them too. You take care."

"You too Deacon Pickett."

With the phone still firmly in his grasp, Chauncey walked over to his nervous wife, who was eager to learn all the details of his conversation with the chairman.

"Get ready Baby, the road has been paved and the only obstacles to me becoming the next pastor of Greater Mt. Carmel are plane tickets and hotel arrangements. We're going to Florida the first weekend in June and if the people like us, I can be voted in as early as the first Sunday in June."

"Chauncey that's great baby, but isn't this process going a little too fast. We haven't even made preparations to leave here yet. We haven't even been able to visit the place to know if it's worth the headache of moving across the country."

"I didn't think of it like that honey but..." Chauncey said before Jada interrupted to further substantiate her argument.

"Have you considered that I will need to find another job or for that matter what is the job market like north Florida? What will they pay you or will they even be able to pay you what I know you deserve? Will they be able to pay you at all?" she said as she got up from the table and begin to put away Lizzy's scattered toys.

"This is a major move Chauncey and major moves require major sacrifices. I always knew that this day would come, but I didn't know it could be as early as the first weekend in June."

"Jada, now you're stressing."

"No I'm not stressing. I'm just being realistic Chauncey"

"Yes you are. Whenever you just get up and start cleaning the house and start looking at me with those pop eyes, you are beginning to worry about something. I know you and you should know I wouldn't be so excited about this unless I knew that it would be good for us. I know that major moves require major sacrifices, but I also know that great risks can yield great rewards. I don't see it as a sacrifice anyway. I see it as obedience to God and you know that the scripture says that obedience is better than sacrifice."

"But what if we don't like the people? What if there are no good schools for Lizzy? OK... I'll admit Chauncey, I'm a little scared. Other than school, I've never really been on my own or dependant on anybody but my daddy and of course you. But if we move I'll have to depend on people I've never known or seen in my life."

"I know you're scared baby but I just trust that God won't ever lead us into any situation that he won't provide for us in or provide for us an escape from. I know it seems a little quick, but this is just God's way of further confirming his call. Don't you see baby, he's cutting out our path for us. Think about it. A year ago we didn't even know what God's plan was for our lives, but now it's plain and clear. What was once distorted from our vantage point is now slapping us right in the face. This process seems so quick and easy to you because it is. Which gives me a greater belief that, if God be for us who can be against us."

"Chauncey, just be sure that this is God. That's all."

"I think I'm sure Jada."

After his passionate plea for understanding, Chauncey walked up behind his doubtful wife, who by this time was rearranging the ornaments in her China cabinet, and massaged her tensed shoulder blades and assured her that worrying was not the answer. As he slowly caressed her with his strong hands he turned her around so that he could look directly into her eyes to get a sense of the effectiveness of his argument or any hint of cautious optimism from his wife. That's when he noticed that Jada had tears forming in her eyes. She appeared to him as a little child who was too afraid to talk about it, but too afraid to allow her fears to go unnoticed. Chauncey knew this feeling all too well, because he too had faced uncertainty and fear and on many occasions it was Jada who comforted him. Now it was his time to comfort her. As he prepared his lips to utter the words that he hoped would ease her fears, Jada positioned her fingers over his lips and whispered, "I trust you."

Looking down at the floor as if to gather her thoughts, while masking her emotions, Jada reached up and grabbed her husbands face and continued, "When I married you I knew you were ambitious and I knew you would always look after me. I'm sorry for doubting your ability to see the whole picture."

"Baby there's nothing to be sorry for."

"Let me finish Chauncey." she said as she wiped her eyes and cleared her voice.

"I want to be wherever God leads you. I want to be wherever you are. I made a vow to you on our wedding day that I'm committed to you and God's call on your life. And if he's calling you to this church, a place I've never known, I may not be prepared but I'm ready to go. What you said is right. I know God will provide for us."

With his eyes staring intently at the living room ceiling as if he was thanking God for divine intervention, and his face alleviated from the strains of knowing that his wife was uneasy about the potential problems of a seemingly premature move, Chauncey hugged Jada tightly and promised that the best years of their lives were yet to come.

After the brief conversation, he knew that Jada was still a little apprehensive about the abrupt transition, but he also got confirmation that a little apprehension wouldn't keep the love of his life from whole heartedly supporting God's direction for their lives. With Lizzy in her mother's arms after finally getting the attention she so desperately tried to garner during her parents intense conversation and Jada's head resting upon his broad shoulders, Chauncey smiled with pride and hugged the two women he loved most in the world and said, "Let the strange roads of life take us where they will and wherever we end up let's just trust that God will provide. As long as I make the two of you the happiest people in the world, I'll always be the happiest man in the world."

CHAPTER 10

"Hello"

"Deacon Pickett"

"Uh huh!

"Chauncey Pennington, how's it going?"

"Oh. How you doing young fella. Is ya'll here yet?"

"I'm doing fine and our plane arrived safely a little over an hour ago. But I haven't spotted your welcome committee yet." Chauncey said as he waited patiently with his wife and daughter in an expensive airport restaurant.

"You ain't. You mean to tell me ain't nobody from Mt. Carmel found ya'll yet."

"Well, no Sir. But it's really no problem, we've just been enjoying this beautiful Tallahassee weather and watching the planes come and go."

"No Reverend, that's a big problem." the angry deacon said before he uncontrollably muttered to himself, "I told Lula's big behind to be at that airport by 1 o'clock and here it is going on 2."

"If she's not there in ten minutes you call me back and I'll come get you myself."

"We're fine Deacon and if we need to, we can just rent a car and just drive ourselves over to meet you. And that might be best anyway, since my wife and I want to do a little sight seeing while we're here."

"Well I understand that, but, we kinda had a good weekend planned for ya'll ourselves son. When Lula get there with the rest of the committee you'll see everything is all planned out. You and your family will enjoy. This afternoon we've planned a welcome meal for you and your family back here at the church, you'll get a chance to see Mt. Carmel and meet some of the members. Tomorrow, me and you gon' do some fishing before we meet with the rest of the board and of course Sunday is the big day. Now once Lula get there and get ya'll settled in the motel, ya'll come on over for the welcome dinner."

"Deacon Pickett that sounds awesome and my family and I are extremely excited to be you all's guest."

As Chauncey and the now subdued deacon continued to exchange pleasantries, he was interrupted by a scuffle nearby, in the airport lobby. "Security!" yelled an obese, deep voiced, black woman whose rants were as big as her girdled waistline and wore enough make-up to make Tammy Faye Baker proud.

"Ma'am we are security and you can't leave that van illegally parked liked that."

"I was just gone be a minute."

"Ma'am, after the bomb scare we had last week, we're ordered to ticket any illegally parked vehicle and/or handcuff anybody exhibiting suspicious behavior."

"Do I look like a terrorist to you." she said as the security officers grabbed her oversized wrists and onlookers begin to gather around the chaos.

As Chauncey and Jada looked on in sheer astonishment at the conflict, they held on tightly to Lizzy and waited anxiously in the nearby restaurant.

"What have you gotten us into Chauncey? This trip is not starting off good. Maybe God is trying to tell us something again?" Jada said as she rolled her eyes at her dumbfounded husband.

As the fearful couple watched and listened in horror with their daughter securely in their grasp, security officers had begun to usher the woman into a debriefing room in the airport when she shouted, "I ain't going no where, I am the Lord's and ya'll gone get yall hands off me! I just came to pick up a preacher for my church and I'm already late!"

The Day All Hell Broke Loose

When Chauncey heard the irate woman's assertion that she had come to "pick up a preacher for her church" and remembered Deacon Pickett's description of Lula, he immediately told Jada "Wait here, I think that's our lady." Afterwards he rushed onto the scene to aid in what had become an increasingly ugly circumstance.

"Excuse me. Are you Sister Lula Penny from the Greater Mt. Carmel Church?" Chauncey said as he tried to catch his breath.

"Sir, you have to be advised to leave immediately. We are in the process of questioning a suspect."

"Yes, I'm Lula Penny and I'm praying that you a good lawyer."

"No Ma'am. I'm Reverend Chauncey Pennington. I think you are here to pick me up."

After nearly thirty minutes of security questioning and edgy waiting by the Penningtons, Sister Penny was finally released around 1:30PM and finally had an opportunity to officially welcome the potential first family to the state of Florida.

"I'm so sorry for all of this Reverend. Let me introduce myself." She said as she swiftly led the way to the newly purchased church van. "I 'm Lula Penny, the head musician and lead singer of the United Voices of Greater Mt. Carmel. Welcome to our state and in about thirty or so minutes I'll be able to officially welcome you to Greater Mt. Carmel." She said with an embarrassing smile. "I'm the welcome committee."

"No, Mrs. Penny I'm sorry. That shouldn't have happened to you." Chauncey said as he paused to appropriately introduce his wife and daughter. "This is my beautiful wife Jada and my darling daughter Elizabeth Yvette."

"You all are a gorgeous couple and that little girl has the brightest eyes I've ever seen. It's really nice to meet you but I guess you know I'm in plenty of trouble with the head deacon because I was supposed to have ya'll at the church by now. I'm afraid that we're gonna have to just skip the hotel and go on over to the church because the people are all waiting for you. We all so excited."

"That's OK. We can't check into our rooms until after four anyway."

During the thirty minute drive to the Greater Mt. Carmel church, which was in a little town, just north of the state capital, the van remained relatively quiet except for Sis. Penny's occasional "are you all OK?" and Jada's playful renditions of are we there yet. But on one particular stretch of interstate highway, conversation opened up a bit between the ladies, when Lula shared that many accidents had occurred "right up in here." as she slowed down and pointed toward three crosses marking deaths that had occurred just this year.

Jada was intrigued and asked several questions about the accidents but Chauncey was in very intense thought and used the time as a reflective moment, remembering special times he shared with his parents and wondering how might his father feel about the great possibility that his son would soon walk in his shoes. It had been months since he had thought so deeply about his deceased parents, but the quiet ride to what he perceived as his destiny uncovered some feelings that he thought he had suppressed.

"What's going on in that brilliant mind of yours Chauncey? Jada asked as she rocked Lizzy to sleep on her lap and gazed into the eyes of her husband, who appeared to be slightly nervous.

"Nothing honey. It's just all hitting me now and really there's no turning back."

"You look a little nervous baby. If you don't want to go through with this I'll understand," Jada said as her tone lowered to a whisper to prohibit Sister Penny from eavesdropping.

"No. No. It's just that we're so close now and everything is moving so fast and I was just thinking how much easier this whole process would be if my mother was here or if my daddy could give me some advice. I know a difficult challenge lies before me and I guess I'm just gearing up for that challenge. I'm not nervous, just extremely focused."

"It's gonna be just fine. I'm here, Lizzy's here and Aunt Eunice is only a phone call away."

"Reverend and Mrs. Pennington this is our exit and the church is only five minutes from here. I'm sure the Mt. Carmel family is anxious to meet you. Are you all excited yet?"

As the church van came upon the densely populated community of what was otherwise a very small town, Chauncey and Jada peered out of the windows of the van to take in the sights of the landscape and verbally imagined what living in this part of the country would be like. Small, but very well kept houses, lined Old Blossom Trail, the street which bent around the tall north Florida pines and hovered over the clear fresh water streams near the church. As they journeyed onward and got a little closer to the church, they noticed a steeple hiding just behind some pines at the top of a hill.

"Is that the church's steeple?" Jada asked as Lula drove slowly around the winding road in the residential area only three miles from the church.

"That's it baby." Lula said proudly as Jada woke Lizzy up to view the exciting sight with her now anticipatory father. "We are the church that sits on a hill, a light that cannot be hid. That is Mt. Carmel and we'll be there in about a minute or so."

The remainder of the drive was a confidence booster for Chauncey and just before the van wrapped around its final curve before reaching the church he received the only other confirmation he needed. As he looked out of front windshield of the van, only seconds before reaching the church parking lot Chauncey fell into a brief daydream wherein he saw the people of Mt. Carmel gladly welcoming him. But what was odd about this uncommon visualization was that as the members of Mt. Carmel greeted him he saw his mother who was dressed in an immaculate white dress and his father who was dressed in his traditional pin-striped suit walking around the church as if they were angels preparing to protect their son's inheritance. As they pulled into the church parking lot, Jada noticed her husband's eerie silence and glazed stare and nudged him saying "Hey, is anybody home?" When Chauncey refused to answer her initial inquiry she grabbed his face and sternly said in a soft but authoritative voice "Chauncey Pennington."

"Huh," he said as he snapped out of his daydream.

"We're here. Are you OK?"

"Oh Yes." Chauncey said as he grinned at his concerned wife. "I was just daydreaming."

"OK Reverend and Mrs. Pennington, at long last we've made it to the Greater Mt. Carmel Church."

As they exited the church van, Chauncey and Jada were pleasantly surprised to know that the church wasn't as small as they initially suspected. Matter of fact it was twice as big as they imagined and from the looks of the outside of the church, it was well taken care of. The big red brick building sat on the very top of what was known to the locals as Pleasant Hill in a little residential area. With dark stained glass windows, a grand white steeple, and stairs that led to a great oak and stained glass entryway, the church's first impressions on the Penningtons would certainly be a lasting one.

As they looked in amazement and appeared to Sister Lula to be extremely happy, she ushered the inspired couple to the dining annex where the faithful of Greater Mt. Carmel anxiously awaited their entrance. Before reaching the dining annex, they were led through the church's beautiful sanctuary. The pews where white with purple cushions and appeared to the aspiring pastor to seat at least three hundred people. As the couple walked down the long purple carpeted isles of the sanctuary they viewed the immaculate edifice in awe, prompting Chauncey to wonder who wouldn't love to pastor a church like this. With crystal clear chandeliers lighting their path to the dining annex, Chauncey got a glimpse of the pulpit where he would stand on Sunday. It was covered with fine oak flooring and white and purple chairs fit for royalty. As Sister Lula led the way, Chauncey, who by this time was walking supremely confident behind his unexpectedly encouraged wife, through the breezeway that led directly to the dining annex, the couple geared up for their long awaited meeting with what could be their new family.

"Now we ain't a big church now ya'll" Lula said as she paused to prepare Chauncey and Jada for a very small welcoming crowd. "But the ones of us that are here are very happy that ya'll are here. So don't be disappointed by the size. Just know that the reason ya'll is here is because we struggling a little bit right now."

As Lula opened the door to the dining annex, fifteen of Mt. Carmel's faithful sat quietly waiting for her to officially introduce the only pastoral candidate.

"Well who do we have here?" said an excited Walter Pickett.

"Deacon Pickett if I may address the members."

"You may Sister Penny."

"We have visiting with us all the way from Odessa, Texas, Reverend C.E. Pennington, his lovely wife Jada, and their gorgeous daughter Elizabeth."

"Reverend I'm the man you been taking to." Pickett said as he shook the preacher's hand and nodded at Jada. "I'm Deacon Walter Picket, the chairman of the board here and what we gone do at this time is introduce you to all the deacons and their wives and the other member of Mt. Carmel. Then we gone just eat and talk and after that we gone let ya'll get on back to the motel so ya'll can get some rest. We got a big weekend ahead of us."

As he ate a belly full of fried chicken, collard greens, and sweet potatoes, Deacon Pickett appeared to be overjoyed to welcome Chauncey and Jada to Mt. Carmel. It took no time at all for Chauncey to recognize this man's powerful influence on the frail congregation. Many of the members present wouldn't utter a word unless they were cleared to address the congregation much like Lula did when she introduced the couple. But that didn't damper Chauncey's spirits at all. He was still in shock after finding the community and church in much better condition than he thought initially and he was equally as shocked to find that Jada, who was once leery about the possibility of relocating to small town America only to start all over again, was now accepting the possibility and embracing what could be her role as first lady of Mt. Carmel. After seeing the church and community for the first time she fell instantly in love and wanted nothing more than to enhance her husband's chances of being chosen. Jada was brilliant. Unlike Chauncey who was very regal and sort of reserved at the dinner, Jada unleashed her southern charm, sharing and trading recipes with the deacons wives and allowing Lizzy to bounce from arm to arm as the ladies and gentlemen alike took notice of the baby's mannerable characteristics.

The welcoming celebration couldn't have gone any better for Mt. Carmel or the Penningtons. Chauncey and Jada were pleased to know that the small church that had sparked their interest only a month or so ago turned out to be what they considered to be a diamond in the rough. The young and the old men of Mt. Carmel seemed to be impressed with Chauncey's calm demeanor and his undeniable command of the English language while the women gleamed and whispered among each other about his incredibly good looks. Jada was equally as impressive and was so charismatic that she had convinced some of the ladies to delay their normal Saturday chores to go shopping with her the next morning. Lizzy played her part in the successful dinner as well by being as sweet as Sister Lula Penny's prize winning sweet potato pie and as calm as north Florida's pristine fresh water streams.

"Well I guess we can let the Reverend and his wife go on back to Tallahassee for a good night's rest," Deacon Pickett said as he got up from the dinner table. But before ya'll go, I'll like to open the floor for any final questions that ya'll or the congregation has."

"I don't have any questions." responded Mother Snelling "But I just wanted to stand and say it's been a pleasure meeting you all and I pray that this experience for you all is as beautiful as you all have been to us."

"Thank you so much." Chauncey said as Jada nodded in agreement. "We have really enjoyed ourselves too and we can't wait to see what the rest of the weekend has in store."

CHAPTER 11

After the all inspiring Friday evening spent with the faithful few of Greater Mt. Carmel, Chauncey and Jada went back to their hotel and had a night of happy conversations about their impressive first impressions of the church and the surrounding area. Excited about their unexpected find in north Florida, they called Aunt Eunice and the Blaylocks to share the good news about the place their loved ones considered too far away and unsuited for the college graduates. As Elizabeth played on the floor of the five star hotel suite they'd booked for themselves, Chauncey and Jada stood together next to the window overlooking the near skyscraperless college town and wondered together about the great blessing that God had put on the edge of their fingertips. They'd sleep this Friday night with smiles on their faces and strategies in their minds of how to make Greater Mt. Carmel home.

After a night of sweet dreams and a morning of high expectation, Jada dressed Elizabeth and prepared herself for a day on the town with her new found friends as Chauncey ironed his Dickey trousers and prepared for his day with the chairman deacon. About an hour after the church van stopped by the downtown Tallahassee hotel to retrieve Jada and Elizabeth, Deacon Pickett was not far away when he placed a call to room 645.

"Hello," Chauncey said as he answered the phone and pulled his camouflage cap over his eyes.

"Good Morning Reverend are you ready for yo' trip to the river?"

"Yes Sir. The only thing I need now is a life vest and a good fishing rod," he said as he chuckled.

"Well if that's all you need you're ready cause I got all that back at the loading dock. I should be there in the next five minutes or so, so go head and make your way down to the lobby."

"Done deal".

As Chauncey waited for the deacon in the lobby, he feasted on the remnants of the hotel's free continental breakfast and placed several calls to Jada, who was having as much fun as she could possibly have spending the couple's limited resources.

"Where are you all at now?" asked a curious Chauncey during his last phone conversation with his wife before Pickett picked him up.

"Chauncey we're still doing the same thing we were about two minutes ago, shopping," Jada responded. "Aren't you fishing yet?"

"No, not yet but I think I see Pickett driving up now. Yea that's him. Have a nice day honey and I promise not to call back this morning."

"That's OK. It makes me feel good to know that you miss me. Be good today and I'll talk to you later."

As Deacon Picket gestured to Chauncey to get into his silver and chrome laced Cadillac he smiled from ear to ear as he told the young preacher that he had made a "hell of a impact on those folk at Mt. Carmel last night." As they drove northeast back to the fishing sight, the two gentlemen talked extensively about everything but church, as if they had known each other for years. The comfortable nature of the conversation even paved a way for Chauncey to reveal that some of his family including his mother and Aunt work on Pickett Plantation, supposedly the same plantation that the deacon's white father owned.

"Say what?" Pickett said in astonishment.

"My Aunt Eunice told me that years ago my granddaddy and mother actually worked near Tallahassee on a tobacco farm called Pickett Plantation and I wanted to know was there any connection."

"My daddy owned that property and it's up near where we headed to go fishing. Me and my brothers inherited the property when that bastard died. Excuse my language Reverend. But I really didn't know him and from what everybody told me he was a racist old heathen. He was white of course. Now who is yo people?"

"My Granddaddy's name was Edgar Dawkins and my grandmother's name was Udell. I'm the son of their daughter Suzanne and it was my Aunt Eunice who told me there might be some distant connection."

"Distant connection?" Pickett replied. "There's no distant connection son, I am one of the only surviving connections. But the name Dawkins don't ring a bell to me…"

"Well you probably wouldn't remember any of my family," Chauncey interrupted as Pickett scratched his chin. "When my mother and aunt were young they all moved to Ohio when my granddaddy got a job at some steel factory or something like that."

"Now I remember!" Pickett shouted as he averted his fishing plans to drive by the old plantation. "They called your granddaddy Buck. Everybody knew him and respected him because he was as strong as an ox and did not hesitate to buck if somebody rubbed him the wrong way. Reverend I don't mean no disrespect, but if I'm remembering correctly that man had two of the most beautiful daughters I know I had ever seen. But if he caught you saying two words to them girls he could turn nasty in a heartbeat. No one ever said a word to them girls and when they left here I always knew they'd be some kind of special. How are they doing?"

"We'll my mother passed when I was seven."

"I'm sorry to hear that Reverend."

"No, it's O.K." Chauncey said, not revealing that he still had struggles dealing with the circumstances surrounding his parents' deaths. "My Aunt Eunice raised me."

"Well I didn't mean to bring up old memories for you but your family, from what I remember, was very fine people and I'm sure you are too," Pickett said as he brought his Cadillac to a halt. "Right over there was the plantation."

As Chauncey let down the passenger side window to take a closer look at the towering but, brown, weathered tobacco barns and the seemingly endless fields of green grass he noticed what Pickett referred to as shot gun houses his daddy allowed workers to rent while working on the farm.

In a moment of silence, Chauncey opened the door of the car and breathed in deeply as if to take in essence of a place his ancestors and especially his mother and aunt once roamed.

"Deacon Pickett if you don't mind, I'd like for you to tell me more about this place and if possible take me to some of the places my mother and aunt would've gone while they were here."

"I'll tell you what, if it's alright with you, let's go fishing another day and we can just talk here. I'll show you around town and we'll get some lunch at my friend's seafood restaurant before we meet with the rest of the board and you can still tell yo wife you caught some fresh catfish. How 'bout it?"

"That's just fine with me Deacon."

As Pickett gave the young preacher an extensive history lesson about the property and its legacy in the community, Chauncey listened interestedly often stopping to rest on the broken down porches of the scattered shot gun houses. Although Pickett couldn't give Chauncey any concrete evidence that his mother or aunt actually lived on the property his keen knowledge of "Old Man Pickett's" business dealings and relationships proved that his ancestry once stood on the very ground he now stood. Chauncey often gazed across the vast property with a smile on his face thinking to himself, how great is this, that he's in a place he's never known but feels as though he's been forever and to make it so much sweeter he's forged a lasting bond and fellowship with the chairman of deacons at the church he knew he was destined to pastor.

After their nearly two hour conversation Pickett felt comfortable enough with the preacher to give him some pointers for a successful meeting with the deacon's board and shed light on the direction the deacons visualized for the church. And before they left the plantation for a long awaited catfish and cheese grits afternoon dinner, Pickett stopped short of his car, which was parked near the dirt road entrance to the plantation, and said,

"Reverend I normally don't do this but I like you. When we meet with the rest of the board it might be a little rough. They gone ask you some tough questions and tell you some thangs that they expect from you. Now don't you talk too much; just listen. Even if you disagree with some thangs they say, you just be humble and listen. A good pastor has to listen to his leaders and sometimes do what they say; especially if they don't want to get voted out like Woodrow. Woodrow coulda still been our pastor, but we couldn't tell him nothin. Don't you be like that. You just be humble like the bible says and remember Acts 6:4; trust

The Day All Hell Broke Loose

yo deacons to handle all the business of the church. If you don't hear nothing else I say remember this one thang, yo job is to preach to the people and let yo' board take care of the business. You hear me son?"

"Yes Sir." Chauncey replied as he stared at the deacon who apparently cared enough about him to take the time to aid him in his interview process.

"Alright let's go eat and we'll get this short meetin' out the way and we can let you reunite with that beautiful wife and daughter of yours."

Leaving the plantation, Chauncey sat back in the cozy leather seats of the deacon's clean ride and breathed easily, knowing that his quest to become a pastor was now inevitable. He had won over the deacon who had the most influence in the church and the only things that stood in his way was as delicious lunch at a country seafood restaurant, a meeting he'd already been given cheat notes to, and a Sunday sermon that he was poised to deliver.

While dining in the little downtown restaurant, Deacon Pickett introduced his fine, out of town catch to the town's people and with Chauncey, invited some of the diners to Sunday's service to witness his initial sermon as the church's candidate for pastor. Deacon Pickett was pleasantly surprised that Chauncey had no problem luring people to the lackluster church, especially the women because if for nothing else they were coming to see what that handsome, young, fine, sexy eyed, among other adjectives the female diners used to characterize the preacher, was all about. Chauncey, in all his charismatic flair, caused a stir in the restaurant, much to Pickett's delight and some even wondered what Pickett had done to get "somebody like that" to come to a "place like Mt. Carmel."

After the delicious and interesting lunch, the skinning and grinning, potential power couple rode the short distance to the church where the six other members of the deacon's board were patiently waiting for their chance to personally address the man they already knew would be their pastor. They had met almost an hour before Pickett and Chauncey arrived, which was a customary practice and tactic used by the deacons to ensure they'd be on one accord before meeting with the pastor or other members. They were ready for what Deacon Phillips, who often referred to himself as "the next man in line" to be chairman of the board because he'd been a deacon longer than any of the other deacons except Pickett, called the "little nigga's first show down"

"Don't be easy on him ya'll," Phillips ranted. "That's how Woodrow got out of hand. This boy is young and from all indication he's a horse of a preacher. But we got to keep the bits in his mouth."

"You shole' right Eddie" agreed the always agreeable deacon Wilford Mallard. "We got to keep them bits in his mouth."

As the deacons continued their sometimes hilarious conversation, Pickett walked in side- by-side with Chauncey. As the two men got closer to the fold out table in the dinning annex, often referred to as the conference table, the other deacons wiped the friendly grins off of their faces and glanced at Chauncey only briefly before looking away as if none of them could stand to look innocently at a man they knew they were about to attempt to hang.

"Brethren, as Psalms 133:1 says, behold how good it is for brethren to get together to do God's business," Deacon Pickett said as he prepared to offer the opening prayer.

"Before we get started I just want to brang' back my report from my meeting with the Reverend. We didn't go fishing but, I found him to be a honorable man and he's very easy to get along wit. And I even found out that his family is no strangers to this area. Now if you want to address him you may at this time. But gentlemen let's not wear him out today 'cause he's had a long day and I'm sure he misses his wife and daughter."

"Bro. Chairman," Deacon Phillips said as he addressed Pickett.

"May I take the floor?"

"Yes you may," Pickett replied as Chauncey looked on in silence, wondering within himself what was the purpose or point for all the formality.

"Bro. Chairman we've met and we only have two questions for the Reverend."

"You may proceed."

"Reverend, as a board we want to know if we select you as our pastor what can you offer us and what do you expect us to offer you?"

"Well brethren" a confident Chauncey said as a more confident Pickett looked on and listened for the answers he'd already given the preacher.

"First and foremost I am a preacher and I believe that my job is to preach the gospel of Jesus Christ and compel dying men and women to meet him while they have time."

As Deacon Pickett nodded in agreement with the highly intelligent candidate, Chauncey continued in oratory excellence.

"But not only am I a preacher, if I'm chosen to be your pastor, I'll be just that, a man that garners the respect of his congregation through humility and lead us to the place that God will eventually give me through his vision."

"That's a gooood saying there preacher. You shole right" said Dec. Mallard, who was often used by the deacons as a pawn, due to his lack of education and evident lack of confidence.

"Shut up Wilford!" sternly whispered a visibly displeased sixty-three year old Connie Maxwell, who was known for his intimidating nature and recognized by the board of deacons as Pickett's enforcer.

"Now Reverend I heard everything you said and it sounds like to me that if we get you as our preacher you gone thank you in charge by yourself." Phillips rebutted as he look wearily into the eyes of Deacon Pickett who by this time was holding his peace though thinking to himself that his little talk with the young preacher had fallen on deaf ears.

"Deacon Phillips that's not what I was saying at all. I know, understand, and appreciate the role and responsibilities of a strong deacon's ministry and no great pastor has ever attained his greatness without the strong advocacy of a credible leadership team. I was only trying to convey that you can rest assured that I'll be just as strong and together we can build a greater Mt. Carmel."

"I understand that," Deacon Phillips said as he opened an envelope containing the church's light bill and passed it over to Deacon Norway Cox, who was a sensible but submissive fifty-eight year old chicken farmer who served as the treasurer for the church. "But I want you to understand that this is a board, and we take pride in leading and guiding this church and that man over there is in charge."

"Understood," Chauncey replied reluctantly but respectfully, as Pickett rubbed his back, assuring him that he'd said was enough.

As Deacon Phillips concluded his tough but impressive question and answer session, Chauncey could breathe a little easier as the soft spoken Cox asked permission to address the tensed preacher.

"It has come to our attention that you has a degree and we don't know if we gone be able to pay you what you make in Texas. I guess what I'm asking is, how much you gone charge us a month to pastor the church."

"Deacon Cox, I have no idea of what the financial situation of this church is and before coming here my wife and I understood that we'd probably see an initial marginal decrease in our income. But as the church grows I anticipate that my salary will grow. With that being said I'd be more than willing to accept the salary of the last pastor until we could come together again and analyze our financial status. I would in no way want to be a burden to this church."

"Now we ain't never heard nothing like that from no preacher. Is we ya'll? This boy good, real good," said Deacon Mallard, who looked around the table for approval of his comments, but only found hard stares and silence from his colleagues.

"Now that's a damn fool," muttered sixty-six year old Clausell Ellis to himself, who sat next to Harold Belford, the church's youngest deacon who often sat silently during board meetings to learn the right way to lead.

"Well Reverend I'm real glad to hear that," said a relieved deacon Cox "because by now you know we want you, but keeping you is another story. I wasn't sure if you'd take what we'd have to offer. But since you 'greed to take what Reverend Elliot got a month, I'm glad to announce to the board that if the church 'proves you to be our next pastor you get $775.33. which is way more than Elliot got."

As Chauncey's eyes widened, he gasped for air and did everything in his power to mask his disbelief in the church's less than stellar compensation for a pastor. "What have I done?" he thought to himself as the deacons begin to shake hands and prepare for dismissal. "My wife is going to kill me." he thought as visions of those shot gun houses and broken down porches raced through his head. "I got to say something. I got to say something quick," a stunned and utterly disappointed Chauncey said to himself as he begin to sweat profusely at the thought that he had made the second worst decision of his short life.

The Day All Hell Broke Loose

"Um… Um…"

"What is it Reverend?" Deacon Pickett asked as he smiled widely at the man who had obviously taken his counsel and passed the daunting first meeting with the deacon's board. "Speak now or forever hold your peace 'cause I'm bout to close out with the Deacon's Creed. Go head Reverend. We should have asked you for closing remarks anyway since you gone be our preacher."

"Um, I really don't have any closing remarks," Chauncey said as the deacons sat back down to the table to listen to his questions or concerns. "I'm just interested in knowing, um, how did you all come up with that salary?" He questioned with a cautious but confused look on his face.

"Well, I can let Deacon Belford answer that young fella. He just studied that in his last deacon board training," said Deacon Pickett. "Go head Harold you know this."

"Deacon Pickett may I address the board?" said the slow, deep talking, goofy voiced muscularly built, thirty-nine year old security guard.

"Yes sir you may but make it quick."

"The new pastor's salary was gone be $800 dollars but we done decided to take out twenty dollars for his dues, and four dollars for our building fund and sixty-seven cents for chillen trips, and dat makes a total of sevun hundud, sevundy five dollars and thudy three cent. That's right ain't it Brother Chairman?"

"That's right son," Pickett said as he proudly shook the young deacon's hand in affirmation. "Is there any more questions Reverend."

"No, not really," said a deflated and disappointed Chauncey.

"Well boys we can close out another chapter and remember what Proverbs 123: 2 says; "It's 'bout time that the church do what the church gotta do to be pleasing in His eyesight and not man's and oh don't forget God bless America. Now let us recite our Creed we just made up."

As Chauncey disappointedly waited for the recitation of the Deacon's Creed he closed his eyes and appeared to Deacon Eddie Mallard to be uttering prayers, which only solidified Mallard's contention that Reverend Chauncey Evansworth Pennington was a "Gooood Boy!" But the truth of the matter was; Chauncey was really just ready to leave so he could clearly think of a way to apologize to his unknowing wife.

"Let us say it together brethren."

"As long as I'm a deacon, I will try my best to do what's right.

Every day I live I must try not come up here to the church to fight; cause that ain't God.

We as humble as little ole lambs trying to do God's bidness.

And if the preachers, the choir and the ushers and the members just listen to what our voices tell um we ain't never got to do what we did to Woodrow. Amen!

CHAPTER 12

After the unfortunate enlightening meeting with the board of deacons, Chauncey traveled with a pleased Deacon Pickett the thirty miles or so back to the lavish downtown hotel in utter shock, disbelief and subsequent silence. His stomach was in knots, his palms were sweaty and his demeanor was uncharacteristically sour as he longed to be in the presence of Jada, who not only had the innate ability to recognize his anguish, but also to soothe his troubled mind. He really missed her now and wanted so badly to see a familiar face and hear a comforting voice. Chauncey was well aware that his final judgment was only a few hours away but his anguish was only compounded by the fears of actually being attractive to a church, who if their courtship was any indication, would prove to be an unworthy bride. He also feared greatly the reality of revealing to his wife that what she had warned him of was actually coming to pass. Chauncey felt in some ways like a failure for the moment and clutched his cell phone much of the ride, contemplating seriously the thought of calling Jada to admit he'd let her down.

Conversations they had only months ago rang out in his mind and he could hear her tender voice and see her worried expression as she asked "…isn't this process moving a little too fast?..." "…do you know if it's worth the headache?" "…will they be able to pay you what you deserve?"

He thought internally on several occasions during the mostly quiet ride that he should call her, but finally gave into his fears and decided that his bad news and his ill feelings toward the "deacons from hell" and their lack luster efforts to provide an adequate salary for their pastor would best be revealed behind the closed doors of their suite. As thoughts continued to race through his head, Pickett's ego swelled and he mistook Chauncey's silence for the speechlessness of over excitement.

"Now Reverend don't you be scared now. You did just fine in yo interview and you'll do just fine tomorrow, O.K."

"Thank you Deacon Pickett and to be honest I'm really not worried about tomorrow." Chauncey said as he gazed into the open fields along the interstate. "I'm just ready to see my wife and kid and rest up for what I know will be an adventurous day of personal decision making."

"Personal decision making Reverend? I thought you had already prayed about coming."

"Oh yes Sir, I did pray about being a candidate to be your pastor, but I mean my wife and I will still have to choose if this place is for us. This weekend has been an eye-opening experience to say the least and before we allow the church to vote on us tomorrow we have to decide whether we want to be voted on. Mt. Carmel seems to be a great church and full of great people, but deacon I'm no longer sure if my wife would support a move to north Florida on such a lean salary."

"Now look Reverend you said…."

"I know I said I'd take what the last pastor received for a salary, but I think that may have been a mistake. I can't expect my wife and kid to live below the standards that I envision for them just so I can live out what I perceive to be my destiny."

"I understand that Reverend and if that's the least of yo worries don't worry any longer. Let me admit to you that I really want you and that little ole family of yours to be our first family. Trust me," Deacon Pickett said as he parked his car in a vacant lot adjacent to the hotel entryway.

"As Chairman Deacon I just about do what I want to do. You and me have struck a bond, son and together we can turn this church around. If you choose to do this, I promise you won't regret it. I'll make sure yo' salary is increased in a short while and you can live how you want to

The Day All Hell Broke Loose

live. I really don't know for sure how the vote will turn out tomorrow, but if it turns out in my favor you'll be happy, wait and see."

"Thanks for that reassurance. I needed that." Chauncey said as his right leg preceded his body in a hasty exit of the car in anticipation of telling Jada all about his less than eventful yet adventurous day. "I'll talk to my wife tonight and before Sunday school tomorrow I'll have the verdict for you."

As Chauncey exited the clean car of the chairman, Deacon Pickett sat calmly with his head firmly planted against the leather laced head rest, staring through his windshield, thinking of one final thing he could say to sway the preacher's evident declining confidence.

"Hey Reverend!" he shouted out of the driver's side window as Chauncey trotted across the street to the hotel.

"Yes Sir." He yelled back across the busy street.

"Whatever you do remember what Proverbs 3:5-6 say " Trust in the Lord with all yo heart and lean not to yo own understanding, In all yo ways knowledge him and he will tell you what to do."

"I will."

As Deacon Pickett drove slowly away from the vacant lot wondering what went wrong, Chauncey entered the lobby of the hotel and wondered what he could've done differently to make more go right. As he waited patiently for an elevator headed towards the sixth floor he thought to himself that, just maybe, God hadn't spoken to him after all. Because God wouldn't allow him to feel so despondent if it was really destiny that he was on the brink of; would He? Quickly approaching the sixth floor, Chauncey had fond thoughts of holding his wife and daughter and just being close to people he knew loved him for all the right reasons. With his electronic key in his hand, he inserted it into the lock and couldn't wait for Jada's expression as he walked through the door a tired but "happy-to-be-home" man. But Chauncey was in for a surprise himself, because although it was a little passed six o'clock PM, Jada and Lizzy were nowhere to be found.

After placing his shoes in the unusually large closet and flopping his weary body on the bed, he reached for his cell phone and dialed up his missing in action wife.

"Hello." Jada answered as laughter and fun conversation was heard in the background.

"Hey. Where are you all at?" Chauncey said as he slowly reclined on the plush pillows that he had strategically arranged to be more comfortable to his back and neck.

"We're actually at this little restaurant across the street from the hotel. Where are you?"

"I'm at the hotel."

"Well that was quick. How did things go?"

"Well let's just say they went."

"Chauncey Pennington you sure do sound dry."

"Not really. I'm just worn to a frazzle. I do kinda of wish you were here with me though."

"Are you lonely boy?"

"Yea. That, among other things." Chauncey said as he smiled at the thought of lying in Jada's arms.

"O.K., we're wrapping up our little trip anyway and Sister Belford just rocked Lizzy to sleep. That means I'll be there really soon and you can have all my love to yourself O.K?"

"Alright. I love you."

"I love you too and Chauncey you are not going to believe the thing these ladies have told me about that church," Jada said as she giggled but lowered her voice to protect what she said from listening ears as her classified conversation with Chauncey continued.

"What Jada?" he said as he rolled over to retrieve a pre-poured glass of water from the nightstand.

"I'll tell you all about it when I get there. But put it like this…our chances of being here are looking real good and if these ladies have anything to do with it, our stay won't be like their last pastor's. We're leaving now. See ya in five or ten minutes. Bye."

After Chauncey flipped off his cell phone and repositioned himself comfortably on the bed, he grabbed the television remote and channel surfed for a while before he heard the sound of high heels, plastic bags, and jubilant voices; which often signaled the return of women who had spent too much and enjoyed doing it. And in this case it was Jada and the young women of Mt. Carmel, who by all indication, were enamored with his southern belle.

"Girls, thank you for a wonderful evening and I'll see all you at Sunday school?" Jada asked just before Chauncey opened the room door for his wife and daughter.

"I ain't never really went to Sunday School. But after talking to you First Lady, I think tomorrow is gone be a lovely day. Plus I can't wait to show off my new outfit," said Deacon Phillip's daughter-in-law Kiesha, whose husband Ronnie rarely attended church services.

As Chauncey opened the room door and pleasantly greeted the overjoyed ladies he told them how thankful he was that they took his wife out for a nice day on the town as Sister Belford handed Lizzy over to him as the two year old slept soundly.

"You all have a good night and we'll see you all in the morning," Chauncey said as Jada stood in the doorway along side of him smiling.

"You too Reverend and Mrs. Pennington, it was our pleasure."

As Jada waved good-bye to the young ladies of Mt. Carmel, Chauncey laid Lizzy in the bed. After he watched for a few seconds to see if his little girl would remain asleep he motioned for Jada to join him on the maroon and gold sofa in the living area of the suite to have the conversation with his wife that, previous to his latest phone conversation with her, he dreaded to have.

"Well baby," he said, as he sat next to her and placed his long arms around her body to provoke a similar response. "I don't know if this is my destiny after all. Those deacons are really not all there and my view of this whole situation changed a bit after they told me that they only intend to pay their next pastor seven hundred, seventy seven dollars, and thirty-three cents."

After hearing those chilling details Jada sat straight up and looked at him as if he was crazy. "And Jada I really don't want to go through this, especially if it means you and Lizzy would have to suffer because of my bad judgment. And I say that because, when they asked me what it would take financially for me to be their next pastor, I ignorantly said I would gladly take what the last pastor was offered until we could analyze the church finances at a later date. How stupid could I be?"

"Chauncey, that's awful. You mean to tell me that that's all they have to offer."

"Yes. And what makes it so bad is that I was really feeling this place until that deacon's meeting. They showed me why this church can't grow. I don't know if this is our place after all baby. I should've listened to you."

"What happened Chauncey?"

"Well they asked me a couple of questions, one of which led to a tirade by Phillips who stressed the point that the deacons were in charge, which made me question what Deacon Pickett told me earlier in the day."

"Which was?" Jada said as she looked up at Chauncey.

"He told me that the preacher's job is to preach and teach and leave the business to the deacons. That's not how I've been trained, but in my foolish effort to befriend the chairman, I listened to that foolishness, thinking that maybe that was his personal opinion. But it seems to me that maybe all of these people have bought into that nonsense. I know all of those deacons have."

"Well, finances aside, I do know from my conversation with the ladies today, that most of the good members had already left the church due to a lack of leadership and many have said they are ready for a change at the church and would come back under the right circumstances. Deacon Phillip's own daughter-in-law told me herself that if a man comes in that church with a backbone to stand up to those deacons he'd have the support of the rest of the membership."

"I'm a little torn now because Pickett did make me feel a little easier when he told me that he would ensure a substantial raise if I accepted the job."

"But can you trust that?"

"Baby he's the chairman deacon and he can do whatever he wants and to be honest, other than Deacon Cox, Pickett seems to be the most reasonable and yes, I believe that I can trust him. I think he's a little misguided in his thinking sometimes, but I've looked into his eyes and underneath that sometimes harsh exterior is a man who I believe really loves his church and knows how to treat a preacher well."

"This may sound crazy Chauncey, but before coming here you know I was really skeptical, but truly after today with those women, I feel right at home and I feel challenged to make a difference in their lives. I even begin to look at this situation as our opportunity to do foreign missions or something. I know we're still in the states but trust me, being in this neck of the woods and around these folk is like being in another world. And by the way, what preacher told these women that it was an abomination to wear makeup?"

"I don't know the answer to that, but I do want to know what you're feeling in your gut because mine is malfunctioning right about now."

As Jada straddled Chauncey's thighs, she grabbed his ears as she normally did when trying to boost his confidence and said "Listen Chauncey, you and I both knew what we were potentially walking into. When I got here I took it all in and I've come to the realization that this will be a major challenge for you and me. But if anybody can conquer a place like Mt. Carmel, it's you Chauncey. You're smart, everybody who meets you falls in love with you, you are a great preacher and I personally feel that it would be more rewarding for you to have to walk into a place that's badly run down and fix it up yourself than to walk into a place like you father's church and live off of his legacy. This is your turn, your time and I'm believing God for a major turn around in that city and for that church and you're gonna be the man who spearheads it. Do you believe what I'm telling you?"

"I hear you." Chauncey said as he pulled her closer to him and kissed her on the face and neck. "But what about money, what about living? I thought I had all of this figured out but after talking to those deacons about my salary I don't have anything figured out."

"What would you do without me Chauncey?"

"Die probably," he said as he stood up to take off his shirt and prepare for a shower.

"You wouldn't die. You'd probably have another Mrs. Pennington before my body got cold." Jada said as she smiled at Chauncey and prepared to give her unsuspecting husband her answer to his financial questions.

"I was talking to Mrs. Lula today and I found out that she's actually the cafeteria manager at the local elementary school and that she could almost guarantee that her principal, Mr. James, would hire me before the summer is out because of a severe shortage of teachers in their county."

"Is that right?" Chauncey said as his spirits perked up.

"Yea, but that's not all Mr. Skeptical. She even called him for me and set up a meeting after church tomorrow. He and his wife live here in Tallahassee but agreed that they would come over to church tomorrow to meet us. Lula lied a bit and told the man she was inviting him to your first service as pastor. But the best part is that he told me that if I agreed to teach at his school, I would be paid at least twenty percent more than the average salary because the school has received failing state governmental grades in consecutive years.

"If Lula could pull that off it would definitely ease some of my discomfort." Chauncey said.

"And… I thought about this too. Tallahassee is not such a bad place to live and it's only a short drive from the church. I know you want to be full time in the ministry, but what if you get a small job until the church is able to give you what you deserve. I figure the cost of living here is not that bad and we could make it if we gave it a chance. Remember what you told me when I was feeling like you're feeling now."

"I told you so much back then." Chauncey said as Jada walked over to Lizzy who by this time squirming and apparently waking up from her lengthy nap.

"You told me that God won't lead us into any situation that he won't provide us an escape from. The faith you instilled in me that day is the faith that I have today and it is the same faith that I'm pouring back into you right now. We can always walk away and thank God for the people and places we can always run back to. But, I'm convinced that this is a challenge you and I must face and this little lady is ready for it. This is going to be the greatest experience of our lives. Think of it as going off to school for the first time. We were scared but we knew we had the brains to make it through. We may be scared right know but we know that we have God on our sides and we will make it through one way or another, on our feet or on our behinds." Jada said as she bounced an awakening Lizzy up and down in her arms and watched her husband undress for a quick shower.

"You are amazing Jada. I couldn't make it without you. When I came back to this hotel room, all I could think about was that I let you down. Sex wasn't even on my mind but girl when I get out of this shower you and me need to leave our mark on this expensive room."

"Boy, Lizzy will be wide awake by the time you get out of the bathroom and besides I need to be rested for my big day tomorrow," she said as Chauncey walked into the bathroom and closed the door.

"Oh yea, and Chauncey, when you get out of the shower try on those shoes, I know they're your size, but they looked a little small to me for a size thirteen."

"Alright."

Chapter 13

Saturday afternoon proved to be rather eventful for Chauncey and Jada even if their days were headed in opposite directions before they met back at the hotel for an evening alone. After talking out the issues that could've possibly prompted Chauncey to back out of his so called chance meeting with destiny, they both showered, one after the other, as they took turns watching their baby girl and prepared for some well deserved family time. No Church folk. No Church Business. Just family enjoying each other and waiting for Saturday night to turn into Sunday morning. After a brief discussion about what they should do for the remainder of the day, they both decided that they were really too excited to do anything much and chose room service and pay-per-view late night boxing on HBO.

"Aren't you sleepy yet Honey," Jada asked as she rebounded from an unexpected nod.

"Yea, I think I'm about ready to turn in. It doesn't seem like De LaHoya is gonna knock this guy out any time soon."

After watching a few more rounds of the somewhat boring fight, Chauncey turned the television off and turned toward Jada, who was already fast asleep and took his familiar position, behind her with his pelvis area positioned like the piece of a puzzle next to her butt and his left leg sprawled across her thighs. They slept harmoniously for most of the night, except for Lizzy's few tosses and turns. They rose early the next morning to the great Florida sunshine and the singing of native birds which used the subtle downtown winds as a microphone to be heard through their open sixth floor window.

"Good morning Baby."

"Good morning Chauncey. How did you sleep?"

"Oh I slept just fine." Chauncey said as he let out a yawn and stretched out his lengthy body as he stood beside the bed while Jada and Lizzy slowly tried to fight off morning drowsiness.

"What time is it?"

"It's about a quarter past seven. We better get moving Jada. Sunday School starts at 9:30 I think."

"Yea it does. We really need to get a move on. Hold Lizzy for a moment and I'll go down to the Lobby and bring us back some breakfast. What do you want?"

"It doesn't matter. Matter of fact I don't think I need anything to eat. I'm so excited or nervous… or both that if I eat anything it'll probably come back up anyway."

"Chauncey is that a good thing or a bad thing."

"It's definitely a good thing. I felt this way before I married you and even before I preached at my daddy's church that Easter. Remember?"

"Yea, I do. But back then I was probably a little more nervous than you were."

"What about now. What are you feeling right now Jada?

"Honestly, I don't feel anxious or nervous or for that matter scared or intimidated. I know that you're gonna preach great. I've come to grips with the fact that we may be moving here and I like that idea. I may already have a job if I can trust Sis. Lula. That means our finances will be O.K. Chauncey, I'm just ready, ready for whatever happens."

"Well baby I feel a whole lot better too especially after our talk last night. And my excitement and nervousness is more about who'll be there today. Of course I've only met a handful of the members. It's not a bad feeling as if I feel like I'll fail, but I guess I'm just ready too".

"Well I'm ready to eat," Jada said as she smiled at Chauncey and stroked Lizzy's rosy cheeks.

"How about this, why don't we all go down to the lobby?"

"There's no need to go with me Chauncey. I'll be right back"

"No ma'am. I'm going and Lizzy is going. You spent all day by yourself yesterday and I need to show these country boys that you have a man. I'm afraid that if you smile at them like you just smiled at me you may have stalkers." Chauncey said as they both laughed at his ridiculous assertion.

As Chauncey and Jada got their morning started early with great anticipation of what this first Sunday of June 1994 would bring, just thirty miles north of the capital city, the Greater Mt. Carmel family was preparing for a wondrous day as well. Excitement filled the little town as the smells of a brewing feast penetrated the near cloudless sky. The hard working members of the Senior Women's Mission ministry, many of whom rarely came to Sunday School or regularly attended Sunday services, rose early on this first Sunday to cut and clean collard greens. They put their final touches on the dinning annex as the dew gave way to the sun. Then they returned home to put on their traditional First Sunday white dresses. But no one could have been more excited or more proud than the Chairman Deacon, who by this time was being heralded as a great leader for his role in getting this preacher from "Outta Town" to come all the way to the country and actually get him to agree to be "Ourva Pastor". And early this Sunday morning, unlike other Sunday mornings that were filled with arguments with his wife over why she hadn't washed any damn tee shirts, Deacon Walter Pickett wasn't argumentative at all. Matter of fact he was down right pleasant and actually cooked breakfast for his wife and made and poured his own coffee. As he stood gloatingly next to the breakfast table with his overwhelmed and uncharacteristically happy Eloise, Pickett looked at his wife and said "You know what Eloise? God is show 'nuff good, ain't he?"

"Yes He is Walter. He answers prayer too. A blessing delayed ain't a blessing denied. He may not come when you thank but he comes on time. He'll make yo mountain yo footstool. Love covers a multitude of sin. He make yo enemy have to do right by you. He…"

"Alright, Eloise, I get yo damn point. You shole do know how to mess up a man's morning."

"Shut up Walter and drank yo coffee that you made all by yo self. Soon it's gone be time for us to go get them chullun for church."

"You right Eloise. I need to call the Reverend now to see if he getting ready. Hand me my little black book over there out the drawer."

As Eloise retrieved Pickett's little black book and searched to find the Reverend's phone number, back at the hotel, Chauncey and Jada were returning from the hotel Lobby after a small but meaningful breakfast together. The time now was about 7:55AM and the couple knew they had to rush to be fully dressed and ready to meet the deacon by 8:45. As Chauncey hurriedly ironed his white, Italian cuffed shirt and Jada sat on the bed with a quiet but growing impatient Lizzy on her lap, placing berets on the child's pony-tailed head, the phone begin to ring and Chauncey knew it had to be Pickett.

"I'll get it Jada." Chauncey said as Jada completed Lizzy's Sunday hair do and began to give attention to her own Halle Berry styled hairdo. "That has to be Pickett." He said to himself as he put on his shirt and walked over to the phone.

"Hello."

"Good morning Reverend."

"Back at you Deacon Pickett, how are you doing?"

"I'll be better after I can stop calling you Reverend and start calling you my pastor." Pickett said as Chauncey chuckled, playing along with the deacon's evident optimism. "Are ya'll getting ready for Sunday School yet?"

"Yes Sir. We're well on our way and should be ready before too long. What time should we expect you?"

"I should be at you about a quarter to nine. That'll give us enough time to get back over here in enough time for you to relax a little just before Sunday school starts."

"8:45 it is. We'll be ready. And Deacon Pickett, I'll take the job if I'm chosen today."

"That sound good son. This is yo day then and we gone make it real special for you and yo family. You just preach God's word and remember what I told you over at the Plantation and ya'll will have a long stay at Mt. Carmel. You hear me Son?"

"Yes Sir. I remember, and again I appreciate all of your advice and I pray that you continue to be as much of a help as you've already been and continue to trust in my ability to lead. And if I'm chosen by the people as the next pastor I'll work hard to prove I'm worthy of their confidence too."

"O.K. son, I'll see you in about one hour."

After Chauncey's brief conversation with the confident deacon, he and Jada finished grooming themselves and we're finally dressed for success on a day that couldn't have started out any better. Jada was decked in a brand new pearly white flowing knee length Ralph Lauren dress and for the first time ever the expectant potential first lady wore a specially designed hat that appropriately completed her southern first Sunday church look. Her shoes were to die for and with those white alligator skins right out of the box, on her feet, Jada's walk down the isles of Mt. Carmel should garner her just as much praise about her elegance as she did on her wedding day.

Lizzy looked spectacular as well and the two year old beauty was poised to make her greatest impact on her father's candidacy. She was dressed in the most gorgeous gleaming white laced dress and little sparkling white heeled shoes that she barely knew how to walk in. Her hair looked as if it was done by Hollywood stylists and her little "I Love Jesus" hair bows accented her dress and affirmed her parent's strong Christian influence on her life.

Chauncey, on the other hand, chose a little more classic look. No pin-stripes, no fabulous colors, just powerful navy and white. The tall, handsome preacher didn't need much to accentuate good looks, nor did he choose to be over bearing in his appearance. But rather he chose to be simple, wearing only a navy blue, three buttoned Claiborne suit, white Italo Mondo French cuffed shirt, a simple, navy, white and gray striped tie, and in classic Pennington style, the always appropriate black Stacy Adams. Together they looked impressive and smelled terrific too.

As they walked out of the hotel room, possibly for the last time as just plain old Reverend and Mrs. Chauncey E. Pennington, they left the scents of what Aunt Eunice might refer to as an Italian Fume Factory. They were all set for the day that could change their lives forever.

Moments after returning to the Lobby and waiting patiently for Deacon and Mrs. Pickett to arrive to pick them up for service, the couple spotted the deacon's Cadillac about a block away as they looked at historical landmarks that could be seen in downtown Tallahassee from where they sat. Noticing that their ride was only seconds away, the couple exited the hotel and stood curbside for the preservation of precious time.

"Get on in ya'll and good morning," Pickett said as Eloise looked on with a grand and very pleasant smile on her face.

"Boy, don't you all look nice this morning," she said as she looked into the back seat to take a better look at the grinning couple.

"Thank you Mrs. Pickett. You look rather ravishing yourself," Chauncey said as Jada agreed and touched Eloise's foxy new white dress.

As the couples continued to exchange compliments, Deacon Pickett sped off and made his way back up I-10 for Chauncey's long awaited date with destiny. The ride over to the church was sort of quiet because it seemed as though the Picketts and Penningtons were very focused and exchanged only sporadic conversation. But before too long they were approaching the town's Interstate exit and butterflies began to fill Chauncey's stomach as Pickett turned on his blinkers and slowed down for his right turn off of the unusually busy highway.

Holding his wife's freshly done French manicured hands, Chauncey geared up for his grand entrance into the city where he finally began to visualize himself as their long overdo savior. He was a little nervous, but as he had stated to Jada back at the hotel, this was a good nervous; a nervous that spoke volumes about his eagerness to get busy doing God's business. As Deacon Pickett drove into the church parking lot, Chauncey and Jada looked at each other apprehensively when they noticed only four cars. Their eyes were saying what their mouths couldn't say about what they thought such a lack of attendance meant about what the people of Mt. Carmel felt about their arrival and Chauncey's potential pastorate.

"Where is everybody?" Chauncey whispered to Jada as Shirley Caesar blasted on Pickett's stereo from the local AM Station.

"Reverend, Mrs. Pennington, don't you be discouraged by the lack of cars here," said Eloise sensing the couple's uneasiness after she glimpsed their befuddled expressions in her vanity mirror as she powdered her nose just before exiting the car.

"These people are late starters and besides, many of the regulars might be running a little late today cause they want to impress ya'll. They'll show up shortly," she said easing the couple's apprehension.

"Yea Eloise is right. They always come late and I tell 'em 'bout it every Sunday during the lesson. But it's only 9:25 yet. If you'd like

Reverend, you can go on round to the pastor's study and I'll come get you when we ready."

"Ladies and Gentlemens in radio land, this is the Gospel Crusader," interrupted a sniffling, slow talking, and sinus-infected radio announcer on the AM station that was blaring in Pickett's car.

"This what I been waiting on ya'll. These is our church announcements on the radio. I wanted ya'll to hear ya'll's name on the radio. I called it in this morning. Here it go. Listen everybody."

"I would like to thank the honorable Deacon Walter Picket for calling in this monin'. They gone have a great big day over at Greater Mt. Carmel, where deacon Walter Pickett is the chairman of da bode and they gone have a young boy outta Texas, yes Lord that's right, a boy outta Texas comin all da way from Texas to preach. His name is Reverend Chumley Pennyworth and from what I hear, you gon' miss a treat if you miss this preacher. That's right. All roads lead to Greater Mt. Carmel on today and Deacon Walter Pickett, chairman of da bode at Mt. Carmel, told me to let everybody know that after da service they'll be selling fish and poke chop samiches and dinnas to all visitors. Yes five dollas will get you some of Betty Carmicheal's famous food and tater pie to boot. That's right and yours truly will try to be in the house. All roads lead to Mt. Carmel. And now back to ourva regularly scheduled broadcast with none other than the Hollering Prophet. Yes, that's right the Hollering Prophet, and for those out dea who don't know; that's me."

"Did ya'll hear that? We was on the radio! Did ya'll hear it?" Pickett said excitedly.

"Deacon Pickett, that was an excellent publicity stunt. Did you think of that all on your own?" Chauncey said as he squeezed Jada's hand to keep his inner laughs on the inside.

"Yes sir Reverend that was all my idea."

"That boy needs some sinus medication," rebutted Eloise. "That was the most horrific thang I've heard since I was a little child."

As Chauncey and Jada got out of Pickett's car, Eloise asked if it would be alright if she gave Lizzy a soft peppermint ball. The little girl graciously accepted after her parents' approval and accepted Mrs. Pickett's invitation to walk with her into the church for Sunday school. Surprised by Lizzy's willingness to walk with a "stranger", the

Penningtons laughed, and waited for Deacon Pickett to retrieve his briefcase from the trunk before entering the church. But, before Pickett could close his trunk Chauncey, Jada, and Pickett were all pleasantly surprised as cars begin to stream into the parking lot.

"Reverend we better go on in before all these people try to get a hold of you. You need to be left alone before service," Pickett said as he hurriedly ushered his prize catch into the back door of the church as if he were the sole body guard for a celebrity.

After they entered the church and the Penningtons were invited into the cramped pastor's study, the buzz on the outside of the church was just getting started. Mother Snelling, who was driven to church by her granddaughter, was overtaken by the massive amount of cars that begin pour in the church's parking lot. In all of her years of membership at Mt. Carmel she had never seen so many cars or for that matter people during Sunday school. If you didn't know any better you would've surely thought a rock star was some where in the building. Men, women, and children were all dressed to the tee. And though some of them hadn't been seen for years, if at all, Mother Snelling was as proud as a peacock and did her best impression of a valet at a five star hotel and warmly greeted each family as they approached the stairway near her handicap parking space.

Sunday school began with a hymn by Deacon Eddie Phillips and an awfully long prayer by Deacon Clausell Ellis who rarely attended Sunday school. Those deacons and regular dues paying members of Mt. Carmel were absolutely astonished by the huge turn out for Sunday school.

"It shole God is a lot of folk here Norway," said Deacon Mallard.

"Just hush Willie," rebutted an always tensed up Deacon Maxwell.

"Leave him alone Connie, Willie is right. It has to be at least fifty folk here," whispered a normally quiet and subdued Norway Cox. "Ya'll know we ain't never seen nothing like this."

The Deacons sat with their backs straight and their chins high in their "deacon's corner" as each thought to himself how lucky these people must be to have them serve as their leaders and how proud they were to be responsible for causing this great day to come to fruition. Occasionally, one of them would scan the room to see who all of the folk were, but for the most part they maintained their "we in charge" demeanor and kept their "no smiling in church" policy in tact.

Finally, Pickett left the sanctuary as if he was a court bailiff to retrieve the preacher and his wife. For the first time, Chauncey and Jada saw the impact that they were already having on this church. Chauncey walked with power and confidence. From the very moment he walked through the door he commanded everyone's attention and exuded the confidence of a man who undoubtedly felt like he had authority. Jada smiled as usual and added her warmth to a room that was full of anticipation by many and eased the fears of others who came just to make sure that this "city slicker preacher" wouldn't come and fleece their little church. Chauncey didn't teach the Sunday school lesson but his presence was felt in the class and his background in Theological Studies aided in his articulation of what was a confusing attempt by Deacon Phillips to teach the lesson.

"Jesus was humble." Phillips taught. "He wudn't like so many of us who always want every thang for ourselves. You ain't got to live in no mansion to be somebody in God's eyesight. That's why this lesson in Matthew 8 and verse 20 show us that even Jesus didn't have no where to lay his head. He said that foxes have them a hole and birds have nests and he didn't even have no where…" he said as he paused to see if anybody other than Willie Mallard would say "you teachin now."

"That's the key." He continued. "You got to be humble. It ain't no where in the bible where it say no preacher ought to be paid. But it do say that he a servant of the Lord. And the choir ain't got no bidness marchin' in. We got to be humble church. It ain't but six of ya'll anyway. What you doing marchin' in?"

"Well Deacon Phillips I understand your argument but I beg to differ as it relates to the context of this particular passage of scripture." Chauncey disagreed as his wife and others looked on fearfully. Jada didn't know it but her worries were substantiated because no one ever challenged a deacon's authority to teach the scripture; especially Deacon Eddie Phillips.

"That boy just hung his self," said Deacon Maxwell, who was always poised for confrontation and smiled widely at the very thought of having an all out church brawl at Sunday school.

"When Jesus spoke these words," Chauncey continued, "He wasn't speaking about a preacher's choice to drive a Cadillac as much as he was talking about the sacrifice it takes to follow him. Matter fact if you look up at verses 18-19 of Matthew 8 you'll see that Jesus was actually explaining that it takes selflessness and sacrifice. This text does not tell us we have to be poor to follow Jesus or that the choir can't march in or that the preacher shouldn't receive a salary." Chauncey continued as he rose to address the now interested congregation. "This text in essence says to us today that if we are to follow Jesus we can't allow what we have or don't have to prohibit us from humbly serving the Lord. Whether you make $100 a week or $1000 dollars a week, we're all somebody in God's eyesight and how pleasing is it to know that we serve a God that is able to give us exceedingly and abundantly above anything we could ask or think. I submit to you today that this Sunday school lesson empowers us to be followers but yet compels us be willing to give up something that we might gain when our work on this side is done. And in the words of my beloved brother Paul, when I've finished my course I want to hear the Lord say to me servant well done."

As Chauncey took his seat among a now eager to learn congregation, a shocked deacons' corner stared at their fallen comrade with their mouths on the floor. Deacon Phillips, who had never heard such oratory exquisiteness in his life, was too shocked to comment although his pride was visibly weakened. Phillips was in so many words embarrassed.

When Deacon Pickett, who would've normally chastised anybody, including a preacher for debating another deacon during Sunday school, looked out over the congregation and only saw smiles from people who wanted to give the preacher a standing ovation but didn't because they didn't want to cause further embarrassment to Phillips, he quickly gave in to his urges to clap his hands in support of statements he really didn't agree with. He boiled on the inside because he saw first hand how this church could slip from his grasp with a preacher like Chauncey being the leader. He saw how the people instantly fell in love with the young preacher and for a brief moment thought to himself how difficult it would be to stay in control of the church, especially if all of these people chose to follow Chauncey's leadership. But Pickett felt confident that he had enough influence over the young man to ensure that the over exuberant preacher would never have an out burst like that again.

The people, on the other hand, now believed that this was the guy who could turn their church around. They noticed and appreciated his fearlessness and his keen scriptural knowledge and for once they had an opportunity to have a pastor who, as Kiesha put it, could keep those "ignorant deacons in check". After seeing the chairman's reaction to the pastor's eloquent teaching, the entire congregation excluding the deacons and Mother Ellis, who was afraid that Clausell would slap her when they got home, clapped thunderously and applauded Chauncey's courageous and valid scriptural explanation.

"People of God we have heard for the first time the man of God. I told ya'll this boy is somebody. And oh, let us give our own Deacon Phillips a rousing hand for givin' it his best this morning," Picket said as he walked to the podium in the center of the church.

"People of God, I see this church making a U-turn and finding her way back to where it use to be and with my leadership along with this board and Reverend Pennington helping us out, we can continue what we started today. God Bless all of ya and although I ain't seen some of you in a long time, it's good to have you back and to our first time visitors, we want you to stay for church service too. And after church we gone eat. Let's be dismissed and get ready for a high time in the Lord. Again God bless you and oh, I can't forget to say this; God bless America. That's my motto."

With Sunday school over and the members and visitors alike being pleased with their initial hearing of the preacher, they were poised for what the 11:00 hour would bring.

Chapter 14

As Chauncey went back to the pastor's study to gather his thoughts one last time before he delivered his big sermon, Jada charmed the appreciative crowd and spent very intimate time sharing with the women and the men of the church, especially those who hadn't been in a while.

"I really enjoyed your husband," said one young man who was compelled to shake her hand. "I almost rededicated my life after that speech. I feel like God needs me in his army."

"Well… He does," Jada replied as she held his hand and comforted the wayward corn-rowed hoodlum like character in the sanctuary after Sunday school. "Don't let anybody fool you, you are important to God and the greatest attribute of the Lord, I think, is the fact that he's able to look beyond our faults to see our needs. None of us are perfect, but God does expect us to repent when we need to."

"Like David?" he questioned.

"Just Like David." She answered and smiled. "Now what is you name?"

"My name is Chris and I grew up in this church, but I just got caught up in the game you know. But I'm real glad I came even though I didn't have no church clothes. I really just came because the people on the streets said there was a new preacher up here and food was up here today."

"Well I tell you what, my husband would be glad to meet you and share more about the Lord with you after service and we believe that it doesn't matter what you have on, on the outside as long as you're ready for a change on the inside."

"Thank you ma'am."

"Choir members! Choir members!" shouted Lula Penny, the piano player and lead singer of the Voices of Mt. Carmel. "We need to stop socializing and consecrate ourselves. Church starts in five minutes. Go on out to the front and line up so we can march in."

"Now Lula," ranted a frustrated and still embarrassed Deacon Phillips, "it ain't but seven of ya'll sangin this monin. Tell me why ya'll got to march in and waste all that time. Ya'll ain't got to march in."

"The same reason ya'll deacons sang all them dry behind hymns and pray like God gone get mad if you cut it off'." With a sniggle and a chubby finger pointed at Phillip's face she continued, "Now move you old fool before I call that preacher in here to set you straight again."

Slowly but surely, Jada was able to break away from the throng that sought to say a word to her and found her way back to the study to encourage her husband one last time. But, as she exited the sanctuary, more worshipers poured into it. The regular church goers were astonished, yet again, at the number of people that showed up for the service.

"Woodrow Elliot ain't never got this many folk to come to church, even for funerals," recounted Deacon Mallard. "Now did he Norway?"

"Naw, he show nuff didn't Willie."

On a normal Sunday morning during the eleven o'clock service you could count on about thirty people showing up, but on this Sunday morning they exceeded that number in Sunday school and by the time Chauncey sat in the pulpit at least a hundred and fifty people would be scattered abroad in the three hundred person capacity sanctuary. Many of the worshipers were long time members who only returned because they wanted to see and hear the new preacher and of course eat and others were complete strangers who were invited by members or heard the announcement on this morning's radio broadcast. Included in that number, was Lula Penny's guests Dr. Adolph James, the principal at the

The Day All Hell Broke Loose

Great Pines Elementary School and his wife Anita, a successful realtor from Tallahassee.

"Good morning Mr. and Mrs. James," said Lula as she ushered her guests to the front row just before taking her position at the finely polished but old black Baldwin piano near the deacons' corner. "Now ya'll just make yourselves at home. I'm sure you'll enjoy our new preacher and afterwards you can meet him and his wife. She's adorable and from what I hear she'll be a great addition to our staff at the school."

"I'm looking forward to that," said the fifty-two year old Dr. James, a very polished professional with aspirations to run for political office in the near future.

After seeing the James' to their seats Lula walked tiredly over to the piano and waited for deacon Pickett's signal to begin the church service. However, Pickett hadn't made it back to the sanctuary just yet, because he spent his final moments with Chauncey giving his last bit of advice.

"The people already love you Reverend and I know you saw that this monin. You ain't got to overdo it and for God sakes don't preach too long. And always remember to give honor to your deacon's board and of course single me out cause I'm yo chairman. The people love it when a preacher is able to give honor where honor is due. If you make a good showing in there like you did for Sunday school, I can guarantee that you'll be our man when the day is done."

As a focused Chauncey fingered through his concordance to find a reference scripture, he never looked Pickett in his eyes, but did respond to the deacon's advice as Jada folded his white inscribed handkerchiefs.

"Thanks Deacon Pickett. I appreciate that," he said somberly as the hour quickly drew near of his last hurdle.

"O.K. Now that we done squared that away, I guess we can get this show on the road. Are ya'll ready?"

"As ready as we'll ever be." Chauncey stood and grabbed his wife's hand as they prepared to enter the sanctuary.

With his bible in his left hand and holding Jada's left hand with his right, the Reverend Chauncey Evansworth Pennington walked into the sanctuary primed and ready to give the sermon of his life. But just before he took his seat in the center chair of the pulpit and as he released Jada's hand so that she could take her position in the mother's corner,

Deacon Pickett in his traditional role as "church starter", nodded his head twice at Lula, which signified that the choir could now march in and boy did they. Unlike any Sunday that they've seen in recent years, the choir actually sounded pretty good as they marched in and sang to the C chords of the song "We Have Come this Far By Faith".

Lula led the choir with a thundering, yet angelic voice. She was in a zone and if the first selection of the small choir would be any indication, this would turn out to be a spirit filled Sunday. The congregation stood as the choir marched in and sang along eagerly to the tunes of the familiar anthem. Matter of fact, one couldn't really distinguish if the choir was sounding that good or if it was the congregation, who was undoubtedly filled with great voices. To be honest, it was mostly the congregation, the choir wasn't that good. But, the harmony that the choir didn't have, the congregation's altos, tenors, and sopranos definitely had. They sang in unity. It was a sign of things to come and as Chauncey would later state in his sermon "As brothers and sisters we ought to stand in the gap for each other and strengthen each other when we find insufficiencies. It's not our responsibility to pick at a person's faults, failures and frailties; but how powerful is it when we're able to love each other and pray for each other through our faults, failures, and frailties."

They continued singing "Leaning on the Lord." Lula led "And Oh I'm Trusting" as the choir answered, "Trusting in His Holy Word."

"He's never failed me," Lula sang on.

"He's never failed me yet." As Mother Snelling begin to shout and others wiped tears from their eyes in great joy, the congregation continued on with the choir as they marched into the choir stand "Oh,… Oh, Oh, Oh,…Oh, Oh, Oh…can't turn around, we've come this far by faith."

Deacon Pickett and Connie Maxwell led the devotional services that began the worship hour. Greater Mt. Carmel received another surprise when they noticed Deacon Maxwell wiping tears from his eyes as he sang the hymn "A Charge."

"Sang it Deacon!" shouted members of the congregation as he sang with spirit. The otherwise hellish old womanizer had become overtaken by what was happening in that church. After the hymn, Deacon Pickett himself, who never showed emotion at church, pulled

The Day All Hell Broke Loose

out his handkerchief and acted as if he, too, was overtaken by the spirit. Some in the congregation thought this must be a move of God but others, including his own wife, knew that Walter Pickett was just acting so that that he might garner the same praise as Connie, who was visibly moved by the words of the hymn. As he sat back down at the old wooden Deacon's Table at the front of the church, he beckoned for Deacon Mallard to come pray in his stead. Mallard who couldn't read or write, or for that matter articulate or pronounce many words correctly, gave the sweetest, shortest prayer you would ever hear from the normally long winded, hooping and hollering deacon from the south.

"Lord we thancha for this hourva, and we pray dat chu bless us on this day. Give us a wud from on high that ourva soul might be changed. AAAAAmen!

His amen was longer than his prayer, but Deacon Mallard had set the tone. The congregation, some laughing and others crying, appreciated the sincerity of the deacon's prayer, and clapped thunderously and shouted Amen with him.

Connie, who just moments ago was overtaken by the spirit was still on his knees for prayer. However, he quickly snapped out of the spirit and snarled at Willie as he thought to himself "Now I know Willie is a damn fool."

The table had been set. With an A & B selection from the newly inspired choir the atmosphere was perfect. Chauncey was about to deliver a word to one hundred and fifty or so anticipatory church goers.

After a prepared introduction by Deacon Pickett and a charge by the elder statesman to the people of Mt. Carmel to "be kind to the young preacher" and "listen carefully to the Word of the Lord.", Chauncey took the podium for the first time and was greeted warmly by the congregation.

Immediately they felt his authoritativeness and just from his regal appearance alone, these people knew that this man was special and meant business when it came to preaching. He was a clean shaven, well manicured, proud father and husband, which was evident by his enchanting references to his beautiful wife and daughter; the "loves of his life." The women in the congregation were especially taken aback by his extraordinary looks and if for no other reason; they were going to pay close attention to this man just so they could witness first hand the closest thing to Denzell Washington ever visiting their city.

"He is gorgeous" a few of the younger women thought to themselves. "That girl better stay close to that man." thought some of the older sisters of the congregation, after noticing how some of the women begin to gawk at the preacher's seemingly caramelized lips. But, for the most part all in attendance knew their purpose for being present. If you were a member, you were there to evaluate. If you were a visitor you were there to congratulate if congratulations were in order. Or of course, you were there because you heard about the five dollar fish and pork chop dinners on the radio that would be sold after service.

As silence came upon the sanctuary, Chauncey took a deep breath, composed himself and begin by acknowledging God, his family and the leadership and members of Greater Mt. Carmel.

"It is an honor to stand before you today, not just because I'm a candidate to be your pastor, but because I always feel honored that God thinks enough of me to allow me into His house and in His presence. I want to thank Him for that. I would also like to thank my wife Jada, who as many of you know by now, is a woman who loves the Lord and I'm a witness that she loves and cares for her family. Without her, I don't believe I'd be where I am today. And I don't know where my daughter Lizzy is" he said as he scanned the sanctuary and the congregation generously chuckled, knowing the little girl was bouncing from lap to lap, "but she's been a princess throughout this whole process and Lizzy, wherever you are, I want to thank you too."

As Pickett sat back with his arms folded and eagerly anticipated the moment that the preacher would give praise to the deacon's board, Chauncey finally found time to acknowledge the famed preacher taming crew.

"I also want to acknowledge this great staff of deacons who have been gracious hosts to me and my family. To all of you who played a part in making our weekend a spiritual adventure, thank you as well."

As he concluded his acknowledgements, Pickett was a little disappointed that his name wasn't called out during the acknowledgments, but he felt confident that if the Reverend was chosen as the next pastor of Greater Mt. Carmel he'd have plenty of time to train him in the appropriate manner to acknowledge a chairman. With all the preliminaries out of the way, the moment that the congregation had waited for was at long last here.

"If you would be so kind, please turn with me now in your bibles to the book of Joshua chapter one and let us read together verses two through six"

As the congregation joined Chauncey in the reading of the very familiar passage of scripture, many in the crowd nodded there heads as if to agree that this was the sermon that this church needed to hear. Other's read intently wondering to themselves, how was this preacher going to preach this passage of scripture any different from any of the other preachers they'd heard. But after the reading Chauncey gave the interested congregation his sermon topic and when he did the people erupted in cheers, knowing that this was going to be one of those sermons that put everybody in check.

"Today, if you'll give me about seven minutes of your time," he said jokingly "I'd like to preach from the subject "It's A New Day" and if I were to use a subtopic today it would be "The Enemy Can't Do Nothing To Stop Me."

The audience was buzzing as they waited on this sermon to unfold. Before Chauncey uttered a word members whispered among themselves. Some of them even stood and proclaimed, "It show is preacher" or "Tell 'em bout they selves."

Chauncey opened the message slowly, carefully alliterating his points for maximum absorption in the hearts and minds of the listeners. As he systematically worked his way through the text he carefully orchestrated and gave his first point.

"The first thing I want you to understand is that **Seasons Change**. Verses one and two substantiates that contention because after years of being led by Moses, the children of Israel had to deal with his loss, but Joshua represented a new thing that God was about to do in their lives. I don't know about you today, but I've had some Moses' to come and go in my life, but is there anybody here who's thankful that God allows the winter to turn into spring and our nightmares to turn into pleasant dreams. Aren't you glad that when you were in your weakest moments after you'd lost somebody or something, that God stepped in and gave you a new lease on life?" he said as he pointed toward heaven to the shouts "Yes Sa" and applause of the congregation. "I thank God for the Joshuas in my life."

"But I don't want you to get too happy right there" he continued "because my second point deals with **Scattered Children**. One word in verse two changed my whole outlook on the text as I studied a little this morning. In verse two Joshua is told by God that Moses is dead. It's a new season and it's your time to rise. But Joshua I don't just want you to go over into the promised land by yourself, you are commissioned to take… watch this…" he said as most of the congregation stood and others sat on the edge of their seats waiting for the answer. "…**ALL** this people. That means that in God's house there are no big I's and little you's. Everybody is somebody in the eyesight of God and we are commissioned through this text to bring everybody to the place where God has us to be. It not only should be a new season for you, but it ought to be a new season for everybody in shouting rang of your voice. Grab your neighbor by the hand and tell them; you're going with me."

"Now you talkin preacha!" yelled Willie Mallard, who often said less than the other deacons due to his lack education. Others continued to stand and shout Amen, as they all waited on the inspiring preacher's crescendo.

"My third point, and I'm almost done, is we all must be **Strong & Courageous**." Chauncey said with sweat steaming down his brow onto his, already soaking, shirt and jacket.

Slowing his pace slightly to prepare for the close of what was already a message for the ages at Mt. Carmel, Chauncey continued. "Verse six argues my last point for me. All you got to do now is just believe what it says. Good evening Mt. Carmel, long fare ye well, I thank you for being kind to me," he said as he begin moan in between his words. Lula accompanied his moans with the sound of the piano. "But if I never see you again, don't worry about me. Because my hand is in God's hand." he proclaimed as Mother Snelling jumped straight out of her seat and ran towards the altar, shouting "Yes Lord, Yes!" The preacher hooped his way to a close.

"And as I leave you today I want you to know that if God be for you, who in the world can be against you. The bible says in verse five of our text that the Lord will not fail thee nor will he forsake thee. And that text reminds me of what the only mother I've really ever known told me," he preached as tears fell from his eyes as he remembered how Aunt Eunice helped him through the loss of his mother and father.

"She told me, that you may not have a mother, you may not have a father, but as long as you live you don't ever have to be afraid. She told me to remember what David said in the twenty third Psalms. She showed me when I was just a little boy that even though your parents can't be here with you, you always got a Shepherd." He continued as Deacon Pickett sincerely wiped his eyes and walked slowly toward the pulpit to tell the preacher he had done enough.

As Pickett made it to the pulpit and wrapped his left arm around Chauncey's waist to convince the overjoyed preacher he'd done enough, at least twenty other members of the congregation, including Chris and Dr. James' wife Anita, shouted as they inched their way to the altar to join an already passed out, Mother Snelling. "The Lord is my shepherd," he continued "and I got to leave you when I tell you that if the Lord is your shepherd, you don't have to worry about crying too much longer because weeping may endure for a night but joy! Joy!" he shouted as he lifted his right leg and fell back into Pickett's arms "joy will… come… in the morning." After he had lifted himself out of the arms of Pickett, who by this time was genuinely overtaken with emotion, he leaned across the lectern, and told the jubilant congregation to look at their neighbors and shout "It's a new season. It's a new season. It's a new season."

As a weakened and spiritually drained Chauncey was ushered back to his seat by Pickett and given a glass of cool water by Deacon Norway Cox, most of the congregation stood and praised God. As the people clapped and praised uncontrollably, some fanning other shouting saints, Lula tearfully burst into an old southern favorite. "This Joy that I have," she sang. "The world didn't give it to me; Oh, Oh, Oh, This Joy that I have, the world didn't give it to me; Oh This Joy that I have, the world didn't give it to me, Oh the world didn't give it, the world can't take it away." Over and over Lula sang the verses of that song that everybody seem to know and it was evident because the ones that were not slain in the spirit or standing in utter shock at what had just taken place, sang joyfully and loudly to Lula's suddenly pleasant to the ear piano.

With Chauncey refreshed after a drink of water, he slowly stood to greet what now looked like a battlefield. People were everywhere and most all in attendance were still moaning and weeping with looks on their faces that ranged from sheer joy and deliverance to pain over not knowing if a man that can preach like that would ever stay in a place like this. Some figured silently, that as soon as he realized that he was taking up residence in Payton's Place, a term commonly used to refer to the church's hellish nature, he'd surely seek higher ground. But Chauncey was resolute and in a moment of satisfaction, knowing that God had enabled him to do all he could on this particular Sunday morning, he offered the invitation to discipleship. And as Lula softly sang "Come Unto Jesus", Deacons Harold Belford and Clausell Ellis walked to the front of the church, as was customary during the invitation period of the service. The deacons pulled out two chairs and placed them at the altar for potential converts. If every deacon had pulled out chairs on this Sunday morning it would not have been enough. On this day alone more people come to Christ than had come in the past six years. At the beckoning of the man who would be their new pastor, seventeen people, mostly those who had left the church years ago, came back home, four of which actually desiring to be baptized.

God had definitely moved during the service and for the first time in nearly a decade, Deacon Pickett did something he hadn't fathomed he'd ever do. In the wake of the carnage left by Hurricane Chauncey and for the sake of time that was already well spent, Deacon Pickett made a decision only a chairman of the board could make.

"People of God, I know its communion Sunday, but to tell you the truth, I'm already full from that sermon. What we gone do now is cancel the communion," he said as his deacon's board and congregation nodded in agreement. "And we gone just let the man of God do the benediction. Then we'll just move right on in to the bidness potion of the service. I would ask, however, for all the visitors to exit the sanctuary. You can either go to the dinning Annex or just wait outside for a few minutes, so we can take care of church bidness."

As the visitors begin to joyfully exit the sanctuary after the benediction, anticipating the church might select a new pastor on this day, the remaining forty or so members sat silently in the church solemnly waiting on Pickett for further direction.

"Now I don't mean no harm ya'll, but you know if you been paying yo dues or not and if you have, you welcome to stay. But if you ain't we gone have to ask ya'll to leave …Charles you excused,… Mandy you too,… Ida Mae, Rita, Ulysses,… who else ain't paid Norway?" he said as the persons whose names he called got up in embarrassment and walked out.

"I could beat his ass," mouthed a five foot five stocky built, frustrated and angry Ulysses Greene, who only moments ago had to be pulled off the floor after he fell out in the spirit.

"And you too Shirley. I don't mean to hurt nobody feelings but right is right."

"You show right Bro. Chairman," shouted the always agreeable Deacon Mallard.

"Now Willie if you had kept quiet, I woulda forgot all about you. But what I'm bout to say next gone hurt me more than it gone hurt you," Pickett said, grimacing at the idea of being the bearer of bad news.

"What dat?"

"Well you and yo wife is delinquent too. By how many months Norway?" Pickett asked as the deacon shook his head as if to say "you can't be talkin bout me."

"You can shake yo round head all you want to, but Norway say ya'll is behind too. You dismissed Willie."

After all of the delinquent dues payers had been excused, the specially called conference meeting was brought to order as Chauncey and Jada sat nervously in the pastor's study waiting for a word from one of the deacons.

"Bro. Chairman, if I'm in order," Eddie Phillips said as he asked for permission to take the floor. "I'd like to offer motion that this conference officially opens."

"Yes you may."

After exhibiting proper protocol according to their Baptist manual, often referred to as "the discipline", the conference meeting officially began with a prayer and the floor was opened for discussion. But, before the floor was opened for discussion, Deacon Pickett offered some very helpful and truthful words of wisdom.

"Now we know what we here for and I just don't feel like it ought to be no long drawn out debate. Either you like the boy or you don't. I ain't gone let this take all day."

"Deacon Pickett if I may," said Mother Snelling as she slowly rose from her seat with the aid of her cane, "I'd like to take the floor."

"Go head Mable."

"Well, you know I've been a member here for a long time…"

"Go head Mable!" Pickett said urging the elderly, but strong willed member to make it quick.

"Now Walter Pickett, I have the floor," she said sternly as she stared at Pickett, who sat calmly but uninterested as he pulled on his right ear with his eyes planted in his manual.

"As I was saying, I've been here for a long time and I ain't never seen nothing happen like that in this church and I want to be the one to offer a motion to take a vote right now to make that young man our pastor."

"That's the best thing you've said in all the years I done knowed you," murmured Pickett. The old deacon also chuckled under his breath as he visualized the great time he'd have molding the young preacher into his personal servant.

"Wait a minute, I have sumpt to say," rebutted Deacon Phillips who failed to ask Pickett for permission to talk. "This boy did preach a good sermont, but I thank he arrogant and too uppity for this church. I just don't know bout this."

"Sit down Eddie," Pickett said calmly. "Strike every word that came outta his mouth from official church records cause he ain't had sense enough to address me," he continued as if someone was actually taking notes for official church records.

"Mother Snelling you can make yo motion. But it don't take no speech, you hear?"

"Yes Sir." She said gladly, as her voice crackled with glee. "I make a motion that we name Reverend Chauncey Pennington our new pastor."

"I second that motion," Lula said as Pickett stood to carry the motion.

"The motion has been properly made and properly seconded and now the floor is open for question."

"Question," chanted the congregation in unison, as tensions mounted about the outcome of the vote.

"All in favor signify by standing."

With all standing but, Deacon Phillip's and his wife Lucille, the motion was resoundingly carried, much to the delight of Pickett. He led the people in thunderous applause and cheers and he readied himself to make his final report.

"Mt. Carmel, it gives me very great pleasure to announce on this the fifth day of June in the year of our Lord 1994 that this church has called my friend and my new son, Reverend Chauncey Evansworth Pennington to be our pastor. Let the church say Amen." Afterwards he smiled and grabbed his bible and manual from the offering table.

"With that being said this meeting is adjourned and we are dismissed. God bless all of ya'll. And Oh, Go bless our troops cross this land and country."

CHAPTER 15

Aunt Eunice's Recollection of the First three years

At the tender age of twenty four years and twenty eight days old, Chauncey Evansworth Pennington became the youngest pastor that Greater Mt. Carmel had ever employed and from the moment he walked into the pastorate of the church that was long overdo for a breakthrough, his presence prompted an immediate impact. The Sunday of the official vote was a very special day in the lives of all that were affiliated with the ministry of Greater Mt. Carmel, but for Chauncey and Jada, especially, they knew it was, a dream come true. And at a time when their financial status and living arrangements could've caused panic and mass confusion, they literally trusted God to make a way and on that very day He began to do just that.

"Chauncey has never been one to get overly excited about anything" said Aunt Eunice who sat in her living room recounting Chauncey's first three years at Greater Mt. Carmel "But I remember like yesterday when he called to let me know how his trip to Florida had turned out. We'd talked from time to time and I knew that there was a possibility that he'd have to move again, but to be honest, I was praying real hard, because I really didn't want him to rush into a situation that he or his young family wasn't ready for. But, on that particular day in June of ninety four, He called me screaming and yelling like he had just won the lottery and I asked what's wrong boy?" she said as she chuckled remembering her nephews uncharacteristic excitement. "I kind of figured it was good news about the church, but something deep down in my spirit told me it had to be more."

As she got up from her brown, leather living room recliner to stir a pot of neck bones that she had boiling on the stove she continued, "I heard Jada's crazy self in the background and it sounded like even my precious little Lizzy had lost her mind too. That's when he started yelling, "Auntie, I got it, I got the job." He was so happy and for a moment I rejoiced with him and told him how proud I was and how much I wished his mother and father was here to see what their boy had become. But as for me, naturally, I was a little worried, not because I didn't feel like he was capable of doing a good job or making another transition in his life. But, he and Jada didn't really have anybody to look after them like I would or her parent's would. They were alone, in a strange place, raising a child, and Jada hadn't even found a job. My concern was how were they gonna make it until they got settled in? Eventually me and the Blaylocks did go down there to help them out for a while, but my burdens were lifted later on in that week, when Chauncey called me and told me that Jada had got a job at a school not far from the church he pastors. He had told me that Sunday that he and Jada had been introduced by the church's piano player to Mr. and Mrs. James, who I still love to this day and even though I've sent them Red Velvet cakes the past two Christmases, I can't ever repay them for what they did for my children." she said as she placed the lid on her boiling pot and wiped her aged but crafty hands on her beige, wrinkled apron.

"Yes Lord. I know God is good." she said as she sat back down into her recliner. "Now, Mr. James, the principal at the school, told Jada to stop by the school on that Monday, before they went back to Odessa to wrap up some personal business and get their things packed to be moved, you know, so that he could talk to her and so she could fill out an application. They went by Mr. James' office and Jada filled out the application. And while they were still in Texas the woman from the school board personnel office called Jada to tell her she had the job. And thanks to Adolph James, who is already grooming her to be his assistant, Jada walked into that position as a fourth grade teacher making almost double what she did back in Odessa. Now ain't God Good?" she said as she shook her head, stomped her feet, and clasped her hands at the reality that all her worst fears were being diminished at such a rapid rate and the fact that God still hears and answers her prayers.

"I couldn't have been happier, or at least I thought." she said as she composed herself and gathered her thoughts. "Mr. James' wife, Anita, a very spiritual woman put the icing on the cake for me. That lady, who I consider as Chauncey's and Jada's angel, offered to let them rent a little house that she'd just bought. She's a realtor you know. Now the house was in Tallahassee and in an area that I wasn't too keen on at first, down near the college, but when I saw that dump Pickett and his crew!..., I'll get to them in a minute" she said as her tone swiftly transitioned from alleviation to outrage at the very mention of the name of Chauncey's nemesis "They wanted my babies to start out, as he put it, slowly and live in a house, behind his ole house, that he'd built after his daughter moved her mobile home off his property.

All that was left, from what he said so proudly, was a concrete slab that he'd previously poured for a porch on the trailer. He built about four rooms onto the porch and thought it could be prime real estate. That thing had one bedroom one bath room and if Jada was in the living room she was in arms reach of the refrigerator, her bed and the toilet. It was a mess to say the least." she said as she chuckled. "But Anita got them started and told them that after they'd been on their jobs for a couple of years with sustainable income, that she'd help them get into something a little bigger and a little closer to where they work. And she did. Honey, when I tell you, I ain't never been in a house so nice in all of my years. Well Wallace and Suzy had a nice place too, but that was different, this is my Chauncey I'm talking about." She said as her eyes lit up as she recounted her summer visit to the immaculate home, nestled in the pine trees on the seventh green of the prestigious North Florida Golf and Country Club at Penelope Pines.

"What's interesting about how the whole thing went was that, when Chauncey came to pastor that church he was making less than eight hundred dollars a month and I didn't know that until he told me bout the next thing I'm about to tell you. If I had known that that clown had accepted that mess, I would've strangled him and then told him to pack his bags and leave that hell hole. But it got better." she said as she smiled and rocked slowly in her recliner. "I talk a lot of trash about Walter

Pickett and those old stubborn deacons down there, but I really do believe that Walter loves that boy. They just don't know any better down there. But when I came down for Chauncey's installation ceremonies I got a chance to see him for the first time in more than fifty years and he was real kind to me and I knew he'd pan out to be a good help to Chauncey as Chauncey begin to train them. But at the installation, which was the first Sunday in August of ninety-four, Pickett stood up before the congregation and announced that he was "using his authority as chairman of the board" she recounted laughingly "to give Chauncey a raise. Chauncey was shocked and Lord poor Jada could've had a fit sitting there on that front pew. But Walter declared before all the people that the pastor's new salary would be $2500 a month with no money taken out for church dues, the building fund, or the children's trips."

"Now some of the folk were a little displeased with such a large amount of money going to one man, but I thought he deserved more than that. And a whole bunch of other folk did as well. After all, on that Sunday, the church was packed to capacity, and out of the two hundred and fifty or so that were there all but a hand full stood up and cheered what Walter said, including this ole wooly head man named Bishop A. W. Tanyhill, who preached one of the longest, most bad English laden sermons I'd ever heard in my life.

But three years later, and knowing what I know now about Walter Pickett, who occasionally calls me, with his perverted self, I'm starting to believe that he only did what he did only to grandstand and to make his own self look good. Matter of fact I know that he had a motive for giving Chauncey that kind of an increase and that was to keep his good deed hanging over my baby's head so that he could influence decisions Chauncey would have to make. Chauncey has even told me on many occasions that Walter and those deacons have threatened to lower his salary or get rid of him all together if he didn't stop moving the church so fast. The fact is; they're just afraid of loosing their power," she said as she raised her eyebrows and got up again to turn off the heat from her piping hot pot of neck bones.

"But they can't do it though, because so many folk have joined that church, and most of them are young, influential, people that's in full support of Chauncey. Like that Billy and Ruth Anne Dunn. I got a chance to meet them when I came to visit Chauncey and Jada in the summer of ninety-five and honey I tell you that, that couple is on fire for the Lord and they have really been a blessing to Chauncey and Jada. From what Chauncey tells me, they were once members at the church where he's at now, but left after a big fall out during the time that Walter and those deacons ousted this other poor pastor. But they came back to the church after they saw the positive changes that Chauncey made and they have been very faithful to Chauncey's ministry ever since. Matter of fact by this time next year, Billy will be a deacon and Chauncey has already appointed Ruthie as the new church finance director, much to the dismay of the deacons after the deacon who used to do it died of cirrhosis of the liver. I think his name was Norman Cox but that ain't the point. I just need to know how in the world does a deacon of the church, die of cirrhosis of the liver?" she said as she chuckled at the thought of a deacon also being known as the town drunk.

"Chauncey could never understand why those deacons, especially Walter, gave him so much trouble for choosing Ruth Anne. She was well liked by the congregation. She was a tither. And better yet the girl is an award winning accountant. And unlike any of those deacons, she had plenty of her own money, so folk wouldn't be accusing her of putting her hands in the cookie jar, if you know what I mean. Who better to take over as finance director?" Aunt Eunice questioned with a perplexed look on her face.

"Oh and I can't forget to tell you about my new grandbaby Daphne, that's Ruth Anne and Billy's daughter who has called me grandma' from the very first day she met me." Eunice said smiling as she thought of the playful antics and fond impression she has of the now fifteen year old. That's a picture of her right over there on the mantle piece, next to Lizzy's. That's my Daphne in her little cheerleader uniform. She's a fine girl and does a good job babysitting Lizzy, who's five now. Daphne tells me that Jada and Chauncey gave her a key to let herself in when she house sits for them when they're out of town. Every now and then she calls, but I get my greatest laughs when Jada tells me that Daphne's head is swelling from all the attention she's getting from all those high school boys, but I'm not worried about my Daphne. She's a sweet girl and very responsible."

As Eunice placed Daphne's photo back onto the mantle piece, she turned her focus back to her delight over knowing that Chauncey and

Jada were surrounded by relatively good people and for the most part, supported whole heartedly his vision at the church.

"All in all it's some very fine people down there and I'm confident that they won't let nothing happen to that boy. They really do love their pastor and his wife and child and anybody who stands in the way of what God is doing in that church, will have hell on their hands as Walter and those deacons have found out. Remind me to tell you about them" She said doing her best to remember to share her thought about the deacons at Mt. Carmel.

"But I can't lie though, all of them in there aren't wholesome or Holy." she continued as she rolled her eyes as only a big black woman could. "The last time I was down there, I saw some ole hoochie mommas too, with their skin tight dress wearing, no panty hose wearing, draws too little for their behinds wearing, wanna be First Lady, nappy head selves. I'm convinced that some of those women that are coming to that church ain't in it but for one thing and that's to try to offer my baby something that he don't want. But, I always tell Jada that she has to let those women know where she stands." Eunice said pointing her pudgy finger. "And I tell Chauncey too, that he needs to make sure that he lifts her up from his pulpit every Sunday to let them know that they don't have a chance.

But, honey to make a long story short; on any given Sunday it's hard to find a seat in that place and from what Jada tells me, they have a lot of tithing members too, and they've cut out all that dues mess. And now, from what I hear, the church finances have increased from something like $3,500 a month to almost $9000 a month and that's real good for that area. I'm proud of what they are accomplishing. But it hasn't been easy on him though."

"I can tell that he's changed a little bit, he's not as cheerful as he used to be but, I guess, being a pastor has hardened him a little bit, and maybe that's a good thing. Chauncey used to be more outgoing though. He used to be more of a socialite, but now he really just sticks to himself and he and Jada rarely accept any company at all other than Billy and Ruth Anne. I ask him sometimes if he's still happy doing what he's doing and he always assure me that he is and he insists he's just growing and being more independent for a change. I can appreciate that and I can really tell that he's grown not only as pastor but as a family man too. He's twenty-seven now and I guess, I'm just having a hard time dealing with the fact that my little naïve boy, who use to cry at the very thought of me leaving him with a baby sitter, has gone, never to return. He's strong though. He reminds me a lot of how his father used to be. Wallace was very authoritative and demanding, and Chauncey looks more like him and acts more like him everyday. I guess that comes with the strain of being a pastor and I really do believe that if he hadn't developed such a tough skin so quickly, he wouldn't have made it a day at that church."

As the evening progressed and swift autumn breezes gave way to the still of the night, Eunice moved the conversation setting to her bedroom, where she reached painfully and slowly, due to oncoming rheumatoid arthritis, under her well arranged and well kept canopy bed that was adorned with a crisp, lavender and white bed spread and an assortment of rose themed pillows, and pulled out a shoe box containing letters that Chauncey had written her over the past three years. She had looked intensely through a stack of about fifteen or so when she managed to pull her self up and continued the conversation.

"When I read this one" she said as her voice lowered and showed visible signs of emotion. "I cried a lot that day. I didn't even call, because I didn't know what to say. I didn't know if I should say anything. All I know, is I just wanted to get down to Florida a fast as I could to check on my baby and just hug him. This letter made me feel like he didn't have nobody in the world he could turn to. I'll read it to you, if you'd like." She said as she sat on her bed and reached over to her nightstand to grab her bifocals.

The letter was dated May 8, 1995 and Eunice thought that it would be some kind of thank you letter, since it was his birthday and he should've gotten his new cappuccino maker by then. But it was everything but a thank you letter as Eunice quickly found out.

"Auntie," she read as she paused to breathe deeply in an inadequate effort to harness her emotion.

"On a day when I should be celebrating, I find my self in tremendous despair. I feel so alone here and nobody other than Jada and a few people at the church, even realized that it was my birthday. The church is doing great, but that is the object of my frustration. In a time when we all should be enjoying what God is doing, I find myself fighting against people who never see the good in anything I try to do and who only harp on things they feel like I've done wrong. It's not everybody. It's only a few. But those few are the ones I have to meet with on the first Friday of every month and even though half of them only come to church twice a month, they never miss they're opportunity to raise hell at a conference meeting. This past Friday, I had my regularly scheduled meeting with the board of deacons and they really showed their true colors. They raised sand about everything from the way I merged the choirs to accusing me of calling them stupid from the pulpit." she read, pausing briefly to mention that Chauncey probably should have called them stupid.

"I didn't remotely say anything like that, nor will I ever. They even told me that they have been told by credible witnesses that a girl in the church is pregnant with my baby, which is a total lie. They raised hell about my salary again and told me that I was going to bankrupt the church like Woodrow Elliot did. I didn't ask them for that raise, they gave it to me and besides, the church's revenue has doubled in the last six months and we even don't have any major outstanding debts.

Walter Pickett even had the nerve to show me a letter that was mysteriously being circulated in the community that supposedly proved that I was trying to change the church name so that I could add my name to the church bank account. All of which is a bunch of foolishness that I don't have the energy or time to prove untrue. But what bugs me more than anything is that they sit there like every word that comes from their mouths is Gospel, like they are actually right. And no one in the meeting ever challenges the authenticity of their claims even if they feel in their hearts that another deacon is wrong.

They're all cowards if you ask me and to be honest, I'm really just tired. My mind is weary and my spirits are extremely low. I've never been so hurt but one other time in all my life and that's when my momma died. I just don't know how to handle all of this and maybe, this place isn't for me. All I've tried to do in the months since I've been here is make this church grow. I've been honest. I've been trustworthy. But none of that really seems to matter to these people. I visit the sick and shut in. I've even made visits to the jail for some of their own family members and the only thing I hear from these deacons is that they don't feel that I treat everybody fair." She continued reading with an anguished look on her face.

"One deacon, Connie Maxwell, even had the audacity to stand over me as I sat in my chair, and put his finger in my face and threatened to "whip my little ass," because he says that I have his grandchildren coloring Jesus white in Sunday school books. If it wasn't for Deacon Mallard and Deacon Cox, I probably would have had to embarrass myself to protect myself. But instead, I just sat there, held my peace, and bit my tongue as any good pastor would as the other deacons found great amusement in what appeared to them as my fear of the always feared Connie Maxwell. Auntie, I guess it wouldn't be so hard if I could talk to somebody about these problems. For the past two nights I've had nightmares. For the first time in years I'm waking up in cold sweats again." Eunice read as her eyes welled up with tears.

"I wish I had somebody to talk to, somebody who understood. I know Jada is always there, but I really don't want to burden anybody, especially Jada, who I don't even want to know how these people really are. She's so happy working in the ministry and it makes me angry me to know that the same deacons, who give me so much hell behind closed doors, walk out into the public, among my wife and the congregation, smiling as if they really supported what's happening and as if it were they're own ideas to that has caused such great positive change in the church. I know you're tired of reading about all of my issues and I'm tired of writing about them. Thanks for the cappuccino maker. That really made my day." She read as she smiled at the thought that she'd done something to brighten Chauncey's day. "I don't mean to burden you or make you feel like I'm not going to be O.K. but I just needed to vent my frustrations and you drew the lucky number this time. I miss you so much and I can't wait for you to come down for the summer. Always your Baby boy, Chauncey."

As Eunice folded the letter and placed it back into its envelope, she sighed as though it was a relief to finish reading the letter of her heavy laden nephew, but she quickly explained that she wasn't tired of reading but, she's just glad that for the most part things are looking so much brighter for Chauncey and Jada.

"Those days are long gone for my baby. Those deacons, all except the one I told you about that died, are all still there. But they are like bulldogs with no teeth right now. Those people have rallied around Chauncey and Jada, and I think he has no intention of leaving anytime soon. He has a nice home, Jada is making her mark on the education system down there and will soon be an administrator, with the help of Mr. James. And that's really the only place that Lizzy has ever called home. She's growing like a weed too by the way. She's a smart little girl, and very talkative like her momma. And at age five, that girl has even memorized a few scriptures and can name all the books of the bible. And boy does she love her daddy. She just can't seem to get enough of Chauncey.

"When they first moved down there, Chauncey told me that there was a river not too far away from the church that he would take Jada and Lizzy to so they could relax a little and spend family time. But, now–a-days, Chauncey spends a lot of his time on the road preaching across Florida and other parts of the country. Jada knew when she married him that preaching was his passion and besides, she's been busy launching her own successful career and Lizzy is well alright spending time with Daphne.

"They don't get a chance to do a lot of family stuff like they used to, but Jada has been a good support to Chauncey, and just a couple of months ago, while I was down there visiting, Chauncey surprised both of us when he drove home in a brand new 1997 E320 four door, Polar White, Mercedes-Benz that he'd bought for her. I could have just died when I saw that boy driving up in that thing and Jada, as usual, just lost her crazy mind. Jada looks good driving in it too. She looks like a little business lady strolling around in that small town in that big ole car. Now Chauncey on the other hand, still drives that old beat up, Blue Ford Explorer, and Jada has tried to get Mr. Frugal to get him something a little nicer and more reliable, but he always reminds her that the best riding vehicles around are the one that's already paid for."

Wrapping up her recollections of the past three years, Eunice did admit, that it had been some trying times for Chauncey. He'd had some good days, but he'd also had some hills to climb. He'd had some weary days and some sleepless nights.

"But you know when I look back..." she said as she looked at Chauncey, Jada, and Lizzy, whose family portrait sat on Eunice's dresser, "...and think things over..." she continued with a smile. "...all of his good days to this point has outweighed his bad days and Chauncey ain't got no reason to complain. If he continues the way he's going and keeps the Lord first, he's going to do what he always set out to do and that is to be greater than his daddy ever was. You go head Auntie's baby."

Chapter 16

In the fall of 1997, Chauncey and Jada were living in utter bliss, as they thought they might be, after listening to and heeding the voice and direction of God. They had moved far away from the relative comfort they'd experienced back in Odessa, where Jada's father and step-mother served as their safety nets, to explore what life would be like without the certainties it had previously afforded. Thoughts of moving away to a foreign place, with no certainties available to assure them, almost paralyzed the couple and could have caused them to miss out on what Chauncey would later consider as his "personal slice of Paradise". But they trusted God and eventually reaped the benefits of only those who believe whole heatedly in the promises of God. They were extraordinarily blessed. Living lavishly in a home built just off the plush and well manicured greens of the Golf course at Penelope Pines, Chauncey and Jada enjoyed the type of pleasantries only entitled to the elite in their community. And to accentuate what God was doing in north Florida, Chauncey and Jada were living large in a place bent on being small. Who would've ever imagined that any pastor of little ole Greater Mt. Carmel could live in a 3,500 square foot five-bedroom, three and a half bathroom, two-floor, mini-mansion and have his wife rolling in a polar white, four door, Benz. That reality was sometimes hard to deal with though, by some in the surrounding area of Greater Mt. Carmel, and often, Chauncey was accused by the small minded folk, who were inoperative towards God's Will for their lives, of peddling in drugs or other elicit and illegal activity. The truth of the matter was that Chauncey believed God to do the impossible and taught on a consistent basis, the power of choosing to believe that God was able to do exceedingly above and more abundantly anything we can ask or think. Having Realtors and Mortgage Brokers as close associates didn't hurt either.

Chauncey and Jada practiced what he preached, and for the most part many of the members, new and old, of Greater Mt. Carmel, grabbed hold to the prosperity that the third year pastor regularly taught about. Other than not being able to convince many of his young supporters to show up for Sunday school, it was evident that the ministry had grown remarkably. Empowered by his teachings, many of the members of the congregation experienced great growth in their personal lives and finances, due to faithfulness to God's Word and consistent tithing. Christopher L. Blocker, who was once considered a thug by the residents of the small town, but was ministered to by Jada on the first Sunday Chauncey ever preached at Mt. Carmel, turned his life around and became an entrepreneur, successfully maintaining an in demand lawn care service.

Chris is a proud symbol of the new Greater Mt. Carmel, which exemplifies to the world what can happen when you put a little faith with a whole lot of faithfulness. The former Miss Keisha Phillips, the twenty-five year old ex daughter in law of Deacon Phillips who was a high school drop out and had two children out of wedlock with the Deacon's son before the age nineteen, was so inspired by her chance meeting with the First Lady during their welcome committee shopping escapade and so enlightened by the dynamic hopeful messages of her new pastor, that she finally divorced herself from the mediocrity that her ex husband portrayed and married a man who "loved the Lord"; Mr. Kenneth Dupre. She got her G.E.D, and successfully launched, with her new husband, a hair salon from their own house, after they both received certification and licenses in barbering and cosmetology through the local vocational school. Now they've set up shop downtown on Main Street, where even the pastor and First Lady regularly get their hair done.

Because of such heart warming testimonies, Chauncey has never been daunted by the nay sayers or the negative rhetoric spewed by the community or the few rebellious church members at Greater Mt. Carmel. But he kept on ministering and by year three of his ministry, he had enough proof that his messages of hope and prosperity was resonating deep in the hearts and minds of all that took a chance to make a choice to take God at his word.

Though calculated and sometimes marginally successful attempts had been made by bitter church members and citizens who didn't even go to church on a regular basis, to assassinate his character, Pastor Pennington had become rather popular throughout his small community, working diligently in his church and alongside community leaders, whose goals were to change the image of the predominantly low socio-economic area. Chauncey was a great motivator and was often chosen to chair various committees, including the County Wide Ministerial Alliance.

His prominence quickly matriculated throughout the state of Florida and his valiant efforts to empower his community were often and appropriately lauded by local and state officials.

For the previously stated reasons, Chauncey's travel calendar was filled with appointments. At least twice a month he was away from home, speaking at conferences or conducting revival meetings. He was a man in demand and didn't mind one bit or neglect an opportunity to share with the world the secrets of his rapid ministry growth and development. But it was evident, that though he had a very successful, young career, the pastor's rigorous lifestyle had taken toll on what was once a perfect marriage and household.

There were no outward signs of fractures in their relationship yet, but it just wasn't the way it used to be. Chauncey and Jada used to struggle together to make ends meet and prayed together about the path their lives would one day singularly take. Chauncey was deep into his long awaited, but sometimes stressful calling and Jada too, was entrenched in her own aspirations of becoming one of the county's youngest education administrators. That aspiration was assured if her boss Mr. James had anything to do with it. Like Chauncey, Jada was excellent at what she did and garnered high praise of all that knew of and appreciated her hard work and dedication. In just two years she single handedly spearheaded Great Pines Elementary school's resurrection from an embarrassing, failing status by working long after her work day was done and even spending some weekends at the church tutoring students who remained below grade level on standardized tests.

Chauncey knew Jada's passion for education and supported his wife's lofty ambitions whole heartedly, much in the same way she had always supported him when he aspired to do great things, even when it meant making tremendous sacrifices. And by this time they both knew that the grind of work had taken its toll on their relationship, but also felt that one day the grind would cease. And with minor adjustments made here and there, they were confident, that what was now deemed as a not so perfect marriage, would still remain a very solid, marriage.

On a clear Friday evening in October, Chauncey shared a rare intimate and romantic cuddling session with his wife in their cozy, and roomy second floor bedroom. The bedroom that overlooked the small pond and fountain flanking the eighth hole on their prestigious golf course property. Chauncey told Jada of his plans to take her down to the river for more romance. It had been a while since they had been able go down there, but Jada was excited to be going to a place that had so much meaning to her. It was during expectant conversation about their drive to the river, when the phone rang and what was initially meant to be a day of "us time", turned out to be any thing but. As Lizzy played down stairs, under the responsible, careful, and watchful eye of Daphne, Chauncey answered the phone against the will of his now sexually charged wife.

"Hello."

"Reverend Pennington," answered a very business minded, but pleasant speaking Adolph James.

"How are you Mr. James?" Chauncey responded.

"I hope I didn't catch you all at a bad time"

"No Sir, Jada and I was just here taking it easy."

"Well I hate to even ask but may I speak to Jada for a moment. I'm a little confused about some reports that she left on my desk. It'll only take a few minutes."

"O.K., hold on just a second,"

"Thank You Reverend."

"Jada, its Mr. James." Chauncey said as he slid the phone across the bed toward Jada and got in return, one of her angry stares of disapproval.

"I told you not to answer that phone," she whispered bitterly with her face overtaken by the strains of knowing her day of quality time with her husband had all but ended.

As Jada poised herself to converse with her boss, who evidently had a hard time distinguishing when the work day ended, Chauncey's cell phone begin to ring. As he, in a panic, went to retrieve his phone from pants that were nestled in his dirty clothes hamper, he stubbed his toe on the post of the bed. In agony, he answered the phone in the couple's fragrantly scented, African themed, bathroom to give Jada a moment of privacy.

"Pastor speaking," he said as he gritted his teeth, not knowing who the caller was because he was in too big of a hurry to check his caller I.D.

"Reverend this is Deacon Picket and I thank, we need to have a little talk"

"Deacon Pickett today is a really bad time. I just got back in from Daytona and I haven't even had time to wind down with my family yet." Chauncey said as Jada continued her seemingly endless conversation with Mr. James, aiding the supposedly befuddled principal.

"Well, this can't wait and as chairman of the board, I've called a emergency meeting." Pickett said with the voice of a man that was frustrated and angered.

"An emergency meeting for what, Pickett?"

"We just need to talk. It's time for us to come together and talk. And me and all the deacons and a few of the other members is already at the church and it is in yo best interest if you just come on over here."

As Chauncey's stomach began to tie up in knots and his rage began to mount at the very thought of what these people could possibly be trying to do now, he quickly put on his pants and a polo shirt, grabbed the keys to the Mercedes and rushed down stairs to find Jada. She was putting on her own clothes for an unexpected office visit with her boss.

"Jada that was Pickett. I need to run over to the church for a minute."

"But Chauncey!" Jada said in anguish, as he reached for the door leading to the couple's two-car garage. "Mr. James needs me to come to the school. I know what he needs. I'll only be about twenty minutes or so. Can't you just wait until I get back?"

"Jada, this is important and I really need to go right now," he said with bitterness nestled just beneath his breath.

"Well what am I supposed to do about Lizzy and Daphne?" she said as she walked toward an entryway closet wearing only a skirt and bra, hurrying to find her candy apple red blouse and put on her matching red stilettos.

"First of all, this is my job," Chauncey said as he raised his voice slightly, showing the signs of a man who was anxious and worn down by the rigors of pastoring.

Pointing his finger uncomfortably close to her chest, he continued his uncharacteristic display of emotion, "What ever James wants can wait today! As of five minutes ago I'm back on the clock and what I do is important for a whole lot of folk."

"Chauncey Pennington this is my job too. And what I do is important for a whole lot of folk," she said calmly, as she grabbed his wrist to remove the finger that was too close for comfort, wondering what had snapped into her husband.

Taken aback by what he considered to be Jada's lackluster response, Chauncey paused briefly just before unleashing his fury over his wife's inability to understand the urgency or importance of his plight. Chauncey was now about to escalate his already heightened state of emergency.

"Jada your work hours are from 7:45AM to 3:45PM, Monday through Friday" he said slowly, but sternly, as he lowered his voice momentarily to ensure that his point was well taken. "Mr. James has a secretary and if he wants overtime, he'd better damn well pay you for it. My job hours on the other hand, are from sun up to sun down seven days a damn week," Chauncey said as Jada looked at her husband in shock. He was obviously out of character and way out of line with his enraged comments.

Chauncey was under stress. And his actions, though, not yet understood by Jada, were the result of the pressures associated with his pastorate.

Snatching his wrist from Jada's grasp, who had grabbed him again to minimize his anger, and repositioning his finger purposely in her face this time; Chauncey continued his uncharacteristic outburst and shouted to the disbelief of Lizzy and Daphne, who by this time wondered together what was going on. "I'm about sick and tired of all these after hours appointments with Adolph James and if you must know, this is the last day that he calls this house and disrespects my right to spend time with my wife. I'm not having it anymore. You're not going anywhere and if you can't give that fruity Uncle Tom what he needs over the phone then so be it. Screw him! And screw that damn Elementary School." he shouted as his tantrum continued. "Now, I have to go to a legitimate obligation with a bunch of hellions that I can't stand, but get paid to deal with, and only hope that when I get back home, I can come to a house where I can get some comfort after I try to spare my job for the millionth time!"

As Chauncey stormed, condescendingly, out of the door in his gray slacks and matching black and gray, Tommy Hilfiger, polo shirt, it seemed as though his black Eastland sandals left smoke in his wake. Jada, on the other hand stood still in magnified disbelief at what had just happened.

For the first time in the six and a half years of knowing this man, she had seen a side of Chauncey Pennington that she never knew existed. He had actually cursed at her. Jada couldn't have possibly known, but the older Chauncey was getting and the more terrible circumstances weighed on him, the more he began to take on the attributes of his deceased father.

But as she finished getting herself together and gave Daphne final instructions just before leaving for her meeting with Mr. James, Jada thought to herself that maybe Chauncey had a point and vowed, that she would be more attentive to the needs of her obviously overworked and under appreciated husband and talk to him extensively when he returned about the frustrations of being a pastor or any other issues that had caused him to exhibit such perplexity. In a moment of reconsideration, Jada thought twice about her spur-of-the-moment meeting with her needy boss and decided to call him in stead to tell him that she couldn't come back to work.

"Great Pines Elementary."

"Hi Rosa, this is Jada. May I speak to Mr. James please?"

"Yes ma'am, Mrs. Pennington, hold for a moment" said the bubbly, attractive, young secretary.

As Jada waited for Mr. James to answer his page, she thought to herself how silly she must've been not to have noticed Chauncey's change for the worse over the past three months. She wondered how she could possibly halt what she perceived as the beginning stages of an imminent bout with depression.

"Dr. Adolph James speaking," answered the principal, who chuckled as though he'd just heard a good joke.

"Hi Mr. James, this is Jada."

"Yes, Jada" the principal answered as he cleared his throat. "I thought you would've been here by now."

"That's what I'm calling about. I'm afraid that I'm not going to be able to come back in this evening. I'm really sorry about this, but my husband was just called into the office to handle an emergency at the church and had to rush out unexpectedly..."

"Oh that's fine Jada" James interrupted. "As long as everything is O.K with you, everything is fine with me."

"Thank you.,." a relieved Jada answered back. "It's just that, while he's out taking care of business, I really need to be here with our daughter at least until he returns."

"Well it's nothing that we can't take care of on Monday. I just figured that since I was here, virtually alone, you and I could've tackled this little project privately; you know without all those interruptions."

"Now if you'd like, we can do this over the phone. I have copies here and I can walk you through the documents. This particular grant is not that difficult," Jada said as she wondered if James was trying to turn this business matter into an opportunity to be flirtatious.

"Don't bother yourself over this Jada. I am a little disappointed that I didn't get a chance to see you" he slyly said, "but I... I mean that business can definitely wait. There will be more opportunities for us to get together and finish up."

"O.K. that's fine. I'll see you on Monday," she said hurrying to hang up the phone to avoid what was quickly turning into an overt attempt by her boss to smooth talk her.

"Alright," the principal said in the sexiest voice that he could muster. "And oh, I've been wanting to tell you this for some time now, but never really got the opportunity. I know how difficult it must be, being married to a great man like Reverend Pennington, he wears so many hats and I figure that you must get lonely sometimes. And, if you ever just want to talk, or if you ever feel the need…you know… to just relax, I'm only a phone call away. Ok."

"I appreciate that. Thanks." Jada answered back with confusion etched on her face.

"Don't thank me Jada. You've helped this school district, this school and for that matter, me so much that I think it's about time you get what you deserve. I'll see you on Monday. And here's my personal cell phone number if you ever need me after hours."

CHAPTER 17

Over at the church, Pickett and a few disgruntled members, mainly deacons and their spouses, and a handful of the remnant from the old regime of Mt. Carmel, prepared for what they thought would be a wake up call for the young pastor. They had a specific reason for calling this special meeting and that was to serve notice on their "overconfident preacher" that they were still in charge of the establishment of Greater Mt. Carmel. Much in the same way they prepared for the impeachment of Reverend Woodrow Elliot, these people were resolved to offer Chauncey the same ultimatum "get in line or get the hell out." But they knew that their attempt to tame this pastor wouldn't be as easy as it was in years past. Because, unlike Woodrow, Chauncey had the support of the majority of the congregation and unless they could coax him into resigning or hoodwink him into believing that he needed to change his "wicked ways" they would have a difficult time, at best, putting the bits in this horse's mouth. They knew the bylaws of the church and their plan was simple; charge him, convict him, threaten to take him before the congregation for a vote of dismissal. And if he didn't crumble under their threats or fear their influence enough to allow the deacons to reestablish control, get him out.

As Chauncey sped into the church's parking lot, in a Mercedes that had never experienced such high speeds or bad treatment, the members readied themselves for their opportunity to talk Chauncey back into his "right mind."

"What it is Pickett?" Chauncey asked the stubborn old deacon, as he entered the dining annex as about twenty or so members watched resentfully in anticipation.

"I'll tell you what we here for. You just sit down Reverend. Yo coming here this evening shows me a lot bout yo character. We all here know you a good man," Pickett said as he stood as representative for the disgruntled members.

"I'll just stand," Chauncey said as he looked straight into the eyes of the members, folded his arms and took a deep breath, waiting on his nightmare to unfold. He was ready for anything and besides that, he was in a fighting mood anyway and like a prize fighting, counter puncher he couldn't wait for Pickett and his crew to land their first blow. For when they did he was ready and prepared to unveil a Chauncey Pennington that only Chauncey Pennington and now Jada knew was hidden deep inside.

"Reverend you been here for three years now and to be truthful bout it, you really ain't panned out to be what we expected. Now we called you here this evening so that we could try to talk some sense in you or if that don't work we prepared to give you yo official letter of dismissal," the deacon said as Chauncey's heart dropped momentarily before he regained his stance of defiance and silently, but visibly and angrily contemplated his rebuttal.

"I'm representing twenty-three faithful members of Mt. Carmel and according to our by-laws, that's more than we need to sign a petition to get rid of you or any other pastor."

As Deacon Mallard scratched his brow and held his head down, he thought deeply about what he could possibly add to the condemnation of the already condemned pastor. Deacons Phillips, Maxwell, and Ellis, on the other hand, whose faces were etched with the expressions of angry bulldogs, looked on in silence, but in staunch support of their strong leader. The other wayward members of the congregation watched on in silence as well, waiting for the preacher to finally show signs that he was weakening under the mounting onslaught by their calculating and increasingly agitated chairman.

As Chauncey stood still in silence, much like Jesus did when he was confronted by the false accusations of the Jewish Sanhedrin, Pickett waited for a response from the bitter preacher. Seeing that Chauncey was unflappable to this point and seemed committed to his right to remain silent, Pickett continued to lay out his plans of impeachment.

"Now according to our by-laws, we don't just need twenty people to sign a petition, but we need a cause and we have plenty. But we just gone address three here today. First of all, is yo lack of respect for yo deacon board. When I first met you I told you bout that and I told you it could get you in trouble round here. Remember?"

"He ain't got no respect for his bode," murmured Deacon Phillips who finally broke his silence to bolster and validate Pickett's claims that the preacher was insubordinate.

"You don't listen." Pickett continued. We can't tell you nothing. Round here we have rules to bide by and the first rule of thumb is that you respect you deacons. You ain't never done that since you been here and I shoulda known better than to brang you here after you showed yo behind in Sunday school the first Sunday you stepped foot in here, makin a fool outta Eddie when he was trying to teach the people."

"Now you shole right bout dat," verbalized Deacon Mallard, who was obviously just glad to be invited to this kind of meeting for a change. "Preacher you was wrong when you done dat" he continued and looked around the room for affirmation of his agreement with the chairman.

"Because you have chose to do it yo way, many of our good, bill paying members have left this church because of you."

"That's a bunch a bull Pickett and you know it," Chauncey said as he broke his silence and momentarily lost control of his emotions. "This church has seen more financial growth and membership growth in six months than it saw in the previous five years and your records show that. We're not hurting to pay our bills either," he continued hoping to set the record straight.

"Yea, you can act all high and mighty if you want to…" Pickett said as he grinned and picked up his handwritten copy of the by-laws that were written in the sixties. "But the fact still remains that you in trouble boy, big trouble."

As Deacon Harold Belford, who had just gotten off from work and had no time to change from his Security uniform, rushed into the meeting late, he sat next to Clausell Ellis's wife Maggie, who whispered and asked "Where's Tiffany at, Hal?"

"She had to work late," he whispered back, lying about his wife's whereabouts, after unsuccessfully attempting to convince his wife to go along with Pickett's scheme.

"Now that brangs me to the second thang," Pickett continued. "You ain't had no business making Ruth Anne no finance director or what ever the title you made up for her. After Norway died that job shoulda went to Connie. He was spose to be the treasurer. That's what our by-laws say and that's the way we been doing it. After Deacon Thomas died, I was made treasurer over thirty years ago, I had it till I became chairman when Deacon Abernathy died. That was a conflict of interest so I made Norway the treasure and he held it for more than twenty years. Now Connie done waited patiently on his turn and you don't have the authority to make Ruth Anne no finance lady. So Connie," Pickett said as he address the suddenly proud and perky, pleased deacon.

"Yes Su' brother Chairman," Maxwell answered.

"Today since we setting this house in order, I'm takin Ruthy down and you take over as treasurer as of this the seventeenth day of October in the year of ourva Lord, nineteen hundud and nindy- seven. Now preacher I can do that cause I'm following the rules in this here book. These what you call by-laws," Pickett said and his off the wall comments prompted an outburst of laughter from a room of people who thought for sure their enemy was about to give in.

"Where does it say that in the by-laws?" Chauncey interrupted. "Better yet Pickett, you told me that this church has never even had by-laws. You told me that you and the deacons were the by-laws. Which is it Pickett? Tell us," questioned Chauncey as Pickett humbly shook his head and looked out among the onlookers and mouthed repeatedly "He lyin'."

"Oh we got some by-laws and here they go right here, you old dope pusher!" yelled Connie Maxwell as he frowned and prepared his old cigarette smelling hands to do bodily harm to the young pastor.

"Calm down Connie" urged Mrs. Viney Abernathy, wife of the deceased and former deacon board chairman, Nehemiah Abernathy, who served as chairman before Pickett took over. "It's right there on page 2," Viney said as the demanding, seventy-five year old, acting official record keeper gave her Xeroxed copy of the hand written guidelines to

Harold Belford, ordering him to take them over to the preacher, who was now shaking his head disbelief.

As Chauncey began to flip through the pages of a document he'd never seen, in absolute resentment and on the verge of a colossal explosion, the barrage of mud slinging continued.

"And you ain't doing right by yo wife either!" added a furious, Maggie Ellis, who was often referred to by the town gossips as the woman who gets knocked the hell out by her own husband. According to them this occurs at least twice a week. And she can't seem to keep him from between the legs of the young girls in the housing projects on the days that he receives his retirement check.

As members at the preposterous meeting whipped their heads around in shock that Maggie Ellis, of all people, would have the nerve to talk about another man's indiscretions, Pickett interrupted her as he pulled his black reading glasses from his eyes and said calmly, "Now Maggie, you done yo part by coming and I thank you for that, but I think you oughtta let me take it from here."

"But he ain't right!" she interrupted trying to finish her statement that would firmly establish her accusation.

"Lady, you of all people, got to have some nerve talking about how I treat my wife. You don't know me or my wife or for that matter how I treat her. You need to spend more time focusing on your own house," Chauncey said as he tried vehemently to keep his mouth from saying was his heart was convinced that he should.

"I know you ain't talking to my wife like that, you crazy ass preacher!" Clausell Ellis said in defense of his wife in anger as he stood to challenge Chauncey's antagonistic comments. "I'll whip you ass!" the five-foot nine inch, skinny and sickly looking character continued. "You done went too far!"

As Deacon Ellis walked up to Chauncey and put his left, index finger into the preacher's face, he waited hopelessly in vain for reinforcement from his fellow deacons, who were reluctant to help because they couldn't support their comrade in this argument. Connie Maxwell, who was known as the deacon board enforcer didn't move a muscle; at least not to help Clausell. The heavy handed deacon was just too overjoyed and too eager to witness the spiraling spectacle to interrupt what he thought would be the best fight he'd seen at Mt. Carmel since Woodrow got beat up by Deacon Mallard at a similar meeting a few years ago. When Chauncey noticed their evident break down in loyalties and reluctance to save the slowly drowning deacon, he snarled and said in a calm, still, but dastardly voice...

"Clausell Ellis if you don't move your finger out of my face, I swear, I will beat the hell out of you or die trying. Now get out of my face, you worthless excuse for a deacon."

With the gaze of a war eagle and the mind frame of the king of the jungle, Chauncey Pennington had marked his territory and dared the deacon to "be stupid!"

"You better not ever put your finger anywhere near me or I'll whip your ass." the preacher continued as all who heard him looked on in shock and disbelief at his verbiage.

"Maggie, I tried to warn you. But you didn't hear me!" scornfully said Pickett, who took off his John Deer hunting cap and begin to scratch his bushy, gray haired head as he thought to himself about the perfect way to issue the people's ultimatum to the pastor.

"Reverend, this meeting done got way out of hand and that ain't the way we do bidness round here and as Revelations 42:3 says, "All this fussin and fightin can't get nothing solved and it goes on to say that weeping may endure for a night, but hear me now church, if we don't fight gainst one another, joy will come in the monin."

"Amen!" agreed Deacon Phillips, who obviously didn't know that there were only twenty two chapters in the book of revelation. But, Chauncey stood by sweating profusely as he anxiously waited, in silence, for the worst meeting of his life to draw to a conclusion.

"Now Son, we got the goods on you," Pickett said as he talked in a soft tone so that the preacher would understand that the deacons had his best interest in mind. "And even though I thank Maggie was wrong for how she said it, we know you ain't doing yo wife right, cause two or three of dem girls you got runnin round in this church is pregnant and the Negro Times Union say you the man who bigged 'em. Now you can say what you want to and you can buck if you want to, but it's enough of us in here today to make you pick yo poison." Pickett continued with a gentle smile, supremely confident that he had worn down the visibly shaken and now emotional young preacher.

As Chauncey stood deflated and worn out by Pickett's constant barrage of false allegations, his eyes finally welled up with tears brought on by the utterance of senseless lies that viciously attacked the core of his character.

"I see you crying son," Pickett said as he walked over to the young preacher and placed his right hand on his shoulder. "That must mean you starting to understand me and you want to save yo self," he continued as the deacons and members all looked on solemnly at the developing situation that they felt wouldn't have unfolded without their leadership and courage.

"Reverend you can save yo self. Let yo deacons take charge and run this church like it spose to and you won't have no mo' problems. But if you don't straighten up and fly right, we'll just take this petition to the church conference and have you voted out before you can say, "I'm headed back to Texas. It's yo call Reverend, and I can sense through yo emotion that you ready for this board to lead you. Is I'm right Son?"

As Pickett looked back to witness what the people thought of his heroism, he thought to himself that he had kept his word to the people of Mt. Carmel yet again and had successfully humbled yet another one of God's men. As he gently massaged Chauncey's left shoulder blade with his wrinkled but still very strong right hand, Pickett appeared to be comforting the young preacher, who by his assertion, was just going through the growing pains of learning how to pastor a church.

But what appeared to be a rare show of kindness by the deacon was anything but. Pickett knew his arrow had pierced Chauncey's frame and the fact that he was able to put his hands on the preacher sent a message to all that witnessed that Deacon Walter Pickett was still in charge and had beaten the preacher down so bad that he could afford to show the wounded warrior a little mercy.

But in a swift moment, before the proud onlookers could even blink an eyelash, Chauncey reached behind his head, grabbed Pickett's right wrist and squeezed it as hard as he possibly could and slowly led the shocked, elder statesman back around for a face to face confrontation.

As some of the members stood in an attempt to aid the deacon, who was in obvious pain, and Connie Maxwell pulled his hunting knife from his back pocket. Chauncey, wiped his eyes, stood fearlessly in the midst of rumor armed assailants and quoted accurately verses

8-9 of chapter 4 from the book of II Corinthians and added a personal overtone to what was already a powerful and appropriate moment to recite the text.

"I'm troubled on every side," Chauncey said as he turned away from the people and walked toward the exit of the dinning annex. "But I'm not distressed," he continued, looking back to emphasize his steadfastness.

"I'm perplexed, but I'm not in despair," he said as he raised his voice to ensure the hellions heard him as he came closer to exiting the annex.

"I've been persecuted, but I don't, at all, feel forsaken. Cast down, Deacon Pickett," he said as he stopped at the wooden door and turned to look at his would be commanders in the eyes one more time before walking away from the yet to be adjourned meeting.

"But I'm not destroyed," Chauncey said as he stood with his feet firmly on the ground, feeling confident that the people who really supported his ministry wouldn't allow this injustice to continue. "You want a fight; I'm going to bring you a fight. You don't have to call a special meeting to dismiss me either. I'll call for the special meeting myself. I want to take all this foolishness before the church and let the tithing members decide who the real crooks are!"

"Now you messin up son. You ain't got to do all that," Pickett tried to reason, as he thought to himself that his little band of disgruntled saints was overwhelmingly outnumbers by the members who supported Chauncey.

"Let the little nigga do what he gone do Pickett!" shouted an angry Eddie Phillips. "He gone hang his own self, wit his own rope. Go head preacher and do what you gone do!"

"I will nigga!" Chauncey bitterly rebutted in response to Phillips name calling." You all wanted this, so let's just do this. You and me Pickett; my leadership or yours. Let the voices of the people of Mt. Carmel be heard. Come on let's give them a chance to run their mouths like you fools have run yours for the last three years. And Phillips, I just thought about it as you were running your mouth, you and the rest of these people are few in number and the vast majority of the people want me here and support what we're trying to do in this city, while the same majority can't stand you deacons or the people who just stand by and watch you do what you do in your personal lives or the crimes you commit against God at this church every week," he said as he pointed at the deacons, who were standing afar, spewing out words that should never be uttered within shouting distance of any church.

As Chauncey and the other members present traded barbs, Pickett stood in disbelief that his plan had failed miserably. He knew Chauncey was onto something and argued not with his flailing counterparts. Instead he contemplated his next move, which he knew could ultimately make or break his chairmanship.

"Let me serve notice on all of you on this the seventeenth day of October in the year of our Lord nineteen hundred and ninety-seven," Chauncey said, mocking Pickett's flare for the dramatic and overly bureaucratic statements, "that the Chauncey E. Pennington that walked into this church in June of 1994 died tonight just about five and a half minutes ago and you'd better damn well pray that this new one doesn't get a chance to stay around here much longer. If he does you'll all have hell to pay. You better do your best to get him out before he rips into your asses. This meeting is adjourned!" Chauncey shouted as he flusteredly walked out on the unruly, but traumatized clan who shouted obscenities as he slammed the wooden door behind him.

As Chauncey walked slowly to his car which was parked just outside of the dinning annex, he overheard through the commotion Pickett's voice as he screamed to the top of his lungs "I'm still in charge round here and you ain't got no authority to close out no meeting!"

As quickly as he had walked out the door, an eager to give his last statement Chauncey, stormed through the doors again, amid mass confusion and said with a vindictive, malicious voice, "Negro, I just did!" and slammed the door.

Chapter 18

While driving home in a sadistic trance that was brought on by the merciless beating he'd taken from his board of deacons and disgruntled members, Chauncey reached down for his cell phone to call Billy Dunn to make his closest ally in the ministry aware of what had just transpired. As he drove with his left hand, he began dialing Billy's cell phone number with his right hand, when, in midstream, his phone begin to violently vibrate, alerting the furious preacher that he had several messages.

After averting his plans to call Billy for the moment, he dialed in to his voice messaging system to check his unheard messages. Four of the messages were the usual calls for special appearances, speaking opportunities, and Lizzy's predictable calls to say hello and see how he was doing. But two of the messages garnered intensified scrutiny. One of those two messages was from Deacon Harold Belford's wife Tiffany, who called to ask for a "very important meeting" with the pastor as soon as he had an opportunity. The time of the message was interesting too, because, the call came in at approximately 7:30PM, during the same time of his unforgettable meeting with the church's dissatisfied members.

Chauncey accurately recalled that she wasn't present at the meeting, but inaccurately figured that she only wanted to vent her unfounded frustrations as well and mumbled fumingly "These people have lost their damn minds. I'll let her meet with her bode" he sarcastically continued as he begin to review his last message.

"Chauncey! This is your Auntie!" blasted an equally furious Aunt Eunice. "I don't know what's going on down there, but you better call me as soon as you get this." she continued as Chauncey slowed the Mercedes down for a rest at one of the city's three stop lights. As Chauncey leaned his head in agony against the luxurious, gray, head rest of his vehicle, waiting for the light to turn green, he accessed the speaker phone and continued to listen uncomfortably at Aunt Eunice's rants as his phone rested unmanned on his thigh. "I didn't raise you to yell at nobody, especially the people you suppose to care about. If you've lost your mind, I want to help you find it. Quick! Call me ASAP!"

As the light changed from "stop" crimson to "go" green, Chauncey drove off slowly wondering what could go wrong next and what authority did Jada have to call his Aunt to reveal his shortcomings. Disappointed and slightly disheveled, the pastor reached for his cell phone once again and dialed up Billy, who undoubtedly was enjoying an evening with Ruth Anne.

"Hello."

"Hey Billy." Chauncey answered in a falsified cheery tone to mask his evident depression.

"Pastor, what's going on." Billy responded with his usual excitement.

"Nothing much. Are you busy?"

"Ruth Anne and I was just playing a little pool tonight in the basement since Daphne was with you guys. What's wrong? You don't sound like your self. Where are you anyway?"

"Man, Billy, I just left the church and it was absolutely chaotic."

"What happened pastor?"

"I know it may be a bad time but man I need you."

"All you got to do is tell what you need and I'm there," Billy said in a voice of great concern but staunch support.

"If you and Ruthy could come by the house tonight, I'll tell you all about it and just so you can know, Pickett and his crew are trying to get rid of me."

"What!" Billy replied in utter shock and disbelief. "You have got to be kidding me."

"No man, I'm not. You all have been through this before and I just need… I just need to know how I should go about handling this."

"We're on our way right now."

As Ruth Anne questioned Billy, with great concern, about the nature of his conversation with their pastor, he rushed her upstairs to get dressed and explained that "Pastor really sounded sick." and that "those deacons were at it again."

Chauncey, on the other hand, drove his car faster, exceeding the fifty-five mile per hour speed limit by more than twenty miles per hour and in less than three minutes he was already back in his garage, angrier and more bitter than he was when he left the house. The bulk of his anger stemmed from his unfortunate meeting at the church, but his anger was only fueled by what he perceived as Jada's childish attempts to keep him in line.

Aunt Eunice's unexpected phone call and subsequent message took him over his boiling point with his normally understanding and comforting wife, which preceded an inevitable showdown back at the Pennington's home.

As he exited the car and violently slammed the car door, he walked slowly toward the house, contemplating what, if anything he would say to his tattling wife. Jada who was already upstairs, in the couple's rather large and lavish bathroom, preparing their bronze finished Jacuzzi for a cozy, warm, candle lit bath in hopes of cheering up her obviously mentally worn husband. Jada was forewarned of Chauncey's return, because in anticipation she watched through the tinted windowpanes of her bedroom as the lights of the Mercedes careened through the scenic paths of the Golf Course village.

As Chauncey, walked through the entryway of the house and tossed his keys on the white, marbled, kitchen counter, he noticed Lizzy and Daphne sound asleep in the theatre and begin in a torrid pace up the stairs to confront Jada.

As he hastily opened the bedroom door, the aroma of burning, orange blossom scented candles permeated from the bathroom and in a moment of expectation, Jada hurried to greet her husband to give him what she thought was a long overdo night of pampering.

Dressed, lightly, in only a pink and white laced, glove fitting, teddy, Jada's curvy, soft, and well oiled body glistened against the candle light, as the meaningful tunes of Keith Sweat ministered softly in the background. As she reached out to grab him, Chauncey stood as still as a board, and as silent as a snake, trying hard not to explode or expose the insensitive and cruel feelings he harbored in this most inopportune moment and prayed that Billy and Ruth Anne "rang that doorbell in a hurry". In an attempt to provoke affection from the man who she once referred to as the most affectionate person she knew, Jada walked slowly and silently over to him and grabbed his large, well kept, but tensed hands and placed them around her waist, then sang softly and delicately the lyrics of Sweat's Oldie but Goldie. "I will never do anything to hurt you", Waiting patiently on the next line of the song, she looked into his cold, despondent eyes then continued…"I'll give all my love to you…And if you need me baby, I'll come runnin'…. Only to you."

"That use to be the case," Chauncey said in his best impersonation of a coldhearted insensitive man.

"What are you talking about Chauncey?" Jada questioned, as the music continued to play softly as she whispered into his ear, trying hard to circumvent another potentially damaging argument.

Spurning her desperate attempt to drag him into an awaiting oasis in the bathroom, Chauncey violently flipped on the lights, unplugged the radio, and lashed out at Jada, who by this time was all but stunned at yet another uncharacteristic and unseemly occurrence.

"You are not the girl I married." he said as he stormed through the bedroom looking for the pastor's manual, given to him at his installation services by Bishop A.W. Tinyhill, the preacher who brutalized the English language throughout his pathetic sermon at the celebration. "I really don't know what's gotten into you."

"Chauncey, I'm trying!" Jada proclaimed as she stood in unreserved disappointment, looking worriedly at her totally beastly acting husband.

"Yea Jada, you're trying alright, trying, along with the rest of these Negros to ruin my damn life."

"First of all if anybody's changed it's you! I've never heard you curse like this before?"

"Whatever." Chauncey uninterestedly replied as he laid hands on the book he was looking for. "You know what you did."

"What has gotten in to you Chauncey? Have you lost you mind? What are you talking about?"

"You know what I'm talking about!" he shouted as he turned around quickly to confront his much smaller wife.

"Boy, you better start doing some explaining fast, because I swear, after today I'm just about sick and tired of you and this foolishness, blaming the whole world for your problems at that stupid church! I'm the one that's trying to make your life is a little easier and all you do lately is talk about what I don't do! You don't even give me the respect anymore that you give those hellions at that church! You've never cursed at or yelled at Pickett have you?"

"Shut up Jada! You've talked enough for one night," Chauncey said, calculating that his tender-hearted wife would probably soon break down and cry, which would mercifully end his fully brewed tirade.

"Chauncey Pennington its official, you've lost your mind," Jada said as she pointed her finger in his face and laughed sarcastically. "You are officially crazy boy. Mt. Carmel has fried your brain. Get out of my way."

"I guess you'll tell my Aunt that too Huh, Miss talk too damn much."

"What! What did you say?" Jada said in astonishment.

"You heard what I said." Chauncey rebutted as he raised his hands to protect himself from his now enraged wife. "Look woman, its one thing for you and me to have issues at this house, but as long as you and I are married you better not ever call my Aunt to tell her anything that I say or do in my own house. I am not a baby and she couldn't raise me again if she tried. Do you understand me?"

Confused by Chauncey's latest off the wall comments, Jada paused for a minute to think what this man could be possibly referring to or what this man could possibly be going through. In a moment of calm before the storm Jada questioned Chauncey with a confused look on her face and quit in her voice. "What are you talking about now Chauncey?"

"You know what I'm talking about Jada!" shouted Chauncey.

"No I don't!" shouted back Jada. "I haven't called anybody!"

"Well tell me how did Aunt Eunice know we had an argument? Why did she call my phone and chew me out about my business in my damn house? Who else, other than, my childish, unconcerned wife, would have the nerve...?"

"You stop right there!" Jada interrupted. "Don't say anything else. You are a fool and in about sixty seconds I'm going to let you have your business, your house and your Aunt to yourself. I swear, I will not tolerate this another day in my life. Excuse me!" Jada said as she stared at her angry, sweaty faced husband and proceeded to shove him out of her way as she made her way to her closet to get dressed and get out of her husband's presence.

Ding! Dong!

As Jada was getting dressed, Ruth Anne and Billy finally arrived and were eager to help their beloved, but embattled pastor prepare for his inevitable fight with the feared deacons' board of Greater Mt. Carmel. As Jada questioned her husband about any company he was expecting, he dashed down stairs without saying a word, frantically trying to compose himself before opening the door to greet the Dunns.

As Chauncey opened the door he was greeted by his supporters, who both hugged him and told him he has absolutely nothing to worry about. Hearing Ruth Anne and Billy's voices, Jada walked down the stairs to welcome the couple for what she thought was just a late night visit. But, she quickly noticed the look on their faces and asked with concern "Are you all O.K.?"

Feeling as though Jada already knew Chauncey's plight and was just overly concerned about their state of mind in light of what the pastor was going through, Ruth Anne answered, much to the chagrin of Chauncey "We're fine First Lady and we want to let ya'll know that you all aren't going anywhere. They can't just kick you out like they did the last pastor. We're not gonna let that happen."

Offering the Dunns a seat at the couple's large, six-chair, dinning room table, Jada wondered unnoticeably what the Dunns meant by their comments and waited in fear for her husband to explain the impending ordeal.

"Pastor, tell us what happened." urged Billy.

Embarrassed by his argument with his wife and self-conscious about her feelings about his sudden ability to turn his pastoral etiquette on and off, Chauncey answered the Dunns much to the dismay of Jada, who had not a clue.

"They called me into a meeting tonight, and in a nut shell, gave me an option to either leave or allow them to regain control of the church. They even said that they were stripping Ruth Anne of her role as finance director because it wasn't done right and made Maxwell the new finance director."

"They can't do that!" exclaimed an upset Billy.

"They let me look at church by-laws that I never knew existed."

"That handwritten foolishness?"

"It's handwritten Ruthie, but I couldn't tell you if it's authentic or not." Chauncey answered as Jada looked on feeling sorry for her husband.

"Pastor, they pulled that mess together weeks before they ran off Rev. Elliot. Those things were done in the sixties and some of the pages are even missing. They made copies of what was left and gave copies to only the deacons. I'm sure that the members who support the ministry right now don't know anything about their so called by-laws"

"Well, I didn't agree to any of their demands."

"That's good Pastor," Billy said.

"And when they threatened to call a special meeting to vote me out, I told them that I would call the meeting for them. I'm thinking that I may have made a mistake."

"Actually Pastor" alluded Ruth Anne "That's probably the best thing you could have done. You can rest assured tonight that ninety-five percent of the people at Mt. Carmel love what you and your wife are doing and they are chomping at the bits to get a hold of those stupid deacons."

"You may be right, but what I need you all to do is mobilize our base. Tell them what's going on and have them prepared for a meeting this Sunday. Billy, I really need your help man and if you would just be prepared to stand with me and speak on my behalf. I don't feel like I should have to speak for my self in this particular situation."

"You don't Pastor and I promise on my baby's life that nothing will happen to you as long as me and Ruthie and the rest of the tithe paying members of the new Greater Mt. Carmel have anything to do with it. Ya'll rest good tonight because this is as good as taken care of."

"Billy is right Pastor and First Lady. We've been down this road before. But this time the script has flipped. We are in the majority and the majority will speak loudly this Sunday."

"I really did not know that they acted like that." Jada said as she looked at her husband who was staring at his reflection in the freshly polished table."

"O.K." Chauncey said as he snapped out of his daze. "We'll go with that plan and hope for the best."

With fire burning just beneath the surface of Chauncey's now politely smiling face, Ruth Anne and Billy's contentions only bolstered and fueled what had already been birthed in the now agitated pastor's psyche.

As the Dunns rose from the dinner table and proceeded to wake Daphne so that she might return home with them, Chauncey looked at them both in the face with an almost evil gaze and said with the authority of a man who just realized he was in control of the world and said. "If they want to fight, I'm ready and I guarantee this night," he continued as he pounded his fist on the table. "that whatever they do, they'd better be ready for the greatest battle they've ever encountered."

Looking at their pastor with gleams in their eyes, both Billy and Ruth Anne were proud to finally have a leader that was willing to stand for what was right and fight, at all cost, for the noble causes of his people and himself.

"We got your back pastor." Billy said as Chauncey nodded in concurrence and ushered the family to the door.

"Thank ya'll so much," Jada said as she wrapped her arms around the waist of the man she now thought had a reason for his madness. "All of this will be over very soon hopefully."

As the Penningtons prepared for bed, Jada didn't bother to provoke much conversation. She knew that her husband's mind was weary and as he lay quietly in the bed with a firm grasp on his baby girl, she looked at him in the darkness and thought to herself "he's changing, but for the better. He's blossoming into a strong leader, and I need to recognize and appreciate, more, the magnitude of his enormous responsibility, I understand now. I really understand."

As Chauncey and Jada slept on opposite sides of the bed, miles away at the Pickett Plantation, Walter Pickett met a couple of his hunting buddies and his top two deacons under the disguise of darkness for a strategy session on how best to get rid of the blatantly cocky preacher. With only the headlights of their hunting trucks shining on their faces, one by one they uttered their comments of disbelief at the preacher's bold threats and refusal to change his ways.

"Well Walter what happened down there tonight to get you so upset and call me out here so late."

"Shaff Tally," Pickett said to his buddy, the county sheriff, with a big chew of tobacco in his jaw. "I ain't never felt so threatened in all my days. The boy actually rubbed up gainst me like he was crazy, he cussed me and these other boys out too."

"The preacher?" questioned one of Pickett's other Caucasian friends, Matt Helmsly.

"Yea, and that lil bastard called me a nigga didn't he Connie? Now Sheriff, Mattie, both of ya'll is white and I been knowing ya'll ever since we was lil boys and ya'll ain't never called me no nigga is you?"

"Deacon Pickett shole right Shaff." agreed Eddie Philips as he stood with his right dusty boot on the bumper of his muddy Chevy pick-up truck. "That preacher lost his mind over at that church tonight. He told Clausell that if he came to church Sunday he was gone kick his ass. And after me and Connie laughed bout it, we thought bout the serisness of the matta. He lost his mind after we told him we had proof that he was sleepin round wit dem gals and sellin dem drugs. Ya'll done seen him flouncin round hea in that car he bought wit the devil's money. He ain't right I tell ya'll. That bastard ain't right! And he ain't got no bidness telling nobody up there at that church he gone kick they ass under no circumstances, now do he?

"Naw, that ain't right at all," agreed the Sheriff who was enjoying his third Budweiser and chewing on blades of hay from the Fall brown fields as Pickett sat comfortably with him on the tailgate of the county owned Ford 4 x 4 given to the Sheriff exclusively to drive. "Ya'll got to put a stop to him Walter, if you don't he gone cause a whole lot of trouble for ya'll up there, and to be honest with you Walter, ya'll need to act quick. Sounds like to me this boy needs to be put in his place."

"I know we need to act quick, that's why I told you to come out here. Now here is our minutes from the meetin'. This don't show all that cussin he did but it do show where we voted him out tonight by a unanimous vote. Frankly I'm scared to go to that church Sunday to do the job I done had for all these years. I can't let my people see me in that kinda fear for my life."

"What you want me to do Walter?"

"Tally, I need you and some of yo deputies to show up at church by 9:30 Sunday Mornin', that's when he normally show up and I want you to issue him a straining warrant so he can't come back. That's what I gave you them minutes of the meeting for, to prove that on this the sevunteenth day of October…"

"I get the point Walter. But, before I can issue a restraining warrant, I have to get a copy of ya'lls bylaws"

"Here they go right here. Hand them to me Connie… Naw, just go head a read the piece he need to see then let him have it. That'll be yo copy Shaff." Pickett said as Connie Maxwell pulled his handwritten copy of the by-laws from his glove compartment.

"Right here on page one it say, the deacons spose to be in charge of chuch bidness. He vilated dat. Then it say on down lil futha dat he can be voted out at anytime but at least twenty dues payin membas must be present. We did dat tonight."

"Was there twenty there?" asked the Sheriff

"Yes Sir. More than twenny," sternly answered Pickett, who sat patiently, gazing into the open air, waiting for the Sheriff to agree to execute his plan.

"Alright I'll take care of this Walter. But you gone owe me some deer huntin on this property in November."

"Done Deal." Pickett agreed as he scowled and spewed his tobacco spit on the dirt road. "Make sure you and yo boys be in uniform. I thank that'll look better when ya'll get him"

As the Sheriff and Matt Helmsly drove off, thinking of the fun they're going have, deer hunting on Pickett's property, the general of the deacon board at Mt. Carmel grinned devilishly as he continued his unconscious gaze into the darkness of night. With his head pointed in the opposite direction of where his top two deacons were standing, he gave them their final marching orders without ever making eye contact with them.

"Look in my glove compartment, Eddie and pull out them papers. That's a list of all the shit that lil nigga's done did since he came here.

Take that and give a copy to the other three clowns we call deacons and tell them I said for them to take this sheet of paper and go all around town and tell everybody they see that the nigga who committed these crimes is gone be put out this Sunday and they all need to be there to see for they self that Pickett, and of course ya'll too, is still in charge. Ya'll go head now and keep yo nose clean. We got him now." Pickett said in a calm still voice.

Then looking at Eddie and Connie for the first time since giving them their orders, Pickett smiled, grabbed his Red Man tobacco from his pocket for a fresh chew and without the courtesy of saying goodnight walked to his truck singing his favorite southern gospel. "Hallelujah, Hallelujah, I know the storm is passing over, Hallelujah."

Chapter 19

On a morning that Chauncey woke up early and thought confidently to himself that he had had successfully found his way out of the lion's den, Pickett woke up early as well and thought confidently to himself that he had made the perfect trap to snare his once prize catch, who suddenly ran astray. They both had, what they thought were, game winning plans in their estimations, but little did either know that the other was deeply entrenched and prepared for a fierce Sunday show down.

Their respective armies had been unknowingly commissioned to do, in essence, the same jobs, which was to spread their viewpoints throughout the community and if this little town's reputation of "keeping up mess" was to hold true on this weekend, we could expect to see a crowd like Greater Mt. Carmel has never seen. Imagine what Sunday will look like. Chauncey in all of his "righteousness" along with his tithe paying, bible believing super saints versus the "shrewd and calculating, old hellion, chairman deacon" along side his demon possessed, back woods thinking, dues paying delegation. A mess was brewing and soon a major battle would ensue and some group of churchgoers would claim victory, while others would have to admit defeat.

Saturday was typical at the Pennington house as Chauncey worked until about noon on his amateurish golf game and Jada and Elizabeth spent some girl time with Daphne and Ruth Anne at the nearby malls. After practicing with his putter for a little less than an hour and after he'd spent close to three practicing chip shots onto the ninth green which was only a short trek through the woods from his conveniently located home, Chauncey walked, with his golf bag in tow, back into the comfort of his luxurious home, to lounge around a little before Billy and Chris came over to watch some good ole Saturday College Football on ABC. This was a special Fall Saturday afternoon for Chauncey, who rarely got a chance to enjoy football on his fifty-two inch flat screen due to his hectic weekend schedule, because he was finally able to cheer for and watch his favorite team, the Ohio State Buckeyes, who were featured this week instead of the local Florida State Seminoles, who normally dominated ABC's regional coverage of collegiate sports.

But, before Billy or Chris arrived for the game however, Chauncey's cell phone begin to vibrate on the couple's imported white, African themed, glass topped, living room coffee table. It was Tiffany Belford again and again, against his better judgment he allowed the phone's answering system to pick up when the Belford's home phone number flashed across the lime green, back lit screen of his phone. After only seconds, hoping the deacon's turncoat wife wouldn't try to call back, the phone vibrated again signaling that Tiffany had chosen to leave another message. When Chauncey checked her message this time, he hurried to call her back because Tiffany sounded shaken and gave the embattled pastor clues that she undoubtedly knew of something that she was determined to convey.

Anxious and sweating, as he normally did during intense moments, Chauncey waited for Tiffany to answer after he hastily returned her phone call. In the middle of the third ring she answered in a rush and said "Pastor I've been trying to reach you since last night!"

"What is it Sister Belford" enquired the inquisitive pastor.

"Those deacons, and my silly husband included, is trying hard to get rid of you and what they doin is wrong."

"I know, but dear, I think we have the situation pretty much under control."

"You do?"

"Yes. I met with some of the same upset members on last night and we have a pretty good strategy to throw a monkey wrench into their plans."

"I shole God hope you do cause I don't want ya'll to leave. My life has changed so much since you and First Lady been here and Pastor Pennington, ya'll is good for our church. I just hate that my husband is participating in that foolishness. He's a good, hard working man and if it wasn't for Pickett and them other deacons confusing him, I know he wouldn't be playing no part in this."

"Well, Tiffany on last night, Harold really didn't play much of a part..."

"But he is now Pastor."

"What do you mean Tiffany?"

"Well, I'm sure you've seen that paper they been circulating."

"What paper?"

"You haven't seen it?"

"No what is it?"

"Pastor, if you ain't seen this paper then you really don't know what they done put these people up to. I really don't want to talk bout this over the phone cause Harold might walk in any minute, but if you meet me somewhere, I'll tell you everything."

"Listen Tiffany." Chauncey said with his voice beginning to tremble with anxiety, "Can you come to my house in the next fifteen minutes?"

"Yes Sir."

"Do you know where I live?"

"Yes Sir. I've been to your house before. Remember the house warming party?"

"Yea, that's good. Meet me here in fifteen minutes and we'll go from there."

"O.K." She said as Chauncey frantically hang up the phone in an effort to call Billy to expedite his arrival.

After calling Billy and waiting anxiously for about ten minutes Billy drove up speeding through the quiet housing development and met Chauncey, who by this time was standing out on his carpet like Bermuda grass of his front lawn.

"Is she here yet," Billy asked trying to catch his breath after scurrying over to meet his now visibly distraught pastor.

"No. She hadn't made it yet"

As the two men discussed, on the front lawn, all of the possibilities of what Tiffany could possibly divulge about the deacons' plans, Chris drove up in a hurry as well. But Chris, unlike Billy had heard the racket around town and couldn't wait to tell his pastor about the vicious rumors being spread by the deacons."

"Pastor!" Chris shouted as he ran toward Chauncey and Billy "You won't believe the things I heard Clausell Ellis saying down at the hardware store."

"What?" Billy asked, urging the young, but faithful member to continue.

"I heard Clausell telling a group of about eight men, that they were getting rid of you tomorrow and as I walked by, he was showing them this piece of paper that obviously had a lot of dirt on it because, before I left they were laughing and saying that you had to go if you were doing all of that. What's going on pastor?"

"Chris its all lies and they're trying to get rid of me because they feel like they've lost control."

"But what are they saying? Why are they doing this?" Chris asked worriedly.

"I don't know Chris." Chauncey explained just before Billy interrupted, "I think that's her."

"Yea, that's her."

"Who?" Chris questioned, wanting desperately to know what was going on.

After parking her red Ford Mustang next to the Pennington's mail box near the area that the men were standing, Tiffany got out of her car in a hurry and handed the pastor the little sheet of paper that her husband and other deacons were distributing strategically throughout the community.

"Come on ya'll let's go inside," Billy said as he snatched the paper from Chauncey and ushered his pastor into the house, just before reading the bomb shell accusations that were listed on white composition styled paper.

As Billy began to read the handwritten, worn, from frequently handled and tattered, sheet of paper, Chauncey became infuriated at what the deacons had listed as the...

"Ten Commandments that this preacher done already broke."

The Day All Hell Broke Loose

1. He stealing church money to support his goody two shoes lifestyle.
2. He selling them drugs and bought that car with drug money. That ain't God.
3. He got a plan to take over the church and change us from being Baptist.
4. He having relations with the young girls at the church.
5. Three of which is already pregnated.
6. He cusses right there in the church and have them dope boys coming in there too.
7. He don't even respect his deacons or women at the church.
8. He told Clausell Ellis that he'll kick his ass right there in the church.
9. Threatened to set all ourva asses on fire.
10. Made me believe infractions 9 & 10

Signed: Someone who cares bout the loving people of this fine community and a prayerful man who read his word daily and know infractions 1-10 is dead ass wrong.

"You mean to tell me that this mess is floating around town."

"Yea, It's all over town," responded Tiffany and agreed Chris.

"Well if that's all they got, their plan ain't got a snow ball's chance in Hell of going through does it?"

"That's the problem though pastor." tried to answer Tiffany.

"Who will ever believe all of this foolishness" interrupted the angry and frustrated pastor. "The people at that church know full well that I haven't done all of this stuff and those of you who know better will certainly vote to keep me on Sunday, right?"

"Vote on Sunday?" questioned a still in the dark Chris. "What are we voting for on Sunday?"

"Chris, Tiffany I'm going to call a special meeting after church Sunday to open up Pickett's closet before he tries to brainwash these people that the stuff on this list is actually in mine," Chauncey said as he looked again at the paper, which contained the horrible accusations against him.

"But, Pastor, that's not all of their plan," Tiffany said quickly. She was determined not to be out talked this time. "Harold told me this morning that they actually held a vote last night and that Pickett had contacted the Sheriff to stop you from even coming into the church tomorrow."

"What!" shouted Billy, as Chauncey and Chris, both, held their heads in disbelief.

"Yea, Harold said that Pickett got in touch with the Sheriff last night and Sheriff Tally told him that the vote was legitimate because the by-laws say that all that needs to present is twenty members and it was twenty at the meeting, so the vote is suppose to be final. They are trying to block you from having that meeting. They getting the Sheriff to arrest you pastor."

"They can't do that." a confused Billy said loudly, as he thought to himself what his next move would be. "Don't worry pastor, I'm going to call Leonard, he ought to know about what the Sheriff can or cannot do."

"Who is Leonard?" questioned Chauncey.

"You know Leonard Pastor. Leonard Maywhether, the young deputy that almost beat Tally in the last election. He's been to the church before."

"Oh yea call him and see what he knows."

Much to the dismay of Billy and Chauncey and the other concerned members of Mt. Carmel, Maywhether shed little light on any possible solution to their dilemma. From what the deputy said, if a legitimate vote was taken, and if the deacons had proof that the vote was taken and had by-laws that substantiated their right to call for a vote, the Sheriff had every right to issue a restraining order to the pastor, comforting words only in the sense that Chauncey needn't fear being arrested unless he didn't adhere to the Sheriff's orders.

"Billy," Maywhether continued, "you need to get your hands on a copy of those by-laws in a hurry and see for yourself if things were done properly. If they were you have a problem. If they were not, there's hope that another meeting can be called."

"Thanks so much Leonard. I appreciate you helping out man."

"No problem Billy. If you need again me all you got to do is call."

Billy was still quite confused about his next course of action, but knew without a shadow of a doubt that getting his hands on a copy of those by-laws would be invaluable. But after vigorously questioning

Tiffany about her husband's access to a copy, he was left at square one all over again.

"The truth of the matter is…" Billy said as he rubbed his chin. "…that those sneaky hellions make it impossible for the members to know what's going on at that church unless they feel like it's time to get rid of the pastor. I can almost guarantee that no one but Pickett and his close allies have a copy of those things."

"Billy, Tiffany, Chris, Listen," Chauncey said, as he prepared to rally his own troops. "I've made up my mind that what ever happens happens. I'm no longer afraid about my future here. You all have proven to me that my future here is pretty secure. But, I do want to tell you not to be surprised if things get a little ugly tomorrow, because I won't take this blatant attempt at character assassination lying down."

"But Pastor you can't stoop to their level," pleaded Tiffany.

"Tiffany, I disagree. It's about time we had somebody that stood for us and fought for himself." rebutted Billy.

In a moment of increased anxiety, Chauncey yelled out to them "Just hold on!" as his forehead became wrinkled in angst, finally realizing that this was a battle he had to fight.

"All of ya'll listen." Chauncey said trying to calm tensions as the impromptu meeting was drawn to a close. "If a person is against me and already believes what's being said about me; so be it. Let them come to see me arrested or thrown out or whatever they want to see tomorrow. To hell with them, I could care less about what they think of me. I'm only concerned about the good people of Mt. Carmel. I just hope they'll show up tomorrow and not be intimidated by those deacons." he said as he prepared to issue one final command.

"What I need you three to do is call everybody you know that supports our ministry and tell them to meet me at the Church at 9:30AM and make sure they understand that it ain't gone be pretty."

"Pastor that's as good as done." said Billy, who opened the front door, just after giving his pastor a firm handshake and an assuring embrace.

"Is there anything else we need to be prepared to do, Pastor?" concernedly asked Chris, who finally began to understand the source of the confusion at the church.

"Chris, all I need for you guys to do is just be there. I can take care of myself. I just want to make sure that they know I'm not standing by myself. This date is long over due and they're gonna find out tomorrow that this preacher is not the one to be messed up with"

Chapter 20

When Jada returned home from her little shopping trip with the girls, she was really shocked at what she'd begin to hear from people in the community. Jada was never known to listen to the town gossip, but this was different, this was her husband and in spite of his rather ruthless behavior over the past few months, this south western girl from Odessa was taking Tammy Wynett's advice and standing by her man.

Saturday evening proved to be as perfect a time as any for Jada to do what she hadn't felt compelled to do since their Friday evening and Friday night spats. For the most part Chauncey had remained quiet as it related to conversing with Jada, but Jada knew that before anything went down at that church or any where else, for that matter, her man had to be assured of her full support.

While sitting in his first floor study with his feet propped up on a dark brown, leather ottoman, Chauncey looked in silence at the rose bushes planted just outside the window as he reclined in his oversized office chair and thought to himself "even something as beautiful as a rose has what some would consider a flaw. It can give someone so much pleasure, but the same rose can also cause a tremendous amount of pain, if handled improperly." He thought of the great blessings he'd received since coming to North Florida, but realized his beautiful experience was made a little more unsettling by a few unfortunate occurrences, which he characterized as his life's thorns. Those thorns had momentarily caused a severe lapse in his judgment and put an agonizing strain on the only relationship he'd ever had with a woman that had grown so deep. Jada was his princess and there was no doubt about it, but stress had overtaken his mental stability, even if only for a moment.

He thought too, about his misconceptions about what constitutes strength. As a pastor, Chauncey, for the most part, measured his strength by his ability to mask what he really felt inside. But, through this struggle he would discover that sometimes what one is willing to share about his own fragility shows how strong one really is. Aunt Eunice helped Chauncey understand his shortcomings a little better and talked to him extensively about the responsibility he has to always treat Jada right and include the woman he loved in everything that's going on in his life; the good the bad, and the ugly. After finally returning her Friday evening, frantic phone call, Chauncey got the best advice his aunt could've possibly given the flustered preacher.

"Always treat that girl with the utmost respect. She's the mother of your child for God's sake. It doesn't matter how those folk up there at that church treat you or how much stress you're under, you love your wife and treat her good. When those people at that church get through with you, who do you have to come home to? Jada and she is a good girl, a very good girl. And she's smart too, let her help you baby."

During a phone conversation that Eunice was dying to have ever since Daphne called her to shed light on the fragile nature of Chauncey's and Jada's marriage, Chauncey even realized how wrong he had been to unknowingly accuse Jada of doing something she never even considered. After all, if he'd known that Daphne was the source of the words that caused his aunt to worry about him, Chauncey probably would've appreciated Jada's failed attempt to lure him into paradise to ease his troubled mind. "How stupid could I have been," he thought to himself. "I really need to apologize to her for how I've been acting."

As he pondered whether or not his thorn had come to humble him, punish him, or strengthen him, Jada walked in slowly, not really knowing what to say. Talking had become a chore for the couple and she didn't want to rub her, already agitated, husband the wrong way.

"Hey," she said as Chauncey stared out of his office window.

"Hey." He answered back without overtly acknowledging her presence.

"Can I sit down for a minute?" she asked as she stood looking at a man she barely knew anymore.

"Yea come on in baby."

"Can we talk for a moment Chauncey, or are you in really deep thought right now?" Jada asked tenderly, trying her best not to aggravate her now easily agitated mate.

"Yea, that's cool," he said as he continued to stare at the roses just outside his window.

"I know you're really focused on what lies before us and probably don't want to be bothered right now. But, I just wanted to tell you that I'm sorry for not being able to see what you were going through. I wish I had somebody I could talk to about how to be a good pastor's wife, but I don't and I've really done the best I could. I promise Chauncey, if I had known you were going through this type of stuff, I know I would've responded differently. Why didn't you tell me?"

"Jada, look," he said as he turned toward her and looked in her eyes. "I apologize for the way I've been acting. I shouldn't have talked to you that way. And I'm really embarrassed about it. No amount of stress should ever cause me to treat you like that. If it wasn't for you Jada, I probably would've already lost my mind by now. But you've been so strong for me and on my best day I can't say that I've been as strong for you."

"Yes you have Chauncey."

"No I haven't; not like you've been for me. But I do want you to understand what I was thinking. I've never told you any of this stuff before last night, because when I come home, the last thing I want to do is talk about those people with all of those problems. And besides that, I thought I was protecting you by not talking about it. I never wanted your opinion of Pickett or any body else to suddenly change. Jada, I'm a man and I've always wanted you to feel like I was able to protect you even when I felt like I couldn't protect myself."

"Chauncey I'm gonna always think of you as a very strong and capable man. You don't ever have to feel as though I couldn't support you, especially when things are as bad as they are right now."

"I understand that and I realize that I need you so much," he said as he glanced at her briefly, before looking helplessly, again, at his roses.

"I need you too Chauncey. I need you like you were. I need the man who didn't mind leaning and depending on me every once and a while. I need to know that you feel comfortable letting me into your world again, trusting me enough to tell me what you're going through. I want to know what's on your mind before you have an eruption like you did on Friday. Promise me you'll let me in again Chauncey."

"Jada, I not only promise to talk to you more, I want to be with you more. I miss, so much, all the time we used to spend together before both of became so important to everybody else that we forgot to be important to each other; like when we used to just go down to the river for no reason of all. I miss that and I must admit that I hate, like hell, when Adolph James calls you back into that office or Pickett calls me in for a meeting, especially when it interrupts what I thought was gonna be a day just for you and me."

"Well baby," Jada said as she inched closer to her husband who was still sitting near the window in the darkened room, "tomorrow will be a hectic day and frankly I'm ready for it to be over either way. But can we just cuddle tonight? I just want to hold you. I just want you to know that I support you and you have many more people out there who love you too. And from what I hear from the street committee you're going to have a whole bunch of supporters there tomorrow."

"Jada tomorrow will take care of itself, I'm no longer worried, but I am just so angry at the way they've tried to destroy my name."

"Come here baby, let me hold you. It's O.K. Tomorrow will be O.K."

As Jada massaged her husband's bruised heart and ministered to his worried mind, he slowly gave in to the fact that he couldn't control what others were saying about him or what a few of the disgruntled members of Mt. Carmel was trying to do to him. In some ways this ministerial mishap did for Chauncey and Jada, the very thing they had failed to negotiate into their schedules. It forced them to talk about their fears. It forced them just to talk. It forced them to rekindle the trust and admiration that they each once shared for each other. This trial was turning out to be a blessing and revealed to Jada, that even though her husband was flanked by very capable associates in ministry most of the time, she was still Chauncey's strongest ally and he needed her to be as understanding as she'd always been.

Chauncey understood now, more than ever, the significance of involving his wife in critical ministry issues and vowed to be more forthcoming with his wife. Admitting again to Jada that he had been wrong for the way he'd treated her, Chauncey promised her that she'd never see that side of him again, at least not directed at her. But he did make it plain and clear that the Chauncey that those deacons once knew is dead and gone. Jada agreed whole heartedly that he needed to be more forceful in his administration; especially when it came to them. Now that she understood how cruel they'd been to her husband, Jada called on Chauncey to always be brave and stand his ground.

"Jada, a lion was birthed deep within me tonight. It's like a beast that's raging just under the surface of my flesh. And that beast is willing and able to punish anybody that attempts to attack my marriage, my ministry, or my life."

Contented that he and Jada seemed to be headed, again, down the pathway to happiness, but still very anxious about how tomorrow would ultimately unfold, Chauncey took an over the counter sleep aid and went to bed a little earlier than usual. As he slept like a baby, Jada watched over him for much of the night, anointing his body with oil and praying fervently for God to give him the strength to endure whatever he faced when he rose early the morning.

Back at the Dunn household, Billy and Ruth Anne were sleepless. They both toiled over how best to help their pastor. But, they were also confident that with the type of support and respect Pastor Penning garnered from the majority of the congregation, it was a safe bet that he'd withstand what was about to go down. The three things that worried Billy the most however, was the deacons' authority to dismiss the pastor according to those by-laws, what role, if any, would law enforcement play, and what long term or short term effects this atrocity could have on the greatly popular and thriving, young ministry.

"Do you think the Sheriff will actually show up tomorrow Ruthie?" asked a concerned Billy.

"To be honest, I think he will, because I'm sure Pickett has over exaggerated this whole thing. That's his style. Pickett has a long history of pulling stunts like this to scare people off. If it's not Pickett's way, he'll do anything his power to stop it and besides that he and that Sheriff are rumored to be real close."

"I just don't know how this thing is gonna play out," Billy said as he sat, in his pajamas, with his back against the black, mirrored headboard of the couple's king-sized bed.

As he let out a sigh of exhaustion, Ruth Anne meticulously sifted through some of the church's old financial records for the meeting tomorrow. She was determined to bolster her contention that the church had seen tremendous financial growth under Pennington's leadership and is better off with the young pastor.

"I don't even know if all of this is worth it Ruthie," he continued as his wife continued sifting in silence. "Pastor could leave that hell␣whole all together and start a new ministry somewhere else. He'll take most of the people with him, the good people any way. And he won't even have to deal with that deacon's board."

"Maybe you're right Billy, but I think he think he's doing the right thing. He ought to fight back. I'm glad he's not a pushover and it's about time that that board of deacons dealt with somebody that got just as much sense as they do. This man and his wife has meant so much to that church and this community and in spite of what these people around here say about him, Pastor Pennington is a good man and he hasn't done any of that stuff they say he did. We can't just stand by and let them have their way; not this time. When Pastor Elliot left they laughed at all of us who tried to stop it and I'm convinced that even if Pastor walked out on his own, they'd consider that a victory too. And to be honest I couldn't stomach the looks on those demons' faces if they thought that they were responsible for running off another preacher. Enough is enough and I'm not gonna just stand by and let them mess up the best thing that ever happened to this church since I've been there," Ruth Anne said as she compared last month's financial record with one from 1990.

"I guess you're right Baby." Billy said, finally relaxing a little, deciding to call it a night. "Pastor always tells us, why pray if you're going to worry and why worry if you've already prayed."

"Yea, I know that's right. Go on to sleep Billy. I just have a few more things to do and I'll be joining you," Ruth Anne said just before asking her husband one more question before he went to sleep. "Hey, did you get a chance to get the word to most of the people?"

"Yea," he said as he yawned widely. "We touched bases with everybody we had phone numbers for and for the most part all I got was positive responses."

"That's good. What about Mother Snelling? What did she have to say about all of this?"

"Oh," Billy said as he fought off a yawn to chuckle, "Mother Snelling said she was coming with her pistol, because if they think they're going to make her pastor leave, it was going to be some trouble. Ruthie she even said that she's glad the sheriff is suppose to be there and thought she might call herself to invite the ambulance too. And oh, I forgot to tell pastor, but she also told me that she was gonna invite several of the members to her house for prayer before they come over to the church. She asked me if that was alright, and I told her that a little prayer couldn't hurt anything."

"That's her. She's a sweet old lady, but she's been known to get a little wild at times too," Ruth Anne said as she smiled and vividly remembered some of the elder mother's not so good days. In a more serious tone she continued, "I pray for her sake and people like her that this will all be over real soon."

As Billy dozed off to sleep, Ruth Anne sat up in the bed with her glasses still affixed to her face, wondering how any group of people could be so egregious. With the night turning into the morning, Ruthie finally laid her head down, but unfortunately too many thoughts rushed through her mind about what tomorrow would bring; sleep did not grant her a goodnight's rest.

CHAPTER 21

If the whether at 6:30AM was any indication at all, this breezy, October Sunday was doomed before it ever really started. The crackling of thunder and the brilliant flashes of lightning greeted all those who dared an early awakening and brought with them monsoonal rains that washed away many of the dirt roads that laced the little town. The stormy weather made sleeping in a few minutes late a little easier for most, but the two men that prepared to wage war on this less than stellar day, both woke up early with the exact same things on their minds. They feared that the horrendous weather would cause many of their supporters to stay home today, fueling anxiety that a low showing of support might just as well be a signal of imminent defeat. As the time drew near that they meet their fierce opposition, they opted for their customary morning rituals, Pickett drinking a fresh brewed cup of black coffee made by his wife, and Chauncey, ironing his dress shirt and shining his shoes, just before preparing for his morning consecration hour.

Standing on his back porch, watching the sneaky destruction of the wind and rain, Pickett's focus was noticeable. The old man thought intensely about the battle plan that he was hell bent on executing and after a final call to the Sheriff's office to make sure that his back up was still scheduled to show up, Pickett urged his wife, Eloise, to get dressed a little earlier so that he might stake his claim to the church that he once ruled all by his lonesome.

By 8:00AM, both Pickett and his wife were completely dressed. Before they left their modest, three - bedroom, wooden frame, home for their rain soaked, five minute drive to Mt. Carmel, Pickett called each of his trusty deacons. He told them all what his expectations were and strictly informed them about the times of their systematic arrivals. Chauncey, on the other hand was still in consecration at 8:00AM, which was an eerie sign to Jada, who thought it was rather unusual for husband not to have been fully dressed and putting the finishing touches on his message by now. But, Jada's fears were eased just a bit when Chauncey walked back into the bedroom looking refreshed and poised to deal with the exploits of his manipulative adversaries.

As the rather large rain pellets continued to beat against the Pennington's bedroom window panes and clouds prevented the sun from sharing its light with the morning, Chauncey slowly put on his presidential, white cuff linked shirt, navy blue suit, and conservative red and silver tie. Jada was assisting Lizzy down the hall, when the phone rang. "Daddy, its uncle Billy," said a giggly Lizzy who had beat her mom to the phone.

"Hang up Lizzy I have it," he said as he smiled at his five year-old's antics.

"Pastor, I was just calling to check in on you this morning and let you know that I got a good feeling about today."

"I really needed to hear that Billy," replied Chauncey, who smiled as he sat at the foot of his bed, tying his shiny black gators.

Following the brief conversation with his right hand man, Chauncey felt better than he did before he received the call and like Pickett, hurried his wife along so that they too might join whoever decided to show up early for this Sunday morning showdown.

By now it was 9AM sharp and the key players were already entrenched. Deacon Pickett who had arrived nearly forty-five minutes before the Dunn's or the Penningtons, sat silently with his wife Eloise in the deacon's corner as the preacher and his allies arrived, waiting for his strategy to unfold. Chauncey, who by this time was, once again, visibly anxious, went with Jada and Lizzy, directly into his office for some alone time to contemplate the enormity of the situation at hand. The Dunns, they walked into the sanctuary to prepare for the 9:30 commencement of Sunday school.

The Day All Hell Broke Loose

"Good morning," the Dunns said as they both cheerfully greeted the Picketts and got only cold stares and an evil "Monin" in return.

"Deacon Pickett, when do you think this rain will end?" asked Billy trying to be polite while simultaneously seeking to get a feel of the deacon's mood.

"I don't know son, I ain't God. It'll end when the master say it end. But I can tell you its gonna be a good day whether it keep on rainin' or whether the sun start shinin'." Pickett responded with a smirk on his face, while continuing his cold stare.

The tensions on the inside of the church were as volatile as the weather on the outside and though words were not uttered between the feuding couples over the next ten minutes or so, the pressure on everybody, was reaching a feverish pitch. Silence was broken, however, as Connie Maxwell entered the sanctuary abruptly with his church conference, hell raiser posture already in full bloom.

"Bro. Chairman, Eloise how ya'll doin'?" Maxwell greeted his chairman and wife, intentionally overlooking the Dunn Family.

"Just fine Connie. How you doin'?" answered the deacon's obviously over exaggerative wife as she looked over at Ruth Anne and rolled her eyes as Pickett nodded at his enforcer and new treasurer, acknowledging his earlier greeting.

"Deacon Pickett can I see you over there for a second?" asked Connie, seeking to initiate a private meeting.

After ushering Pickett into the choir stand, Deacon Maxwell questioned Pickett about the success of the plan so far and inquired of the chairman why more people hadn't showed up yet.

"Listen to me Connie," Pickett sternly whispered, "everythang is goin' just like I planned it."

"But where is evybody?" Connie whispered back.

The truth of the matter is Deacon Maxwell wasn't really concerned about who hadn't showed up yet at all, he knew they'd eventually show up. He just enjoyed the idea of being seen strategizing with the chairman of the board at such important times as these. It was simple; the more questions he asked and the longer he and Pickett talked alone in the choir stand, the more significant, those watching would think he really was.

"Dammit Connie they gone be here!" Pickett said as he tried desperately to keep from exploding on his over anxious, number two. "Be patient! It's raining! You know how black folks is when it's raining! Now I was thankin anyway, that even if nobody else show up that's good too, because Shaff Tally and his boys will be up here in ten minutes or so and if nobody from his side don't show up, it would be that much easier for them to get him way from here. Now you go on back over there and sit down somewhere and do what I told you and stop asking me all these dumb ass questions, Connie. You startin to act like Willie. Go head, and take yo position."

"Alright, Brother Chairman, I know what I spose to do," Connie replied with slightly bruised pride.

As Pickett walked slowly and quietly back to his seat, he noticed the rest of his deacons and their wives, with the exception of Deacon Harold Belford and Tiffany, storming through the front door and like Connie Maxwell, none of them even acknowledged Billy or Ruth Anne. Aside from the angry stares and snarls they received, the Dunns were relatively nonexistent in the eyes of their formidable foes, and for the first time this Sunday morning they knew something was up and whatever it was, they knew it was very serious.

"Billy they're up to something," Ruth Anne said as she prodded her husband to get up and join her in the dining annex to strategize.

As Billy and Ruth Anne walked through the breezeway to the dinning annex to make phone calls, they thought about it and asked Daphne to go and get Lizzy from the pastor's office and take her to the car to listen to some music for a moment. They didn't want either of the girls to witness what was about to unfold because it wouldn't be pretty. And from the looks on the faces of the those increasingly confident deacons, who knew their deceptive plan was working even better than they thought it would, this had the potential to get really ugly fast.

Just as they'd begin to glory at the pastor's lack of support and just before Deacon Phillips stood up to sing the opening hymn that signaled the beginning of Sunday School, they got two more incentives to fully carry out their strategy. Arriving over five minutes late, most, but not all, of the crew that had voted to oust the pastor on Friday had finally showed up, conspicuously, with a few of the other members they'd convinced and recruited to war with them against the "evil pastor".

The Day All Hell Broke Loose

What a blessing it was for Pickett to see Mother Viney Abernathy leading a group of about twenty saints that all had hatred in their hearts toward the preacher into the sanctuary to help him "get this church back in order". And to top it off, Sheriff Tally walked in just moments later, in full law enforcement regalia, with six of his deputies. Yes, Pickett was proud of his clan because, unlike Chauncey's, they had weathered the storm and shown up. But with the arrival of the sheriff, he knew that the fate of the rebellious, young preacher had all but been sealed. To the adulation of all involved in the vicious and sadistic overthrow, the Sheriff and his deputies had arrived and they were in no mood to waste time.

"Where's the preacher at Walter?" asked the sheriff, who had a scowl on his face that even scared Connie Maxwell.

"He's back there in his office" Pickett said as if Chauncey was a hog, ripe for slaughter "Let me take you back there so we can go on and get this over with."

As Pickett led the sheriff and his deputies back to the office to confront the totally off guard and still hoping for a peaceful resolution, preacher, a handful of Chauncey's supporters drizzled slowly into the sanctuary and took their seats, waiting anxiously for a chance to support their pastor at his specially called meeting. Totally unaware of what had already transpired, they looked at each other in confusion when they heard the condescending chuckles and saw the gloating gazes from the people they discerned were already staunchly against the man they revered. But before Pickett and the Sheriff reached Chauncey's office, they stopped for a brief conversation.

"This ain't much…" Pickett uttered with the seriousness of a man who knew now he was the church's undisputed leader. He presented Tally with a wrinkled old paper bag full of the church's money. "But, here is a little something for your trouble. I know how hard it is for us leaders to take time out our busy schedules to handle matters such as these."

As Pickett and the Sheriff concluded their brief conversation in the finance room, only two doors down from the pastor's study, tensions continued to mount inside the sanctuary. But by this time Billy and Ruth Anne were back in the sanctuary and had taken their seats alongside the other twenty or so members, who vowed earnestly to defend their right to keep Pastor Pennington on his throne. Waiting patiently for the rest of Chauncey's supporters to show up, who by Chris' account, had unfortunately been delayed by a downed power line on the only road leading from Mother Snelling's house, who called a special prayer meeting of her own, Billy tried to calm the tensions of those supporting Chauncey's cause. Whispering to quiet down the faithful and informing them that the rest of their team would be arriving soon, Billy and Ruth Anne continued to witness the verbal assaults between the sparring squadrons, which caused a commotion that could be heard from the pastor's study, which was yards away from the brewing confrontation.

Hearing a noise that they mistakenly thought was the prelude to Sunday school, Chauncey and Jada exited the pastor's study just before Pickett and the Sheriff and his deputies left the finance room, unknowingly aborting the chairman's plans to catch him before he got a chance to enter the sanctuary. As Chauncey walked into the sanctuary side by side with his wife, prepared to give his customary introduction to today's lesson on forgiveness, he was left in disbelief at what he saw. A little over half of the waiting congregation, all sat in solidarity on the far left side of the church and stared at him obtrusively, as if he was a common criminal, convinced that the Sheriff had already served him his official dismissal papers. As the deacons stared at him without saying a word, wondering why he was even allowed to come out of his office, Chauncey greeted the Sunday school, totally oblivious to what was going on around him.

"Good morning," he said as some in the congregation popped their lips and looked away from the preacher and his wife, as his supporters reverently responded to his greeting.

"Why is you still here preacher!" shouted an angry Eddie Phillips. "Yo days of messin' up this church is spose to be over," he said as he got up from his seat to approach the surprised pastor.

"Yea ova," agreed Connie Phillips, as Pickett and the Sheriff rushed from the hallway to confront the man that they knew now wasn't hiding in the bathroom.

As Pickett and the Sheriff approached Chauncey, much to the shock and disbelief of his supporters, they issued him a sealed envelope that for all intents and purposes ended the preacher's three year assault on the great tradition of deacon leadership at Greater Mt. Carmel.

"What are ya'll trying to do?" questioned Billy as another supporter angrily shouted "ain't none of ya'll right!"

As Chauncey motioned for Jada to go back into his office amid the frantic protests of his vocal, visibly outraged and infuriated cohorts, the sheriff issued the silent, but resolved preacher, what Pickett called "yo walkin' papers"

"This is a restraining order," sternly said Sheriff Tally, as the beleaguered pastor's foes looked on in delight and his supporters wondered where was everybody who said they "wouldn't let this happen." "And here is yo letter to notify you that you are officially dismissed."

"Now wait just one minute!" Chauncey said as he tried, distractedly, to regain his composure. "I know my rights and Sheriff, you or nobody else can just come in here and make me leave my own church without just cause and I'm not going anywhere until somebody in here tells me what in God's name is going on."

"That's right," shouted one angry woman, as Billy and Ruth Anne frantically raced out of the church to see if any of their other combatants had arrived yet.

"I'll tell you what goin' on preacher!" shouted a bold and flagrant Eddie Phillips. "You just got voted out. And we knowed you were gone talk that same talk that Woodrow tried to talk. He wudn't goin nowhere either," he continued to the chuckles of unashamed participators. "But as of this day, yo time is up you ole cussin dope pusher. So get yo hat, yo coat, and leave before Shaff Tally and his boys make you leave."

Ignoring Deacon Phillips' foolish rants, Chauncey asked belligerently again for more clarification. "What is this all about Pickett?" As Pickett looked on with his right hand over his mouth, as if he couldn't believe that Chauncey didn't really know what this was about, Chauncey continued his reasonable rebuttal. "I thought that another meeting was supposed to be scheduled to resolve all of this."

"Son I can't believe yo actin' like this." Pickett said as the sheriff waited patiently for the chairman's parting assault to be delivered. "You and I both know what these deputies is here for," he said boastfully and arrogantly. "You have been dismissed… Fired! Put out like I told you we was gone do if you didn't change yo wicked ways. Frankly, I'm surprised that you even standin up here like you sked now. You wudn't sked Friday when you told Clausell you was gone whip his ass or when you grabbed my arthritic hand and tried to squeeze it off, was you?"

"Pickett you are a bald faced liar and you know it," Chauncey said as he looked deeply into the deacon's eyes as the sheriff's deputies inched a little closer to the preacher at the beckoning of their superior.

"The only person bald in this church is Willie!" Pickett said seriously.

"You shole right Bro. Chairman," Willie Mallard said, finally getting his opportunity to weigh in on the matter.

"Shut up Willie!" shouted the fuming leader as he momentarily looked away from Chauncey to glare at the man he regretted making a deacon.

"Now like I was sayin, the only bald person in here is Willie and the only liar in this church is you!" He said focusing his attention back on Chauncey.

"You been foolin these people since you came here and you even fooled me into believin that you was gone listen and not be bull headed. But we done got tired of yo mess now son and it's time for you to get out. And you can act like you don't know what this bout if you want to but, just Friday, you flounced yo butt round this church like you was high and mighty, cussing and threatening folks like you was God. Now you acting like you don't know? Negro you know. That's the word you like ain't it? Negro?" Pickett continued as he chuckled at his own words and provoked laughter of affirmation from his faithful "bunch of hooligans".

"Let me close out by sayin this. As long as you live you better understand that laws ain't meant to be broke especially in God's house. You hear me boy? You done broke a lot of 'em at this church, but that ain't the point no more. As long as you still a preacher, let this day stick in yo head. Remember what this day taught you" he said as he sarcastically patted Chauncey on his left shoulder, confident that if he tried anything stupid the deputies would arrest him. "Always remember Romans 2:12 that say "follow yo bode and don't never disrespect the people that God done ordained to show you the way. Never!" he said as he motioned for the Sheriff to handle his business.

"Shaff if he won't leave on his own, feel free to use all yo man power to make him get out. And oh, by the way, go on head and take the rest of them crooks over there, out too, before they stir up mo confusion," Pickett said pointing at Chauncey's few but vigilant supporters. "Yea, ya'll crooks too! Ain't no God in none of ya'll; sittin over there havin a fit cause we tryin our hardest to clean up the mess this boy done left behind." he continued.

As the Sheriff's deputies moved toward them to execute the deacon's orders, some of Chauncey's helpless supporters angrily got up and left as others defiantly, spewed revolting and repulsive words at the band of demons that had destroyed their church.

As Chauncey boiled on the inside, angry and disappointed that many of his faithful supporters, including Chris and Tiffany, hadn't shown up at 9:30 as they'd promised, Sheriff Tally gave Chauncey five minutes to clear his things out of his office and ordered his deputies to escort the few remaining non compliant members out of the church for safety precautions.

While deputies walked slowly behind the shocked and dejected members, who were equally disappointed about the contradictory absence of people who had promised to show up, Deacon Pickett continued his arrogant rants as the other deacons stood shoulder to shoulder with their leader agreeing with his every word, sometimes, before they churned out of his mouth.

"This meeting is adjourned!" Pickett said mocking Chauncey's forbidden dismissal of the emergency meeting held on Friday. "Remember that Reverend. You thought you was in charge then, didn't you?" Pickett said as he sadistically chuckled. "Friday night I told you I was in charge and now I'm gone have the last word."

As Pickett and his crew continued to taunt the preacher, who finally realized that his pre-destined pastorate had just about come to an unfortunate end, Chauncey stood still, thinking of his future, as he waited for the Sheriff and his deputies to do whatever they had to do to get him out. He was determined not to walk out on his own and the more Pickett and his band of brethren taunted him, the more resolved he was to stand his ground and not be forced to leave the church he loved, like Woodrow Elliot, with his tail between his legs, even if it meant he had to be handcuffed.

"Where all yo pepus at now?" Deacon Mallard said, continuing the unsympathetic barrage on the now seemingly helpless preacher.

"The Sheriff didn't give you but five minutes Reverend," Viney Abernathy said scolding Chauncey, urging him to go ahead and leave without a causing a scene.

"Don't tell him nothin Viney," Connie Maxwell added as he positioned himself next to the door he thought the preacher would be exiting. "Three of his minutes already gone and I'm countin for the Shaff."

"Don't you want to go on head and leave before they hand cuff you son?" Pickett said trying to expedite the departure of a man who still remained silent and relatively calm during the ordeal.

In the face of the Sheriff's blatant intimidation and Pickett's arrogant victory speech, Chauncey continued to stand still, staring the chairman directly in his face, saying not a word, only brewing hatred on the inside.

"Shaff you need to go ahead and handcuff him," Pickett urged.

"Yea, he ain't goin' no where," agreed Phillips who up to this point had remained relatively quiet.

"I agree Shaff" said Willie Mallard, getting another perfect opportunity to add his two cents without fearing a tongue lashing from the chairman or his designee.

Feeling that the deacons were undoubtedly in support of his timely comments, Mallard continued his Pickett like tirade. "He doin that same shakin and looking at pepus like he was doin Friday night Shaff. Ain't he ya'll?"

"Hush Willie!" Pickett shouted, getting fed up with Mallard's ignorant display of support.

"But I'm sked!" said the ill thought of deacon as he tried to explain himself.

"I tried to warn you Willie. You brought this on yo self," Pickett said as he hung his head in disappointment at Mallard's continuing self embarrassment. "Deputy, take him out the door. And oh take his wife out wit him, before her Alzheimer's starts kickin in."

After the Mallards were escorted out of the church, Sheriff Tally ordered his men to go ahead and handcuff the preacher, discerning that he wasn't going to leave otherwise. As the deputies came toward Chauncey, Jada re-entered the sanctuary and begged her husband to just leave on his own.

"Baby, he ain't gone listen. He don't never listen." Pickett softly said to Jada as if he was really concerned about her feelings. "He didn't listen to his bode either." He continued, provoking laughter from the remaining deacons and members.

"Jada go on out to the car," Chauncey said calmly, as he voluntarily put his hands behind his back. "Get Lizzy away from this hell hole. Let me handle this the only way I know how."

"How's that?" Pickett sarcastically countered. "Like the crooked fool you is." He continued as Maggie Ellis put her hands over her face to smother her boisterous expressions of amusement.

"No, Brother Chairman, like a man. Something you and the rest of these heathens wouldn't know anything about."

"Oh you still got a lil fight in you." Pickett said as he inched closer to the preacher, putting his right index finger as close as he could to his nose without touching him.

With his hands securely cuffed behind his back, Pickett knew that there was little Chauncey could do. But he did offer a summation of his feelings about the hostility they'd shown him.

"I not only have fight in me but what you've done to me hasn't taken God's word out of my heart and if God's word is true, all of you will have hell to pay. First Chronicles 16:22 should've been the only warning you needed not to mess with me"

"Is that a threat preacher?" asked Sheriff Tally as he ratcheted up pressure on Chauncey's handcuffs.

In visible agony and squirming to alleviate the pain brought on by his unwarranted seizure, and with his eyes beginning to turn bloodshot red, Jada looked on in horror and screamed dissonantly, as Chauncey mustered enough strength to finish the statement he previously directed at his oppressors.

"No, that's not a threat Sheriff. It's actually the Word of God. These deacons wouldn't know much about that either. The scripture says, touch not mine anointed and do my prophets no harm and if you think you don't have to pay for what you've done..." Chauncey was saying before an abrupt interruption.

Before he could finish his final statement and as Pickett and his boys looked at the preacher with "whatever" expressions, the sheriff, the deputies and the other participants of this spectacle, were taken totally off guard by the re-entry of Deacon Mallard, who ran back into the church with a pained look on his face, screaming and hollering. "Lawd Ha Mercy! Lawd, Lawd, Lawd Ha Mercy!'

"What is it Willie?" Pickett lividly asked.

"Lawdy Jesus, Lawd I'm so sorry Jesus," he continued his incensed shouting as he fell down at Chauncey's feet.

"Get yo ass up Willie!" shouted an angry Connie Maxwell as he pulled the short and stubby, bald, deacon from the floor by the back of his short sleeved dress shirt. "You better start talkin wit some sense befo I bust you in yo fohead. Now tell us what you talking bout."

As Chauncey stood in shock, watching the once arrogant deacons' worried interrogation of Mallard, who by this time was a bucket of tears, the front doors of the church flung open. A throng of people burst into the sanctuary led by the man the current sheriff only beat by less than three hundred votes in the last election. Leonard Maywhether had been contacted by Mother Snelling to add legitimacy to their claims that the vote to oust Pastor Pennington was fraudulent and that the sheriff had no jurisdiction to intervene in the matter.

"What are you doing here Maywhether?" asked Tally who was taken aback by the large crowd that had followed his noncompliant deputy into the sanctuary. "You ain't got no right to be here boy. I thank you best leave before you find yourself unemployed like this preacher."

"I didn't come as an officer of the law. I'm here as a concerned citizen who knows the law, and according to the by-laws of this church, what you and these people have done is wrong and you have no right to be here either Sheriff," said the young black deputy who aspired greatly to be sheriff to ensure that Tally's historic good ole boy policies would walk out the door with him once defeated. "This is a church matter. No crimes have been committed and these people have every right to defend their pastor."

"By-laws? What by-laws? You ain't got no copy of our by-laws. Only my deacons and a few of my trusted members have copies these by-laws. You lyin now son!" shouted Pickett who lost his cool in the heat of battle.

"Dees by-laws!" cried out a deep, goofy voiced, slow talking male, who couldn't be seen immediately because he was deep in the middle of the crowd. Holding the copy of the by-laws high in his hand as he moved to the front of the angry mass, Pickett recognized the fellow and fainted when he saw enough of the man's face to identify him.

"Hal!" shouted Clausell Ellis as Deacons Phillips and Maxwell rushed to the aid of their fallen chairman.

"Yea dis me!"

"What's wrong wit you boy? Do you know what you doin? You ain't gone never become no chairman after this."

"Maybe I won't Clausell. But I will save my marriage unlike you," the young deacon said to a thunderous applause as his wife, Tiffany, rubbed his back, solidifying her approval.

"Walter Pickett, you wake tale up!" shouted a feeble, but strong willed Mother Snelling. "Ain't nothin' wrong with you. You just shame. We done went over these by-laws and the way you and these deacons have handled this is all wrong."

"Shut up old lady!" shouted an angry Maggie Ellis. "You don't know what you talkin bout!"

"I tell you what!" shouted Lula Penny, who walked to the front of the crowd, being verbally confronted by Maggie's always defensive husband. "If you talk to the mother of this church like that again, Maggie, I'm gone snatch yo wig off and show these people that not only has Clausell beat all yo sense out, but he done beat all yo hair out too. You don't want to mess with me you old rooster pecked fool."

"As I was saying these bylaws do tell you how you can get rid of a pastor, and believe me, I know ya'll know how to do that." she said as Ruth Anne and Billy slowly walked her to the front of the church. "But Leonard showed us where they say somethin else too. I seen ya'lls paper, accusing this man, and if he's guilty he needs to go. But where you went wrong at is when you had that meeting to vote to get rid of him without first giving the chuch two weeks notice of the meeting. And according to the last page of these here bylaws, any such meeting of the congregation should also be announced in church by the church clerk at least two weeks in advance. Ya'll didn't do that cause ya'll knowed we wudn't go for that foolishness. Now Shaff, you take yo hands off my preacher and get out our church before I call on the Lawd to strike all you hellions down in ya mess."

Seeing Pickett was still out cold and his plan had utterly failed, Sheriff Tally thought to himself that his political future wasn't worth the gamble of meddling in this type of church drama. After removing Chauncey's handcuffs, much to the delight of Jada, who sobbed after his release, the sheriff signaled for his deputies to vacate the building, which garnered another thunderous applause. But before he walked out of the sanctuary, he pleaded with the demanding crowd, who he feared would vote against him in a little over a year, and apologized for his unintentional role in this big mess.

"Ladies and Gentlemen, I'm sorry about this." the sheriff said with his sincerest political voice, pulling off his tan cowboy hat and placing it over his heart as the formerly proud deacons and disgruntled members, all held their heads down in embarrassment. "Walter Pickett, who I once had a great deal of respect for, and those two men right over there" he said pointing at Phillips and Maxwell. "…gave me some very bad information about this preacher and this church that unfortunately led to all of this today. I'm a God fearin' man and I should be at my own church at Sunday school right now, and I'm just sorry for letting them fool me into believing that this was a legitimate dismissal. I beg all of you; don't hold this against me in the next election. Ya'll know I've been a good sheriff and have helped a lot of people, even people in this room," he bargained, with November 1998 on his mind. "God bless you all and oh, God bless the children."

After Tally solemnly walked out of the church, much to the chagrin of Pickett who was finally resurrected by some smelling salts given to him by a concerned but unforgiving Lula Penny, the debate, now one-sided in Chauncey's favor, continued.

"Befo ya'll make up ya'lls mind bout this preacher," Reasoned Connie Maxwell, who felt it necessary to clear the record, "ya'll need to know that everythang we put on dat paper is true bout him."

"Connie even if every word of that stuff ya'll put on that paper is true on that paper; and I don't thank it is," countered Mother Snelling, "it ain't nothing no more or nothing less than you and the rest of these deacons have done. If we gone start taking people out of their positions for the stuff ya'll had on that paper let's start with you and go on down the list. Jesus said, he who is without sin cast the first stone. And it's a shame what ya'll have done to this man and how you've made your own selves look."

As the arguing continued in the sanctuary, Chris ushered the pastor out of the church, finally removing him from the horrible scenes therewith, telling the pastor how sorry he was that they showed up so late. Once in the office Chris informed the pastor about the downed power line on Mother Snelling's road and assured Chauncey that his supporters had full control of the meeting now and this was a battle he no longer needed to fight. "Just stay back her with me pastor, Billy and them gone handle them deacons."

Not noticing that the pastor had already been removed from the fracas, the last of the enemy's ammunitions were dispersed.

"Mother Snelling you don't know this man like we do," said Viney Abernathy, who raised her voice to testify of a Chauncey Pennington that most of them hadn't seen. "That man ya'll love so much ain't no real preacher. This Friday he acted like a thug off the street," she continued.

"He shole did," agreed Eddie Phillips "He even told that man right over there," he continued, pointing toward Clausell Ellis "that he was gone whip him like he stole somp."

"He shole did do that. He threatened to kill me too and Maggie. Yes he did!"

"Somebody needed to threaten to kick yo behind you ole drunk," shouted an angry scraggly, obviously disguised voice deep in the crowd. "And stop messing with dem young gals up at that project too. Condoms ain't meant for no married deacon Clausell," the condescending voice continued to a smattering of applause and laughter.

"I tell ya'll what, if ya'll choose to follow that man after all he done did, you ain't never got to worry about seeing my face or my dues no mo round here."

"Mine either!" said Maggie, as a hush came over the room and people, including Phillips and Maxwell, begin to look at each other wondering why either of the Ellis' thought anyone would care if they never came back.

Finally coming to, Deacon Pickett stood slowly with the aid of his wife and said with a whisper, "Clausell, Maggie, shut up. Ya'll is more foolish than I gave you credit for. Hush!" he said as he slowly regained his strength and issued his last ditched attempt to overthrow the pastor.

"I've been doing this for a long time ya'll. I've seen some come and I've seen some go. If ya'll let this boy stay in charge he gone be trouble, big trouble. He don't listen to his bode ya'll," said the suddenly out of breath chairman, who slumped over the chair he previously sat in.

As Chauncey walked, somewhat victoriously, but humbly, back into the sanctuary with Chris and Jada by his side, the congregation cheered respectfully and some even wept as they thought about the disservice done to their totally innocent pastor. As some of the people began to hug the pastor and his wife, Jada and Chauncey too, wept at the outpouring of support received on this unforgettable day.

But out of the corner of his eye, Pickett noticed some of his faithful few as they begin to exit the sanctuary in defeat.

"Viney! Clausell! Where ya'll goin, this meeting ain't adjourned yet. I ain't had the last word. The chairman always spose to have the last word don't he? Ya'll don't leave! We can still win this thang." sobbed the overpowered, former dictator, as he wept uncontrollably. "I'm still the chairman, for God sakes. Don't walk out on yo chairman." he said as a few more of his subjugated followers gathered their belongings and left the sanctuary hastily. "Ya'll forgetting what the scripture say in Malachi 3:9," he continued as he slumped to the floor in despair. "Ya'll know it say don't ever leave yo chairman in a battle by his self."

"No Deacon Pickett that's not what it says," a chomping at the bits Billy Dunn calmly refuted. "That's actually one of my favorite scriptures and it says "that ye are cursed with a curse, for ye have robbed me and verse ten says, bring ye all the tithes into the storehouse that there may be meat in mine house and prove me now and see if I won't open up the windows and pour you out a blessing, something you never believed in."

As Pickett hung his head in defeat and clung to his two remaining faithful deacons, who vowed to die with him on the battle field, Ruth Anne Dunn gave the broken hearted deacon a glimmer of hope when she said, much to the surprise of everyone who heard her, "Deacon Pickett, I want to apologize to you. You were right and I should've trusted you more. I remember, a little over three years ago you and I had a conversation, standing almost in this very same spot we're in right now. It was after the meeting where you all got rid of Pastor Elliot.

Remember what you told me?" she asked preparing to refresh Pickett's withering memory.

"Naw."

"You said to me that night if you turned out to be right about the young man for Odessa, you wanted me to come back, not to apologize, but help build a greater Mount Carmel. Remember?" she said smiling as Pickett dropped his head in defeat as he remembered that day.

"Well you were right and though you didn't ask me for it, I feel I need to apologize. I was wrong and you were right. You wanted Pastor Pennington, I thought he was too young and I left this church in anger because you told us that night that you didn't want to interview anyone else and he was going to be the only candidate. I stand before you today to tell you personally that you made the best decision you've made in all the years that I've been associated with this church. Thank you for overriding my ill-informed judgment and bringing, to our church, the best pastor we've ever had," she said to the applause of many of the bystanders.

Being lifted up and accompanied to the door by Phillips and Maxwell as their wives bitterly walked behind them out of the sanctuary, Pickett shot off at the mouth for what Chauncey mistakenly thought would be his last time in this church.

"Ya'll can do what you wanna now, I done got too old to fight like this and my blood pressure done shot up. Reverend, good luck to you and these bastard heathens, and to be honest I ain't gone miss a damn thang bout none of ya'll. The hell with you all; God damn every, last one of you good for nothin sons of bitches."

"Walter Pickett, you just shut up while you still got a mouth you old ignant fool." said that same scraggly, obviously disguised voice from deep within the crowd. "All ya'll getting just what ya'll deserve. God say in his word that vengeance is mine."

"You shut up! I don't even know you Lady!" Pickett shouted back.

"Oh you know me Walter Pickett." said the woman who finally made her way to the front of the church. "I'm glad you done finally come to grips wit parting ways with this church," the woman said as Pickett turned around one last time to embarrass her. "Now maybe somebody can pastor this church without ya'll negroes on they back." She continued as she began to pull off what was clearly a bad wig, to the shock of an already anxious crowd. "But if it's any consolation to you, you'll be glad to know that even teeth and tongue fall out," the woman said as she threw her wig toward Pickett and unzipped her oversized dress. "And if you don't believe me ask my wife."

As the anxious crowd gasped then exhaled collectively, at full volume in utter shock and disbelief at what they'd just witnessed, Pickett weepingly muttered "Woodrow?" and then fainted again.

A man, who knew all too well, what Chauncey was going through, pulled off the remainder of his costume and walked up to the deacon as he lay lifelessly on the floor again and said in the coldest and most malicious voice he had, "Yea this me Brother Chairman. I told you yo time was coming. You had it coming to you and I'm glad I was able to see it wit my own two eyes. This meeting is adjourned, you old hellish fool. And oh, God bless Walter Pickett's soul."

Chapter 22

"Wait a minute; I need to say something and I want all of you to listen to me very carefully. And Pastor Elliott, if you would, I'd like you to stay as well," Chauncey said as Woodrow slowly averted his stealthy backdoor exit.

As I was sitting back there in my office," Chauncey declared, resuming his spontaneous message with measured authority, even though he knew his fierce rivals had been toppled. "God revealed to me a scripture that I never really understood the full meaning of until right now. Romans 8:28 says that "All things work together for good to them that love God, to them who are called to his purpose." "What happened here today was a divine orchestration by God to painfully prune us and purge us from people obviously controlled by the hand of Satan. But, this is not a time for us to glory in the fall of an adversary. This is a time for much prayer." Chauncey profoundly continued, as the faithful members of Greater Mt. Carmel looked on solemnly in the sanctuary.

"This situation has its purpose and I'm convinced that God wants this church to continue its upward path to holistic growth and development. And I'm also convinced that God needs some people who are dedicated to continuing that growth that I'm talking about. Now I don't want any of you to misunderstand me, but I must tell every one of you that's in reach of my voice, that this is a new day at Greater Mt. Carmel. This is a day that God has proven himself and I'm determined to do everything in my power to make sure that none of us ever have to endure what we endured today, ever again." he said as his authoritativeness became overwhelmingly clear.

"Like Joshua, I've made up my mind that as for me and my house we're gonna serve the Lord. And if it seems evil to any of you to walk in the vision that God has laid upon my heart for this church, you choose this day to walk out of here and never come back. And to be honest with you I believe, with every fiber of my being, that you've already chosen, by your actions here today, that you are ready to help this church reach its full potential. Because of all that's happened this morning, I'm going to cancel the services for today. I know this has been tough on most of you. But, I would like to extend an invitation, to all of you, to stay with me for a while and pray with me that we not be discouraged by what happened today nor be disappointed in the unfortunate acts of a few. It's my prayer that God give us the strength, as he did in the days of Nehemiah, to rebuild this church, from the inside out. Would you pray with me?"

As Lula begin to play softly, the chords of the old familiar hymn, Sweet Hour of Prayer, Chauncey knelt at the altar with Jada, who held his hand firmly in unwavering support. Others welcomed his invitation and, they too, knelt with their pastor, praying earnestly for God to continue the great work he'd began at Mt. Carmel. Even Leonard Maywhether, who wasn't even a member of the church, remained for the prayer vigil. Touched by the words of a man he barely knew, Maywhether was certain that this man knew God. As the prayers continued, Chauncey, with the aid of his wife, took anointed oil from his pulpit and begin to lay hands on every soul in the building, including those who misguidedly partook in Pickett's diabolic disservice. As he meandered through the petitioning crowd he came upon Harold Belford, who noticed the pastor's presence and stood to hug the man he had no idea could be so concerned about their lives.

"I'm sorry pastor," he said, as he laid his head upon the pastor's chest and wept for forgiveness. "Man, I want to do all I can to suppote you and what you doin'. Me and my family ready to suppote you."

"Harold, it's alright," Chauncey whispered as he hugged the once rebellious deacon. "It's O.K."

As Chauncey laid hands on Harold's forehead, Jada and Tiffany embraced respectfully before the pastor moved advantageously through the mass that called fervently upon the Lord to hear their humble cries. It was evident that the people of this church, on this particular morning, were as unified as one body could be. Their struggle had drawn them closer and in the midst of daunting challenges, a new pastor was born, a new family was born.

The outpour of support of the formerly embattled pastor was overwhelming. And if this massive number of people, who came out to defend him and pray with him, was any indication, one could appropriately deduce that Pastor Chauncey Evansworth Pennington was well on his way to the rarified air that preachers in small town North Florida only dreamed about.

Walter Pickett, on the other hand was as exhausted and embarrassed as he'd ever been in his entire life. He never would have thought, in a million years, that the church he loved so dearly would have ever consciously chosen to follow a pastor's leadership, rather than the strong leadership of the chairman of the board. Pickett was a pitiful sight as his wife and a few of his followers encouraged him not to "let them niggas up there run him off." They knew deep in their hearts that it would only be a matter of time before "that womanizing, adulterous, dope pushin' thief of a preacher" would bankrupt the church's account and send "all them lustin heffas runnin back" to the Chairman for his brand of proven leadership.

"I know. They gone see it. Mark my word, By and By they gone see it." Pickett said reasoning with himself that the people at Mt. Carmel would soon see the big mistake they'd made. "And if they thank I'm gone just come back up there to straighten that mess out they got anotha thang comin. As long as I live, I ain't neva settin another foot in that church unless I'm recognized as the leader."

"Brother Chairman," Connie Maxwell said with concern in his voice. "I know how you feelin, but they ain't runnin me off. I'm gone stay there till he make a ass out his self. It gone happen, just wait and see, and when it do, I want to be there to tell all um, I told ya'll so."

"Connie you can do what you want to do." Pickett responded unconvinced. "But it's gone be a cold day in hell before I go back up there to try to help out. I know he gone fall too, and when he do, I don't want my name nowhere in it. As for as I'm concerned I'm still the chairman…"

"That's right," they all agreed, continuing their encouragement of the man who now had an, obviously bruised ego.

"Yea, I'm still the chairman and I guarantee that before it's all over, I'm gone have the last word."

How true Pickett's guarantee or predictions of failure would be, is yet to be determined, but one thing remained etched in stone, Walter S. Pickett was as serious about never returning to Mt. Carmel as long as Pennington remained pastor as he was about trying to get rid of "that ole forked tongued bastard."

As Maxwell tried to convince the ill fated members, who'd been beaten badly by their foes, to return to the church with him, most of Pickett's followers were as determined not to return as their leader was, including Eddie Phillips who vowed to immediately move his membership to The Holy Rock Church of Faith International World Wide Ministry of the One and Only True and Living God, led by the founder, pastor, teacher, and overseer Bishop A.W. Tinyhill.

"Eddie, A.W. Tinyhill is bout as dumb as that Billy goat out there cross that field." Pickett said, criticizing Eddie's apparent misconception that moving his membership will solve his problems.

"Walter you might be right bout that" rebutted Eddie Phillips. But I'd rather try to lead a dummy than try to lead somebody who thank they know it all. I ain't never gone be no part of another church where a preacher thanks he know more than a deacon, not no more. They goin gainst everything the word of God say bout his deacons. Ever since I can remember, the deacons done been in charge of the business dealings of the church. The bible say that is the right way. That's why I'm goin over there with Tinyhill. I know he old, and he may be stupid but, at least he the type of preacher that expect his deacons to lead him."

"Eddie, go on and do what you thank is best for you and Connie you do what you thank is best for you. Frankly, I just don't even care what none of ya'll do no more. Ain't none of ya'll ever got to worry about me tryin to help out no more. Do it ya'lls way." Pickett said in frustration over his followers' betrayal of his commands. "But, as of this the nineteenth day of October in the year of ourva Lord nineteen hundud and ninety seven, I Walter S. Pickett declare that both of ya'll is crazy as hell, and I already knew neither one of you ain't had much sense when I made you deacons." he continued as he stood up and angrily scolded the two men he once considered his greatest allies. "Get out of my house and I don't care if none of ya'll come back!"

"Now Walter you don't have to act like that toward Eddie and Connie."

"Eloise, Shut up!"

"Whatever I choose to do from here on out, I'm gone do by myself. That's what the bible say anyway. First Peter 35:6 say, "He that want it done right must do it by himself." That's the Word. Now if you will excuse me, I'd like to get drunk by myself. God bless all of ya'll. And oh, God bless any man that thank he can make a fool outta Walter S. Pickett and get way wit it."

Pickett was defeated and badly bruised in his encounter with a man he mistakenly thought he could control because of his lack of pastoral experience. But the people who knew him best, worried not about his inflammatory and discomforting outburst, because they understood that a man with as much pride as Walter, would bounce back and bounce back with vengeance.

On the other hand Chauncey, now back home in the comfortable confines of his theatre styled den, sharing quietness after the storm with his wife and daughter, thought internally about his victory and like a proven warrior, relished in his outing as the new man "in charge" at Mt. Carmel.

"Chauncey, I was really proud of you today," Jada said as she proudly stoked the back of her husbands head. "You stood your ground and even though I was afraid of how all of this would turn out, you proved to me once again how great you are."

As Lizzy combed her Barbie doll's hair, Chauncey stared into open space as he thought intensely about the future of a ministry now firmly and undeniably in his control.

"Did you hear me baby?" Jada asked, trying to spark a response.

"Yea, I heard you. I was just thinking though. With those hellions finally put in check, maybe I can finally move this church to the place I know God wants it to be."

"The people showed you today that they want your leadership. I doubt if Pickett or any of those other deacons will ever show up again after how bad they made themselves look today."

"Jada, mark my word, they may not be back this Sunday and it may not even be the rest of this year, but they're coming back. I know they are. I don't know when, but I do know that when they do show up they're gonna meet a man they wish they'd never touched."

"What do you mean by that?"

"Just what I said Jada. It will be a cold day in hell before they ever take advantage me again. Those people have made me who I am. They made me bitter and angry. They made me cold hearted toward them."

"Chauncey, you're not cold hearted. You're just a little angry and…"

"Listen Jada. You really don't know all that I've been through. You don't know how hurt I've been over the past three years. I've been in warfare for three years by myself with men who had no other purpose but to make my life a living hell. Those deacons almost caused me to loose my mind, my family for God's sake. I don't have any place in my heart for any of them and I'm praying, for their sakes, that they don't ever provoke me to have to do or say anything that I might regret."

"That's not you Chauncey. You're bigger than that." Jada said as she chuckled, hoping her husband wasn't serious about his hateful expressions of disdain.

"Oh yes it is. I'll never be so foolish again in my life. I won't ever allow another man's blatant disregard for me to go unnoticed."

"Hold that thought Tarzan, let me see who this is" she said, as the phone begin to ring.

"Pennington residence." answered a perky Jada, who picked up the phone after only the first ring.

"Hi, First Lady Pennington, this is Leonard Maywhether. I was at the church today."

"Oh, Ok."

"Is it any way possible that I may speak with the Pastor?"

"Sure, hold on just a sec," Jada said before whispering to Chauncey "it's Leonard Maywhether," while looking as though she couldn't possibly know what he wanted.

"Leonard Maywhether…" Chauncey answered cheerfully, finally having an opportunity to personally thank the Sheriff's deputy for his role in his Sunday morning victory. "Man I want to thank you for what you did today. What happened for me and the people at Mt. Carmel wouldn't have been possible without you. Man we're all very grateful and forever indebted to you."

"Well Pastor I really appreciate that, but that wasn't why I was calling."

"O.K. Talk to me."

"I was calling to tell you that you really inspired me today. I had been to your church a couple of times before and I've always loved to hear you preach, but today was different. Pastor Pennington, I want to personally tell you that when you stood still in the face of those people, you showed me that real leadership still exists in this part of the world."

"Hey, I really appreciate that Maywhether, I really do."

"Yea, I was just standing there watching you. I didn't say much but I was watching you and I thought to myself that these people over here really don't know what they have. Pastor you are a jewel to this community and I'm praying that you stay steadfast and unmovable and never allow anybody to make you leave here."

"No… man, I'm here to stay and nothing or nobody will be able to come between me and what God promised me this church will be. You can count on that."

"I know you're probably worn out by now, so I'm gonna make this quick. When you called all of your people together today and begin to pray this morning, I was moved and it almost felt like I was one of your members. When I came home I told my wife that it had to be God because I would never think about leaving my chuch. But, Pastor this feeling just won't leave me and I've talked it over with my wife. We want to become members of your church if you'd have us. I see your vision, man, and my wife and I just want to help out in any way possible."

"Leonard, my wife and I, along with all of the members of our church would be more than happy to welcome you and your family into ours. I, personally, count it as an honor that you would even consider our ministry after what you witnessed today."

"Pastor, let me explain something to you. It was what I saw today and what I heard today that made me understand how valuable you are to this community and I don't want Sheriff Tally, Walter Pickett, or nobody else to mess up what I know God is trying to do around here. I guess you know that I lost to Sheriff Tally when I ran for Sheriff three years ago, but you give me hope that things are about to start changing around here and I want to help in any way I can to make sure that change takes place. Thank you for welcoming me and I'll see you on Wednesday night."

"Thank you Leonard, I'll see you on Wednesday and I'm glad that I can call you the newest member of our team."

Chapter 23

With the departure of Walter Pickett and his cronies and the arrival of Leonard Maywhether and his family, 1997 ended better than Chauncey ever could've imagined especially considering how tumultuous much of the year had already been. It was evident that things had begun to change in a positive way, for the most part in Northern Florida. And with a little tweaking of the existing ministry layout, Greater Mt. Carmel was only a few years and a few more members away from becoming the areas first mini mega church. With most of his hellions gone and Connie Maxwell silent due to his stricken role as one of the "leaders of the church", Chauncey had the leeway to make the much needed, adjustments immediately and he did; beginning with a, seemingly, smooth transition in the music ministry.

Being a charismatic people person, it was easy for Chauncey to convince the people of Mt. Carmel that a change was needed and though bruising her ego temporarily, he even convinced life long church musician, choir director, and song leader, Lula Penny that her services would be better utilized in another capacity, maybe even as the new church administrator. Initially Lula did everything she possibly could to persuade the pastor that she could be both a full-time minister of music and work in another capacity at the church, but she failed badly, not having a clue that Chauncey's mind was already made up. Connie Maxwell tried to disrupt Lula's loyalty and participation in the transition and almost succeeded by telling her that this was just the pastor's underhanded way of getting rid of her for better musicians, but after a long heartfelt conversation with the pastor she agreed to move graciously to another area of ministry in spite of what she initially perceived was an attempt to appease the "younger crowd".

In a way Maxwell was right about the pastor's intentions, because in his heart of hearts, Chauncey had always pondered the thought of hiring a more accomplished full-time music minister. But wisdom always led him to patiently wait for the right season to make the changes that he knew, though met with some uncertainty, would eventually be greeted with acceptance and understanding by his loyal supporters.

Now was that season and with one stroke of his administrative pen four new positions were created and for the first time ever Mt. Carmel had a church administrator, though Lula accepted her new role with a bit of skepticism, and a dynamic band to accompany what had quickly become one of the area's largest and best sounding choirs. Keyboardist, Evelyn Graves, guitarist, Tommy Riles, and drummer, Bruce Cameron, were all welcomed additions to the ministry. And coupled with Chauncey's charismatic style of preaching, Mt. Carmel began to jump like "we use to do in the night club" and was a magnet for anyone who desired a fresh and flavorful alternative to the old way of doing church.

Changes in the music ministry were only a small element of what really caused the church's massive overhaul. Much of the difference came in the form of a brand new style of church leadership. Chauncey knew that if the ministry was to flourish in this new season, he had to maximize his opportunity to lead and administrate while he had the chance, in the absence of the folk who formerly damned everything he tried to get accomplished.

He began by banning the often volatile, monthly church conference meetings. These meetings were predominantly fruitless and rarely attended by authentic parishioners who genuinely desired church growth and development. And for the most part, monthly conference was Pickett's soap box; his opportunity to show the pastor who was really boss and a place where it was O.K. to use distasteful language in the sanctuary as long as you were making a good point or telling the pastor "if you keep showin' out you ain't gone been round much longer".

With conference meeting officially outlawed, people like Deacon Connie Maxwell no longer had a platform to cause visionless disturbances. And because much of their voice had been stripped away, through the striking of the illicit meeting, many chose to fade in the sunset of the old Mt. Carmel and joined other church congregations who thought, as they did, that conference meeting was "instituted by Jesus Christ himself" and that "it was a sin if you didn't do it at least once a month". Just the mere fact that a meeting designed specifically to argue over church business was discontinued was impact enough to change Mt. Carmel's image in the community and when word got back to Walter Pickett that the "best part of being a Christian" had been done away with by his arch nemesis, he replied with a grin "now I know it won't be long before all hell break loose."

Pickett's response was primarily based on the warped premise that deacons were ordained by God to be the administrators of church business and that conference meeting was the place where all final decisions, financial disclosures, and future direction of the church was revealed to the congregation. Thus, if there is no conference meeting "Them negroes up there is gone be lost." because they no longer had the right to help shape the church's vision or control the pastor's hand especially as it related to his dealings with church finance.

One member, said angrily just before she left the pastor's office after storming in to ask for her official letter of withdrawal of membership, "If the business of the church won't be done in the open you must be trying to cover up something and I won't give another cent to this church as long as you thank you is the only one with some sense round here. Something is wrong and sooner or later God gone reveal all the stuff that you and the rest of these devils who followin' you is doin'".

The truth of the matter was Chauncey, along with the majority of the Carmelites, knew that conference meetings only led to church turmoil and now was as perfect a time as any to implement a new administrative layout, which put the deacons' roles into biblical perspective and fostered more involvement from the laity. The new staff, which consisted of twelve tithing members, included the heads of all church ministries and the deacons' ministry which now looked totally different with the additions of three of Chauncey's trusted young men.

The additions of Billy Dunn, Chris Blocker and Leonard Maywhether to the previously diminutive "deacon's board" added validity and substance to a band of brethren once deemed the "thrust of chaos at Mt. Carmel". Although Connie Maxwell declined the pastor's half hearted invitation to participate in the churches new administration and a recently discovered aggressive brain tumor prohibited Deacon Mallard's full participation, the new organizational structure was a hit with the congregation and Harold Belford kept his word to support the pastor's new direction.

The deacons now had a newly defined bible based role, which was to administer benevolence to the needy in the church and community and aid the pastor in all areas that would lighten his burdens for purposes related to the preparation needed to preach and teach the congregation of Greater Mt. Carmel. Leonard Maywhether relished his new role as a deacon at, arguably, the fastest growing church in North Florida and in many ways being an ordained servant in what was quickly becoming a respected spiritual institution aided his quest to become the county's first black and youngest Sheriff ever. And by mid 1998 he was in a heated battle with the man who narrowly defeated him just four years earlier. And with Chauncey's influential support and the church's strong backing, Maywhether was giving the incumbent Sheriff Augustus Tally the fight of his life again and if the local polls were good indicators, by the first Tuesday in November of 1998, Mt. Carmel would be proud participants in Maywhether's, inaugural festivities, which would prove to be exactly the case.

On Tuesday, November 3, 1998, Leonard, indeed, became the new Sheriff in town, shocking all that had previously doubted his candidacy and making history in a county, which had only known the lily white, good ole boy, style of law enforcement. As the news of the colossal upset seeped down the courthouse steps to a premature, celebratory crowd that was waiting to crown Tally Sheriff for a record seventh term, jubilation abruptly turned into despair and the once incomparable Sheriff Augustus Federal Tally had officially been dethroned as the county's top man by a "boy" he laughed at when he said "I'm running for sheriff".

Tally was so depressed after his stunning defeat that late that evening, after several beers and a few shots of aged whiskey, he had to be rushed to the hospital for what turned out to be an overnight stay to be treated for symptoms of severe depression brought on by what he knew "had to be a fixed election". Tally was defeated by Maywhether, much like his old buddy Walter had been dethroned by Chauncey only a year earlier and if there was any commonality in both of their surprising defeats, it was that Chauncey's persuasive people skills and influence in the community played an essential role.

By spearheading the campaign that led to Leonard's election Chauncey Pennington was now, not only recognized as the leader of the premier church in the area, but also as a political powerhouse who respectfully produced, through his empowered ministry, young men and women who sought to change an area that, Pre-Pennington, was on life support due to the misguided deeds of the "powers that were". Pickett found out, those hellish deacons found out, and now it was Tally's turn to feel the wrath that had become known by townspeople as "Camp Pennington."

Shortly after realizing that his dream to retire as the most powerful man in the county was temporarily on hold, civilian A.F. Tally made amends with those he had arrogantly discarded as worthless to his campaign and called several to begin his run at redemption to garner any support he'd evidently lost over the past three years. One man he had to call immediately was Walter Pickett. Pickett may have been a thorn in Chauncey's flesh, but one thing was certain in the eyes of Tally, "as long as Pickett was in charge at Mt. Carmel", he could always count on the "black vote" to secure his election victories. With Pickett now out of power and with Leonard Maywhether now a solid supporter and leader in the influential congregation, primarily due to Tally's ill-fated involvement in Pickett's unsuccessful attempt to overthrow Chauncey, the former Sheriff now knew that if he was to regain the position that made him feel like he was the "most powerful man in the universe" he had to work alongside Pickett, the once "most powerful man in the black community", to chip away at Chauncey's glossy, goody two shoes image by uncovering the imperfections that could lead to the resurrection of both their egos and respectability in the county.

Making an early morning phone call, Tally made a plea to Pickett, that if met with a positive response, could change the public perception of the "pesky preacher" and turn the small rural county, now firmly in the grasp of Pastor Pennington, upside down.

"Walter," the former Sheriff pitifully called out to his friend during a post election December conversation. "Now I see why you wanted to get that preacher out. He's done got too big for his britches. If this type of stuff continues round here we gone be in for some big trouble."

"Tally, I don't mean no harm, but I tried to tell you and everybody else bout this boy but ya'll didn't listen. I never thought it would come down to this between me and you but, as of this day…"

"I get the point Walter."

"Well, I don't know if you and me have nothin to talk about," Pickett said preparing to abruptly hang up the phone on the man he once was proud to call a friend.

"Wait a minute Walter. I know what I did was wrong in your eyes but I couldn't afford to go through with that plan, especially after all those people showed up with a copy of them by-laws."

"That ain't what I'm mad about Tally!" Pickett quickly and bitterly responded. "You left me in the middle of that church by myself and you shoulda knowed it was gone come back to bite you in the ass. The word of God say in Romans 43:21 that "what goes around, come right back around." and you found that out when all them people who you thought loved you turned they back on you when you got the hell beat out you by Maywhether. I heard bout how you was up there at the courthouse falling out and shit. You shoulda been thanking bout how you did me."

"Listen Walter;" Tally apologetically rebutted. "I'm sorry for how all that worked out when you tried to get him out the first time but I ain't the sheriff no more, if you know what I mean."

"Naw I don't know what you mean Tally." Pickett answered still angry by Tally's "too little too late" phone call.

"That means I ain't got to do it by the book no more. And between me and you and only between me and you, if you want to get back to where you was before he came here like I do, you'll help me get rid of him once and for all. With your help, Walter, I know that we can hang his ass up by the shoe strangs of his church shoes and make him wish he had never come here in the first place. You know what I mean?

"I hear you." Pickett said, now listening with an inquisitive ear. "Keep talkin'." he said as he sipped his strong dark black coffee.

"Now Walter, listen to me, I still got major connections with law enforcement and I just took a job as a consultant with the Florida Bureau of Investigation. If I have my way we won't have to kill him to get rid of him, naw that'll be too easy."

"What's yo plan then Tally?"

"Put it this way, I'm in a good position to make his life a living hell and before 2002 he'll be sorry that he ever brought his ass to our county."

Revealing his iniquitous strategy to the still bitter and ill willed deacon, the suddenly anticipatory Tally gave Pickett hope that what he had felt about his former pastor all the long would soon be uncovered for all his supporters to see.

"As God is my witness, I'm runnin' for sheriff again, and with your help the next time won't turn out like this time. That's a promise"

"Count me in. That's a plan I can help you wit. You just don't get sked like you did when it was my plan."

Although anxiety, trepidation, and gloom appropriately defined much of what Pickett and Tally were going through toward the end of 1998, Chauncey's year was being defined by the antithesis of those words. He was experiencing a high he never dreamed imaginable after Leonard's upset victory over the unmovable Tally and his own magician like escape from the jaws of the ferocious lions formally known as Mt. Carmel's deacon's board. His marriage once strained by the travails of traumatic ministry experiences was now thriving again and with God's restorative power the couple had transformed into almost the mirror image of what they once were. Life was good now, but they would soon find out that the sun was never meant to shine forever. Just as the sun rises it would surely fall again and the night would stake claim to what the sun had owned only in hours passed.

When Aunt Eunice was asked about Chauncey's sudden development into one of the areas most influential people she responded. "1998 was probably the best year he ever had in Florida. He had finally worn down those folks that had gave him so many problems and for a change I saw him happy to be where he was and he wasn't stressed out all the time, you know? He was happy. But then…I just don't know…"she said as she wiped her brow wondering how things could change so dramatically in such a short period of time. "All hell just break loose."

CHAPTER 24

With the winter slowly turning into spring and life favorably shining upon the Penningtons in every possible way, the beginning 1999 figured to be a carbon copy of what had turned out to be a fantastic end to 1998. For the most part ministry was status quo and from their outer expressions and behaviors, Chauncey and Jada seemed as happy as they'd ever been since moving south. But though good times camouflaged the couple's marital ills from the public's glare, good times were not enough to hide the cracks in their marriage from them.

Chauncey, because of his more important roles in the community, had even fewer opportunities to spend quality time with his wife and daughter. And though the stressfulness of his pastorate had lessened to minuscule levels, Chauncey still exhibited stressfulness over his lack of quality time with his family. When he'd have a moment to unwind with Jada, Jada would be busy working overtime at a place where her roles were becoming important. But, though she worked in an environment that she was becoming more important in, that environment had become increasingly more difficult to work in. Jada was hiding something. She had become less interactive with Chauncey and he noticed slight changes in her demeanor. She was more reserved now, less touchy feely now and didn't feel comfortable at all about talking with Chauncey about this most sensitive issue. She didn't think she was showing her inner anguish and she thought she was quite proficient in masking her true emotions, but Jada had a "little work issue" that made Chauncey believe that something wasn't quite right; a feeling that sparked some heated debates in the Pennington house.

No one other than Chauncey had really recognized it, but for a little while now she'd experienced a bit of uneasiness that if handled properly, should not have caused any major threats to life as she knew it. But handling it properly meant telling her husband and telling Chauncey wasn't an option because he'd already shown instability and lack of control when faced with challenging circumstances. So Jada's "little work issue" was her personal battle that up to this point was a battle she was undoubtedly in control of. But one day real soon her lack of confidence in Chauncey's ability to react rationally to challenging circumstances and her unfortunate failure to alert him of her bouts of work related emotional distress would come back to haunt her marriage, their ministry, and all but halt her flourishing career as an in demand, soon to be promoted educator.

It was a misnomer to many and unfathomable to others but, Jada Pennington, the proud pastor's wife, was struggling to hold her emotions together and on a blustery, moist, late February, Thursday afternoon, what she was so proficient at masking would cause a colossal unraveling and forever change the way she looked upon life and the way life looked upon her.

"Mrs. Pennington?" called out Rosa, the beautiful school secretary, to Jada's classroom on the school's modernized telephone based intercom system as students, teachers, and staff prepared for the pre-scheduled, twelve noon, early dismissal bell to ring.

"Yes Ma'am," she answered as she quieted students who were eagerly waiting for their five minutes to freedom to pass so that they might begin their three and a half day weekend induced by a county wide teacher's planning day.

"Mr. James asked me call you and inform you that there will be a special principal's training meeting going on tomorrow at the district office that you need to attend instead of coming here."

"OK, I kinda figured I would need to go over there." she said, dreading another long, boring, lecture series designed to train up and coming school administrators.

"He also wants you to stop by his office on the way out to review the results from the standardized pre-tests."

"Are they back already?"

"Yes ma'am they are back. Matter of fact I'm on the way to the district office to pick up ours now. By the time you're ready to leave I'll be back with them and the review will only take a minute or so."

"Alright then, I'll see you around twelve thirty."

As she contemplated why she hadn't been told in advance of her expected attendance at the normally calendared principal's training, she also contemplated what Adolph James could possibly think of today to let slip out of his disgustingly flirtatious mouth. Jada had known for a while now that James was somewhat attracted to her but, she never thought in a million years that he would ever muster up enough guts to actually "try me like that."

Shocked by his increasingly vulgar pursuit of her, Jada initially seemed a bit disheveled, but after consistently, constantly, and up until now successfully declining her boss' periodic, inappropriate offers to be "more than just a friend" she felt like she had the situation under control.

When all of James' flirtations began she told no one because she was too ashamed and to be honest she was exceptionally hurt. But then her reasons for silence became more personal. She didn't want to ever be viewed as being akin to Regina Eubanks, the last school secretary who shamefully resigned after unsuccessfully bringing charges of sexual harassment against the flamboyant principal with the "pine sol" clean image. After hearing of what happened to poor Regina who was humiliated in the public square, there was "no way in hell" she would risk her family's reputation or their livelihood for something as fruitless as Adolph James' failed attempts to lure her into infidelity; after all he had never physically abused her, even though in the beginning his words cut like a knife into the core of her consciousness. She had this one under control and over the past few weeks it seemed as though James had finally gotten the point and much to Jada's surprise, he actually lessoned his pursuit enough that she naively felt comfortable again in his presence.

Even though she had previously battled a myriad of emotional distresses, over time she essentially became accustomed to James' now laughable antics and attributed them to "just a result of a major character flaw"; and all of us have at least one. And her reason for not telling the world shifted from being; too ashamed and too fearful of ridicule to plain ole feeling sorry for the old man, who must have been painfully undersexed at home. Jada's silence was her way of proving to herself that she was definitely able to fend for herself in spite of being only 5'5 one hundred and thirty five pounds, but to James that very silence was a signal that the preacher's wife was weakening under his mental pressure and was finally opening the pathway to enter parts of her that he knew for sure "only the preacher had tasted."

No one had ever really viewed James' favor towards Jada as a way of showing his underlying affection for her or questioned his rationale for being so adamant about seeing that she become the school's next assistant principal, after all she was arguably the sole reason for Great Pines Elementary school's sudden resurgence from the states failing schools list. But James knew something they didn't know and if he had his way things between he and Jada would definitely heat up just as soon as "that old tired, tell the superintendent everything", Liz Caldwell retires and Jada moves into her new office only a stones throw away from the office of the "head man in charge".

With most of the campus cleared due to the early dismissal and Rosa out fetching pre-test scores, Jada was now cornered like hunted prey, susceptible to James' renewed vigor for his opportunity to land a woman he wanted to touch badly. And although Jada had successfully fended him off in the past and viewed him as only a pitiful, horny old man, this day would prove to be much more than another futile attempt by James to get into her panties. No this day would be the beginning of the fight that she would ultimately take to her grave.

"I'd forgotten that you were getting off early today," Chauncey said to Jada in a phone conversation just before she prepared to leave her classroom to meet briefly with Mr. James.

"Yea but, I have to stay over a little while. Our pre-test results came in today and I just need to review them before we leave because, I won't be able to do it tomorrow because I just found out that I'll have to go to that darn principal's training at the district office."

"What time are you going to get home?"

"1:00 at the latest. It's just a review session and it'll only take fifteen minutes or so.

"What's up?"

"Well I was thinking that since you were going to be home early that you might go with me to my Shared Services Network meeting at the capitol."

"You mean to tell me that you want little ole me to go with you to a meeting with all those big wigs in Tallahassee?" she said jokingly with an appreciative smile on her face.

"Yes baby. I would take you every where I went if you weren't working all the time."

"I know Chauncey I was just joking. I'll go with you."

"Now Jada, you need to be here no later than 1:15 because it'll take us at least forty-minutes to get to the capitol through all of that lunch hour traffic."

"Ok, I'll be there Chauncey. Just call Daphne and see if she can keep Lizzy. She gets out of class early today too doesn't she?

"I don't think so, but I'll call to make sure. Better yet," he continued, abruptly having a change of plans, "Lizzy can just go with us and we can make a family date out of it. Maybe catch a movie or something after the meeting. That'll be better than just sitting around the house all day being bored."

"Alright, I'll be home by no later than one. You guys be ready when I get there."

"That's a deal. Give me some sugar."

"Get of the phone boy. The sooner I get to the office the sooner I'll be home. I'll see you by 1:00, I promise. I love you." she said as she smiled at the thought of a renewed romance with the man she'd always adored.

"By 1:00 and I love you too."

Not exactly looking forward to her little review session with Rosa and Mr. James, Jada gathered her things together, grabbed her black leather Louis Vuiton handbag, flipped the lights off, closed her door, existed the classroom, and strutted down the hallway, thinking of the afternoon she was about to spend with her husband and "growing into a little lady" daughter.

With a smile on her face, she breathed in the cool crisp air in the breezeway that led to the school's administration wing without a care in the world. She knew that her meeting with James would be brief and with the knowledge that James' inappropriate behavior had all but ceased and the assurance that Rosa was sticking around to help out, she felt confident that she wouldn't have to endure another psychological assassination which would all but obliterate a day that up to this point had been beautiful in spite of the dark, heavy, clouds and sporadic ice cold rain that could've spoiled anyone's day. With her mind at ease and her conscious clear she entered the administration building not even noticing that Rosa had yet to return and poised herself for her brief encounter with the pitiful man she once revered.

Knocking on the principal's opened door and brimming with confidence, Jada smiled just before asking if it was Ok if she came in. Whirling his auburn colored, leather winged back office chair around from his computer desk, James invitingly offered Jada to come in and have a seat to wait for Rosa to return with the pre-test results.

"I thought she would've been back by now but you know how Rosa is." James said as he boyishly grinned, knowing full well he had also sent Rosa on a fruitless expedition for school supplies that would take at least another thirty minutes to an hour.

As he stared into the eyes of the woman he desired so badly to be physically involved with, Jada intentionally rummaged through her purse to avert his undesired attention.

"If she's not back in a few minutes I'll let you go on home even though I don't want to." he said, turning up the heat slightly, much to the amusement of Jada.

"How well do you think we did on the test this time around? Jada said, as she childishly chomped on the piece of gum she had just pulled from her purse, now staring back at James in a blatant way to forewarn him that this time will be no different than the last time he tried to commandeer her affection.

"Well Jada, with people like you on my staff, I know we did as well as we did last year. How about a glass of wine?" he asked abruptly, trying desperately to transition the conversation into one with a sexual overture.

"Now you know I don't drink Mr. James and neither should you. It's bad for your health and besides, you know it's against school policy to even have alcohol on the premises," she said as she carried out her strategic plan to make James feel as though his inappropriate advances had no affect on her. It had worked in the past and seeing that he was putting his wine glasses away made her falsely secure that her counterfeit confidence was wearing the old man down.

"Now what if I turned out to be like Mrs. Caldwell and told the Superintendent about your little stash. You know you know better; don't you?" she continued, treating the "head man in charge" like he was a mischievous little boy.

"I know you won't do that. You're like Rosa. You look out for me. Besides, if you were ever gonna tell anything you would've told by now don't you think?" he said referring to her inability to reveal to anyone that he had made reprehensible remarks to her in the past.

"I guess you're right." she said as she repulsively shook her head and looked down at her watch, carefully noting the time so she wouldn't be late for her date with Chauncey.

"You really do have your way with men; don't you?" James said, taking her lack of fight as evidence that Jada had fell for his sucker punch.

"What do mean Adolph James?"

"That statement was self explanatory baby. I mean…you can make a man do whatever the hell you want him to do if you wanted to."

"What do you mean by that?" she confidently asked, not fearing the conversation would lead to any further inappropriate behavior. After all she was in control and had been for a while now and felt comfortable conversing with James because she knew that at any moment Rosa would be walking through the door and if not she wasn't obligated to stay, ending what she had often internally referred to as "another of his little moments."

"Well baby it's just something about you." he said as Jada placed her hand over her forehead and chuckled, asking herself "how embarrassed does he have get before he stops making a fool out of himself".

"You know you got that thang about you. You're nice to look at, you always smell so good, and it seems like to me you're getting better with time. You know what I mean? It's like I can't get you out of my head and just looking at you makes me want to come over there lay you down on that couch and give you what I got."

"What?" Jada said in sheer astonishment. Have you lost your mind Mr. James?"

Now rethinking her previous assumption that her strategy of forged resilience had caused James desires to deteriorate and feeling that Rosa's return might come a little too late, Jada chose to initiate another mercy killing of James' unwelcomed advances to prevent a potentially devastating display of embarrassing behavior. In a way, Jada was too kind for her own good and her well thought out preservation of James' integrity and reputation would eventually lead to a brief degeneration of her own.

"I really have to be going now." she continued. "I need to be at my house to meet my husband in the next fifteen minutes; so if you will excuse me..."

The very reference of pastor Pennington's name used to make the principal's bones rattle, but James wasn't fearful of being found out because he had figured out over time, that Chauncey couldn't possibly know all that was going on at Great Pines Elementary because, if he did he would have felt some reverberations of his misdeeds by now and because he hadn't, Adolph James figured there must be a reason behind her silence. So he had no problem pressing his way through her intentional mention of her husband and interrupted her just as she was about to conclude what she thought would be her closing statement.

"Wait a minute Jada." he said in the sexiest voice he could utter, abruptly jumping up from his chair, smiling like a cheetah as if he had just told a misunderstood bad joke.

"Now you ain't got to leave because of what I said. I'm just havin' a little fun with you baby. You know that."

"No. That doesn't bother me at all." Jada said with a puckered brow as she reached down for her purse, preparing to walk out of the principal's office.

Now standing in front of James brown leather love seat which was primarily used for parent conferences and the like, Jada continued her statement with a swagger that bruised Adolph James' ego so bad that she permanently crossed the line of boss employee relationship much like James had done a year earlier and breached the man's confidence so bad that she set off the time bomb that was formed in his heart from the very day he met her. With her hands on her hips, Jada brought forth a voice of determination that few had ever heard before and with a forced smile on her face she unleashed words that she had harbored from the moment she unfortunately was made aware of James' psychotic yearning.

"Mr. James since I've been here, I've only tried my hardest to be an educator, a professional. And from the day I stepped foot on this campus you've tried your hardest to break me down like you've broken down several other women around here. Unlike Rosa or Regina or some of these other women, I refuse to allow you or anybody else for that matter to continue to disrespect my marriage, my body or my mind. I'm telling you right now, today you're going to stop and if you don't'..."

"Are you trying to threaten me Mrs. Pennington?" James said, quickly interrupting Jada's attempt to finally speak her mind as he pulled out an empty tape recorder with seriousness now etched on his face.

"Are you trying to blackmail me?" he said as the tone of his voice escalated to a feverish pitch. "Bitch I told you I was just playing!" he continued as he aggressively charged toward the door that Jada's back was now pressed up against with the miniature tape recorder firmly in his grasp. "I done been through this kinda shit before."

Jada, now in utter shock and distress, now knew that she had bitten off more than she could chew when it came down to her choice not to tell Chauncey about what was really going on and her worst fears were quickly turning into a reality that she had hoped she'd never have to face. With her eyes turning red from the anger that she tried desperately to control, Jada prayed that Rosa would walk through those doors before it was too late and quietly urged James to calm down, trying to persuade him that she wouldn't tell a sole if he "just let me leave now."

"I know you ain't gone tell nobody 'cause it ain't shit to tell! Is it?" he said as he inched his way uncomfortably close to Jada whose back was still pressed against the exit door as her heart raced like a chased deer.

Feeling that Rosa could be walking through the door at any moment now, James quickly turned up the heat on Jada, who by now looked and felt like fallen prey. With her back pressed against the principal's door, James inched even closer to her and began to whisper in her ear as his, now, hard penis rubbed closely against the much shorter woman's stomach. Her legs, which strutted so fashionably through the principal's door, were now numb. Her eyes which sparkled just minutes ago when she asked if it was Ok to come in; now looked glazed over and were as wide as the time spent in James' office seemed long. But her mouth was closed shut; not because she didn't want to scream but because she was so stunned and so traumatized, that the muscles in her jaws couldn't receive the signals from her brain which was crying out "somebody please help me!"

Seeing the look of defeat on her face and once again mistaking her silence for approval, James knew that he had accomplished his goal of scaring the twenty eight year old into sexual submission and as quick as Jada's day had turned from beautiful to disgusting, James unzipped his black dress pants, whipped out his old, wrinkled experienced penis and begin to molest the now badly weakened and delusional pastor's wife. As his work laden hands viciously groped the plump behind that only Chauncey's hands had been privileged enough to touch, Jada's tight, black knee length skirt was raised just enough for that perverted old Adolph James to catch a glimpse of the black, rose laced panties that Jada couldn't wait to pull off for her husband when they returned home from their impromptu date.

Feeling and seeing a body that he never thought he'd ever feel or see, James removed his right hand from Jada's butt, while maintaining his firm grasp with his left, and proceeded to rub his fingers against her hairy and now wet from sweat vagina, moaning and groaning like a lucky, male kitty cat having sex in the moonlight. As James rubbed his penis up and down and against her stomach like he was actually having sex with her, he continued to stroke her vagina and he stroked without actually penetrating until he let out a culminating groan that signaled he had given it his best shot.

Hearing Jada's cell phone ringing in her purse caused James to escalate his already ramped pace. In a nutshell, the phone's ringing pre-empted any furtherance of his exotic escapade and James prematurely and embarrassingly ejaculated all over Jada's slick, sweaty thighs. He was done, through, tired, very tired. But Jada, though suffering from more mental than physical fatigue, felt as though she had just been caught cheating, knowing that the ring tone she had just heard was a special ring tone that signaled that her husband was calling. In her mind she thought that "he must be worried" about where she is or impatiently waiting for a preplanned, date that would never be.

Jada was torn about what she should feel about what she had just endured, though, and instantaneously begin to wrestle with the conflicted emotions of elation that she wasn't actually penetrated, fear of how she would handle the situation now that her worst fears had already become a horrible reality, and hate over the fact that this anti-climactic act was ever perpetrated against her by the man she once respected and was once so thankful that she had the opportunity to meet.

She chose to feel all of the above. But above all, she felt relieved that this regrettable ordeal had ended and to be honest it had ended much like the women of Great Pines had imagined it would, which was the very reason why nobody ever gave James the time of day; ejaculating in twenty seconds on a leg without his penis ever touching the real experience.

Out of breath and now thinking painfully sober again due to his ejaculation, James appeared to be a little embarrassed as he starred uncomprehendingly through the pane of the office door that Jada's back was still planted firmly against. With James' left hand still uncomfortably gripping her behind and his right had now gripping the door knob of his office door, Jada wept as the principal hovered over her like a sexed out bull.

"Get off me!" Jada uncompromisingly whispered as she forcefully pushed the principal back. "Someone just came through the door!"

"Shit, that's Rosa." James whispered in a sudden adrenaline rush, realizing that the sound Jada had heard was the office door slamming. "Get your shit on! Hurry up." he said as he hurried to get back to his desk, zipping his slacks and wiping the sweat from his brow on the way.

With her heart racing rapidly from her own rush of adrenaline, Jada hastened to pull down her skirt and tried her hardest to gain her composer and gather her things as thoughts of what could possibly happen if Rosa walked through the door raced through her mind.

"Hurry up! Sit your ass down girl," James whispered harshly. "She'll be in here in a second, Get your shit together."

"I'm not sitting anywhere you bastard, I'm getting my shit so I can leave!" she screamed back in disdain.

Not knowing exactly what to do and fearing that Jada would only leave his office to tell her side of the story anyway, James helped her get her stuff together and intentionally yelled out loud enough for Rosa to hear what was really going on "Get out of my office right now!"

"I ain't going through this with none of ya'll heffas no more." he screamed as he opened his door in an unashamed and deliberate performance to cover his own behind.

Weeping as she walked slowly out of James' office, Jada held her head down, much to the surprise of James who now felt that his attempt to make himself look like the victim had been successful. She walked out of the office, never shifting her eyes, once, towards Rosa's closed door. James on the other hand, backed his way into Rosa's office with his eyes angrily fixed on Jada, murmuring as she exited "I can't believe this shit is happening to me again!"

After lividly admonishing the broken young women from Odessa, who now faced the greatest difficulty of her adulthood, James whipped his neck around toward Rosa's desk for her sympathy only to be shocked to find that Rosa wasn't at her desk at all. Matter of fact James was more shocked and downright worried to find that Rosa wasn't even anywhere near the administrative wing. In an anxious moment James ran back to his office grabbed his phone and said to himself in a scared, shaky voice while dialing Rosa's cell phone number "She's probably just over in the supply room."

With the phone now on the second ring and the third fast approaching, James began to worry even more, but what he heard when she finally answered would almost cause him to have a conniption.

"Hello." answered Rosa in a sultry sexy voice, which was her usual way of answering when she knew for sure that it was her boss calling her private line. "What's up?"

"You know what's up. Jada Pennington is crazy as hell. That's what's up." he said to his naive secretary in a quiet but angry voice, knowing in his heart that she had already heard the commotion in his office and seeking a favorable response that would let him know that she understood his plight.

"Why...what happened?"

"I'll tell you about it when you get over here." James said with worry and weariness in his voice, waiting and wanting so bad to give Rosa his spill. "Where are you anyway?"

"You sound like this is an emergency or something."

"It is! Now where are you?"

"I'm just leaving Wal-Mart! I can't be in two places at one time Mr. James."

Chapter 25

At the Pennington residence, Chauncey was livid that Jada hadn't made it home in time for their scheduled 1:15 departure. But what he was even more upset about was the fact that Jada had failed to call home to let him know that she wasn't going to be on time and her failure to answer several calls that he had placed to her workplace and her cell phone. In a jam he wasn't prepared to deal with, he paced the hardwood floors of the den as his anger brewed to a vehement pitch. It was already just past 1:30 and he had heard absolutely nothing from Jada. He had already told Daphne that her services wouldn't be needed for the evening, meaning, by now, she probably had other plans, and he knew that making it to his meeting on time was all but out of the question. Chauncey was mad, real mad, but had no earthly idea of Jada's predicament and by the time Jada did finally get home he'd be in no mood for her explanation.

Rushing home in a mad dash, knowing that Chauncey was probably already boiling over, but eager to tell her husband of the horror she had just experienced at work, Jada dashed into the driveway, choosing not to redo her make up, which was what she normally would before meeting her husband or anybody else, nor did she make any attempt to adjust her skirt or blouse which were both uncharacteristically tousled from her traumatic tryst with James. She didn't care. All she was concerned about doing, at this moment, was finally telling her husband and allowing him to handle the situation the best way he knew how; even if it meant a, well deserved, beat down for a man she now prayed would fall dead in a heartbeat. After all, the Sheriff was a member of their church and she was certain that before this day was over with, Adolph James would get what was coming to him.

After exiting her Mercedes, Jada paused for a moment, just before entering the house, as a rush of emotions came over her. She didn't know what was about to happen, but she knew something was about to happen and what ever that something was, would, without question, shake the very foundation that their lives were built upon. Oh yes, she was still ready to get Chauncey involved, but now, being on the verge of telling her husband what she'd been experiencing at work, Jada understood the enormous impact of what she had to say would really have. Even though she was the victim of a crime and would be undeserving of any public scrutiny, Jada knew that once what had happened between her and James hit the streets of small town north Florida, she would be victimized yet again and the squeaky clean image that she and her husband both shared in the community would be tarnished in the twinkling of an eye.

Entering the house with her keys dangling from her hands, with the appearance of a woman that had just seen a ghost, Jada was unexpectedly met at the door by a man who had the scowl of a bald eagle and the mindset of scorned lover.

"Where have you been? It's almost 2:00!"

"Chauncey calm down, I'm about to tell you where I've been." Jada said calmly but fearfully, with horror worn into her face and astonished that her husband came at her so aggressively.

"My meeting starts at 2:00 and you didn't even have the common decency to even call me and tell me that you were going to be late again! You told me you would be here no later than one!"

"Chauncey, I need to tell you something. Calm down and just give me a second! Please."

"You need to start talking fast! I got to go!"

Figuring that she finally had her opportunity to tell her horrific story, Jada held her head down in shame and said softly before being interrupted "Mr. James…"

"Mr. James what; kept you at work late again? Jada just stop. Give me the damn keys." he said as he walked toward the dining table to retrieve his black Kenneth Cole briefcase. "We haven't had much time lately to do anything together and the one day that we do, you come home late again, with another lame behind, Mr. James excuse."

"If you just give me a moment, I'll tell you exactly why I'm late, Chauncey!" Jada screamed like a badgered animal, signaling to Lizzy that her much wanted day with her parents had all but been spoiled, which caused her to rush up the stairs to her room in an effort to avoid hearing the progressing day shattering argument.

"To be honest, I don't care to even know exactly why you're late. All I know is that I called your job at approximately 1:15 and the answering service came on. Then, I called your cell several times and your answering service came on. Are you trying to tell me that Mr. James had you so tied up that you couldn't even answer my phone call?

"Yes he did and that's not all he did Chauncey! Mr. James…" she said, passionately trying to explain before Chauncey rudely butted in again.

"Wait a minute, we've had this discussion before and you know exactly how I feel about Mr. James! I just can't believe that you're standing in my face trying to validate why you couldn't take one second… one silly second just to answer your phone and let me and your daughter know that you weren't gonna be on time again. That's all I need to know. All that other stuff you can keep to your damn self."

Firmly restraining her response due to the pain she was feeling internally over her husband's distinct lack of concern and anger over her tardiness, Jada stoically replied with little or no emotion due to a double dose of shock, "Chauncey if I could have I would have."

"And look at you! You're not even ready to go anywhere. And why is your shirt all outside of your skirt? That's not how you left the house this morning. What the hell were ya'll doing; making passionate love on his desk or something? …. Look, don't even answer that. I got to go and I hope you're happy that you spoiled your daughter's day."

In total disbelief and actually miffed by Chauncey's irrational response to her undesired belatedness, a stunned Jada, who was already feeling abused and violated by James, felt even more abused and violated because the man she was sure would be there to comfort her and aid her in her quest for vindication, didn't even have the "common decency" to even hear a word she had to say.

With tears streaming down her face and her body shaking like pine needles from the brisk February breeze, Jada stood quietly, starring straight ahead as Chauncey walked right past her, through the door, and regrettably not even acknowledging her visible agony. She felt him pull the keys out of her hands, she also heard the harsh statements he made just before leaving, she even heard the door slam just behind her, but nothing at this point was registering. Chauncey didn't know it, but Jada Alexia Pennington had slipped into a trauma induced trance that was clear cut evidence of her coming emotional fragility and long after Chauncey had snatched the keys, stormed out the door and driven off for a pointless meeting that he was already late for, Jada turned to the door her husband had just existed and let out a pathetic plea, that if heard by Chauncey would have warned him of the seriousness of her mental struggle.

"Chauncey, he raped me!" She exclaimed as she pitifully cried and stood helplessly in front of and stared at the closed door as if her husband would somehow hear her and walk back through the door to rescue her.

"Adolph James put his hands on me Chauncey!" she continued, pleading her case to nobody's ear.

Realizing that Chauncey had already gone and, for what it's worth, neglected his responsibility to fulfill the promise he had made to her daddy, years earlier; which was to always look after and protect her, Jada's helplessness turned quickly into hurt, which led her down a one way path to rage over her husband's inability to see and feel her evident pain. "Please Chauncey… don't leave me here by myself." she screamed as she cried and her body shook violently "He raped me!" she continued, as she began to bang viciously on the solid wood, cherry finished door.

Feeling neglected and abandoned, and in a potentially, irreversible state of bemusement, Jada slowly turned from the door, as her tears mounted, and walked up the stairs leading to the couple's bedroom. Once inside she entered the bathroom, feeling sorry for herself and somewhat blaming herself for what had happened. And in dejection and resentment, she filled her oversized, oval shaped, Jacuzzi styled bath tub with scorching hot water and soaked herself, not for any relaxation, but in a purging effort as she thought of how bad this situation had actually become. She knew that there was no place to turn or for that matter, no place to run, because the only person in the world she would've confided in had left without as much as a "What happened to you?"

As she looked down at her naked body, and continue to cry over the fact that she wasn't pure any longer because of James' violation, her eyes were drawn downward toward her thighs, which still had the nasty residue of her struggle in the principal's office. Seeing the foreign, snotty, sticky, substance that clung to her thigh as though it had planted a flag signaling ownership, Jada had flashbacks of what James had done to her, and remembered that the "sick man" had actually masturbated on her left thigh.

In a panic she splashed out of the water, and without ever thinking of the danger of what she would do next, grabbed a previously used porcelain cleaning, scrubbing pad from one of her overhead bathroom cabinets before slithering back in the tub with contaminated contemplations. Feeling as if she was the scum of the earth, Jada mixed up a little lather and begin to scrub both her thighs, as if to wash away the disgrace she felt. She wanted to be clean. She wanted to be pure again; the way she was when she went to work this morning. But it seemed as if the harder she scrubbed the more she thought about what James had done, and in a way, it was as if she was scrubbing away the fear of loosing everything she'd worked so hard for, scrubbing away the anxiety of finding out what others thought of her, scrubbing away the hurt that she felt over Chauncey's abandonment. What she couldn't perceive at the time though, was that no amount of scrubbing could ever wash away her fears. No amount of scrubbing could ever wash away her anxiety or hurt, but none the less the poor woman scrubbed. And she scrubbed until her scorching, but clear, bathwater turned into to a murky pink from the blood she had drawn from her thighs.

Seeing the fresh blood in the water and feeling the excruciating pain of the scorching hot water and cleaning substance, which agitating her fresh wounds, Jada caught herself, threw the porcelain cleaning pad down into the water, held her head in her both her hands as her chin rested on the upper part of her chest, and cried even the more "Lord, why did this happen to me?"

Chapter 26

"Deacon Pickett?" a woman's shaky voice whispered on the other end of the Pickett's home phone line.

"Um huh. This me." Pickett said after snatching the phone from Eloise and looking angrily at her for handing him the phone in spite of the fact that he had told her he didn't want to talk anybody before the phone even rang. "How can I help you?"

"I need to talk to you and I need to do it as soon as possible and in person." she continued.

"First of all who is this? And why you talkin like that?"

"You know who this is Pickett, It's me. I need to see you."

Taking a few seconds to accurately discern the owner of the voice on the other end of his line, that he'd obviously heard before, Pickett rubbed his chin and chewed harder on his tobacco before agreeing, "Yea, now I know who it is," in an angry voice "and hell naw, you can't see me," he said, shaking his head in objection as he reached for his spit cup. "You don't need to see me and even if you did, after what ya'll did to me up there at that church, I ain't got no need to see you or none of the rest of ya'll no more. Now I'm hangin' up this phone. I gots work to do!"

"Wait a minute Pickett." she interrupted. "It's about Pastor Pennington." she said, figuring he would change his mind and listen, knowing his steadfast disdain for his former pastor.

"What about him?" Pickett condescendingly questioned. "His bidness ain't my bidness no more. He ya'lls problem now, not mines."

"It's something that I know you been looking for and if you meet me somewhere, I promise it'll be worth yo while. I need to talk to you and only you, cause something real bad is goin' on and I'm plum scared to handle this by myself."

"Well why you just can't tell me right now if it's so bad. Better yet; why you ain't done told ya'lls Shaff bout it? I ain't the law and ya'll voted out the real Shaff."

"I just can't. Now listen, what I have to tell you will give you what you need to get rid of him and I know you want to get rid of him and I do too now. But, I need you to meet me cause, I don't need nobody else getting involved in this before you get it. My job is at stake and I don't want no parts of this after I turn it over to you."

"I tell you what, I'll meet you somewhere, but I ain't comin by myself. Ya'll ain't bout to set me up for dat nigga to try to kill me…"

"Pickett, I ain't got no time for no foolishness. Either you comin or you ain't."

"Listen lady, I'll come but, this better not be no trap; you hear me?"

"Look, brang whoever you want to brang, but meet me in thirty minutes out at the truck stop out on I-10 and I'll show you it ain't no set up."

Confused but captivated by his unexpected conversation, Pickett quickly spit out the remainder of his Red Man chewing tobacco and dialed up Augustus Tally to see if he'd be interested in accompanying him to his, out of the blue, meeting with the woman who evidently held some juicy information about the pastor that could possibly lead to a quick character assassination which could spell the end of Pennington's three and a half year reign as Greater Mt. Carmel's top dog. Securing Tally's positive response, Pickett jumped into his old pick-up truck without even notifying his wife that he had left and drove over to the plantation through the now driving rain, to join forces with his old buddy in what he considered to be a perfect opportunity to uncover the preacher's previously unseen seed of corruption. It seemed as if the harder the rain fell, the faster Pickett drove. By now his growing anticipation and need to find out a negative nugget about Chauncey had taken over his need to drive responsibly in the bad weather and in less than the original thirty minutes allotted by the woman to meet her, Pickett had picked up Tally from the plantation and had driven the twenty miles or so to the truck stop near an I-10 exit, just two small towns away.

Spotting the woman's vehicle in the overflowing parking lot, Pickett backed out of his parking space and sped over to a vacant space adjacent to where she was parked. In a dash, Pickett and Tally, both, jumped out of the pick-up truck and scurried, under the guise of secrecy, over to the woman's car, as if they were C.I.A. agents. Reaching the charcoal gray, 1992 Ford Taurus, they both entered the car quickly, avoiding the persistent, cool rain and begin a shocking dialogue that had the potential to bring Chauncey Pennington to his knees.

"Lula, this better be damn good," Pickett said to the former musician and current bitter and reluctant church administrator of Mt. Carmel as Tally leaned over the back seat to listen carefully.

"Deacon Pickett, I'm gone tell you exactly what happened today, but first I need to tell you why I'm coming to you. After you left the church, I thought you were dead wrong about the pastor. But as soon as you left, that man lost his mind. He started changin' everythang. He even fooled me into becomin' the new church administrator but then turned right around and brought in another piano player to take my place. Connie tried to tell me about what he was tryin to do but I wouldn't listen.

"Well now, Lula, I was bout to say that ain't God but to be honest I don't too much blame him for that. And if that's why you called me out here in this thunder storm, I'm goin back home. Hell, I tried to get rid of you right after you came to the church. You just sangs too loud and I told you that, years ago."

"That ain't why I called you, but if you gonna keep insulting me, I don't have a problem with telling you or that white man to get the hell out of my car. Now do you want to hear what I have to say or not?"

"Yea, Lula. What you thank I'm here for?"

"Calm down Walter." Tally interjected. "Mrs. Penny, I apologize for Walter's insulting remarks, but what is it that you really want to tell us."

"Well today around 11AM, my staff had just got through with cleaning up and everything and I had counted all the lunch money up early because we had a early lunch today, cause school was going to turn out at 12. So, as the lunchroom manager, I just told everybody that since all the work had been done early and since school was gone turn out early anyway, that we was just gone go on home early too, cause it wudn't no sense in staying round with no work to do. So I told Lucile, Gary, Eugene, Alice, Willie Ruth, and …"

"Dammit, Lula! Tell us why you called us out here in this thunderstorm?"

"Go ahead Mrs. Penny never mind Walter."

"As I was saying I told all my staff to have a good weekend and I did what I normally do."

"What was that, Mrs. Penny?" Tally questioned like the seasoned investigator that he was.

"I put the lunch money in my glove compartment so that I could take it around to the office so I could turn it in to the bookkeeper. But, on the way round there, I lost my train of thought and plum forgot that I even had the money. So after I went home, I remembered that I didn't turn it in and I ran back over to the school and when I got there I didn't see Rosa's car, who is our bookkeeper, but I did see Mr. James' car. So because I didn't want nobody to thank I was tryin to steal that lunch money or nothing, I just went in quietly to put the money on Rosa's desk. But when I got in there I heard, what I thought was people having sex in Mr. James office. So I sneaked over to his door and what I saw almost made me have a heart attack."

"You probably gone have a heart attack anyway like you eat, but go ahead." Pickett uninterestedly mumbled under his breath, without Lula never realizing that he had just insulted her again.

"What happened next, Lula? What did you see?" asked Tally who was now sitting on the edge of his seat.

"Sheriff Tally, I saw Mr. James through the little window in his office door and he had the pastor's wife up against the door giving her the business."

"What you talkin bout Lula?" Pickett asked as he sat straight up in the front seat, now totally interested in what she was saying.

"They were having sex," she said with a voice of certainty.

"Are you sure that's what you saw Lula?" asked Tally, still not totally convinced that this could be true about the pastor's wife.

"I'm as sure as I am black. They were having sex. They was kissin and touchin and moanin like they ain't never did it before."

"You mean to tell me they were doing all that and didn't notice you come in the office?" Pickett said seriously, but making a direct reference to Lula's always noticeable corpulence.

"Deacon Pickett, Sheriff Tally, I was too shocked to make a noise and I just eased out the door. I just would've never thought that our First Lady would've ever been caught cheatin. I always thought it would be the pastor that would get caught up in something like this cause Jada just didn't seem like the nasty type. But that little lady shole made a fool out of me" she said shaking her head in disgust. "That woman was lettin that man touch every inch of her body and from the look of the back of her head she was enjoyin every bit of. I'm just shocked." she continued in disbelief.

"Are you sure Lula?" Pickett asked again with his eyes stretched to capacity and his heart now pounding furiously at the hearing of Lula's astonishing revelation.

"I promise to God and I hope to die."

"Can you prove any of this Lula?" asked Tally, seeking concrete evidence of Jada's alleged infidelity.

"I only have what I saw with my own two eyes. Now Sheriff Tally, you don't really know me but, I ain't never been no liar and I ain't got no other reason to be telling ya'll all this, other than the fact that I want the truth about our pastor and his wife to finally come out. I know what I saw and I'm telling you as truthful as I know how, that I saw the pastor's wife and Mr. James having sex in that office. Now that's that."

After hearing Lula's rather convincing testimony, Pickett and Tally reasoned, however, that without the presence of actual physical evidence or more solid proof, there wasn't much they could do with Lula's disclosure other than, somehow, make the pastor and aware of Jada's and the principal's infidelity; which could serve as leverage to issue the Pennington's a stern ultimatum. But before they made any attempts to contact Chauncey, or carry out any plans, they wanted to make certain that they all were on the same page.

"Listen to me ya'll." Augustus Tally said, as if he was a four star general leading his troops into battle. "Now this has the potential to be very explosive, but we have to very, very careful when dealing with this man because ya'll know that for the most part he has everybody in this county fooled. It's been proven that when anybody tries to come against him in any way those people at that church always come to his defense. So I suggest that we don't tell anybody about what we know," he continued, cautioning Lula and Pickett not to say a word to preserve the integrity of an impending plan. "Walter you know what happened the last time we tried to get him out and I don't want that to happen this time. Is that clear Lula?"

"I ain't gone say a word Sheriff Tally."

"I hear what you saying, but what is the plan Tally?" Pickett asked, wanting to know what, exactly, Tally had in mind and what each of their roles would be in making sure that carrying out the strategy would end successfully.

"Well this is what I'm gone do…"

Speaking quietly, as if he thought their conversation was somehow being secretly recorded, Tally revealed a plan so Machiavellian, that if carried out exactly the way he had envisioned, would have Chauncey and Jada on flight out of Tallahassee by the break of dawn.

Back at the Pennington house, Jada waited, as she sat on the side of her bed, for the other shoe to drop. With her eyes still streaming with tears and her heart throbbing as if someone had beaten it with a sledge hammer and her body still shaking as if she suffered from Parkinson's, Jada sat, rocking back and forth, knowing full well that she was only experiencing the calm before the storm, the proverbial eye of the hurricane. Although this late February day had turned out to be anything but predictable for her thus far, one thing was definitely for certain; life as she knew it had forever changed and no matter what the outcome would be of any criminal investigation into James' salacious behavior, her reputation as a good, moral and faithful wife, mother, and First Lady was almost over.

This should have been the point where any rational thinking person might scream out against the atrocities committed against them or even begin to strategize to clear their name but, Jada wasn't thinking rationally at all. Evidence of that very point is in the fact that Jada hadn't even called her father yet, who she always sought protection from and would have flown in from Odessa in a moments notice to protect his little girl. And although they talked at least three times a week she hadn't called Aunt Eunice either nor did she contact law enforcement. At this point Jada was anything but a rational thinker and could now, fittingly, be classified as a woman suffering from severe emotional distress, incapable of fully understanding the trauma she had experienced only a few hours ago. By now it was almost four o'clock and she hadn't heard a word from Chauncey either, who was only about a thirty five minute drive from home but so distant that he couldn't possibly imagine the strife in his own home. And soon and very soon the roof, that had covered and protected her from the day that she met Chauncey, would cave in.

Little Lizzy didn't have a clue about what was really about to go down either and she played, as she had learned to do over the years, in her own room, alone, and was thankful, on this day, that all the yelling had ended and the mother that she loved so dearly loved had finally stopped crying. But Lizzy couldn't have possibly known, that tucked away on the second floor in a bedroom that would never see its owners make love again, her mother wept silently, mumbling to herself and wondering aloud, what could go wrong next; and by the end of this night, for Jada at least, it would seem like everything.

Chapter 27

After plotting against the Penningtons with their highly unlikely source, Pickett and Tally knew that they had a foolproof strategy to put an end to the Pennington regime. But, unlike the first time he plotted to rid Greater Mt. Carmel of arch enemy, Pickett didn't dare to enlist the services of "them fools", that he had once considered his closest allies. Nope, this was a job for Augustus Tally and his crew to carry out and Pickett knew that with Tally's strong background in law enforcement and his boundless ties to corruption, the former Sheriff would prove to be, not only, the perfect strategist, but the perfect executioner, a master of disguise and a manipulator of deception. It only took a few minutes to come up with the devilish scheme that they felt would be an affective strategy to alleviate them of the cancer they had come to know as Pastor Chauncey Pennington.

Now eating an early dinner at an exclusive, downtown hotel, restaurant with "important people", Chauncey was totally oblivious to what was going on back at his house or for that matter what was happening to life as he knew it. There was really no possible way he could've known because from the moment he left that house he turned his cell phone off because he was so angry at his wife for being "late" and couldn't even stand the sound of Jada's voice at that particular moment. He knew that once she calmed down she would definitely try to reach him; either to try to explain why she'd been late or to chastise him for yet another inadequately thought out outburst. But he wasn't trying to hear any of that; no right now and even when he reached his destination, he left his phone in the car purposely to escape Jada's explanation and/or her wrath.

Uncharacteristically, after his "power meeting" he appeared to be quite despondent and shied away from the gentlemanly conversation that was going on at the dinner table. While others nattered about politics and the like, Chauncey remained silent for the most part, thinking of a way to ease back into Jada's good graces. It was at the dinner table that he began to realize that he was dead wrong for his unwarranted and overboard chastisement of his wife and knew that he had, once again, caused an uproar in his house that could have been avoided if only he had chosen to listen to her rather than lecture her.

But he was sure that with a little time apart and a lot of time to consider forgiveness, Jada would be just fine when he returned home, which was precisely the reason why he hadn't called her yet. He and Jada had experienced little fights like this before and he was a veteran at smoothing things over, especially when he knew that he was wrong. So after leaving one hundred and twenty dollars on the dinner table to pay for their food and saying goodbye to associates that wondered about his despondency and questioned his premature departure, Chauncey left the restaurant, shortly after stopping by the hotel lobby boutique to purchase flowers and a card, on his way home to a wife he was ready to say "I'm sorry" to.

Pressing his way through bumper to bumper, rain soaked, five o'clock, rush hour traffic, Chauncey drove at a snails pace through downtown Tallahassee with his cell phone in his lap, pondering if now was the best time to call his wife. Reasoning that he should and knowing he would have plenty of time to apologize due to the backed up traffic and subsequent longer than usual ride home, he picked up his cell phone and turned it on for the first time since he left the house. But, before he could key in his home phone number his own cell phone begin to vibrate, signaling an incoming call.

Normally the incoming caller's phone number would flash across his cell phone's green backlit screen, forewarning him of the identity of the caller, but this phone call was different. This time, instead of the actual phone number appearing across the screen, the rarely seen words "Restricted Caller" flashed vibrantly, which left Chauncey clueless about the caller's identity and the call's origination. But because he had just left a highly informative meeting at the State Capitol and because he had given his business card to several seekers of his services, Chauncey totally disregarded his rule not to answer unidentified phone calls and answered the call anyway, with a bit of hesitation.

"Pastor Pennington." he answered in the most business like manner he could, still wondering who the caller might be.

"Yes, Pastor this is Arthur Blankenship," responded a slow talking, hardened voiced, white man that Chauncey realized he had never heard of or spoken to before.

In an attempt to be kind to the strange man, who was breathing heavily into the phone, Chauncey acted as he always did when encountering strangers and continued "Mr. Blankenship how might I help you?" in an upbeat manner.

"Helping me shouldn't be your concern right now," the man unexpectedly snapped back, much to the surprise of Chauncey, who still had no earthly idea who the man was or his reason for calling. "I was calling so that I might help you."

"Ok. Well how can you help me then?" Chauncey snapped right back in a less than serious manner, assuming that maybe this guy was just another prank caller from the local mental hospital; you know, the kind of call he received maybe twice a month from residents of the large state institution that was only a few miles from his church.

"Listen Pennington, I'm a private investigator hired by some of your former parishioners and I have some recently discovered material on your wife that I think you need to be made aware of."

"A private investigator, hired by who?" Chauncey defiantly questioned, now beginning to treat the call with a little more seriousness even though he was still in the dark about the caller's identity or purpose.

Chauncey didn't know it, but the caller was using an assumed name and a fictitious profession in a stealthy scheme designed by Augustus Tally for the underhanded purposes of manipulation, intimidation, and with any luck, the Pennington's evacuation from a town that Pickett and Tally, both, longed to control once again. In actuality Arthur Blankenship wasn't Arthur Blankenship at all, but none other than career criminal Cecil Whitlock, a frequent visitor to the County Jail, who had often traded off jail time in the former Sheriff's "good ole boy" system for secretive participatory roles in many of his corrupt undertakings.

"Look Pastor, I'm gonna make this quick," Whitlock continued with a scary, muffled tone, which startled Chauncey and caused anxiety to take over his mind as beads of sweat began to formulate around his brows. His heart raced fiercely at the very thought that his antagonists were making yet another attempt to destroy his ministry and his stomach became coiled in apprehensive knots as fear of another fierce battled with his adversaries loomed as an imminent possibility.

Infuriated, but uncertain of what wrongdoings anybody could have possibly uncovered to incriminate his wife, Chauncey listened in disdain as Whitlock began to tear at the very fabric of his heart with vicious allegations that if proven true, would totally demolish the preacher's faith in marriage and ministry.

"Today your wife was caught on videotape having sex with her boss in his office at the elementary school."

Already feeling violated that someone had the audacity to hire this man to secretly investigate his family's private dealings; Chauncey became nauseous as his heart dropped and his anguish instantaneously multiplied.

"If this is some kind of sick game you're playing, you better damn well shut your mouth right now because defamation of character is against the law and if I find out that this is what you're trying to do, I will have you strung from the highest pine tree in this state. Now you tell me right now what's really going on Mr. Blankenship."

"Listen Pennington, you don't scare me one bit and if you knew what was best for you, you'll shut your god damn mouth and listen before I have your ass hung from the highest pine tree in your own backyard. I know where you live. Now we've known for sometime now that your wife was sleeping around with Adolph James right under your damn nose and we've waited for solid evidence to be brought forth before we brought it to your attention. And around one o'clock this afternoon we got just what we were looking for."

"I've heard enough of this foolishness Sir..." Chauncey retorted ready to end the conversation, knowing he'd better start preparing for another fierce battle with his rivals. "… and frankly I don't believe a word that you're saying. But, I do want to give you a word to take back to the people who unfortunately thought it would be a good idea to hire you to spy on me and my wife. Maybe you all have forgotten who you're messing around with, but this preacher ain't no fool and you can't force me or intimidate me out of Mt. Carmel." Chauncey replied in antipathy, but reluctantly wanting to know what could possibly be the evidence Blankenship possessed that substantiated his wife's infidelity.

"You can be a hard ass if you want to, but I'm giving you exactly twenty four hours from the time I hang up this phone to get the hell away from here. If you don't, then, I'm totally prepared to act on behalf of the members of your church and everybody else that's sick and tired of your damn ass and send copies of this video tape to every significant authority in this county. By the way, screwing on school property is against the law too. Now get your sorry, two timing ass out of our town before I personally make your life a living hell."

With an earsplitting "Click!" and without as much as a goodbye, Cecil Whitlock hung up the phone, completing the task, just as Tally had asked him to, leaving Chauncey in a whirlwind that signaled only be the beginning of tumultuous times to come. Already irritated by a call that he initially thought was a premeditated hoax designed by Picketteers to distress him, Chauncey became overwhelmed by feelings of hurt over his wife's unfathomable deceitfulness after deducing that much of what he heard from Blankenship was in direct correlation to Jada's earlier, work related, displacement.

Utterly devastated by the allegations, Chauncey thought over and over about several things that had occurred during the day and surmised that too much of the information he had just heard fit too closely with his own twisted timeline and was a perfect explanation of why Jada couldn't make it home in time and why she looked, uncharacteristically, disheveled when she finally made it home. Even though he had been badly misinformed about what really went down at Great Pines Elementary, Chauncey had all the information he needed and talked to himself as if he was practicing for a massive interrogation of his hapless wife.

"That's why she didn't get home by one o'clock." He said, rationalizing his wife's failure to be where she had promised to be. "I can't believe this. That's why she didn't answer the phone." he continued as his emotions began to take over. "Damn it! Why Jada? Why did you have to go and do something as stupid as this? Out of all the things you could've done... Damn!" he shouted, banging his fist against the steering wheel as the brunt of what Blankenship alleged finally hit him like a ton of bricks.

Now, more than ever, Chauncey knew that he was in very big trouble, but never in a million years would he have imagined that Jada, of all people, would be the culprit of his coming demise. He was facing a two headed monster now; his wife on the one hand which was an entirely unforeseen shock and his enemies, on the other, who he always felt were out to get him. With a plethora of emotions flooding his head and heart, Chauncey pulled to the side of the road, gripped his steering wheel tightly and rested his face upon the driver's side air bag, trying to make sense of why in the world would the Lord allow something else so terrible to happen to someone like him. Yes, he was still visibly upset and downright hurt over what he thought Jada had done, but by this time he knew full well that this situation was much bigger than Jada's missteps of infidelity, because in approximately twenty four hours or so, everything thing he'd built since coming to north Florida could all come crumbling down if Blankenship stooped further and allowed one viewing of that salacious videotape.

In a frenzied panic, Chauncey picked up his cell phone off of the floorboard of the Mercedes and dialed home frantically for an answer seeking conversation with his wife, who, by the time he successfully placed his call, would already be in her own answer seeking conversation with her own strange caller.

He dialed his residence, hoping desperately, that some sort of reasonable resolution could be brought to the madness that had become his one way ticket out of town, only to find that no one in the Pennington house was in the phone answering mood. As he slumped over the steering wheel of his still parked vehicle, with his cell phone next to his ear, Chauncey waited anxiously as the phone rang for an eternity, it seemed like, and after five rings, when the answering service should've automatically commenced, his suspicions were heightened because he knew that if the answering service didn't respond after five rings, somebody was on the line and whoever that somebody was, was so preoccupied that his waiting call was of little or no importance.

Realizing that this blustery February day had become too mysterious for his taste, Chauncey turned his ignition key and in haste made his way toward Penelope Pines, leaving dust and debris in his wake.

Before Chauncey finally placed his call, all Jada had done was just sit stoically in her bedroom and wonder how this saga would ultimately unfold. She had begun to think deeply about taking matters into her own hands and start a ball to rolling that she didn't know was already rolling full steam ahead.

She had just sat on her bed, crying sporadically and waiting for her world to unravel. But, though she remained in a state of discernible disillusionment and incomprehensible confusion, her thought process changed slightly over time. With every second that went by, Jada was gradually transforming from what resembled a victimized little girl into a woman in rage, a woman that was mad as hell, a woman determined to make Adolph James wish he had never laid his hands or his eyes on her.

Progressively Jada thought less about what happened to her and more about what would soon happen to James. She still contemplated what the consequences of her catastrophe would be on her marriage and ministry, but with every waning minute she thought less about her marriage and ministry and more about her mission of misery toward her tormenter. Like Chauncey had reacted in times past, when he had taken all he could take from the hellions of Greater Mt. Carmel, Jada was fed up now and had the propensity to exhibit the same vengeful behaviors. But unlike Chauncey, her mind was totally messed up and the recipient of her fury would taste ten times the pain if she ever gave free rein to the pain she, undoubtedly, harbored in her heart.

Nothing had really separated her attention from her brewing anger, which couldn't have been good, considering her deteriorating mental status. Not Lizzy; because Lizzy was sound asleep by now after playing with her dolls alone in her room. Not the television; the television hadn't been on since before she came home and the phone, even though it rang feverishly after Chauncey left, hadn't been answered for the fear of who or what she would hear on the other end. But after hours of stewing in her own volatility, Jada was finally more than ready to share her horrific truths with anyone that would listen and in the mood to unleash her fury upon the fool that dared to have the boldness to question her role in this calamity.

Around five o clock the phone did ring again and finally Jada had the nerve and was furiously ready to speak out, or so she thought. Anxious to talk to anybody that would listen, Jada just picked up the phone without even checking the caller ID as she normally did, leaving her, like Chauncey, totally oblivious to the fact that she was walking swiftly into a sadistic set up.

"Hello," she flusteredly answered, in an unusually monotonous manner.

"Um, Mrs. Pennington?"

"This is she." Jada anxiously, but protectively answered, not knowing who the caller was.

"I'm Author Blankenship and I just got off of the phone with your husband," Cecil Whitlock said in a kind and tender voice about as fake as his made up name, in a blatant attempt to lure in the woman that was in a recognizable defense mode.

"About what?" Jada apprehensively asked, wondering why this strange man would be calling her if he had already conversed with her husband.

She was thinking that maybe this was the call that would signal the beginning of her life's unraveling and in a sense it was, but Jada had no clue that her worst fears were about to get worse.

"What about?" she questioned again as she pulled her robe together and quickly stood up to walk off increasing uneasiness.

With the smoothness of a master illusionist and with the unpredictability of a wild Bengal, Tally's empowered henchman changed his tone of voice without warning, snapping into the same ferocious character that had, moments earlier, ripped Chauncey's bloody heart right out of his chest.

"You know what this is about lady. We caught you and the principal at that school having sex today in his office and we got it all on video tape."

"What?" Jada asked in fear as her face began to bare the strains of the confusion trapped in her mind. But besides asking what, like an aged, labor weary slave, Jada was silent; real silent because she just couldn't believe the enormity of was going on at this moment in her life.

"Just shut up and listen! You thought you could keep your little secret to yourself, but the camera doesn't lie. I've already told your husband that you've been screwing around on him with Adolph James and he's really pissed off at you. Yea, now he knows the type of girl you really are. You whore."

Hearing a beep in her hear, but totally drawn in to Blankenship's allegation laden tirade and in utter shock again, Jada never even looked down at the phone or noticed that it was actually Chauncey trying to get a call through. The beep that signaled a call waiting continued as Jada poised herself for a rebuttal but Whitlock didn't have time to hear her denial. He was on a mission that didn't require a two party conversation.

"I don't even know who you are…" Jada countered before unsuccessfully trying to refute the validity of his evidence.

"You don't have to know me but I know you. You are the slut who that caught red handed having sex at a damn elementary school for God's sake."

"You don't know what you're talking about."

"Oh yes I do." he said arrogantly in a brazen attempt to discredit her integrity. "Now, I told your husband the same thing I'm about to tell you; so listen carefully. Both of you need to have your asses away from here by tomorrow this time or I promise, I will make copies of that videotape and I will send it to everybody in your church and to anybody else who wants it. If you know what's best for you and your family, you'd take my advice and pack up tonight and leave here before you both loose everything you have."

"You don't know what you're talking about! I was raped! She shouted, trying hopelessly to tell Blankenship what really happened to her in James' office.

With conviction and not giving her false accuser any time to respond to her adamant rebuttal, Jada continued her, not yet determined soliloquy as more fear crept into her mind.

"At this point I really don't care about what you or anybody else thinks of me. Adolph James raped me and since you say you have the videotape, go ahead and show it. That'll only prove…!

And she just stopped. She just quit; not because she was done with her attempt at vindication or because she was too miffed to continue, but she heard a long piercing dial tone in her right hear. Arthur Blankenship had already, rudely hung up the phone without ever hearing one word of her desperate disclaimer. Incensed and in more of a state of shock than she was in before she got home, Jada immediately slammed down the phone upon the wood grain flooring of her bedroom and fervently lashed out at the Lord before breaking down in tears once again.

"Why is all of this happening to me? She cried, beginning a pitiful dissertation. "What did I ever do to deserve all this?" she cryingly questioned God, as she threw herself onto the floor in a bathroom that still bore the bright reddish residue of her last tearful visit.

"Why me, God…? Why me…?" She continued with her beleaguered head in her hands.

Sobbing profusely as she now lay prostrate on the bathroom floor, Jada occasionally belted out eerie shrills that sounded as if soldiers were purposely disjointing her shoulder blades in some sort of a vicious act of punishment. She had tried, minutes earlier, to bounce back from her tenacious bout with depression, but after her ill-fated conversation, with who she presumed to be Arthur Blankenship, she once again found herself overwhelmed by the day's events and for the third time in less than five hours she felt as low as she'd ever felt in her life, knowing that her marriage, her ministry, her life would never be the same.

Hearing her mother's screams, Lizzy woke up out of her sleep in utter fear and ran to the bathroom to her mother's aid only to find that the woman that lay flat on the bathroom floor didn't resemble the mother she had grown to know at all. Jada looked worn and abused and although Lizzy had no clue about the source or severity of her what her mother was really going through, one thing was evident; she needed help and she needed help right away, prompting her to tearfully question repeatedly. "What's wrong momma?"

Unresponsive, but visibly in a great deal of internal pain, Jada continued to lay face first on the bathroom floor as Lizzy hovered over her, helplessly and hopelessly looking for answers that up to this point where nowhere to be found. She heard her daughter's constant pleas to "Tell me what's wrong momma", but the only thing she could do was just cry and it seemed as if the more Lizzy caringly questioned, the more sorry she felt for herself and the sorrier she felt for herself, the greater the outpouring of her bitter born tears. Jada, in a nutshell, was a mess; especially considering her tattered, state of mind.

Noticing her mother's despondency and her continuing unwillingness to reveal if or how she might be best helped, Lizzy considered the urgency of calling her father.

Realizing that she couldn't wait any longer for an adequate response from her mother, the very mature for her age, six and a half year old, momentarily left her mother's side to look for the master bedroom based cordless telephone only to find that the cordless phone had been broken to pieces, shattered about the floor, near the shower door.

Running frenetically down the hallway in an instinctive effort to find her own cordless phone, which was tucked away near the toy box in her bedroom, Lizzy thought to herself how badly she wished that her father was already home. By now that's all she wanted because she knew that if anybody could possibly calm the situation that had become about as tempestuous as a mighty, raging sea, it was her daddy. So in a panic, but in hope, she dialed her father's cell phone which was answered on the very first ring.

"Why haven't you all answered the phone? I've been trying to call for at least thirty minutes!" exaggeratedly yelled Chauncey, who by now was in his own state of emergency and was so angry that he didn't even care to know which one of the Pennington women was on the other end of the line.

"It's me daddy. It's Lizzy!" she said tearfully, thankful that her daddy had responded quickly to her insistent cry.

Hearing the trepidation in his daughter's voice Chauncey quickly changed his tone and in concern asked "What's wrong baby?"

"Daddy its momma!" she answered, bursting into an exclamatory outreach for her father's tremendously desired assistance.

"What's wrong with your momma Lizzy?"

"She's just laying on the floor in the bathroom crying and I can't get her up. She won't say nothing. She's just laying down crying," she said, as she continued her heartbreaking cry for help.

"Where are you?" he asked with concern, realizing that his daughter was suffering great grief.

"I'm in my room."

"Where's your momma?"

"She's in the bathroom. She won't get up."

"Stop crying baby. Your momma's OK," he said, trying desperately to calm his daughter fears and ease her troubled mind. "I'm only five minutes away. I'll be right there. Ok?"

"Please hurry daddy. I'm scared!"

"I'll be right there baby. I promise. Take the phone to your momma baby. Let me talk to her."

As Lizzy ran back to the bathroom, as fast as she could, to see if her mother would respond, at all, to her father's expected appeal, Chauncey formulated his own response which, unfortunately, was born in his disgust over what he erroneously thought was Jada's deliberate plea for pity. Disregarding his previous plan to talk sensibly to her in an effort to seek truthful answers and going against his earlier desire to allow Jada to participate in the recovery of both their characters, Chauncey took this opportunity to take one last jab at his punch drunk wife, who by the time Lizzy returned to the bathroom was sitting on the toilet stool with a blank stare and fool's grin locked into position on her tear dried, insipid face. Once again startled by her mother's uncharacteristic, scary looking, appearance, Lizzy slowed down, as if she was approaching a stray dog. In fear of getting to close, but free from the anxiety caused by her mother's continuous crying, from a distance and in silence, the inundated little girl tried to hand the phone to her mother.

"Lizzy put down the phone. I'm OK," she said in a still voice as if she had found some diluted form of inner peace.

"But Momma, its daddy..." The little girl, tranquilly, countered in an equally subdued voice, trying to persuade her mother to take the phone.

"Why did you call your daddy?"

"Momma, I was scared!"

"Give it here Lizzy," she said as she paused for a moment, preparing to tell her husband the truth, the whole truth and nothing but the truth.

As Chauncey fumingly listened to the rather calm, but border line contentious, discourse between Jada and Lizzy, he anxiously awaited his opportunity to speak with his wife for the first time since the devastating news that Mr. Blankenship had rendered. He was becoming more and more incensed, however, over Jada's unhurried effort to get the phone from Lizzy and in his own hurry, turned off onto a dusty back road, speeding furiously to expedite an already short drive, the rest of the way, to his residence, which was, by now, in discernible peril.

After the brief exchange, though, Lizzy did give the phone to Jada and breathed a sigh of relief, because she felt in her heart that God had heard her little prayers. Feeling as though her tempestuous storm was, at long last, coming to a standstill, Lizzy stood at a distance, listening and waiting for any evidence of her mother's relief.

"Jada I know all about what happened today!" Chauncey sternly shouted. He was now only a few minutes away from home, but frustrated because a slow moving tractor trailer from a nearby chicken farm had negligibly pulled out in front of him, stopping the progress of his high-speed race toward Penelope Pines. "That's real stupid Jada. How could you do something so stupid?" he questioned as his anger mounted.

"Chauncey, whatever you heard was wrong." Jada answered back in a disconcerting and docile voice, as if she had no feelings left in her heart, provoking even more defamations from his mouth.

Feeling as though her parents were about to engage in another heated argument Lizzy disappointedly walked back to her room hoping and praying for a resolution. Her presumption was correct, but although she hoped and prayed that whatever was going on ended swiftly, what came out of her father's mouth next would only cause an already bad situation to get worse.

"All those niggas needed was somebody to slip up and out of all people you chose to do something as foolish as cheat on me with your boss in his damn office. How could you?" he angrily questioned as Jada begin to weep again, preventing her from responding the way she so badly desired. "What the hell were you thinking?"

"Do you hear me talking to you?! Damn it, answer me Jada!" he shot back again ferociously, hearing his wife's groans over his alleged adulterous exploits, but not knowing that she had placed the phone on her lap to shield her ears from any more attacks against her dignity.

Closing her eyes and bowing over as if she had a terrible stomach pain, Jada couldn't help but hear Chauncey's insulting and downright slanderous smear though, and mid sentence of another, Jada picked up the phone and lashed out at her unjustly critical husband.

"Shut up Chauncey! You don't know what you're talking about! If anybody's been stupid today, it's been you!"

"What? Have you lost your damn mind Jada?"

The truth of the matter was, Jada had lost the only mind she had ever had and the only thing Chauncey's quarrelling was doing was fueling her already heightened vengeful state of mind. By now she was all but through trying to state her case to her husband, because up to this point he hadn't even offered to lend an unbiased ear; nor had he taken the time to notice that something was severely wrong. So she reasoned that it was time to take matters into her own hands and in a voice as subdued and as the one she initially answered the phone with and as resolved as a woman bent on vindicating herself, Jada ended Chauncey's one-sided tirade and made declarations of her own that sent the preacher's blood pressure sky high.

"I thought I knew you Chauncey." she said, as she composed herself and dried her eyes.

"What are you talking about Jada? You're the one who messed up. How dare you."

"Jada, you're talking crazy."

"And you're talking stupid. You're arrogant and you're selfish and evidently, you don't know a thing about me, because if you did, you would know that…"

"What? That you love me?" He responded in the same type of arrogance that Jada had just described and interrupting her again, just as he'd done at other critical times during the day. "You better not let that come out of you mouth?"

Totally infuriated by Chauncey's interruption and failing to hold back the tears of anger and anguish that she had desperately tried to dam, Jada lost total control of her emotions once again and screamed…

"Believe what you want to about me! Believe whatever they said about me! But, the truth is, I was raped, you selfish bastard! Adolph James assaulted your wife; you pathetic excuse for a husband."

"What did you say? What…"

"I've been trying to talk to you all day!" she said as her voice trembled and her face was once again flooded with her tears. "I'm tired of trying to get through to you Chauncey. And just for the record, I'm not some loose floozy that would just cheat on my husband in a principal's office at an elementary school or anywhere else!" she said as she broke down again. "I was raped!" she tearfully shouted.

"Jada talk to me. Talk to me!"

"Damn you Chauncey!" With piercing words she screamed, "Damn you!"

And just like that she hung up the phone in fury, with her focus now totally drawn into a not so well thought out plan to vindicate herself, leaving Chauncey confused and in an even greater sense of emergency.

"Jada!" He screamed as the phone suddenly went dead from another earsplitting "Click!" "Jada!" he cried out hopelessly, as the thoughts of not making it home before something really bad happened tormented him even the more.

Lizzy thought that when her mother ended the contentious, but presumed beneficial, conversation with her father, that the worse of the worst was almost over. If nothing else, her daddy was on his way home and her daddy had always been her problem solver. Bearing that in mind, Lizzy waited, without worry, in her bedroom as her mother stormed about her own bedroom in total retribution mode, viciously slamming doors and opening drawers before hollering across the hall at Lizzy "Put on your shoes Lizzy!"

"Where are we going Momma?"

"Hush girl and put on your shoes!"

"But, daddy said he's on his way!"

"Hush and hurry up girl!"

In a rush to make it out of the house before Chauncey's likely "in the next second" return, Jada dashed down the stairs, dragging an uncooperative Lizzie behind, to grab the keys to an old Explorer that she had always felt was too big for her to drive. The hour of atonement had come for Adolph James and unfortunately, Chauncey's arrival would come a little too late.

Chapter 28

Chauncey was only about a country mile away from his neighborhood's south side entrance, which is one of the three entryways, to Penelope Pines, when Jada unexpectedly left the house. But, because he chose a slightly different route home on this particular day to expedite time, as Jada was pulling out on the, more frequently used, east side of the sprawling, housing development, Chauncey was pulling in through the little used south side entry way. In a nutshell, he had already missed her and it was evident that he had from the moment he pulled into the pine tree laced drive and opened the garage door with the remote control that was mounted on the electronics panel of the Mercedes. His heart raced as he pulled into the garage and for a moment he was baffled about what his next move should be. Like a mouse caught in a maze, Chauncey's confusion escalated, as he finally brought the car to a screeching halt.

"Dang!" he grunted to himself as he gritted his teeth in extreme anguish over his failure to make it home before his wife, potentially, made matters worse. Flinging the car door open and sprinting up the stairs leading from the garage as if he was a paramedic racing to an accident scene, Chauncey knew he'd better locate Jada fast. Because, from the sound of her voice during their last conversation and her inability to respond rationally to what he felt were warranted concerns, he knew that she was in no condition to drive her self anywhere nor was she in any condition to be solely responsible for Lizzy's safety;

especially in the dangerous and dreary road conditions on this cold February day.

He also had new fears that his wife, the love of his life, may have actually been assaulted by a man he knew was no good from the start. And his anger toward her for doing something "so stupid" slowly turned into fear that he had actually been the stupid one for overreacting and not recognizing his wife's plight; a fear that was substantiate when Leonard Maywhether would later call him to bear more unbearable news on this, the most difficult of days.

After entering the house, Chauncey made several unsuccessful attempts to reach Jada's cell phone, hearing only her cheerful voice mail greeting time after time after time. "Hi this is Jada but you missed me. Leave a message and I'll be sure to get back with you. And have a blessed day."

Almost out of breath and totally out of his natural mind due his lack of knowledge about what was really going on, Chauncey entered the bedroom and saw the evidence of Jada's prior rage.

Drawers were uncharacteristically left hanging open as the clothes that Jada had rummaged through earlier lay sloppily on the floor. The bedroom, to say the least, was in a mess. The bathroom door, which normally remained closed, was wide open and like the bedroom it too was uncharacteristically in a complete mess. Chauncey walked toward the bathroom with his right hand on his right hip and his left massaging his head as he whispered "God" continuously.

Just inside the bathroom doorway, he noticed the remnants of the phone that Jada had smashed just before she left the house, which was even more cause for Chauncey to be concerned. But what he saw next literally made the preacher sick to his stomach. The stench of the blood stained water that Jada had soaked in hours earlier still remained in the bathtub and the very sight of the stale, pinkish brew caused Chauncey to vomit in disgust over what may have actually happened in that tub.

He was now afraid for his wife's life. "What did she do?" he questioned himself in agony, wondering if she had harmed herself due to the distress she was undoubtedly under. But more than that, the last words that Jada spoke to him, kept on ringing out in his mind's ear as if she was standing right there beside him as he stood limply in the bathroom doorway "evidently you don't know me."

Chauncey should have known better, earlier, because he had a history with Jada and should've known that it just wasn't her nature to do something as foolish as what was alleged by Arthur Blankenship. Jada would never cheat on him, nor would she ever jeopardize their ministry. She hadn't done anything detrimental to their relationship from the day they met.

So as he thought about his next move he surmised that something wasn't right, but he just couldn't put his fingers on it. But before he had the opportunity to make anymore assumptions about his wife's guilt or innocence or what he thought the truth really was; his cell phone rang again. But this time the phone number was recognizable. It was the Sheriff, who bore news that would sadly clear up many of his unanswered questions.

After telling the pastor that he'd been trying to get in touch with the family all day to discuss this rather unsettling issue, Maywhether disclosed to Chauncey that there had indeed been a sex crime that occurred on that school campus and the very act had, indeed, been captured by a surveillance camera that had been secretly placed in the principals office by district security to monitor Mr. James' most recent alleged workplace harassment with another employee.

"Evidently they've had him under surveillance for a while Pastor and they believe that First Lady is the person he assaulted," the incensed Sheriff said, as Chauncey showed his own anguish over hearing of the atrocity that his wife had experienced at the hands of a man he could kill if he saw him.

"Aw Man! Don't tell me that Leonard," he said, as he fought back tears as he paced throughout the bedroom, imagining what Jada must've gone through.

"He's already in custody. We picked him earlier, but I really need to speak to First Lady. Can ya'll come down here to…" Leonard said before Chauncey interrupted, "I don't know where she is."

"I had a meeting and she wasn't here when I got here." he explained through his tears and as his blood boiled at the thought of not proving to be his wife's greatest protector.

"Calm down Pastor, I got it under control, but as soon as you here from her you call me."

In a panic and totally willing, now, to listen to and provide the security for his wife that he failed to provide earlier, he hung up the phone with the Sheriff and dialed Jada's cell phone number yet again without a care in the world about the church, Author Blankenship, or what anybody else thought about him or his wife. After what he'd heard from Leonard Maywhether all he cared about was seeing that the girl he loved was Ok and that she knew that she had all of his love and support.

But today wouldn't be that type of day. Of course she didn't answer her cell phone; she was still heated over his selfishness and inability to come to her rescue when she needed him most. Yea, she heard the phone's repeated ringing, but answering Chauncey's calls wasn't her priority at this moment, but something was, somebody was, seeing Adolph James suffer was; which was precisely the reason why she was on her way to his house to personally let him know that he wasn't going to get away without paying a hell of a price for what he'd done to her.

Adolph James had all of Jada's attention at this point because after carefully deliberating who could possibly be behind such an evil scheme, she felt confident that she knew who the culprit of Blankenship's character attacks was. And why shouldn't she think that Mr. James would be behind this palpable smear campaign? Think about it; he was the only one, other than her, who knew what really happened in his office today. And he would be the only person with a need to viciously attack her integrity by having "some man" to call her husband with nasty allegations of an affair.

It made sense to her now. James was trying to destroy her credibility because he knew that she would go to the police and he had too much to loose to just allow her to tell her story without administering some form of damage control. He was the only person imaginable, in her mind, who would have a motive to humiliate her publicly. And his motive was saving his own behind. Jada had figured it all out. It was Adolph James who had set out to ruin her life and no one else and reasoned that this must be the same kind of tactics that he used to discredit and destroy the testimony of Regina Eubanks. But little did she know, the man she vowed to harm with her own bare hands before telling police her side of the story, was already in shackles needing only her collaboration to ensure that he'd spend a substantial amount of time behind bars for what he'd done.

Driving at least eighty-five miles per hour during some stretches on a rain soaked interstate highway to confront him in front of his own wife, Jada murmured to herself "You won't get away this time; you bastard."

While Chauncey waited in anguish for any sign of his wife and daughter's whereabouts and Jada drove alone, after dropping Lizzy off at the Dunn's, through the bitter cold and driving rain, the masterminds of another failed corrupt and manipulative plan met at Pickett's farm as the dreary day slowly turned into an even dimmer and drearier night.

"Pickett the damn girl was raped! And Lula's fat ass didn't know what she was talking about!" Tally yelled at his counterpart as news of James' arrest and Jada's victimization circulated through the small town. "They've already arrested the principal. Damn!"

Cecil Whitlock had already been paid for his role in their plan, but even he was angered as he thought of how foolish Pickett and Tally were for initiating his involvement in a situation that they never had full proof of.

"What we gone do now Tally?" Pickett asked in concern, knowing that if their involvement was divulged they'd have hell to pay too.

"Nothin." he said as he stared in to the night. "None of ya'll say nothin' either!" he scornfully demanded. "Damn it I mean don't say a word! This is bad, Real bad."

And with that, at dusk, the three walked off ashamed, putting what they thought was a seal on the dastardly deed that would have at least one of these three men repenting to Chauncey before sunrise tomorrow morning.

By now it was about 6:00 and for a little over thirty minutes now Jada had been driving, on average, seventy five miles per hour in the driving rain and was only about seven minutes away from her desired exit before her quest for exoneration suffered a momentary but, timely interruption. Jada's fierce driving didn't calm her nerves at all and if it did anything, it made her even more upset that the other drivers on the road didn't understand her urgency to get to her destination, which prompted many of them to honk their horns to display their own anger.

On several occasions during her malicious mission obsessed drive toward vindication, she dangerously ripped passed slower traveling vehicles and in a slapdash fashion, cut through clusters of others that were, understandably slowed a bit from the normal speed limit of seventy miles per hour for weather provoked precautionary reasons. Luckily, little Lizzy didn't have to sit through her mother's unusual expressions of road rage because before Jada even ramped onto the interstate, she had sense enough to leave her daughter in the care of Ruth Anne and Billy, who thought something was strange about her behavior, but dismissed the bizarreness she exhibited as just work related stress. So, now free of childcare responsibilities and unable to subdue her newfound darker nature, she drove as fast as she could toward the James' home, without any regard for her own safety or anybody else's, which was exactly the case when a Florida State Trooper, appeared from behind the brush, where he had been hiding, to detect speeders and erratic drivers.

Jada fit both of those descriptions and by the time the trooper spotted the dark blue Ford Explorer coming toward him, he couldn't believe how anyone in their right mind could be driving so recklessly in weather as bad as it was on this day. So spinning his wheels in haste, he pulled from alongside the shoulder of the westbound highway in a cloud of mud, darted across the intersection to join the eastbound traffic, flipped on his blue lights and drove in excess of eighty miles per hour in an effort to track the older model SUV that was undoubtedly driven by a maniac.

Seeing the blue lights flashing in her rear view mirror, Jada's heart dropped and her mindset shifted from anger to fear almost instantaneously. Because, now the prospect of actually running afoul of the law was looking more and more like a grim possibility. She thought to herself that maybe Adolph James had already called the police and that maybe this officer was about to take her to jail on a charge that would make her situation look even worse than it already looked. It was a troubling moment for Jada, a moment of intense contemplation. "What will Chauncey think now?" she thought as she gauged the progression of the officer's pursuit in her rear view mirror, not knowing yet whether it would be best for her to attempt to flee or just pull over and surrender.

Reasoning that her life couldn't possibly be made worse by a trip to jail, she slowed down and pulled to the right shoulder of the interstate highway and waited for whatever was going to happen to run its full course. Thankfully, for Jada, none of what she thought about the trooper's presence was correct. He was actually just doing his job. She was speeding and driving recklessly, but maybe her speeding and recklessness on the highway had come to save her from herself. Finally coming to a complete stop, Jada leaned her head lackadaisically against the headrest, strumming her hair with her fingers, in total disbelief that something else so serious was about to happen to her on this forgettable day. She waited, miserably but silently, to be arrested as the tall, fully uniformed, burly, white man, slowly and cautiously approached her parked vehicle in rain gear.

After knocking on her window with his flashlight to get her attention and waiting in the drizzle, for her to roll the driver's side window down, the trooper asked with concern, "Ma'am, do you know how fast you were going?" in a resonant southern voice.

"No Sir. I don't. But, I know I was going too fast," she answered in full compliance to the trooper's questioning, feeling as though it was only a matter of time before she was arrested for harassment or the like.

"Too fast. Ma'am, when I clocked you backed there, you were going right at eighty-two miles per hour. That's twelve miles over the speed limit and in this weather you're trying to commit suicide if you keep doing that."

"Officer I'm really sorry. I was just in a hurry and didn't notice…"

"But, ma'am that's not the only reason I stopped you." he said sternly as Jada's heart raced at the very thought of what could come out of the trooper's mouth next. She knew that she could deal with getting a fine for speeding or even revocation of her driver's license, but even though she had prepared herself for the worse, deep down inside she really didn't want to go to jail.

Waiting for the trooper to reveal his real reason for stopping her, she contemplated telling him her side of the story first, but before she could finish thinking that possibility through, the trooper told her what his real purpose for pulling her over was.

"Look lady, I pulled you over because you were weaving from lane to lane like a bat out of hell," he said as Jada placed her left hand over her chest and breathed an undetectable sigh of relief. "And if I didn't stop you, you were either going to kill your self or somebody else. Now you were well over the speed limit and I'm going to write you a citation for that. But, because what you were doing was so dangerous and reckless, I'm also going to have to give you a sobriety test. So the first thing I'll need to see is your driver's license and your vehicle registration please."

By now, Jada was just relieved that she wasn't headed to jail. So without hesitation she subjected herself to any and all of the trooper's request, responding "Ok." to his every demand.

For the moment, at least, her little traffic ordeal had subverted her attention from her intentions of making James pay, which could prove pivotal if the traffic stop permanently disabled her malicious plans.

After receiving her driver's license and vehicle registration, the trooper ordered Jada to exit her vehicle under his watchful eye. She was dressed in a rather nice, charcoal colored skin tight dress which was usually accompanied by a fancy blazer and black winter boots. But on this night, fashion was the least of her concerns. She had actually walked out of the house with a tee shirt on top of her dress that read "God's Property" and slippers with no socks.

Complying with the officer's orders, Jada climbed wearily out of the explorer and followed the man to his patrol unit where she was asked to wait in the back seat as he conducted a standard check for outstanding warrants. The warrant check, which only took a few minutes, seemed like an eternity to Jada, who sat silently in the back of that car and stared helplessly straight ahead, feeling as though she had been victimized all over again. But slowly, however, she began to decompress. She began to release all of the anger and anxiety from her system. She didn't cry, maybe because she had cried all she could cry, but, oh what a relief it was for her finally to think soberly about her life again. No, not about what happened in this particular day, but her life her whole life. Doing so made her consider that even including what happened today, all of her good days had outweighed her bad days and that's what came to her remembrance as she sat in the back of the patrol unit.

Yes, when she left home she was angry as hell. And by the time she was pulled over by that state trooper, she was fearful. But, now, as she sat helplessly waiting for the trooper to conclude his precautionary background checks, Jada was more reflective than anything else and thought favorably about how comfortable she would be if she was in her own home, out of the cold and rain, in the loving arms of her husband, hearing Lizzy's sometimes annoying but laughable demands.

She thought of how bad she just wanted to get on with life. Understandably, her initial response to James' violation was great disgust which led to what one might consider temporary insanity. But as she sat there and waited for the trooper's verdict, she reasoned that what Adolph James had done to her wasn't reason enough for her to loose everything that she had worked so hard to gain and maintain. What he had done to her wasn't worth loosing the two people that she loved most in the world. After all, what was the worse that could come out of all of this? She knew Chauncey really loved her and surmised that the only thing this could do was make each of them and their relationship stronger. She knew that her church family loved her and wouldn't ever believe that she was as slutty as James' tried to portray her. After all Adolph James had a history of this kind of behavior and Jada knew that once the people she cared about weighed and considered her testimony against his, he wouldn't have a snowball's chance in hell at saving face. "I'm going to do this the right way." she said to her herself, finally bringing closure to her need for vengeance. She wasn't in any way OK with what had happened to her, but thanked God that she was caught speeding before she did something she'd regret for the rest of her life. She could've never imagined it but being temporarily under arrest was one of the most purifying experiences she'd ever had in her life. It was a cleansing of sorts for Jada and she peacefully smiled as she mapped out in her head what she'd do once she was released. Calling Chauncey was at the top her list.

Chapter 29

While Jada patiently and peacefully waited alongside the interstate highway as her traffic ordeal was drawing to a close, she seemed refreshed, as if the sun had somehow defied nature's rhythm and shined through the dark of night into her mind's cloudiness to give her a sense of direction. She had made up her mind that after she talked to Chauncey, she was ready to go to the police to allow them to hand down any retribution to Mr. James if there was to be any handed down. This was too big for her handle alone and to be honest the only way to handle this situation without perpetuating any further problems was to let the men and women in uniform do what they were trained to do. Upset, yes. Hurt, yes. Abused and humiliated, yes. But, as far as Jada was concerned, the worse was already over and she couldn't wait to get home to her family and on with the rest of what had already been a very privileged life style. However, in stark contrast, Chauncey waited for his wife in unrest, as his own mind became cloudier by the minute and his hopes of finding a resolution before becoming the subject of ridicule become more of a reality.

He was still at home, but by now, word had already spread about what had happened to Jada. Lizzy, who was now back at home with her daddy hadn't a clue, but the Dunn's, who were in utter shock over the news about what had happened and subsequent rumor mill that had begun after word hit the street, sat dejectedly and silently with Chauncey as he waited for any word from his missing wife.

To Chauncey, calling Jada wasn't even an option any longer. He had been calling, it seems like, forever and she hadn't answered up to this point. So he painfully rationalized that when and if she was ready to talk she'd call. And when she's ready to come home, she'd come home. He thought of how upset she must have been when she left the house and blamed himself for not engaging her in the type of conversation that could've possibly changed the questionable activities of the day. But he was resolved to wait, all be it in a terrible cold sweat, he was resolved to wait until his wife either called or came home.

What he didn't know was that Jada was saying her good byes to a Florida State trooper that had shown her great favor and was waiting and wanting to hear his voice as much as he wanted to hear hers.

"Mrs. Pennington, I checked out everything and you don't have a criminal history and our records didn't show anything that would suggest that you've even had a traffic ticket. And…your tag is good and you don't smell like alcohol and you don't appear to me to be under the influence of any drugs, so I'm going to give you a little break today, Alright."

"Yes Sir. Thank you." she said humbly, as she looked down at the ground, not yet believing that this was the end of this ordeal.

"I don't know why and I don't normally do this but I am," he said, shaking his head as if he couldn't believe what he had just said. "But I must ask you, where in God's creation were you trying to get to?"

"Officer, I had a day at work that I care not to describe at this point," she said as she managed to smile even though her heart was feeling a tremendous amount of pain. "But I just wanted to blow off some steam and to be honest I'm glad you stopped me. It was almost as if God placed you here at the right time to protect me from myself. And because of that I thank you; not just because you gave me a break but because you protected me."

"Well ma'am, I don't know about all that, but just slow it down and be a little more careful. I've seen a many of accidents on this stretch of highway and it's never pretty. So be safe and you have a good night."

After the trooper said "good night" Jada was free to go, not to her initial destination, but home. She was tired by now, and was actually developing a painful tension headache. She was uncertain about what her immediate future would hold and was quite unsure of how her husband would react to the news she had to share, but one thing was for certain; she knew now, more than ever, how important Chauncey was to her and desired to call him immediately. But due to the decreasing visibility brought on by the darkness and the now even heavier, driving rain, Jada decided not to make any phone calls while she was driving. So in an act of safety, though delaying her homecoming a bit, she exited off of the interstate into the huge parking lot of a truck stop that had, ironically enough, been visited earlier in that day by Pickett, Tally and Lula Penny to discuss a plan to destroy her.

At a complete stop and in a secure, well lit area, Jada reached down into her purse and grabbed her cell phone as the sounds of big rigs and city style hustle and bustle noised through the old Explorer's broken vents. She thought briefly about calling Billy and Ruth Anne first, to tell them that she was on her way to get Lizzy, but she knew that Lizzy was in good hands and figured that it was more important, at this time, to call her husband.

"Where in the world could Jada be?" Chauncey thought, as Jada dialed her home phone almost simultaneously. "Why hasn't she called?"

But in the middle of his thoughts, and totally out of the blue, the phone rang as Billy and Ruth Anne sat quietly in another room, watching over a totally oblivious, Lizzy. And when it did it was if Chauncey had heard a fire alarm.

Jumping up from his chair with a tom cat's quickness, he answered his desk phone with the anxiety of a big game hunter, as important church documents were scattered as a result of his mad dash and Billy and Ruthie rushed in.

"Hello, Hello!" he breathlessly answered, hoping and praying that he would hear Jada's voice on the other end of the line.

"Hello?" she answered back in a soft, unassuming voice, hoping and praying, herself, that Chauncey wouldn't exhibit the same type of temperament that had provoked their previous dissension.

"Jada, is this you?" he asked, knowing full well that it was indeed his wife's voice, but wanting to be certain it was before he breathed a long awaited sigh of relief.

"Yes, it's me," she replied as he did just that.

"Baby where are you? I've been worried about you. Where are you baby?" he pantingly questioned as the Dunn's hugged each other in relief that their prayers had been answered.

"I'm just outside of Tallahassee, parked at the truck stop; the one near the interstate."

"Jada, I miss you and I love you and I just need you to come home, baby. I promise I'm not upset. I know about what happened to you. I know baby and they got him locked up. Just come home."

As Jada cried while hearing her husbands comforting words, she was left speechless, knowing now that everything would be OK. She had heard Chauncey say that James was already locked up, but she was so relieved that he was finally listening to her that she didn't even ask how anyone else even knew about what happened. She was just glad that he said he knew the truth.

"Why are you crying baby?"

"I can't help it."

"Do you want me to come get you baby."

"No, I'm fine," she tearfully responded to the tender offer of her husband.

"I didn't know what to do Chauncey. I don't know what to do. I…"

"Shhhhh…Hush baby," he whispered, wanting so badly to hold her in his arms.

"Chauncey I feel so bad and I'm scared. I didn't want to…"

"Hush baby…I know Jada. I know. Baby just crank up the car and come home baby. Come on home. We can get through this baby. Just come home."

For about ten seconds or so, not a word was uttered by either of them. The only sounds that could be heard through their respective earpieces were those of the cars and trucks that noisily meandered through the truck stop and of course, that of the pounding rain and the howling winds that had, unfortunately, picked up steam over the course of the few minutes that Jada had been stationary.

Her silence was borne out of relief that she had finally released herself from the pain of having to hold something so tragic, inside of her for so long. But, on the other hand, Chauncey's silence was a product of the sheer pain of knowing he wasn't able to protect Jada from such an egregiously malicious episode and fury over what he visualized James had done to her. But with the strength of a man resolved to make things right for his wife and the propensity to become Adolph James' legal nightmare, Chauncey dried his eyes and broke the silence and gave his wife reassurance that, like Jesus, he'd never leave her or forsake her again.

"Hey Jada…"

"Huh," she softly answered as she dried her own eyes, feeling a little better, now knowing that she was no longer alone in this all important battle for her dignity.

"Girl, I love you so much… more than you'll ever know," he said sincerely to the echoing of "I know," from Jada. "And nothing that could ever happen in this world will ever stop me from loving you as long as I live. I'm sorry baby, I'm sorry that this happened to you and I'll never let anything like this ever happen to you again."

"I know Chauncey."

"Just come home, baby. I just want to hold you. And I'll call Leonard when we get off the phone and by the time you get here, we'll know exactly what to do next; Ok?... Just come home, baby."

"I'm on my way. I should be there in about twenty minutes."

"It's storming baby. Don't rush just be careful."

"I love you Chauncey."

"I love you too. I'll see you when you get here."

With that being said, Jada bided farewell to Chauncey, put down her cell phone, turned the key in the ignition, and ventured intrepidly into the storm and rain to reunite with her husband, felling, now, that, at long last, this horrible day was coming to an abrupt end; with her family still intact, with her integrity only marginally marred, and with "that damned" Adolph James paying an appropriate price for what he had done to her.

Chapter 30

After Chauncey hung up the phone with Jada, he called Leonard to make him aware of Jada's momentary arrival to which the Sheriff responded, "I'll be there in thirty minutes."

After talking to his wife, he seemed somewhat relieved of some of the tremendous amount of stress he was under. And although he was still undeniably furious and terribly tormented over what had happened to Jada at the hands of Adolph James, he along with the Dunn's was comforted a bit, primarily, because he had finally heard her voice. He knew that she was safe and he was very thankful, that after a long day of many failures on his part, he had finally been able to give Jada the kind of comfort, love and support she needed, so badly, to be able to deal with a trial as tumultuous as this one. In four words, Jada was coming home.

He should've known, from the very beginning, that something more serious was going on in his wife's life, because everything she did or said during the course of this day was totally out of character for her. And as the rain pitter pattered against his office window pane and the wind blew boisterously through the trees, Chauncey sat down at his desk once again, but this time in a revelatory moment, realizing that his relationship with his wife meant more to him than that church, those "important" people, and everything else that had caused a strain on his marriage. Jada meant more than life to this man and he'd prove that fact to everyone.

After his brief contemplations, Chauncey walked upstairs to the bedroom, as Billy and Ruth Anne sat anxiously awaiting their First Lady's arrival, to revisit a sight that had devastated him only an hour or so ago. It was still a mess and it bore signs of the day's struggles that he didn't want the woman he loved to revisit. So he set out to clean up a bit before she came home.

It was only a short time before her expected arrival, but for the next fifteen minutes, Chauncey walked through the couple's bedroom and picked up the clothes that had been strewn about during Jada's fit of rage and shut drawers that were left hanging open as a result of her haste to get out of the house before he came home. It was painful to put his hands on the panties and bras and outfits that used to make his wife feel so good and empowered and it was even more painful to pick up the clothes that she had actually worn to work today. He didn't want to touch them but he did, dropping the sweaty sex smelling skirt and blouse that she had worn to work into the dirty clothes hamper in the bathroom. He wasn't thinking about the forensic value of the clothing at the time, but law enforcement would need those clothes a little later to substantiate video evidence against James to aid in an impending trial.

As he finished tidying up the bedroom he entered the bathroom, where he was presented with an equally daunting task. The floor was still littered with the shattered fragments of a broken telephone. The tub was still filled with the stagnant blood ridden water that had stood as still as time had seemed to stand, unbothered, from the moment that Jada got out of it. But none the less he cleaned, glancing at his watch occasionally as he swept up phone fragments and drained and wiped down the downright filthy tub, wanting to be done before Jada arrived. It wouldn't be a complete cleaning job but he would accomplish his mission of leaving the master suite in better condition than he found it.

In a way, Chauncey's cleaning spree was therapeutic. It was almost as if the more he repositioned misplaced items the more he felt as if he was actually putting the pieces to Jada's life back together again. The more he wiped away stains from the tub the more it seemed as if he was cleaning her life's slate. It seemed as though the more he straightened the mess that she had made the more he felt as though he was beginning to straighten out the mess that James had made for both them. But as he put the finishing touches on his spur-of-the-moment sprucing, spraying a fresh air fragrance into the air, he felt as though Jada's arrival was imminent, which, in itself, caused a flood of emotions.

He was a bit apprehensive at first, because, though he longed to see her, he didn't know if he knew the right words to say to her. But, at the same time his heart raced in excitement because he couldn't wait another second to hug her.

After he left the bedroom he walked back downstairs to join the Dunn's in their ever increasing anxious wait for Jada. But he couldn't just sit, motionless, with them in the living room. Chauncey had too many emotions flowing through him to just sit around. So in a moment of expectation he got up and meandered out to the couple's large, farm house styled, front porch. He wasn't just too anxious to sit down but he wanted to be the first person that Jada saw when she pulled into the drive.

So he paced as he waited and waited, periodically stopping to rub the finely finished wood of the rarely used, antique, rocking chairs that Jada had always said reminded her of the first time she met Aunt Eunice. And as the rains and wind subsided a bit, he watched for her in the bitter cold, knowing that he should see signs of her arrival at any moment.

He waited, as time passed, staring expectantly into the dark gray night, looking for the glimmer of headlights. But as he waited, anticipation quickly turned into trepidation as his eyes shifted from Jada's path to his watch, which by this time showed that the twenty-five minutes he had reasonably allotted for Jada's return had passed by almost ten minutes.

And by the time he looked at his watch a second time, ten more minutes had passed and Jada still hadn't shown up and surprisingly, Maywhether was noticeably late too. This really wasn't making any sense to Chauncey, but he reasoned that the weather must be holding them both up. As his worry escalated, he contemplated calling her cell phone again. But in a sight that must've resembled that of Paul's Damascus Road experience, Chauncey's trepidation turned into unspeakable joy as lights began to slowly careen down the curved path towards the house.

"Billy! Ruthie! I see her! He called out to the equally overjoyed Dunn's as they ran towards the front porch to meet her.

Breathing like he did the day he saw her walk down the aisle and with as much anticipation as he had when he was waiting for her father to utter the words "You may now kiss the bride.", he looked on excitedly as the Ford headlights continued their slow but onward path to the Pennington estate. But as the lights unhurriedly came closer, Chauncey's smile gradually fell away from his face, because what he thought was a sure sign of Jada's homecoming was anything but.

"That's Leonard," he said to Billy with slight disappointment voice. He now noticed that the headlight he saw were those of the sheriff's specially outfitted Ford pick up truck.

After pulling slowly into the confused pastor's drive he got out of his vehicle just as slowly. He greeted the Dunn's as he pulled off his hat but refused to make eye contact with his pastor.

"Leonard we thought you were Jada," Chauncey said with a forced smile on his face. "She should've been here by now, but I'm glad you're here…" he nervously rambled before Leonard abruptly cut him off as Billy and Ruthie looked on with worry.

"Pastor," he said calmly in a practiced, sheriff's voice. "I need you to come with me. And ya'll probably need come too," he said as he gazed at the worried couple signifying that something was evidently wrong.

With his anticipation deflated and confusion written all over his face, Chauncey was downright disappointed. He had thought that Jada was arriving and he wanted, so bad, for it to be Jada because he just wanted to hold her and begin her process of healing. He was glad to see Maywhether, but he would've preferred if it was Jada at the door and to make matters worse he didn't understand why Maywhether had asked him to leave his house.

With his palms outstretched as if to signify he didn't understand, he addressed the Sheriff, hopeful that his wife would be pulling up any minute.

"She'll be here in a minute Leonard," he continued as Maywhether held his head down with an awfully sad look upon his face, "she hasn't made it in yet. Come on in." He pleaded as the look on Leonard's face began to trouble him. "She'll be here in a minute. I know she will because I just talked to her." He continued, purposely not giving Maywhether a chance to respond.

The look on Leonard's face was horrible and it spoke volumes about what he felt in his heart. And Chauncey knew deep down inside that something was wrong and the longer Leonard stood silently, unable to look him in the eyes, his suspicions grew grimmer and grimmer. Without waiting for a response Chauncey tried again to offer Maywhether inside only to be spurned again.

"Pastor, I need you to come with me. It's about First Lady."

"Man, don't tell me she's in jail. Is she in jail? Did she do something wrong?" Chauncey asked, hoping Jada hadn't done something they'd both regret.

Taking a deep breath, but not totally willing at this point to divulge the seriousness of the matter, Maywhether spoke in evasive terms to persuade Chauncey to get into his waiting, county purchased, law enforcement vehicle as Billy and Ruth Anne retrieved Lizzy and prepared to follow the men.

Maywhether who was already visibly shaken, seemed to become more dejected than he already was when he saw that little girl smiling as she walked out the front door. It was as if his heart literally broke right before their eyes. And Chauncey knew from Leonard's facial expressions that no matter what his news would be; it wasn't going to be good. As they got into the running truck and drove off of the Pennington property, followed by the Dunn's who had Lizzy, Chauncey prepared himself for the worse, thinking that if he had only listened to his wife, this situation would've never come to this; whatever this was.

As Maywhether drove as if he was responding to a national catastrophe, Chauncey continued to think, never even questioning Maywhether about where they were actually going. All he knew was that they were going somewhere and that somewhere had answers about Jada's immediate future. Little did he know, though, Jada wasn't in the Sheriff's jail and Leonard had no intentions of taking them there. He was on his way to the county's rural, rarely visited hospital where he would find out just how bleak his future with Jada really was.

Entering the emergency room parking, lot Chauncey's eyes gaped open as his blood pressure began to rise. It was at this point that Chauncey began to ask Maywhether questions about what had actually taken place from the time that he had last spoken to her until now. Now ready to give Chauncey the devastating news, Maywhether parked his truck just outside the small emergency room's door and told his pastor that Jada had been in a serious car accident on the interstate and that he didn't know her current status.

Hearing those words, Chauncey all of a sudden unlatched his seatbelt and ran towards the emergency room entrance leaving Maywhether behind and the truck door hanging open.

"Oh my God." he repeated continuously, as he raced toward the double glass sliding doors. "Oh my God."

He was traumatized, but for the first time today he actually prayed. It wasn't a formal prayer and he wasn't on bended knee, but he prayed as he frantically walked through the emergency room doors. It didn't take him long to get to the waiting room entrance and when he did he could've cared less about noticing all of the other waiting patients. But if he had, he would've noticed all of their grim stares as they looked upon him with grave pity. "Where is my wife?" he shouted as the strains of worry wore heavy on his heart and face, questioning a smiling receptionist at the front desk.

"Sir, calm down," she said, trying to control a situation that she felt could quickly get out of hand.

"Now who are you looking for?" she asked as she poised herself to enter a name into the computer as the Dunn's trotted in with Lizzy.

"Jada Pennington. She was in an accident..." he said, before being interrupted by the now serious looking paraprofessional.

"Ok. Just calm down Sir and have a seat. Someone will be out to speak with you in a moment." She had already been made aware of Jada's condition, but hospital protocol required that someone more seasoned in dealing with cases like this, be responsible for addressing family members.

"All I want to know is is she alright?" he said, composing himself, calming down a bit, seeing no emergency on the woman's face. "Just please tell me where she is. Is she even here?" he continued as Leonard stood afar in grief.

"Yes Sir, we have her. But, if you would have a seat, a doctor will be out to talk to you in just a minute" she answered, not wanting to involve herself in the further obliteration of Chauncey's world.

Chauncey was fearful that his wife was already in surgery. What other reason would the receptionist have to tell him to wait on a doctor for? So as he poised himself to be informed of the nature of Jada's injuries, Ruth Anne began to walk outside with Lizzy, who had become fretful during her father's chaotic quest for answers only to be called back in by her pastor, who felt the need to hold on to his daughter. He knew that Lizzy was old enough to know what a hospital was and he also knew that she was mature enough to handle the fact that her mother was there. So he whispered in her ear and told her. "We're waiting for the doctor to tell us how momma's doing. She was in an accident, but she'll be fine. Remember I told you that God gave us doctors to help us when we're sick?"

"Yes Sir." the little girl replied as she clutched her father even harder. "Well, they're going to make momma feel better, OK?"

"OK." she answered, as Leonard rubbed her back for reassurance, as she sat in her father's lap.

Just as Chauncey finished giving Lizzy an update on what he thought her mother's condition was, out walked three individuals donned in white lab coats. They each had clipboards and the only woman of the three carried a bible.

Not knowing who among the people sitting in the emergency waiting room, was actually Jada's family, one of the doctors asked.

"Is the family of Jada Pennington here?"

"Yes, we're here." Chauncey stood up and said as he handed Lizzy off to Ruthie.

"Sir may I ask your relationship to Mrs. Pennington?"

"I'm her husband. Could somebody please tell me what's going on with my wife. I need to see her...she needs to know that I'm out here."

"We will Sir, but first we're going to have to ask you and your family to come with us to the family counseling room," the doctor said kindly, understanding the fragileness of a husband's mind at such a time as this.

Without hesitation, Chauncey willingly followed the woman and two men, understanding that the doctor's would want to talk to them privately about Jada's condition. As he walked slowly behind, he beckoned for Billy and Leonard to come with him and told Ruthie to bring Lizzy along as well. As they walked down the long, quiet hallway, they all heard the pitter patter of feet coming up just behind them and much to their surprise it was Daphne who had heard, from a friend that Jada had been in an accident.

Finally, after reaching the family counseling room, Chauncey along with his daughter and friends were encouraged to have a seat on the couch that was located in the center of the cold cream painted hospital room. It was a bit uncomfortable, but with the exception of Leonard, who braced himself against the wall, they all crammed onto the couch, waiting for one of the three individuals to give them any information that would bring them closer to the realization of what had happened to a woman that they all loved so dearly.

With the family finally seated and as comfortable as possible, the lady opened her bible and recited "Come unto me all ye that labor and are heavy laden and I will give you rest." Nodding their heads, but not fully understanding the magnitude of what she had just read, they all waited in silence for more information and they got more from the tall dark haired, doctor who said as solemnly as he could in a thick Arabic accent…

"Mr. Pennington, your wife was in an accident tonight," he began as Chauncey looked on as if to say go ahead. "She suffered tremendous head trauma and we had to attempt emergency surgery. We did all we could do and I'm so sorry to inform you that your wife has passed away."

With that Jada Alexia Pennington had just been pronounced dead and the curtains that had opened on a life only a short time ago in Odessa, Texas were closed.

Chapter 31

It was silent for a brief moment and the darkness of the night couldn't qualify as an adequate description of the darkness that had just fallen in that room. The coolness of the late winter February air couldn't do justice for the portrayal of how cold an already air conditioned hospital conference room really felt when the news of Jada's death fell upon her loved ones like a ton of brick. The news was unexpected to say the least and to use verbiage like unbearable would be a terrible understatement and it wouldn't be long before pure chaos erupted.

Shaking their heads "No!" as if they could not believe what they had just heard, everyone in that room except Chauncey begin to sob uncontrollably. What was even worse was the fact that, in the midst of all of the pain and suffering, was a little girl who cried but hadn't yet grasped that magnitude of what she had heard, not even understanding, at this time, that she would never see her mother again. And poor Daphne; she screamed so loud that it was scary. It was piercing. It was eerie. That girl was in so much pain. And as Lizzy begin to cry, due to the overwhelming emotions that were overflowing that room, Leonard, who shook his own head and cried uncontrollably himself, did his best to keep Daphne from injuring herself as she jumped up and down and pounded her fist against the solid cinder block wall.

As for Chauncey, it was almost as if he was stuck in time; for the moment at least. He heard exactly what that doctor had said and he heard all the crying and commotion that was going on around him. He even saw the doctors as they walked out and grief counselors walked in. But, he sat there, motionless as he gulped and stared straight ahead as his visibility slowly began fade due to the tears that were unconsciously beginning to flow.

He hadn't screamed like Daphne yet and he hadn't even flinched since the doctor said what he said. But it wouldn't take long before he lost all control too. It was his daughter's little hands that triggered his hidden emotions.

Lizzy was still crying, but when she noticed that her daddy had also began to cry she did her best imitation of her mother, trying desperately to wipe every one of his tears from his eyes. It was at that point that he reached out and grabbed his daughter and held her so tight that she cried more from the pain of his grasp than she did from the pain of seeing her father's grief. That man was hurting. Just looking at Lizzy was so hurtful, so painful and the news that he had just lost the only woman that he had ever loved, placed him on the brink of a serious emotional breakdown.

Everyone in that room was completely devastated. Everyone in that room was visibly shaken to the core and it wasn't long before that very room was filled with even more sorrowful visitors, who like those before them, lost complete control when they heard the news.

News had spread quickly that Jada had been in a serious car crash. And one family at a time, the townspeople began to converge on the hospital emergency room to hear any more news of the First Lady's fate. But as they were escorted toward the secluded area where Chauncey expressed his sorrow, no doubt was left in their minds about her fortune. Chris Blocker was one of the last to show up on this fateful night and he lost complete control too after he asked, "What's going on ya'll?" and hearing "She's gone Chris." from one of the sorrowful mourners.

By now, at least twenty-five people had crammed into the room which had the capacity to hold only twenty. And in all the chaos, Chauncey's emotional sate continued to deteriorate quickly. He was hysterical by this point, mumbling words that no one could possibly understand, holding his head in his heads as the veins in his forehead protruded as if he had been given a lethal injection. Although no one knew exactly what the words were that came out of his mouth, it was clear that he was crying out for Jada. "She gone ya'll." he mumbled uncontrollably at times and "I want my wife ya'll." at others as some of the older women, including Mother Snelling, rubbed his back and reassured, "She alright son, she alright now."

By now Billy and Ruth Anne had removed Lizzy from the room and took her outside into the brisk air to explain to the little girl that her mother had died. "Your momma passed away tonight baby." Ruth Anne said as Lizzy looked helplessly into her eyes as if she didn't fully understand what her "Aunt Ruthie" was trying to say. "She's OK though, she's with the Lord OK."

"I want my momma!" the girl screamed as she cried at the thought of not being held by the woman who always wiped her tears away. "I want my momma," she cried.

"I'm so sorry Baby." Ruth Anne pitifully answered in condolence.

As Lizzy cried in the arms of Ruth Anne, Billy sought out to find Chauncey, who was deep into the mass of people that had gathered at the hospital. It was a difficult task because by the time he tried to find him, at least seventy five people had converged on the entryway to the emergency room, all of whom were extremely devastated by the news that had ripped through their small community like a ravenous hurricane.

Among the throng of mourners, however, sat the man who was in the throws of the most devastating day he had experienced since he lost his own mother and father to an unreal murder at age seven. Jada had become that man's life, his everything and had given him the most beautiful years of his life. And as he sat there in the arms of a big breasted older lady that he didn't even know personally, rocking back and forth, and sobbing profusely, he thought about his purpose for living. "She was all I had." he would say intermittently. "I came down here by myself, she was all I had."

In one crazy day he lost it all though; his best friend, his sounding board, his confidant, the mother of the most beautiful daughter in the world. In one day he lost it all. And his mind was slipping away from him too. He was too sorrowed to feel spite over what had potentially caused all of this, too bereaved to point a single finger at any person responsible for Jada's agitated state of mind before she died. So sorrowed and bereaved that for a split second he even thought about just ending all of his pain by taking his own life. After all what was his purpose of living? In all of the hysteria, the very man who had always proclaimed the Goodness and Mercy of God, slowly begin to stray away from his own advice of "giving God the glory no matter the circumstance." Yes the Reverend Chauncey E. Pennington even began to question the very authenticity of God's protective hand. "She didn't deserve this!" he would scream out. "Why Lord? Why?" he continuously questioned the master.

But after briefly contemplating ending his own pain and suffering he thought of how selfish it would be to leave Lizzy in this "damn crazy world" all by herself.

So in as much misery and with as many tears flowing down his face as were flowing the moment he realized that he had forever lost the love of his life, he sought out to find his baby. He was desperate to find Lizzy.

"Where's Lizzy?" he asked as he finally stood up and looked through the ever growing crowd, wiping his eyes, trying to show a semblance of strength.

As the room quieted momentarily as if Jesus had entered the room, Chauncey asked again "Where's my baby?" as those who had tried to gather themselves to be strong for their pastor lost it all over again as the realization of little Lizzy's loss became evident.

The weeping continued at even a greater pitch now, but Chauncey was resolute, wanting to be the one to comfort his daughter. Slowly pressing his way through the crowd, the bewildered pastor was ushered toward the light that shined from the hallway through the exit door, which was where he found the arms of Billy Dunn who was on a frantic search of his own for Chauncey. It was at that time that Billy just held his friend, crying as he assured "I'm here with you. I'm here for you man."

Ushering Chauncey outside to be with his daughter Billy continued to cry as he watched his pitiful leader's countenance shrivel before his eyes. As they walked down the same hallway that had previously led them to the unfathomable news of Jada's death, Chauncey and Billy shared no conversation; only thoughts about the grief that had not only taken hold of their lives, but the pain that had evidently gripped the emotions of a whole town. Feeling Billy's gentle pats on the back, Chauncey, almost unconsciously, made his way through the drizzle and chill to find his daughter who was still in Billy's running car in Ruthie's loving arms. By the time he reached the car Lizzy was still crying and shivering from the effects of a tragedy that one wouldn't wish on his worst enemy.

Chauncey immediately grabbed her and held her close, kissing her forehead continuously as if he had seen her for the first time in years. He occasionally whispered into her little ears word's that not only comforted her, but gave him a momentary false sense of strength as well. "Momma's OK now baby," he whispered. "She's alright."

Deep down inside he really didn't believe a word he was saying and if only Lizzy had looked up into his blank face or looked into his hopeless tear filled eyes she would've immediately known that her strong father wasn't as strong as his words made her believe he was. But Chauncey knew that saying those words were essential to his daughter's faith in a brighter day and if masking his weariness would help her cope with the loss of her mother any better he would do it all over again. And in a way it did help because the little girl stopped crying, ceased her shivering and clung to the only parent she now had.

With Lizzy dealing with her pain a little better, Chauncey urged Ruth Anne to take the girl home. She had been through enough and Chauncey knew that the worst, for him was just around the horizon. He hadn't even called Jada's father, nor did he know how to begin to tell him that his only daughter had been killed in what he thought was highly preventable car accident. He hadn't called Aunt Eunice yet either. Chauncey knew it would just break her heart once she found out. But more importantly, Chauncey knew that at some point real soon he was going to have to make decisions concerning Jada's remains. It was all too much for him and asked Leonard Maywhether, who had resurfaced from the depth of mourners, to assist in making phone calls to the people he dreaded revealing the news to. Little did he know, though, the Blaylocks already knew. Aunt Eunice already knew and both were flying in on the first flights out of their respective cities. Maywhether had possession of Chauncey's cell phone and had called both the Blaylocks and Aunt Eunice, because he knew that Chauncey would need all the help he could get in this most difficult of times.

"Pastor I know its rough right now." Leonard said, as he gripped Chauncey's shoulders with his right hand as the defeated looking Pastor used both his hands to cover his lowered head. "But we need to identify the body and then we'll need to call a funeral home to remove her remains," he said somberly, choking up again as Chauncey shook his head and whispered "I can't do this man."

When he said that he couldn't do it, he wasn't referring to identifying Jada's body as much as he was making reference to his inability to live through yet another life altering experience and unwillingness to go on with life without Jada. But in a brief moment of fabricated strength he reasoned, "You're right Leonard. I need to go see her." He didn't want his wife to spend another second alone in such an unfamiliar place.

And with that they walked. Chauncey led the way as Billy and Leonard walked slowly behind as if they were walking to the death chamber for their own executions; silently with heads down, bracing for the worse of Chauncey's emotions.

By the time Chauncey reached the room where Jada's lifeless body laid, he had already made up his mind that he had to be strong for her. It sounds a little silly to those of us not in Chauncey's shoes, but he really didn't want Jada to see him cry. Bracing himself for a sight that he knew was horrific and insisting that he must go in alone, Chauncey walked into the operating room and pulled back the curtain that had hid his wife from the world's eyes and opened his own eyes to find her, almost unnoticeable.

Her body was badly mangled, but the impact of seeing her in that way was minimized a bit by the nursing staff's quick attempt to make her body as presentable as possible. She had been thrown from her vehicle at least a hundred and fifty feet into a densely wooded area and her hands, black and blue, bore the evidence that she had tried desperately to save herself. A drizzle of some type of watered down bloody liquid was still dripping from her nostrils onto the bed sheets. Her head laid limply and close to her right shoulder. Her eyes stayed fixed in a wide open position as if she was staring at the wall.

One of her arms, which was badly bruised and cut up from the encounter with the windshield and towering pines, was visible, hanging just from underneath the white linen covering that was intended to prevent any one from seeing that kind of atrociousness. Her feet, which bore her freshly painted, candy apple red, toe nails, stuck out from under that sheet as well. One of her toes had already been donned a toe tag, which was even more proof that there was no life left in that little body.

Not knowing what to say or how to react, Chauncey just stood there by his wife's side, crying, blaming himself in the same fashion that he did when his parents were killed. His emotions were running high; so high at moments that he couldn't even swallow. As if something was caught up in his windpipe. Chauncey would gasp at times as he looked upon the girl that had made almost all of his dreams come true.

He was sad and at times he was very reflective, thinking to himself about the first time he ever laid eyes on the bubbly cheerleader from Odessa. He reflected on the many days and nights that they cried together and shared their longings for parents they never really got to know. They had so much in common and they brought each other so much happiness.

Shaking his head in utter disbelief that she was really gone, he screamed to the top of his lungs, "No! …No! God no!"

Hearing their pastor's tormented cries just beyond the green privacy curtain, Billie and Leonard agreed that it was time to go in and comfort the man who was hurting so bad. They walked in silently, though they continued to wipe their own eyes, and consoled Chauncey, rubbing his back at times and whispering encouraging words at others. It was an undeniably tough moment for them, but neither man could possibly fully understand the type of pain their downtrodden leader was in.

It was after his comforters walked in the room, that Chauncey begin to open up and talk to and about his lost love. He told her that he'd always love her as walked closer to her bedside and rubbed her forehead. He told her that he wished it could've been him and not her and that he was so sorry, as if she could hear him. Those that could hear; heard a man that was in the throws of depression; one who was, no doubt, bordering a severe state of depression. "Man this girl was all I had." he would say over and over, as Leonard allowed him to rest his weary head on his shoulders as they held each other closely. "She was all I had."

"I can remember the first day I asked her out," he said with a strained chuckle as he reminisced about his college days. "She told me no at first, she said that we could be friends though, then…"

For a moment it was just too tough for him to continue to speak, but as Billy patted him on the back and uttered repetitiously "Its alright."

he found the strength finish telling the story of the day he got the girl that already had his mind. "Then one day she walked up to me and out of the blue she just said Ok. I'll never forget it. She had been to a dance rehearsal and she was all sweaty with black tights on. That's the day I said to myself she belongs to me. She still belongs to me. She'll always belong to me."

It was at that moment that he reached out to grab her left hand that dangled from the side of the bed. He had noticed the ring that he had put on her finger on their wedding day. It was unharmed though her hand looked as though she had been battling gladiators. That sight triggered even more tough emotions, but just before representatives of the funeral home made their way into the suddenly crammed operating room space where she lay, Chauncey found just enough strength to lift her left hand and remove the ring that had symbolized their union till death do us part. Death had parted them and it was only a short time later that those who had come to retrieve her remains parted them again.

Billy and Leonard left the room again because they knew that, though seeing Jada put on that stretcher would probably cause another outburst, this was a personal and tender moment that their pastor needed to share only with those responsible for taking her away. Chauncey aided the men as they tucked her lifeless limbs neatly under the hospital bed sheets, ignoring their insistence that they do it alone, arguing "She belongs to me. I want to be the one to do this."

It didn't take long to prepare her body to be placed in the black body bag that laid open and waiting for her on the gurney next to her death bed and once she was ready for the transition, they lifted her with Chauncey's help and placed her carefully into the black bag initialed CM which were the initials of Crawford Mortuary. In the bag and on the gurney that would lead her from the hospital to her funeral preparation, there was only one thing left to do.

The bag had to be zipped and Chauncey asked if he could do it just before asking to be alone one more time with her before he did. It wasn't the usual practice, but the body retrievers granted his request and respectfully stood just outside the curtain to afford the preacher his desired private moment. He talked to her before he zipped the bag, telling her to go ahead and rest and not to worry about Lizzy. He assured his wife he would always take care of the little girl. He also told her one last time that he loved her and began to zip the bag when he was moved to kiss her one last time. The bag was zipped to her chest area when he pulled backed the covers that hid her face and kissed her gently on her badly scarred forehead and said as if Lizzy was standing in the room. "She'll always belong to you and me; Always."

With that, he completely zipped the bag and called in the funeral staff to, at long last remove his love from the hospital that by now had the stench of death laced through its halls. "Come on ya'll. She's ready." he told them as he nodded in confirmation as he unconsciously wiped his eyes.

As they began to roll her body down the hall toward an awaiting hearse parked just outside the emergency room door, Jada's coming was heralded as if she was a queen being welcomed back home after visits abroad. "Here they come ya'll," some woman whispered the news after she caught a glimpse of the black clad gurney rounding the final corner that led to the long stretch of hallway that led to the exit door where the hearse waited. Chauncey and his friends walked just behind the gurney that was respectfully pushed by funeral home staffers as if they were soldiers protecting a presidential casket.

To their surprise, once they rounded the corner, they were met with a throng of saddened well wishers. Some stood at attention and wept as Jada's gurney journeyed toward the hearse. Others waved goodbye when the beloved First Lady passed by them and even more cried as they noticed the teary eyed pastor walking behind his wife as if he just didn't want to let her go. It was truly a sad spectacle, but it was necessary that she leave the hospital and once they reached the exit doors, they noticed even more people weeping and wailing as they surrounded the already opened back door of the waiting hearse.

Chauncey, who had never stopped weeping since he had began again when he saw her for the last time, began to weep even louder, moaning and groaning as the funeral staffers forcefully lifted the heavy gurney and pushed it into the back of the hearse and secured it to the floor. As unbelieving onlookers continued to sob, Chauncey gathered himself to give his wife one last honor before she left. He insisted that he closed the hearse door. It was a symbolic gesture, because he always respectfully opened and closed doors for her and he would be remiss if he wasn't the one who literally closed the door on this particular chapter in their once cherished lives.

After he had closed the door and before the hearse drove off, one of the staffers thanked Chauncey for his entrustment of his wife's remains to them and let him know that he'd be contacted first thing in the morning to begin funeral preparations.

"Mr. Pennington, we're sorry for your loss, but we're honored that that you chose us to assist you in, this, your time of bereavement." he said in a rehearsed professional tone. "Someone will call you tomorrow morning so we can begin to make arrangements for Mrs. Pennington."

Chapter 32

Jada's sudden and untimely death had gripped the small community, but the reverberations from her death would survive long past the day that her body would eventually be put into the ground and laid to rest. Everything about this day was horrendous; from her horrible workday experience with Mr. James, to her battle with Chauncey about being late for a stupid meeting, to that other man, Cecil Whitlock who had threatened to spill the beans about something that could've had catastrophic and irreparable consequences on the Pennington's squeaky clean reputations if it were true.

It was all crazy to Chauncey and up until this point he hadn't really found enough time to reflect on why any of it had happened. But after leaving the hospital around 9:30PM, the still miserable new widower, came to grips with it all as his friends tried desperately to console him at his, soon to be, forever empty home.

Not much talking was going on, but one would think that their presence alone was comfort enough for the man who needed everything they had to offer and more, especially since it would be at least midday tomorrow before his Aunt or the Blaylocks were able to fly in. But after an hour of shock induced silence and even more dreadful thoughts on his part, Chauncey asked if the Dunn's could take Lizzy for the night and pleaded with Maywhether that he was well enough, at this point, to be left alone to deal with his loss privately.

"I just need to be by myself ya'll," he said trying to convince his friends that he would be better served if he had the house all to himself. "I'm alright," he pleaded to the responses of "Are you sure?" from Billy and Leonard. "I just want to be by myself. That's all."

Convinced that their pastor knew what was best, the Dunn's gathered their belongings and beckoned for Daphne and Lizzy, who were upstairs dealing with the loss of Jada in their own way. As they left, after giving Chauncey consoling hugs, Leonard stood by him for a separate but equal embrace. With the house finally cleared and both cars slowly driving away from the house, he was finally alone as he wished; to deal with his grief by him self; in his own sick way.

But Chauncey had lied. He wasn't alright in the least. And at a quarter past 10, without fear of anyone feeling more sorry for him than they already did, he let out the long eerie scream that he had held, so protectively, from the people that loved him as he stood in the very spot where he had, earlier, criticized Jada for being late.

"Oh God, please help me!" he would cry out as he repeatedly and ferociously bang his fist on a front door that he longed for his wife to walk through again even if she was late again. "I can't take this no more!" he would say at other times, longing for somebody who really knew the depths of his past struggles to hold him. The problem was nobody really knew the depths of his past struggles. No one knew of the pain he couldn't deal with again. No one knew the blame or the shame he'd felt in times past. So, alone, he cried out for no one to console him. He felt by himself, just like he did the day he waited for his aunt to show up to a house that held the dead bodies of his own parents when he was just seven. It was almost as if he was turning into that little boy again. And like a child, he sought refuge. But the refuge he sought wasn't the refuge he needed.

Totally unable to mask or control his anguish, Chauncey grabbed the keys to the Mercedes and drove as fast as he could to no where. As he drove, depression sat heavily upon his heart and blame increased in his, already, troubled mind as anger began to besiege his spirit; neither of which he was strong enough to deal with by himself. He just couldn't take it any more. And in a self medicating effort, Chauncey did something that was completely atypical for a man of stature and character, but somewhat justifiable for a man going through this kind of anguish.

Without shame or any thought of what anyone else would think of him, he drove into the parking lot of a dusty, back street, all night juke, a few miles away from his house and walked right through the front door of the liquor store and purchased a substance that had never entered his blood stream before, but was sure would take some of his pain away.

With a fifth of Crown Royal under his arms and anger now mixed with his grief, a concoction for more disaster was waiting to be blended as the beleaguered pastor hurried back home to commence his own pitiful self help strategy.

Back at home, he began to drink heavily, having no regard for the ramifications of drinking too much, throwing down glass after glass of the sneaky intoxicant into his system. But the more he drank, the angrier he became, and the angrier he became the more he shifted from what Adolph James had done to bitterness at what his God had allowed to happen to him once again. He didn't hold back on his choice of words during his tirade either; repeatedly shouting "God damn you!" with noticeably slurred speech as he sat on the floor in complete darkness in what was, now, a lifeless and loveless bedroom. "I don't deserve this. I've never done anything to deserve this!" he shouted as if God had actually killed Jada with his own powerful hands.

God understood his outbursts, though, and if anybody knew Chauncey Evansworth Pennington it was Him. God knew that the bewildered preacher was a under tremendous amount stress. God knew that he was depressed. And God also knew that he was failing to maintain any control over his emotions because he had failed to let Him take control.

After he had screamed all he could scream and after he had cursed God with almost every profane word he knew, by 11:30PM Chauncey was totally drunk, occasionally dozing in and out of consciousness, amid less frequent insults thrown at a God he no longer trusted. But as his seemingly lifeless body lay across his bed, what happened next would ultimately lead him on a destructive path that only God knew could've been on the horizon.

He was lying across his bed in a drunken stupor when his daughter's whereabouts and condition crossed his inebriated mind. He smelled horrible at this point and he could barely get simple sentences out of his mouth when he mumbled to himself, "I want my baby girl" with a bad slur. "Baby girl where you at?" he called out to no one's ear. "Lizzy! Where you at?"

Remembering that Lizzy had been taken for the night by Billy and Ruth Anne, Chauncey reached, lethargically, toward his waist to pull his cell phone from its holster and fumblingly dialed the Dunn residence to ask them to bring his daughter back home.

"Ruthie?" he asked in forced composure, but still slightly slurred manner, upon her prompt answering of the telephone after noticing her Pastor's cell number on their home caller ID.

"Pastor, are you OK?" she asked with concern, detecting that he didn't sound quite like his normal self.

Reasoning that he was probably just worn out by the dreadful experience of loosing his wife only hours earlier and physically and spiritually drained due to his attempts to deal with it all, she continued the conversation as usual when he asked that they please bring Lizzy home to be with him.

Without any hesitation and still figuring that he knew what was best for him, she told Chauncey, in a rather comforting tone, that she'd have Daphne to bring the little girl home and asked if it would be OK "if Daphne just stayed over" to ensure that he'd be able to rest if he chose, fearing that Lizzy could, for some unforeseen reason, be left unattended.

With the pastor's unknown drunken approval, Ruthie and Billy allowed their daughter to leave with Lizzy, urging the teenager to call when she got there as they walked the girls outside and further instructed her not to hesitate to call if she thought they needed to come over for more support. After those final parental instructions, the Dunn's saw the girls off, kissing them both, before walking back inside.

Daphne was very responsible and her maturity level was well beyond her years, and the concerned teenager felt like her parents' request was a good gesture. So she drove with Lizzy to the Pennington house so that Chauncey could spend the night with the only real family he now had, feeling in her heart that she was doing her part to bring some relief to this devastated family. But by the time they got there shortly after midnight and walked upstairs to see him, Chauncey had managed to drink even more than he had previously and was already in a liquor induced deep sleep, uncharacteristically snoring loudly as he lay across his bed with his clothes and shoes still fastened to his worn out body.

After quietly walking Lizzy over to her own bedroom, in an effort not to disturb the seemingly pleasant sleeping pastor and seeing the little girl off to sleep, Daphne reentered his room sorrowfully and with great concern, to pull off his shoes, as evidence of his alcoholic binge rested noticeably on an untidy night stand.

"Good night, Pastor." she whispered, feeling even more, sorry for him than she did before.

With Lizzy and Chauncey fast asleep, Daphne showered and put on her night gown before she walked over to her oft used guest sleeping quarters. But she couldn't get to sleep though. Exhibiting understandable restlessness as she sat in the silent second floor bedroom, her mind raced as he she thought of how miserable her pastor and Lizzy must've been. And though she lay across the bed and closed her eyes, her heart was in turmoil as her own grief began to wear heavy on her. But silence was broken around two o'clock early that Saturday morning, when the soon to be college freshman, was startled by the abrupt moaning and groaning she heard coming from the master suite. It was evident that the man she had always respected for his strength and tenacity in ministry was suffering mightily and struggling to come to grips with his sudden loss.

It was out of the blue. No warning. No nothing. He just began to moan and groan. Daphne couldn't have possibly known but, Chauncey was deep into that dream that had haunted him ever since he was seven, but one that he hadn't had often in some time now. This episode, however, was undoubtedly brought on by this traumatic day.

On this night, as he dreamed of that nightmarish June 1977 day, he would moan, and would groan too, and even eventually let out that scream that Aunt Eunice knew all too well.

The dream began, as usual, with visions of photos that depicted happier times during his childhood; like the photo his parents took on the day he was born and family photos that were taken at his daycare graduation ceremony when he was five years old. The photos that he would visualize would often put a smile on his face as he slept, but his dreams didn't end with those happy photos though. They always ended with graphic visuals of exactly what happened on the day his parents died; every gory detail.

This night he saw, again, those visions of his mother as she walks into the living room where his father stood, waiting anxiously for his wife to enter the house. It all began as Chauncey was riding with his mother, who was very angry after leaving the church on that particular day.

Like his father, his mother was just as anticipatory of the living room confrontation because she had found out that his father had been carrying on a strange affair with one of the church musicians that just so happened to be a young man. It had been rumored before they married that he was gay, which is exactly what she found out the day that she surprisingly dropped by the church to see him. She used her office key to get in and stumbled across Wallace making out with the boy on the desktop in his pastoral suite.

His parents started arguing at the church as Chauncey looked on in anger at the boy who played the piano for their church grabbed his clothes and ran right past him. And the arguing only escalated when both his parents reached the house in separate cars.

He dreamed of and heard his own cries of helplessness and his pleas for the fighting to stop, only to see his father punch his mother in the face after she vowed to tell the world that he was a "damn faggot."

The punch actually knocked her into the wall, bloodying severely, the back of her head as blood also flowed from her nose due to the ferociousness of the punch. She bounced back though and began to strike back his father in self defense only to be driven into the wall yet again as Wallace forcefully grabbed her head, ripping out patches of her hair from the root.

It was then, that Chauncey tried to save his mother only to be slapped and threatened by his daddy and told to go to upstairs to his room. Though weeping and scared as hell for his mother's life, he did go upstairs just as his daddy had asked him to, but he didn't go to his room though. From the distance, he stood and watched as his father continued his fit of rage, throwing his mother down on the living room couch, repeatedly punching her in her broken face and calling her unseemly names, occasionally wrapping his unwashed, nasty hands around the woman's delicate throat.

He dreamed of and heard his father's continuous slurs as the man he grew to hate called the mother he loved so much and wanted to help so bad "stupid bitches and nosey mother fuckers" as he stood, helplessly, in the stairwell sobbing, wanting it all to stop.

It was at that point that the little boy had seen enough and had heard enough. And in a rage, Chauncey ran to his parents' bedroom and got the gun that his father owned. After he got the, already loaded, easily handled pistol from under the bed, he ran back down stairs and pointed it at his daddy, screaming "Leave my momma alone!" He was only seven, but with that gun in his hands he stood tall as his mother's only defender.

Wallace still had his hands around his mother's neck when he finally glanced up at Chauncey and saw that he had a gun. "Put the damn gun down boy!" he urged as he loosened his grip from Suzanne's neck. As Wallace got up and focused his attention on Chauncey, who had a gun and was ready to shoot, Suzanne's body laid on the couch, as bloody as a butchered hog and as unconscious as a corpse. He visualized it all as he dreamed. It was almost as if he were in the moment all over again and by the sweat that formulated on his brow; one could reasonably deduce that his emotions were as intense as the day all of this happened.

As if with the natural eye, he visualized his mother lying lifelessly on that chair all bloodied and bruised, honestly believing hat his father had already killed her, which kindled the anger that he had within for him.

Wallace yelled over and over again as loud as he possibly could "Put that damn gun down boy!" as he walked slowly toward Chauncey, who aimed the gun directly at his fathers head. Noticing that little Chauncey was unresponsive; Wallace lunged at the boy still screaming and yelling. And then, BANG…Chauncey pulled the trigger, striking his father in the forehead, killing him with one shot, splattering his brain all over the floor. The blast was so forceful that Wallace's dead body was blown from the edge of the living room into the entryway of the kitchen.

Crying and in a panic he ran to his mother's side looking for a hug or to hear his mother say it was Ok. But she was drowning in her own blood, dying as he tried to get her up. "Momma, Momma!" he cried "Momma, get up Momma!" the little boy would prod to no avail.

His dream would always end with him trying to desperately get his mother up. But this time his father spoke to him just before the curtains on this nightmare came down, maliciously infusing Jada into an already unbearable hallucination.

"You deserve just what you get Chauncey," his father's grizzly voice rang through his head as he visualized him with that gaping hole in his forehead. "That girl is dead because of you. You are reaping what you've sown," he continued as Chauncey begin to toss and turn and moaned "No!" repeatedly in his sleep. "You had no right to interfere with me and your momma and because you did both of us are dead," he said as Chauncey's tossing and turning increased. "But isn't it funny that because you chose not to interfere in your own wife's life she got raped and killed herself on that dangerous highway. You were more concerned about a meeting than you were about your own wife." He continued his verbal badgering as Chauncey begin to moan even louder. "You were selfish when you were a boy and you're even more selfish as a grown man. That's why you're by yourself. That's why your momma is dead. That's why that girl is dead. You didn't come to her rescue when she needed you. But you killed me trying to save your momma."

It was at that moment that Chauncey abruptly woke up out of his nightmare as beads of sweat dropped from his body like water off of a ducks back. He yelled and screamed "No. I didn't mean to!" as if he'd lost his mind. "I can't take this no more!" he cried out into the darkness. Though he was out of his nightmare he was still in liquor induced delusion.

And he was in mid-sentence of a defiant rebuttal to his father's assertions when he saw what appeared to be a vision of Jada which appeared to him from just outside the bedroom entryway coming toward him slowly with her hands outstretched in an effort to comfort him. "Jada?" he called out incoherently to no answer as the walking female figure made her way closer to where he sat on the bed. "Jada!" he called out louder as he was overtaken by the female's presence that made him feel as though his wife had somehow heard his cry and come back to him. He felt her as her small, but sure hands, rubbed his back as she whispered "It's OK." He even felt her as she began to wipe sweat from his brown and held his head close to her breast.

Little did he know, the figure he saw, wasn't Jada at all. It was actually Daphne who had innocently walked into the room shortly after hearing signs of his evident struggles, to console her pastor as best as could. She didn't answer when he called out for Jada because she just didn't know what to say. It was just hurtful that he longed for someone that was no longer available. So she was just silent, feeling in her heart that she was doing the right thing. She loved her pastor and respected him so much and couldn't stand to see him in the shape that he was in. And she went in unto him, summoning maturity beyond her years, hoping that her consolation would be enough to get him through the night; even if it meant that he thought she was his long gone wife.

But, what she didn't know was that Chauncey was in a drunken daze which was made even worse by his nightmare. He didn't know what was really happening for sure and when she entered that bedroom, he was actually thinking that she must be his wife; he was still dreaming or at least he thought was. All he was certain of at this point, however, was that whatever was happening to him, made him feel better and it wasn't long before he fell even deeper into what he thought was an awesome after life experience with who he presumed to be Jada and reached out to touch and embrace her.

Though completely silent, she felt real. Even her back was tender and felt moist from the sweat that he foolishly thought was born out of passion. He touched her face too and her face felt real, which proved to be the last sign he needed to let his, supposed dream, take its course. So he grabbed her face as if to kiss her only to be let down easy to his dismay.

It was when Chauncey held her face tenderly in his strong hands and gazed longingly into her eyes that Daphne became a little uncomfortable about what was happening, starring nervously, but silently back at him. It was as if her pastor was now looking upon her in a sexual manner. She wasn't scared, but she was a little tense, having never felt the hands of a grown man in such a provocative way before.

Now panicky about the possibilities of what could happen next, yet in silence, she slowly pulled away from him, tenderly grabbing his wrist with her own hands, to which Chauncey responded "What's wrong baby?" to a rapid response from the girl who now knew she had to act quick.

"Pastor, you're dreaming." she said, pantingly, as her body began to send her signals that she knew her mind couldn't handle."

"I know baby, but come on." He persistently begged but Daphne tried to respectfully resist his efforts to kiss her lips, as he forced her to her back.

"No, Pastor." She moaned, turning her head away from the awful smell of his alcoholic breath as she pressed against his chest in an embarrassed, half hearted attempt to restrain his sudden urges.

But with every "No!" that Daphne moaned, the more determined, Chauncey was, not to let this moment, with who he still envisioned was Jada, end. So in a desperate attempt to feel more than she allowed, he just took what his marriage vows said was his and ripped off the girl's night gown. Amid her desperate but docile cries for him to stop, her breathing grew deeper. Her resistance was docile because she didn't want to arouse Lizzy. None the less, she pleaded for him to stop. She wasn't pleading because her body hadn't began to respond more positively to his more experienced hands, but because, she knew that what was taking place was very wrong. And by now she knew that her pastor was out of his natural mind, prompting her to push even harder against his chest, as her requests for him to stop grew louder and more authoritative.

Unable to handle, what he now perceived was, strong resistance from the woman who never resisted, Chauncey became more aggressive, forcefully kissing her against her will, as she squirmed in uneasiness. But then, in a moment that would ultimately force him to the brink of insanity, he grabbed both of her wrists with only his strong left hand and stretched her arms over her head as her squirms became more violent and her cries for it all to cease grew weaker because she had intentionally closed her mouth in an attempt to fight off his protruding tongue. With his right hand, he squeezed her ever so soft waist and occasionally allowed it to grasps breast that had never been touched in that way.

By now Daphne was in total disbelief as she dared not to look upon the face of the man she couldn't believe was on top of her.

Powerless against his passionate kisses against her unyielding sealed lips and unable to prevent his occasional sucks on her sweaty neck and breasts, the girl just cried as her body shook in trepidation. She wasn't crying because she was scared for her life nor because she feared she wouldn't be able to endure whatever he did to her this night. But she cried because she knew that whatever he did do to her would be irreversible and feared that she wouldn't be able to endure the feelings she'd have the morning after.

Feeling as though this regretful encounter was nearing an end and couldn't get any worse than it already was, Daphne's crying and shaking eased a bit, as she reluctantly allowed her pastor to suck on her lips, neck and breasts as he pleased. She mistakenly thought that his slower pace meant that he was almost done. But his slower pace only meant that he was becoming more passionate, measuring every kiss as he tried to make a moment, that shouldn't be, last forever.

As she lay there helplessly on her back with her arms still restrained above her head she couldn't help but to moan feverishly every time his tongue slowly stroked the hot spots, she never knew she had, and moaned even louder when his lips would sensitively massage her, never before licked, nipples. Daphne did her best to handle that part of her ordeal and she was handling it as if she was, unenthusiastically, carrying out a civil service.

But it was during one of her long irrepressible groans, as Chauncey sucked on her breasts, that the inexperienced girl literally went into a trance, as her body's response to what was happening, momentarily took over cognitive function of her brain and her eyes rolled to the top of her head. She wasn't enjoying what was happening in the least, but she couldn't help but give into the demands of a body that was too overwhelmed with powerful sexual charges she'd never felt before. It was at that point that Chauncey loosed the right handed grip he had on her tender and smooth waist and seductively eased her, now yielding thighs apart. She was still moaning as if she was in a trance as he spread her thighs, but quickly snapped out of it in a shriek of pain.

Without any warning and before Daphne could realize what was about to happen to her next or do anything about it, Chauncey violently pierced inside of her, thrusting his rather large, fully grown penis into a vagina that had never been penetrated by anybody before. She bled profusely as his undesired entrance ripped away any signs of her virginity.

The pain of feeling, the piercing penetration made the hurting girl scream out with every ounce of strength she had "Pastor please stop! Please!" she pleaded as she squeezed her thigh muscles together and tears abruptly burst from her ducts just as quickly as Chauncey busted his way inside of her. She breathed hard as her face bore the strains and pains of a young girl who couldn't take the man's repeated pounding against her already sore and hemorrhaging vagina. "Stop!" she cried as loud as she could, as the pastor's forcefulness increased with every cry.

She screamed and she cried and she helplessly fought back. "No Pastor! No! Please God mo!" But her cries up to this point hadn't been heard by anyone; especially Chauncey, who forced his way inside over and over again. That sick man relentlessly pounded the girl that he thought was Jada, as if he was punishing his dead wife for walking out of his life. The more he pounded on her small frame the more chilling Daphne's cries for help were. And then ...hearing all the loud screams, Lizzy woke up and ran towards those screams and walked through her father's bedroom door, flipped on the lights, and found her daddy on top of Daphne, which prompted the scared little girl to plead "Stop hurting Daphne Daddy! Daddy, get off of Daphne!" In the middle of ejaculation, as he viciously gave his passions to Daphne, and amid her evident screams of rejection, Chauncey heard his daughter's pleas, forcing him to snap out of his trance and immediately come to the harsh realization of what had just happened.

As Lizzy looked on astonished, the suddenly embarrassed father, in a pitiful attempt to hide himself from his daughter's tear filled view, jumped off of the girl that he truly envisioned was his wife. In a panic he tried frantically to cover him self in the same bloody sheets that Daphne held onto in an equally pitiful attempt to cover her own naked body.

Finally freed from Chauncey's dreamy assault, but still gripped by the trauma of it all, Daphne jumped out of the bed, and ran as fast as she could out of the bedroom, bumping Lizzy as she fled. She was as naked as the day that she came in the world and as miserable and tormented as she'd ever be in it.

In a panic and totally out of his wit, Chauncey jumped out of the bed with those bloody sheets still draped around his, soaking in nervous sweat body, depressed and starring at an innocent little girl who had no idea of the severity of what she'd just witnessed.

"Lizzy go back to bed," he urged in a flustered tone, as he anxiously scratched his head, hoping his daughter wouldn't ask any questions. "Everything's alright," he said pathetically, trying to persuade his starring, sleepy eyed daughter to leave his bedroom. "Go to your room Lizzy!"

She did exactly what her father asked and walked back to her room, immaturely gathering that yet another surreal episode had come to an end in a house that seemed to always be tormented by something. But Lizzy had no idea of knowing that by day break, all hell would've already begun its push for freedom and would be on a sadistic path to destroy the Pennington's remnants of normalcy.

Feeling more than ever that God had forsaken him, Chauncey hurriedly put on the same smelly clothes that he'd worn all day Friday and grabbed that less than half full bottle of Crown Royal, immediately putting it to his mouth.

As he stood, before daybreak, within arms reach of his car keys, which were still on the nightstand, Chauncey guzzled down every ounce of what was left in that bottle without even stopping once to breathe through his mouth or alleviate his scorching esophagus.

It was after he swallowed the last bit of liquor, that he lashed out at God all over again and became increasingly enraged at all that God had allowed in the less than twenty four hours it took to ruin his whole life. It was as if his grief had been magnified to the tenth power and he acted as if he had totally lost the grip that he once had on life. And to be honest, he had lost his grip.

In a refreshed state of drunkenness, Chauncey grabbed his car keys from the night stand and stumbled out of his bedroom door with that empty liquor bottle still in his grasp.

After he staggered down the stairs in an effort to get away from the horrors that had occurred in his bedroom and escape the pain of hearing Daphne's muffled cries, Chauncey stopped at the bottom of the stairs, near the foyer only to find that he couldn't run away from what he was feeling or hearing. Though she was locked in a bedroom, a floor away, Chauncey could still hear the girl's pitiful whimpers, but he couldn't deal with the fact of knowing that he was the source of those tears. It was at the bottom of those stairs, as he stood only a stone's throw away from the kitchen that his metamorphosis into the mad man that always hid just beneath the surface was completed.

As if he was demon possessed, he screamed out in pain, as if he was trying to exorcise the devils that were attacking his soul. Unable to control his emotions and incapable of redoing anything that had gone wrong since a little after 1PM on yesterday, in a rage, he viciously threw the massive, empty liquor bottle into the ceramic tile kitchen floor, busting some of the floor tiles and shattering the bottle.

By now he was completely drunk again, looked a complete mess, smelled ridiculous, and scared the hell out of Daphne and Lizzy when they rushed downstairs after hearing the glass shatter and embittered screams, only to find that the man they both loved had already staggered through the broken glass and out of the front door.

Chapter 33

Before Lizzy or Daphne could do anything in their power to stop him, Chauncey had already exited the once happy home, in an effort to run away from the battles he fought in his own mind. Daphne knew that things could only get worse from this point, so she hurriedly looked for a phone to call her parents. She had to let them know that things were totally out of control in that house and that they needed to come over "right now" before something really bad happened to the pastor. She didn't tell them that she had been brutally assaulted though. Nor did she even make mention of the fact that Chauncey had been drinking. But by the sound of her voice, her parents knew that whatever had taken place was reason enough for them to act expediently.

By the time Billy and Ruthie got to the house, Lizzy and Daphne were worried sick, clutching each other as if they were the last thing they each had on earth and afraid to go any where near the broken glass in the kitchen. It was a little after 3AM when the Dunn's made their panic stricken entry, but when they did enter, they almost immediately noticed the broken liquor bottle splattered across the cracked tile of the kitchen floor; which signaled that they had walked into what could already be characterized as a grave situation.

Once they saw that the girls were in a reasonably stable emotional state and showed no overwhelming visible signs of post traumatic stress, their attention swiftly transitioned, to the condition and whereabouts of a man they knew was having a difficult time dealing with all that had happened to him. So in panic they questioned Daphne about, what, if anything, had been said before Chauncey left. Billy reached for his cell phone to call Maywhether, as Ruth Anne ushered Lizzy up the stairs to prevent her from witnessing any more of the drama that was unfolding in a house that the little girl no longer felt secure in.

But it was as Ruthie walked Lizzy to her room, that she noticed small drippings of blood that led to even more blood drippings that seemed to come from the pastor's bedroom. Without hesitation and without knowing that the drippings she saw were actually those of her own daughter's obliterated vagina, Ruthie took a closer look only to find that the dripping led to a small pool of blood in the middle of his bed. Worried that her pastor had tried to hurt himself, Ruthie rushed back down the stairs and whispered as her eyes pointed toward the stairs. "Billy I saw blood."

Ruth Anne didn't want the girls to know of her discovery, but when Daphne heard her father's hushed "Oh my God." and saw that her mother's eyes were communicating that something was wrong upstairs, she became fearful of having to tell her parents about what had actually led up to Chauncey's departure. She feared that if her parents' knew of what Chauncey had done to her and that the blood that they saw was actually hers Chauncey's condition and whereabouts would become secondary. She still loved him enough and was concerned enough not to allow what he had done to her life to overshadow what he could possibly do to his own. So she just kept quiet and allowed them to believe that the blood they had both seen, by now, was Chauncey's attempt to harm only himself.

After seeing for himself, the bloody evidence in the bedroom, Billy made a second early morning call to the sheriff, telling him of their disturbing findings, which prompted the Sheriff to avert his hurried trek toward the Pennington estate so that he might comb the streets for any sign of that polar white Mercedes before he put out an all points bulletin.

Little did any of them know, by the time Leonard started combing the streets for any signs of him, Chauncey would have already driven to what he hoped would be the last stop on what had been a rather miserable life's journey. He had driven to the river that he and his wife had frequented during happier times and had parked the Mercedes just off of a boat loading ramp. He just sat there contemplating in the pitch black darkness of the before day morning as tears of sorrow streamed down his face.

His eyes were extremely sore and blood shot from his tear laden night and over indulgence on Crown Royal. His head was splitting with pain, not just from the hang over he was enduring, but also from the tension of the thoughts he had. He blamed himself for Jada's death. He was embarrassed and blamed himself for what had happened to Daphne. And he thought to himself, it would be better if he wouldn't have to face another day in misery without Jada or the faces of people he knew he'd hurt. He felt as though the whole world already knew about what had happened in his bedroom and couldn't fathom seeing Billy's or Ruth Anne's hapless expressions. He felt as though Lizzy would be better off without him and knew that he could never bear the pain of seeing that little girl cry again; especially after what her little eyes had seen him doing to Daphne in that bedroom.

Besides all of those feelings, he felt like God had let him down. His faith had all but diminished and any hope of a brighter day wouldn't emerge on this day. To him, the hour had come that he just ended it all. No more pain, No more suffering. No more worrying about all the people who were worrying about him. No more worrying about what the world would think of him after they found out about what he thought Daphne had already told her parents. "I can't do this no more." he would say over and over again as he contemplated driving off of the boat ramp into deep dark waters. But he just couldn't force himself to do it.

As most, who worried about him, remained asleep, waiting for the hour to come that they might shower him with all their support, Chauncey sat wide awake in a car that he wished he had the courage to drive into a bitter cold lake. His daughter, the Dunn's, and Maywhether worried that he wouldn't even make it to the morning.

He was pitiful and defeated after again thinking about all that he'd loss. But, it was during his persistent sobs that he began to loose his fight to maintain consciousness. As he muttered about his atrocities in weariness, the anger that was lodged in his mind and the sorrow that had engulfed his heart begin ease away or so it seemed. The truth of the matter was that the alcohol had begun to take control and confiscated his body functions again. Unable to continue his rants of pity and without the strength or courage drive his car into the lake, Chauncey drifted out of consciousness. He was completely drunk again and more dysfunctional and more depressed as he'd ever been in his whole life.

As Chauncey dove into another perfect set up for a nightmare, another man was waking up out of his own. He couldn't sleep. And he couldn't rest because visions of a woman he'd only seen pictures of haunted him. He felt as though the woman's death was in direct correlation to a plan he regrettably playing a part in. He had to contact "that woman's husband" to apologize for what he'd done and tell him of all the others that participated in the scheme to ruin his life; a decision he would regret more than his participation in Tally's plan. He thought he had to relieve himself of the guilt he had over what he'd done. And though it was difficult for him to wait the four hours or so he knew it would take for the preacher to get out of bed, he vowed to call "first thing in the morning."

As the man waited on the appropriate time to call Chauncey, Billy and Ruth Anne made several unsuccessful attempts to reach him on his cell phone and Maywhether drove, hopelessly, up and down country roads looking for any sign of him. Lizzy was asleep by now without the slightest idea of the gravity of her father's plight. And Daphne was in the bathroom for what seemed like the hundredth time, wiping to make sure no blood came out of her freshly wounded vagina, which could possibly tipped off her parents to the real problem.

Chauncey was asleep in his car at 4AM, but would wake up again only to try to finish what Crown Royal had prevented.

THE DAY ALL *Hell* BROKE LOOSE

CHAPTER 34

By daybreak, but before the onslaught of phone calls of condolences by well wishers, every one that knew of Chauncey's disappearance sat in his house waiting for him to return their calls or return home. They were more worried than ever that something bad had happened to him. But Maywhether, who had concluded his preliminary search, had seen this type of behavior many times during his law enforcement career. His rationale gave the Dunn's a little hope as the sun's rays crept through the shades of the living room window where they all sat in unrest. He reasoned that the pastor is probably just blowing off steam, because if something was wrong or anything worse had happened, he or his deputies would've already been notified by now. "Let's just be patient and wait a little longer." he said with dying hope, knowing that if he didn't hear from his pastor in the next few hours he'd have to involve law enforcement; something he really didn't want to do.

"But Leonard, do you think we should tell his aunt…the Blaylocks?" asked Ruth Anne, going on to tell him that the Blaylocks and Aunt Eunice had called and were concerned because they couldn't reach him either. "I told them that he just wanted some alone time."

"Good. Let's just try to handle this from our end. The last thing we need is for those poor people get more upset than they already are. They'll be here soon enough. And hopefully by the time they do get here Pastor will be back. He'll come back. Let's just wait." the sheriff said before he left to comb the streets again.

As Billy, Ruth Anne, Daphne and Lizzy continued their, less than patient, wait, Chauncey was waking up in misery with a scowl on his face as the sun peered through his windshield. His eyes were still bloodshot and very sore and his head was hurting even worse than it was before he uncomfortably drifted off to sleep. And he was shivering too. It was cold outside and he had gone to sleep with the car turned off and a window partially down.

As he squinted to protect his eyes from the sun's vibrant ray, he confusedly looked around as if he didn't know where he was before he turned his car on to generate some heat. But he knew exactly where he was, he was just perplexed about his next move. If he was too scared to kill himself and too embarrassed to return home to face Billy and Ruth Anne after what he had done to Daphne, what else was there for him to do? He was miserable and probably wouldn't want to return home even if he knew that Daphne hadn't told her parents a thing about what had happened, because Jada wouldn't be there.

Daphne had told Lizzy a complete lie about what really happened last night and hadn't mumbled a word to her parents, but Chauncey couldn't have known of the girl's protective measures. He literally thought that bounty hunters were after him and he was scared. But the truth of the matter is, everyone that knew he was out of pocket wanted that man back home safe and sound and couldn't care less about the blame game he was playing with himself.

As he rubbed his arms to try to warm his frigid body and stared blankly through his windshield at the white capping water that he wished was already his death bed, the things that weighed heaviest on Chauncey's heart though, was never seeing Jada again and why God had allowed it to happen in the first place.

He was in deep depressive thought when he reached toward the back seat to grab the cell phone that he had thrown over his head before he drifted off to sleep, in an attempt to rid him of phone's persistent rings. By the time he retrieved the phone, however, it was already vibrating, sending that familiar signal that alerted him that he had a boat load of unheard messages. But he wasn't interested in hearing any messages or returning any of the calls that he'd missed. By now he knew he needed to try to reach his aunt to tell her that he didn't want to live anymore. He didn't want her to try to talk him out of what he thought was best, but he felt as though if anybody would understand why he couldn't take life's trouble anymore it would be Aunt Eunice. She had been with him through the thick and the thin and he just wanted to talk to his aunt, who by now was sadly standing in line in an Ohio airport, waiting to board a flight to come see about him.

It was as he thought about what he'd say to his aunt that the phone rang for the first time since he had opened his eyes. It shocked him in a sense because it was almost as if someone was watching him and knew that he'd just picked the phone up. He didn't want to look at his caller ID because he was fearful that the name he'd see would be one that he'd be too ashamed to talk to anyway. But he did venture to look, hoping that his Aunt somehow knew of his need for her and was on the other end.

But to his surprise, the name Cecil Whitlock appeared across the screen. It was a name that Chauncey hadn't ever seen before and he had put the phone down in the passenger's seat to ignore the call, when he suddenly thought that maybe Cecil Whitlock was the person in charge of making Jada's funeral arrangements. He felt like the least he could do before he did anything stupid to himself was to make sure his wife was buried in a way he thought was befitting. So in a panic, trying to flip the phone open before it stopped ringing, Chauncey answered, only to be greeted by a scraggly voice that he would remember all too well.

"Hello." Chauncey answered with artificial respectfulness, figuring the caller was from a funeral home staffer.

"Mr. Pennington?" Whitlock answered back in an apologetic tone, making sure he had the right man before he began his well thought out confession.

"Yeah, who is this?" Chauncey asked, beginning to recognize the voice but not the name.

"Mr. Pennington, my name is Cecil Whitlock and I spoke to you on yesterday."

"I recognize your voice, but I can't remember. Are you the guy from the funeral home?" he asked as he sat straight up in his seat and put his left hand on his forehead in careful thought.

"No Sir. I called you yesterday and I told you that I was a private investigator." he said as Chauncey's heart began to pound as the voice became more familiar. "I told you my name was Arthur Blankenship" he said slowly in embarassment.

And then there was silence. Silence. Complete silence. For about thirty seven seconds there was nothing but silence. No words, no wind, no birds chirping; no nothing just silence.

Hearing that name sent chills down that boys spine. That name brought back the reality of the events that had led up to Jada's death and the vengefulness he harbored toward everyone that he thought made his wife's last day on earth a living hell. And in an instant it was as if he had transformed from that depressed man who wanted to kill himself into an even more bitter man who wanted to kill whoever was on the other end of that line. That name enraged Chauncey, but he noticed Whitlock's rather remorseful tone, which made Chauncey believe that the man had something else to say; and he did. So the preacher listened and listened very carefully.

"Mr. Pennington, I'm sorry for what happened to your wife." The man began, as Chauncey sat in silence and starred in fury at the wind blown lake.

"And I couldn't sleep last night because I know that what I did yesterday was wrong."

"You damn right it was wrong!" Chauncey shouted back, unable to control his anger towards a man he felt started it all. "My wife died…" he cryingly and belligerently tried to argue before Whitlock urged the man he'd never met before, to listen.

"Mr. Pennington, please. I just need to tell you what happened."

"Who are you and why did you do this to me." Chauncey whimpered.

"I'm just a common criminal. I ain't no investigator or nothing like that…"

"Tell me why man. What did I do?"

"Mr. Pennington I'm so sorry. I shouldn't have even been involved in this but, I didn't think it would lead to all this. I only did it because Augustus Tally told me to. And he paid me to do what he called a favor for his friend Walter Pickett. They paid me to do it."

"What did you say?" Chauncey ferociously questioned, knowing full well what the man had said, but in disbelief that the two people he hated most in the world had paid somebody wreck his life.

"Mr. I promise I don't know nothing about you and I didn't know nothing about your family. I was hired to try to force ya'll to leave town. I'm sorry and…"

"But, where did you get information about what happened at that school? It was a lie and you knew it. Didn't you?" Chauncey shouted. "Didn't you?"

"No Sir. The information I had was wrong. It was all wrong. But at the time I didn't know nothing about what happened at that school until after I found out later what really happened. It was too late then. That's what I'm trying to get at."

"Well, where did that shit come from? Tell me what the hell happened; you fucking low life!"

"I got what I told you from Tally and Pickett and they got it from a lady name Lula Penny."

"What?"

"A lady named Lula Penny told Pickett and Tally a lie. She's the one who said that she saw your wife having sex with the principal in the office. Now I know that everything she said was nothin but a lie. Pickett wanted you to leave their church. But, Mrs. Penny wanted you out too because you had took a position from her or something." Whitlock continued as Chauncey rocked back and forth in the driver's seat, becoming angrier by the second as he listened to a man that seemed to be credible.

"So you're trying to tell me that Pickett and Tally put you up to this shit because of a lie that Lula Penny told them."

"Yes Sir. I was only involved because they paid me. I needed the money." he pleaded as Chauncey revved his engine with thoughts of retribution on his mind. "Mr., I'm telling you I'm sorry. It wasn't supposed to happen like this."

Chauncey hadn't heard everything that Whitlock had prepared to say, but by now he was in no mood to listen any longer. He had heard all he needed to hear and what he heard had made him angry as hell. As he revved his engine more furiously, Chauncey's mind wandered in wrath, trying to figure out what he'd do to settle the score with everybody that Whitlock had named.

Without even saying good bye and without a calculated plan in mind, Chauncey hung up the phone on Whitlock and left that river for a date with pay back.

CHAPTER 35

By the time Chauncey's conversation with Whitlock came to a screeching halt it was a little past 8:30AM and no one that waited in his house had heard a word from him yet. They didn't know it, but Chauncey was on a mission. And after driving down a long back woods dirt road to a single wide trailer that sat on an unkept acre of land only five good minutes, or so, from the river, he reached his first destination, fully committed to issuing some form of punishment to Lula Penny for her involvement.

After he walked up the old rickety wooden steps that led to the front door of the dingy looking single wide mobile home, he knocked politely, as if he was making a not so routine pastoral visit.

"Who is it?" asked Lula, as she walked over to the door in a holey white night gown with pink hair rollers still in her hair. Chauncey could tell by the sound of her voice that she thought it was too early in the morning for anybody to be knocking on her door, but he didn't care. He just needed to look into her face to confront her for what he knew she had done.

"It's Pastor Pennington." Chauncey replied in a rather somber tone as he stood just outside the door, looking as raggedy externally as his heart was internally.

Recognizing the Pastor's voice, but not knowing the purpose of his early morning visit, Lula was taken aback, fearing that her pastor knew more than she had ever intended for him to know about what she had said about Jada. But she opened the door anyway, praying that he would receive any words of consolation that she could think to offer. She had no way of knowing for sure that Chauncey knew of her involvement, but she was guarded in what she thought to say, because she felt that his awkward hour, Saturday morning visit had something to do with her false testimony.

After opening the door, Lula greeted the pastor without ever looking into the man's face. She didn't look into his face because she didn't dare to look into his eyes. And she didn't want to look into his eyes because she feared that he'd be able to see beneath any attempts she would make to hide that sick feeling she had about the role of betrayal she'd played in Pickett and Tally's failed plan. She didn't want to look at him because she didn't want him to see through her. But if she had looked into his face she would've noticed the cold gaze and angry scowl of a man who was hell bent on giving the retribution he felt she deserved.

Unable to perceive the very present danger she was already in and with her head held down in embarrassment rather than condolence, Lula offered her sympathy, "Pastor Pennington I'm so sorry for what happened to our First Lady," praying her pastor wouldn't respond negatively.

But without even giving the remorseful obese woman an opportunity to lift her head Chauncey said to her in a nasty voice, "I know you are, you lying bitch." And then out of nowhere, he punched the 5'2 three hundred pound former choir director, landing a solid blow directly on the bridge of her nose. The punch was as ferocious as he had seen his father punch his own mother years ago and so forceful that it actually lifted her heavy body a foot from the floor before it snapped her head backwards.

Blood gushed from her face as Chauncey pushed his way into the house and pushed her down into an old food smelling couch, grabbing at her throat as she screamed and tried to explain how sorry she was. She knew exactly why he was coming after her and tried to explain her way out of it, but Chauncey wasn't trying to hear it. And she could tell that his intentions to hurt her were real because she could see hatred ripped into the veins of his blood stained eyes.

"Shut up you lying mother fucker!" he sadistically scolded as he choked her with every ounce of strength he had in his hands. "You still

The Day All Hell Broke Loose

want to fuck up my life?" he would repeatedly ask, as curse words he barely knew how to say slid through his gritted teeth. "Huh? You still want to fuck with me?" he questioned at others, with a grimace on his face as the woman's eyes bulged out of their sockets but stayed focused on his.

He had her by the throat and she could tell that he was literally trying to choke the life out of her. But she couldn't say a word. Though she screamed, she wasn't making much of a sound because her wind pipe was literally being crushed by the forcefulness of his penetrating thumbs. She tried to fight back, but as she scratched at any part of his body that was in arms reach, he squeezed on her neck even harder, rendering her efforts useless.

After loosing a fierce battle to fight him off because she had grown weak due to a gross lack of oxygen, Lula just knew she was about to die. She was helpless and she wasn't fighting back but Chauncey's grasp, on a throat the fat lady wished she hadn't used to defame Jada, was as firm as it was when he began choking her. And then… just before she drifted out of consciousness… he just let her go, abruptly releasing his tight grip from her neck.

No, he wasn't trying to alleviate her from any of the pain that he knew she was in nor did he begin to feel sorry for her when he loosed his grip, but he thought twice about "letting her ass die." That would be too easy. Lula Penny needed to suffer for the lies that she had told and if he killed her his actions would be the sole reason for her peaceful rest. He wanted this "bitch" to suffer and he thought he knew the best way to intensify that suffering: Take her back to the very person she felt she had to run to in the first place.

Lying in blood like a butchered hog on the couch that she restlessly tossed and turned on the night before, Lula's body looked lifeless. But she wasn't dead, nor was she dying. She was now fighting to stay alive, gasping for every morsel of air as she stared up at the man she prayed would just leave. But he wouldn't; not without her at least.

Chauncey was trembling and breathing hard as he watched her gasp in desperate attempts to regain a normal breathing pattern when he angrily but demanded "Get yo lying ass up." By now he knew that he was too deep into trouble to return to any normalcy of life. He had already figured that what had happened to Daphne had leaked out of his bedroom and knew that if Lula lived, he wouldn't be able to explain away his assault on her either. But he didn't care at this point.

Lula was still gasping, trying to fight off asphyxia when Chauncey grabbed her by both of her arms and pulled her to a sitting position on the couch. She couldn't respond to anything he was saying, but he told her that he was going to take her to confront Pickett and that he wanted Pickett to see what they had made him do to her.

"…and then I'm gone give him what he wanted."

As Lula moaned faintly in agony, Chauncey strained as he pulled the hefty woman up from the couch and drug her to and out of the front door, twisting her right wrist to speed up her march toward his waiting car. Once they were at the car, he opened the door and forced her into the backseat, warning her that if she said "a damn word" he'd kill her dead.

Lula was lying on her left side in that back seat in pain as she tried to breathe through a damaged throat; coughing and wheezing as the air that seemed so foreign only moments ago begin to seep back in more freely. She was scared, but she was alive. But being alive was about the only thing she had to be thankful for on this Saturday morning. Her mind wasn't on being alive though. Nor was it on being thankful either. Her mind was on what could possibly happen next.

As Chauncey drove furiously toward a place she had no idea of, she rode in demanded silence, thinking to herself that whatever was about to take place wasn't in her best interest. A call to Pickett, however, made his immediate plans clear to her.

"May I speak to Deacon Pickett?" Chauncey asked; camouflaging his evil intentions with a dismal tone that he knew Eloise would expect from a man that had just lost his wife.

"He ain't here right now. Who is this?" Eloise asked back with that uninitiated hatred that she often answered the phone with.

"Pastor Pennington." Chauncey answered in that same dismal tone.

"Oh baby I'm sorry. I didn't know who you was." she said, explaining away her rather rude behavior. "And I'm sorry for what happened to yo wife."

The Day All Hell Broke Loose

"Yea, I know. Everybody is now." He said as his tone became noticeably colder, somewhat confusing the old lady.

She didn't understand what he meant by what he said and she wasn't sure if he even knew what he meant by what he said. But she reasoned that his "lil mind probably just goin bad", thinking the preacher's confusing behavior was just a result of his grief. So out of concern, she promised to have her husband call him when he returned. But before she would have an opportunity to relay that message, she'd make a crucial mistake. It was standard policy in the Pickett home that whenever Walter Pickett went hunting, no one was to disturb him even if it was a life or death situation. But Eloise figured that the pastor was seeking his former deacon's comfort when she broke the rules slightly by telling Chauncey that Walter was at the Plantation hunting.

"Baby, Walter over there at the farm hunting. Do you want me to tell him to call you when he get back?"

"No ma'am. I'd rather see him anyway."

"Son, Walter been real hurt ever since he heard bout what happened. And…

"Yeah I know. I'll see him and we can talk about it then."

And then he just hung up the phone in Eloise's ear, confusing the woman even more than he had when he made that off the wall comment about "everybody" seems to be now. She didn't know it, but Chauncey had no intentions on waiting for her husband to return home. He was on his way to that Plantation and he knew exactly where Pickett's dear hunting stand was on the property. As he made a u-turn in the middle of a desolate stretch of highway and darted across town towards Pickett's location, Lula continued her agonizing silent ride in fear that if she moaned too loud Chauncey would keep his word and kill her dead.

She had started to breathe a little easier and could whisper a word or two if she really tried, but Lula wasn't stupid; not yet at least. After what had happened to her, she was just content to still be on this side of heaven. For now, as she regained a portion of strength, she just laid there as if the back seat of the Mercedes was her burial place, in silence, praying that some graveyard wouldn't soon be.

As he drove as fast as he could to the plantation, Chauncey already knew what he wanted to say and what he wanted to do to Walter

Pickett. Yea, he had thought about the fact that Pickett would probably have a gun within arm's reach, but he felt that if push came to shove he would have no problem sacrificing his life for his wife's honor nor would he mind his former chairman of the board being forever remembered as the man who destroyed the lives of both he and Jada. But if he had his way on this sad morning, none of the above would have to even be taken into consideration. His mind was churning as he drove and by the time he would reach the Plantation, he would've already concocted a plan that would only be enhanced by what was he saw upon his arrival.

CHAPTER 36

Pickett had gotten out of his bed early this morning because, like Whitlock, Tally and Lula, he just couldn't rest. He just had to get out of the house to clear his head. So he went hunting, not for anything in particular, but just to be out in the woods by himself to think about how he was going to explain away what he had done; if and when word hit the street. But by the time he would see that white Mercedes speeding through a cloud of dust down the only dirt road that led to the property, Pickett was sitting on the back of his pick up truck, chewing on tobacco, in deep thought, having never once ventured into the woods to do any hunting.

He was just sitting there on the back of his truck when he noticed Chauncey's car from afar. His heart was racing as the car sped towards him; but he wasn't overtaken by panic, because he had a gun and if that "crazy nigga" tried something stupid he knew how to "make his journey to his wife short and sweet." So he stood up slowly in astonishment, but prepared and waited for whatever was going to happen when Chauncey got out of that car.

Chauncey had spotted him too and from a distance it was if the two combatants had already made uncomfortable eye contact. Noticing that Pickett saw him and noticing that he had his hand on a weapon he knew how to use, Chauncey brought his car to a stop about fifty yards from where the baffled old man stood.

Pickett didn't know what the preacher, he wanted away from his church, had come to the plantation for and he didn't know how he knew how to find him, but one thing was for certain in the old man's mind; "this boy done come up here for some foolishness and I ain't got time for that shit."

Before Chauncey exited the car he demanded that Lula "better not say a word" and told her not to lift her head until he called for her. She didn't respond to him, but her humbled posture spoke volumes about her intensions to be in full compliance with the preacher's orders; or so he thought. Now sure that Lula would remain hidden from Pickett's view, Chauncey got out of the car and walked slowly toward Pickett with his scratched up hands hidden in pockets, and his lying heart ready to lure the old man into some form of confession.

"Deacon Pickett!" he called out from the distance into the cool morning air.

"Yeah.!" the old man shouted back, as he keenly eyed Chauncey's every step.

"Hey, I just need to talk to you!" he said as he paused to await the armed old man's response.

"Bout what!"

"You know... I lost my wife and I just needed somebody to talk to and I thought..."

"Come on over here. I don't mind talkin." Pickett cautiously urged; still looking intently at the boy's every move, sensing that something wasn't right about him. He knew that something was strange about Chauncey's demeanor but he just couldn't put his finger on what it was. He felt as though Chauncey had shown up to question him about issues he didn't wish to discuss, but he didn't know for sure. So he took the preacher at his word, beckoning for him to come closer, knowing that if he made a bad move he'd have an easier shot to kill him as dead as he had promised to kill Lula.

But by the time Chauncey got to within arms reach of Pickett, the guarded deacon was again sitting on his tailgate, with his loaded riffle only a fingertip away. That's when Chauncey held his head down and said.

"I need to ask you something Pickett."

Mistaking Chauncey's lack of eye contact for bereavement, Pickett reached out to touch his shoulder and entreated "Go head Son. You can talk to me. I know we done had our problems but I'm still yo deacon."

But as Chauncey readied himself for a war of words with Pickett, Pickett noticed arms flailing through Chauncey's windshield. It was Lula. She was trying to get his attention and making gestures that he couldn't understand. The woman had tried to escape from her captor's car but Chauncey had barricaded her in the car with the child lock system. She was thrashing around when Pickett finally made eye contact with her and that's when hell broke loose even the more.

"Who the hell you got in that car boy?" Pickett boisterously questioned as Chauncey looked back, in panic, to find that Lula was violently shaking the car trying to get out.

Chauncey knew now that his plan to avert any altercation with an armed Pickett had all but backfired. And though Pickett couldn't tell who it was, he knew that whoever was in that car was in trouble and trying to escape and he also knew that he was in trouble too. Without even thinking or waiting for Chauncey make another move, Pickett reached for his gun and when he did Chauncey reached with him.

"What the hell are you doing you crazy ass nigga?" Pickett shouted as he tried to wrestle his rifle away from the much younger and much stronger man, who fought for the possession of the gun in relative silence.

Pickett had both his hands on the gun and his strength seemed to increase as his fear for his life did the same. But Chauncey had a crazy man's strength and had a firm grip on the gun too and he wasn't letting go. Amid Lula's muted screams for help, the two men struggled. But in a moment of calculated decision, Chauncey released his two handed grip on the gun for a less comfortable right handed one, freeing his left hand just long enough to slap the hell out of Pickett with the back of his left hand.

It was only one backhanded blow, but it was enough to knock Pickett's false teeth crooked and disorient him long enough for Chauncey to take possession of a gun that might very well fire the shot of his execution. But, Pickett didn't have to fear death though; not now at least. No, death was too good for him too and after he backhanded Pickett once more for good measure, Chauncey used the gun to commence the torture of an old man who still had fight but hadn't yet dared to challenge the crazy man that had a rifle in his hand.

With the rifle pointed directly at the tip of Pickett's nose and in full control of the defiant deacon's destiny, Chauncey chuckled nervously as he questioned. "You still thank you in charge Pickett?" "Huh?" he asked as his voice escalated to a fever pitch. "I know exactly what you did yesterday," he said in a firm voice, as Pickett looked directly into his eyes in silence and scowled more intensely with every word that spewed from his former pastor's mouth.

"And I know why you did it. You thought you could do whatever you wanted to do! You thought you could mess up my life! Didn't you?" Chauncey asked as his loud reproach rang out through the woods.

"Well you did!" Chauncey bitterly shouted as Pickett's continuous cold and unconcerned stare prompted him to smack him across the face with the butt of the riffle. "You fucked up my life!" he shouted as he hit Pickett across his swelling head again without even giving the man a chance to lift his head from the first vicious blow. "And for what; a god damned church that you ain't never did right by. I ought to kill yo ass right now."

One would think that Pickett's defiance would've eased away when he felt blood dripping from his eye brow. But the old man was more defiant than he was before Chauncey bloodied him. And just as soon as he had the opportunity to raise his curly gray haired head, he did slowly, putting his own face back in front of the barrel of the gun and resumed his cold stare.

Then he said in a voice as cold as his gaze was "If you hit me again you better kill me; you sorry son of a bitch.", as he chewed harder on his tobacco, readying his mouth to spit into preacher's face in self defense. And then he did. He spit directly into Chauncey's face, temporarily impairing the enraged man's vision, giving the old man an opportunity to attempt a last ditched effort to snatch the gun from his grasp. But Pickett's futile attempts only infuriated Chauncey more, prompting a beat down that the old man hadn't experienced since he was a child. Chauncey hit that old man so hard and so often that he literally knocked him into submission and sobriety.

"Look son; just don't kill me." Pickett said with a painful groan as he struggled to get to his feet. "Killing me ain't gone make none of this no better. I didn't kill yo wife and I can't brang her back."

"I ain't tryin to make nothing better Pickett. I want your ass to suffer like I'm suffering." Chauncey said, as if he was out of breath. "Now get yo ass up and if you try that shit again I promise I will blow yo god damn brains out!"

By now Lula was in full blown panic mode, seeing that her efforts to escape had failed and her captor had a loaded gun pointed again in the face of her would be savior. Though she had cried out to the Lord, it seemed as if her pleas were in vain. Her worse fears had come to fruition and when she saw Chauncey pushing Pickett in the back and forcing him toward the car with his hands up as if he'd been arrested, she knew that he was coming back to do what he'd promised. And Pickett knew that if he was to escape with his life he was going to have to put down his pride, admit his wrong, and continually beg that boy not to kill him.

By the time Chauncey got back to his car with Pickett, Lula was lying down in the back seat again, crying, knowing that her efforts to get away had made her circumstance worse. But he didn't want to kill her or Pickett. He had something else in mind that he felt he had to do now. So with the loaded riffle pointed at Lula, he demanded that she get behind the wheel and drive to a spot they all knew very well, warning the lady "if you do anything stupid I'll blow the back of yo head off."

As Chauncey sat in the backseat on the driver's side, Pickett sat as far to the right of him as possible with the gun pointed at his rib cage. And Lula drove the speed limit as requested to the place he requested, in absolute submission, feeling as though she'd survive if she cooperated.

THE FINAL CHAPTER

CHAPTER 37

Chauncey had long dismissed from his mind the notion that people were probably wondering where he was, because by this point he was already too deep into a warped state of mind that led him to believe that his only way out of the misery that had become his life was to end it. By now he was sick and demented because of everything that had happened to him and everything that he had already done to others. And he knew that before this saga would draw to a close he would've amassed a wrap sheet so torturous that he'd never be able to recapture the glory days he had once experienced in this small town. He had done absolutely too much to ever recovery his integrity and too much to blame on his dead wife. And what he had done to poor Daphne and the ramifications that he felt was sure to follow only fueled his will to continue to destroy what was left of his life. So he rode toward a familiar destination with absolutely nothing to loose but with the intent of gaining one last thing.

By the time Chauncey would reach the last stop on this tempestuous day it would be a little past 11AM. But before he would get there and initiate the plans that he was putting together as Lula drove, his vehicle would be spotted; a sight that prompted a call from a concerned member.

As Billy and Leonard prepared to leave the house again to search for any signs of their pastor, Lizzy fought off her suffering by trying to watch Saturday cartoons under the protective eye of Ruthie as Daphne hid away in an upstairs room, still claiming that her despondency was a result of Jada's death rather than admitting Chauncey's unconscious assault on her. Hope of finding the deeply depressed preacher without the public's intervention had all but diminished. But then they got the big break they thought they were looking for.

Ruth Anne had been answering the phone all morning and she had actually spoken to Mother Snelling earlier and told the seventy-six year old the same miserable lie she had told Aunt Eunice, the Blaylocks and everybody else who asked to speak with him. "Pastor's not here right now. But he's doing as well as can be expected. He just wanted to be alone."

But Mother Snelling called back to the house a little before eleven, because what she had seen looked real strange to her. She told Ruth Anne that while she was on her way to the grocery store with her granddaughter she had noticed the pastor's car on the highway near where the church is but "Lula was driving" the pastor's Mercedes and "Pastor and some other man was ridin' in the back seat. That just didn't look right to me. Lula still had her hair rollers in her head."

Ruth Anne was so relieved that someone had actually seen Chauncey alive that she cared not about the awkwardness of the sighting, but asked in elation before telling Billy and Leonard the good news. "Now where did you say they were Mother?"

"They were down near the church and I don't know for sure but it look like to me they were bout to turn to go down by the church."

"OK Mother we'll check it out. But don't worry. I'm sure there's a reasonable explanation."

"It might be baby, but Lula ain't the best company for him right now. He need to be home resting with ya'll. I done been there and I know," she said with concern, having lost a spouse herself and knowing the tremendous amount of pain it brings. "He don't need to be out like that baby."

Immediately after Ruthie hung up the phone with Mother Snelling she told Billy and Leonard about the good news and they all were relieved that their worse fears hadn't come to pass. But, though they received news that he was alive and in the vicinity, Billy and Leonard knew that it would be better if they just tracked him down instead of allowing him find his way back to a house that he had all but forgotten about.

So as Ruthie kept an eye on Lizzy and Daphne remained in her depressive shell, Billy and Leonard left the house with a general idea of Chauncey's location, somewhat confused about why Lula would be driving his car, but thankful that he had been spotted alive. But by the time they'd pin point his exact location, Chauncey would already be inside of Greater Mt. Carmel ritualistically handing back over the reigns to former chairman Walter S. Pickett in a sinister ceremony that Maywhether might have to use fire power to bring to an end.

By 11:10AM Lula had already driven to the church just as Chauncey had asked, but not without trepidation though. She had to drive just how and just where he wanted her to because based upon his previous ruthless actions she knew that he could and would erupt if she wasn't cooperative. Pickett knew that he could and would erupt too and was just as scared and just as cooperative as Lula was. Though it seemed at times that Chauncey was disengaged, the barrel of that rifle never once was taken from the worried deacon's rib cage and his eyes never once looked away from the back of Lula's head. So they both rode silently and were virtually motionless. But though they rode uncommunicatively, both Lula and Pickett felt as though the worst of their ordeal had yet to surface, which made that drive over from the plantation not only eerily quiet but excruciatingly long.

One could easily understand why Lula and Pickett rode silently; they were scared and demanded to remain silent. But Chauncey rode in silence for a different reason. He was in deep thought about a plan he felt he had to execute. His plan involved turning in his keys before turning out the lights on his own life. His plan was to execute himself in the presence of the two people who hated him enough to lie on his wife for the purpose of getting him out of a church that he would've gladly left voluntarily had he known that his wife's integrity or her life hung in the balance. He felt now, that if they wanted that "damned church", they could have it because it had become a symbol of his agony. He didn't want it anymore and today he was giving it back them.

When they arrived at the church, silence was finally broken when Chauncey demanded that Lula hide the car on the backside of the building right next to a seldom used dinning annex door for a surreptitious entrance into the sanctuary.

With the car parked in a spot that Leonard and Billy wouldn't even see when they drove by looking for it and careful not to be seen by anyone else, Chauncey brandished the gun, using it as a pointer to direct Lula and Pickett out of the car and towards the back door. Without even saying a word or putting a hand on them, he forced the two scared to death visibly disturbed cohorts into the door at gunpoint.

Once inside the dinning annex and away from any public scrutiny, Chauncey began to issue his final commands, but in kind of a scary whisper, as if he thought someone had an ear to a window and would hear him if he spoke any louder. "Go on into the sanctuary. And walk slow." he said in a nervous tone as he walked slowly behind Lula and Pickett, with the loaded rifle to their backs.

They didn't understand why he was escorting them back into a church they no longer felt welcome in, but they were compliant and they walked slowly into the freshly vacuumed and polished sanctuary as Chauncey followed and uttered more of the same perplexing directives.

"When you get in there, go to the altar." he whispered as they approached the entrance to the dim, unlit sanctuary.

Once he had positioned them at the altar as if he desired to pray for them, Chauncey backed his way up into the pulpit with his watchful eyes still fixed on Pickett and Lula's motionless bodies and the gun in a ready to shoot position. The stage for his bizarre resignation and handover was now set. He was standing behind a sacred desk that he'd never preach from again as Pickett and Lula stood in front of him at an altar that had never seen so much turmoil. He was ready to turn over his keys to them and take his life in front of them; a befitting punishment for their role in a plan to destroy him, he thought.

But, before he could initiate any of his plans, Lula tried to initiate her own, bursting out in a pitiful plea for her life as Pickett looked on hopelessly, not even knowing that they were no longer the objects of his death trap. It was an act that they'd both regret however; an act that would incite the preacher's more wrathful nature; a wrathful nature that sought to make Lula and Pickett suffer more than they already had.

"Pastor, please I don't wanna ..." she hoarsely tried to plead as Pickett opened his mouth for the first time in an effort to strengthen Lula's plea. "Son we..." But before either of them could begin to beg for their lives, Chauncey became infuriated and put a cease to their unwanted petitions.

"Shut up, god damn it! Shut the hell up!" he mercilessly scolded them as the scared woman threw her hands up in front of her face and trembled hysterically as if to protect herself from his piercing words or bullets she was sure would be flying at any moment. "Don't ya'll think ya'll done talked enough?" he asked to no answer as Lula whimpered uncontrollably. "Answer me damn it!"

"Yes Sir." Lula answered as Pickett fearfully responded, "Yea."

"Naw, I tell you what…" he said as he began to pace the pulpit floor. "Since ya'll want to talk I want ya'll to tell me something before I blow ya'll damn brains out. I just need ya'll to tell me; what did I ever do so bad to make ya'll want to mess up my life like this?" he questioned as his more vengeful disposition resurfaced. "Tell me!" he shouted as the pitch of his voice rose to match his current level of his intensity. "What was it?" he asked with his left arm outstretched as his right kept a grip on the riffle. "Was it because the church was doing good without you? Tell me! What was it?"

As Pickett gulped repeatedly and feared to look upon the preacher's face or say anything, Lula slowly held her head down in agony, preparing a potentially life saving explanation as her tears begin to liquefy the blood that had dried around her nose and mouth.

"Pastor, I know what I did was wrong," she pleaded as sincerely as she knew how as Pickett looked under eyed toward her with pity, feeling sorry that Lula was ever drawn in to this mess. "But I didn't mean for all this to happen and I…"

"Wait a minute. I got it," the now psychotic behaving preacher said with a panicky voice, abruptly cutting short another one of Lula's sad attempts at an apology as Pickett fearfully held his badly bruised head up again to see what was about to happen next.

"Ya'll wanted me out because I took control," he said sarcastically. "Yea that's it. Pickett you wanted to be chairman and Lula you wanted to be the choir director and I hired somebody else. That's why you wanted me out; ain't it Lula?" he said as he chuckled at his reasoning.

"No Sir. I didn't…"

"Shut up! You lyin'!" Chauncey interrupted again, gesturing as if he was a hair away from pulling the trigger. "You wanted your position back…" he said as if he was pondering what he'd say and do next. "OK… I'm gone give it back to you right now and Pickett, I'm gone give you back your spot too."

"Pastor I don't wanna die. I'm sorry. Please."

"Go to the piano Lula." he said motioning toward the new white baby grand piano as if that riffle was a pointer. "I want you to sing that song for me; that song that you sang at funerals. You know what I'm talking about." he said before muttering to himself "Somebody 'bout to die anyway."

"Please Pastor, I can't half talk. Don't make me sing. Please." begged Lula in a raspy voice.

"Get yo ass to the piano Lula!" he demanded. "That's what you wanted ain't it? And Pickett you go on over there to your deacon's corner. Sit where you used to sit. I want you to be chairman today." he said with a devilish grin, mocking the old man's former status.

As Pickett walked toward the deacon's corner to sit in the seat of the chairman, he shook his head in sadness over what had become of something that was only meant to scare the preacher off. And Lula…she didn't want to go to the piano, but she knew she had no choice. So like Pickett she walked nervously over to her post, wiping her eyes with that holey bloodstained night gown as she went. She knew she couldn't sing because her throat felt like Chauncey's fingers were still ripping away at it. Nonetheless, she went to the piano, sat down and played the music to one of the saddest funeral marches known to man, preparing to sing it as best she could.

As soon as Lula began to play the music to that song, Pickett burst into an awful gut wrenching cry as he sat on the pew that he had once sat so proudly on as chairman of the board of deacons for so many years, in deep sorrow, wishing he could take back his efforts to get rid of a man he now knew was out of his natural mind. But when she began to sing the words to the song, his emotions erupted, even the more. It was a song that he had heard way too many times over the years and he never really heard that song unless it was an extremely sorrowful day. Well this too, was an extremely sorrowful day and Lula sang that sad song.

After she coughed to clear her throat, Lula hoarsely uttered the lyrics that would bring forth an outpour of emotion from Chauncey as well.

"Oh I want to see him, to look upon his face.
There to sing forever of his saving grace.
On the streets of glory let me lift my voice.
Cares all past home at last ever to rejoice."

After virtually crying out only the chorus portion of the gloomy hymn, Lula paused as if she was done and wiped her eyes again with the upper portion of that blood stained night gown before Chauncey urged her to "sing it again" as tears streamed uncontrollably down his face.

It was at the hearing of those miserable lyrics that Chauncey finally realized that nothing he could ever do to Lula, Pickett, or anyone else would bring back his wife or erase all the horrors that he had faced during his short life. That song had brought him back to the sad reality that his life had been filled with too many days of trouble; troubles he no longer had the strength or the will to endure.

As tears flowed freely he thought about the fact that he was the one that had killed his own father. And though he shot his father in his mother's defense, he blamed himself for everything that had happened on that day. He thought about how bad he always missed his momma and how sad he was when she didn't get up when he begged her to. He thought about all the times Jada would ask him about that nightmare he would periodically have and all the moments he missed to share the whole truth about his past with her. But he couldn't now because the love of his life was gone and she wasn't coming back to him. She hadn't been dead a full twenty four hours but he thought about how bad he missed his wife and how wrong he felt for not hearing her when she cried out for him. He blamed himself for everything that had happened to her and he sobbed profusely as he thought "she wouldn't be dead if I had been there for her."

He was tortured even more as his mind replayed the sexual torture of an innocent girl who only wanted to console him. He felt bad because he knew Daphne didn't ask for or deserve what had happened to her and his baby girl didn't ask for or deserve to see him doing what he was doing to "that helpless girl" or hear Daphne's horrid screams.

He had never dealt with the events that had shaped his past. He only ran from it and hoped that it wouldn't follow him. But it did and now the circumstances that shrouded his future were added to those past burdens. They were burdens that he didn't want to live with. He wanted the words of Lula's song to come to pass.

> "Oh I want to see him, to look upon his face.
> There to sing forever of his saving grace.
> On the streets of glory let me lift my voice.
> Cares all past home at last ever to rejoice."
> And then BANG!!!

With a blast that could be heard from across the street and would prompt one resident to place a desperate call to the sheriff's office, Chauncey had inadvertently fired a shot that actually hit Lula somewhere about her torso, knocking her off the piano stool onto the floor.

He was in the process of pulling a ring of keys from his pants pocket to hand over to Pickett when he mishandled the gun. It just went off, striking the woman so precisely that no one would ever believe that he didn't aim to kill her. He didn't mean to shoot her, but he had. And because he had, lights flashed and sirens blared as Leonard Maywhether, Billy Dunn and a convoy of sheriff's deputies rushed toward the scene.

"Oh my God!" Chauncey hysterically and repetitively screamed as Lula tried to breathe but bled badly as she lay not too far from the piano. "I didn't try to shoot her," he appealed to no one in particular as he stood in shock in the pulpit.

The moment Pickett saw Lula fall backwards he immediately and without hesitation hurried over to her without any fear for his own life and held her head in his arms as he kneeled beside her and yelled at Chauncey "Put the gun down Son!"

After dropping the gun as if it was hot, Chauncey fell to his knees in the middle of that pulpit and totally broke down screaming "No!" as Pickett helplessly rocked with Lula's head held in his arms and looked at the preacher with a "What the hell has happened to you?" look on his face.

"I didn't mean to…Oh my God…I didn't…"

Too overcome with emotion to finish any of what he was trying to covey, but in full knowledge that he had crossed a threshold that he'd never be able to return from, Chauncey picked up the riffle from the pulpit floor with his left hand, thinking it was best to kill himself before someone else did. But before he would aim the long gun at a portion of his body that would surely kill him, he felt as though he needed finish what he was trying to do when he mistakenly shot Lula; which was give those church keys back to Pickett.

As Pickett looked upon him with contempt, but in silence and in complete and utter astonishment, Chauncey pulled his church keys from his right pants pocket and tossed them toward Pickett and said "I ain't gone need these no more. You can have your chuch back. I don't want it no more. You got what you wanted. I'm leaving."

But then, just as suddenly as the horrible events in that sanctuary had unfolded, sheriff's deputies kicked down the front door to the church and stormed in yelling "Put your hands up!"

Leonard and Billy were only a few steps behind and nosey neighbors had just begun to gather outside the church when they rushed in to see a sight more gruesome than they would've ever imagined. Like the other uniformed officers, they saw Pickett kneeling on the floor near the piano holding Lula's bloody body and they saw a man that they couldn't believe was their pastor on his knees holding a gun and ready to do deadly damage to himself. They were in shock and they were both in visibly disillusioned. But both men knew now that the ultimate fate of the man they loved was no longer in their hands but his immediate fate remained uncertain.

Billy shook his head in dismay as Chauncey disobeyed repeated deputy orders to drop his gun, but Leonard pressed his way through his officers, demanding that they hold their fire, hoping that he could possibly talk his friend and pastor out of putting a bullet into his neck.

"Oh my God, Pastor, hey…man please don't do this." Leonard begged as he undesirably placed his right hand on his own high powered firearm. "Put the gun down Pastor. I'm here for you man" he continued as he inched a little closer and EMS staffers waited for clearance before they entered to aid the wounded.

"Naw man you don't understand," Chauncey replied as his long arms braced the long gun against his neck.

"Yes I do man. Please."

"Man you can't understand!" Chauncey said as he sobbed. "I can't live like this no more."

"Live like what Pastor? You can make it through this. Man we're here for you."

"I've been through too much and I've done too much."

"No you haven't Pastor. Just put the gun down. We can work this out."

As every deputy in that church tensely prepared to pull their triggers if necessary and Billy stood in distressed unbelief at what he was witnessing, Pickett continued to console Lula, who was alive but bleeding to death. He occasionally whispered into the dying woman's ear, "Hold on." And Chauncey…he was preparing himself to give them all his reasons for refusing to live.

On his knees and with that loaded riffle to his neck, Chauncey began what he considered to be his final argument for his self imposed death penalty as everyone in that church looked upon him pitifully. He knew he was going to die one way or another, but he couldn't leave this world without giving up a ghost he'd held for twenty years.

Having composed himself as if he was about to deliver a sermon, Chauncey gave up a secret that he thought no one in the world knew. He had stopped crying for the moment and looked to be more peaceful, though the gun was still aimed at his jugular. It was as if he was relieved that he could finally disclose what had tortured him since he was seven. And he did and then some.

"When I came down here I was trying to get away. I wanted to get further away from what I left in Ohio."

"What did you leave Pastor?" Billy asked trying to encourage Chauncey to release his demons.

"I left my father's legacy. He was an adulterer and he was gay and he beat my momma to death. I thought when I came here that I could be a better man than my father and a better pastor than my father."

"Pastor you are."

"I killed my own daddy when I when I was a boy," he said as his speech slowed dramatically and as if Leonard hadn't uttered a word. "I wasn't but seven years old and I've had to live with it ever since then. I killed him because I watched him as he beat my momma down. I watched him kill my momma and he killed my momma because she caught him having sex on a desk with a damn man. He was killing my momma" he said as tears dripped from his eyes but his face remained expressionless.

"So I went and got his gun and I just pulled the trigger. I didn't mean to kill him" he said as that once expressionless face began to breakdown as he sobbed at the remembrance of killing the man he had always looked up to. "I just wanted him to stop killing my momma. She was telling him to stop but he just kept on hitting her and choking her. I think about it everyday and not one day has gone by that I haven't thought about the look on his face when that bullet hit him. Not one day. I still have nightmares about that day.

Man I loved my daddy," he continued as Billy and Leonard cried and felt sorry for him.

"I've been running from that day my whole life and I'm tired of running." he cryingly said as he closed his eyes and slowly tilted his back. "It's my fault that I don't have a daddy. It's my fault that I don't have my momma and it's my own fault that I don't have my wife."

"No it ain't, man." Leonard interjected, trying to keep him from believing that Jada's death was a result of anything he did. "Pastor it wasn't your fault man. You didn't do nothing."

"I know…" he said as his voice began to drift away as if he was in a fog. "I didn't do nothing… She tried to talk to me before I left… She tried to tell me…But I was mad because she was late for my meeting. If I had listened to her I would've known that she was late because…she didn't have to die." he said as his voice faded away. And then he paused and sighed as if he was already detached from this world and said. "I've lost everything; my wife; I lost my baby man, she was my whole life…"

And then he held his head down, and tightly shut his eyes… and BANG!

In a moment that shocked everyone that witnessed, Chauncey Evansworth Pennington had pulled the trigger, executing himself in front of a man who had done everything in his power to get him out of that church. In a very sad way he had succeeded. With one blast that could be heard by the onlookers that stood beyond the taped off perimeter of the church, Chauncey had shot himself in the neck, nearly ripping his head off of his body. He was dead.

As deputies and Emergency Management staffers rushed in to aid Lula, Billy and Maywhether rushed toward Chauncey only to find that he was nearly decapitated; a sight that neither man could stomach and immediately turned away from in great grief. Billy immediately ran out of the sanctuary in tears because he couldn't bare the pain of what the man he loved had just done to himself. He was miserable and he was sick and the very thought of how that man's family would react when they found out that he was dead absolutely made him dread having to be the bearer of such grim news. Leonard went out after Billy in just as much pain and as his officers and medical staff filed into that church, he just stood by his truck with his head down contemplating how something so bad could happen to a man as pure as Chauncey was and a family that had only meant good for his community. They both cried as they watched from a distance, wishing the nightmare would just end and what they had seen with their own eyes wasn't really true.

Inside the church technicians were tending to Lula as they purposely bypassed Chauncey's body, knowing there was nothing that they could do for him. Lula had all their attention because Lula was the one clinging on to a life that was almost gone. Though she was drowning in her own blood, the little sign of life that she had shown was reason enough for on site medical technicians to radio in for a helicopter to expedite her journey to the nearest hospital.

And Pickett... he tearfully watched as technicians loaded Lula onto a stretcher, preparing her to be air lifted. He was just sitting there, despondently in his chairman deacon's seat in absolute dismay, feeling partly responsible for what had just occurred and completely sorry for a boy that he could've never known had endured so much pain.

And then, as everyone in that church looked over the boy's body as if he wasn't even lying there, Pickett got up slowly from the pew where he sat, and walked even slower over toward the pulpit where Chauncey lay, just so the man he thought he hated wouldn't have be all by himself at such a time as this. When he got to the pulpit he ran his bloody hands through his beaten gray head in agony and in evident sorrow, feeling sorry that hatred had ever brewed in his heart for a boy he didn't know had gone through so much. He was real sorry now and in a pitiful attempt to treat Chauncey as if he was the father he had promised the boy he'd be to him upon his arrival from Odessa, he cried as he knelt down to hold what was left of the preacher's partially blown away upper body; whispering pitifully and repeatedly "I'm sorry Son". As he held Chauncey's, still dripping with blood, body in the cradle of his arms he rocked him as if he was putting a son to sleep; as if he was the daddy that the boy always wished he had.

As crying onlookers made their way toward the chaotic scene and Billy and Leonard called everybody they knew would be sorry, police officers roped off an even greater portion of the area and pushed back the throng who knew, by now, that something horrible had happened to somebody in that church. Something had indeed happened. All hell had broken loose. And the "somebody" it had broken loose on was Chauncey Evansworth Pennington, a boy who thought that he could run from that demon called past that always lurked near.

After Lula had been attended to and been readied for her emergency evacuation by helicopter, Pickett put his bloody fingers over what was left of Chauncey's unseeing but still gazing eyes and closed them as he hummed a hymn that he wished were true for him.

Hallelujah
Hallelujah
I know the Storm is passing over
Hallelu.

THE END

The Author's Message

I pray that this book touched you and helped to bring you to a place of personal reconciliation and understanding of the fragile nature of life. Chauncey Pennington was only a figment of my imagination, but his life and the people and circumstances surrounding it, represents the very real complexities of a life and how every choice we make effects the very core of our being. Struggles are inevitable, but when dealt with appropriately can only serve as mechanisms to make us stronger. Pains and sufferings shall occur, but with God's help we can endure them all.

This book was designed so that the reader would confront often overlooked, but prevalent personal issues so that a thorough examination might be initiated to look deeply into every detail that may very well determine futuristic outcomes. Though humorous at times and sorrowful at others, this book's real purpose was to provoke serious considerations about how we treat others, how we react to others' treatment of us, and the value of allowing everything that happens to us in life to work out for our good in life.

I pray that you were, in some way, empowered through the characterization of Chauncey Pennington's rather sad experiences. And I pray that his failures don't become yours. But, if by chance Chauncey's failures are already yours or become yours, you have time to correct them. You've read this book, which means that you're still alive and if you're still alive, that only means that God still has an opportunity and enough time to work out any situation you might be faced with. Thank you for reading and live a long and empowered life.

Clarence M. Jackson, II

3 Points For Conversation

1. Lack of Communication...

"Pursuit of Success and the struggles that come with that pursuit should never overshadow the value of those who are trying to help us get there."

-Clarence M. Jackson, II

Discussion Questions

A. What do you think led to the breakdown in communication in the Pennington marriage?
B. How did you feel when Chauncey walked out on Jada before she had an opportunity to explain what had happened to her?
C. Does Jada bare any responsibility for not telling Chauncey about what Mr. James was saying and doing to her at work?

- So many times we get so wrapped up in our pursuit of what we perceive to be success that we forget how important those closest to us really are and how, essential a communicative relationship with those we love really is. Evidence of this negligence is found in the later stages of Chauncey and Jada's marriage as they both became more involved with career development than maintaining healthy relationship with each other.
- Because of that career focus there was an evident breakdown in communication; a lack of trust. Jada didn't even feel comfortable enough to talk to her husband about her workplace difficulties and Chauncey failed to value his wife's encouragement when things were toughest for him.
- If they were able to talk openly about what was happening in their lives, maybe things wouldn't have unraveled so destructively. Even when Jada came home and tried to tell Chauncey about what she had been through at work in Adolph James' office, he totally disregarded her outcry because he was too concerned

about public perception and/or duties unrelated to being the protector that he'd promised to be.

2. Too Little Too Late...

"You never really know how much what you say and do affect a person until that person reacts to what you've said or done. In some cases their reactions are regrettable and your guilt comes a little too late."

-Clarence M. Jackson, II

Discussion Questions

A. In your opinion, who was to blame for all the chaos that ultimately destroyed the lives of so many of these people in the small town and church depicted in the book. Was any one person responsible?
B. Can you imagine the pain Chauncey must've been in after learning of Jada's death before he had the opportunity to hold her and apologize for his unwarranted behavior?
C. What are your feelings about Walter Pickett's role in what ultimately happened to Chauncey and Jada? Do you think that his love for his church was greater than his love for his fellow man?

- How often do we walk away from people we love without them actually knowing how much we really love them. How many times do we argue over fruitless matters and not take into consideration that this could be the last time I ever see this person alive.
- By the time Chauncey realized that Jada had a reasonable explanation for being late for a scheduled meeting, he had already verbally assaulted her, which proved be as damaging as what Adolph James had already done to her.
- Chauncey couldn't have possibly known that his argument with Jada would actually be his last face to face meeting with her. And by the time he apologetically poured out his love toward her, she was already in a cold hospital on her death bed; and what he said was too little; too late.

- If Walter Pickett had known of Chauncey's prior struggles he probably would've treated the young man with a little more tenderness; like a father Chauncey never really had. But he didn't know and he continuously picked away at a fragile core that he regrettably thought was impenetrable. His apologetic behavior toward Chauncey came at a time when Chauncey couldn't respond if he wanted to. Pickett's "I'm Sorry Son." was too little; too late. Actions that could otherwise be characterized as pointless and petty had spun a web so vast that it trapped more than Pickett's intended prey.

3. Give It To God...

"Your trials are only as great as your reluctance to allow God to handle them."

-Clarence M. Jackson, II

Discussion Questions

A. When Jada died did you think Chauncey would be able to pull through it? What did you think his future was going to be? Would you have ever imagined that he would've done what he did?

B. Did you at any point during the reading of this book, find yourself feeling sorry for all that Chauncey had gone through? Was what he had gone through justification for all of the actions that he displayed after he learned of Jada's death?

C. Have you ever found yourself in a circumstance that was too big for you to handle alone? What happened when you tried to work those issues out alone? What happened when you turned those issues over to God?

D. Did you at any point feel sorry for Pickett or Lula? Do you think they deserved what ultimately happened to them?

- It's easy to talk about faith in God when things are going relatively well. But what happens when all breaks loose? What happens when we find ourselves in situations beyond our control? Chauncey proved to us that it doesn't matter how great you are or how great you aspire to be; trouble will befall you. The question then becomes how will I respond? Will this trial grind me down or will this trial polish me up?

- From the moment Chauncey heard of Jada's death he lost control because he didn't allow God to take control. Jada's death led to depression. And depression led to the drinking. The drinking led to inebriation and the inebriation led to everything else that happened on the day all hell broke loose. Don't allow life you to grind you down. Be blessed and Give your Trials to God.

About the Author

Clarence M. Jackson, II, a purpose driven pastor and teacher by all accounts, was born and raised in rural Gadsden County, Florida. He is regarded by many as a master communicator and motivator; a characterization that has enabled him to minister in cities throughout the U.S.

Mr. Jackson began his collegiate studies at the renowned Florida A& M University in Tallahasse but completed his Bachelors studies in Theology at The Smith Chapel Bible College where he also attained a Masters Degree in Divinity.

Mr. Jackson is currently the pastor of the flourishing Bethel Baptist Church of Chattahoochee, Florida www.gbethelmbc.org and a Job Coach for the Gadsden County School Board.

He, along with his lovely wife Dee, are the proud parents of three beautiful children: Jaelen Allen, Joana Alexandria and Jan Adolphus Jackson.